When the Shark Bites

When the Shark Bites

Rodney Morales

University of Hawai'i Press

Honolulu

Printed in the United States of America

07 06 05 04 03 02   6 5 4 3 2 1

Library of Congress Cataloging-in-Publication Data

Morales, Rodney.
   When the shark bites / Rodney Morales.
     p. cm.
   ISBN 0–8248–2565–9 (acid-free paper)
   1. Hawaii—Fiction. I. Title.

PS3563.O7594 W48 2002
813'.54—dc21   2002017306

University of Hawai'i Press books are printed on acid-free paper and
meet the guidelines for permanence and durability of the Council on
Library Resources.

Designed by Publication Services

Printed by Versa Press

for Hal Carmichael

Contents

When the Shark Bites

Hawaiian values &
way of living.

WEHE 'ANA
The Gatherer

(Kealaikahiki Channel—Summer 1976)

Sunrise

He felt it brush against him again. Even after years of swimming in the shallow waters of Ala Moana, he had not gotten used to that feeling.

Anger kept him going. Anger at those chickenshits who gave up when the Coast Guard called off its search. Did they really think those crew-topped grunts had their hearts in it? After only two days, Keoni, who had challenged him to action, who had admonished him for his lethargy, . . . written off as lost.

Hank had dived off the northeast part of the island, from a point near Kanapou Bay, also known as Obake Bay, a place where the current brought vast amounts of debris. Hank figured that all he had to do was swim easterly in the 'Alalakeiki Channel, faithfully stroking toward Mākena on the eastern end, and let the west-aiming current carry him toward Kīhei. Such was the equation.

His eyes hurt. They were tender, salt-burned, and he struggled to avoid the sun's reflection on the waves. But he had to look on occasion, and reel from the sting of incessant light.

His arms were beyond ache, beyond pain; an eerie sort of numbness had set in. Still he continued his methodical stroking, as his brain constantly reminded him to. And again, something that felt both giving, like flesh, and slimy, brushed against him.

This was excruciating punishment. The question was, became, could an untrained swimmer, albeit a young man in moderately good shape, swim seven ocean miles, fighting current a good part of the way?

He could not see Haleakalā, the mountain that harbored the fugitive sun. Though it loomed beyond, like a grail, like treasure and reaffirmation, he was too brutally committed to the hypnotic steadiness of stroking to recognize it, or to consider the alternating currents he was caught between: the icy water from the north, the comforting warmer southern stream. If he went with the flow and rode Kealaikahiki, *the pathway to Tahiti*, if he really got caught in this channel, heʼd be in the water far too long. Long as in forever *and kiss your ass good-bye*. If he fought against the steady stream, and swam, swam hard, he might surface in the residue of sunrise. One path presented certain death, and the uncertain promise of rebirth; the other, life—and yet a kind of death, if it were a return to business as usual. Did Keoni—like Lono, the grieving, maddened chief, the loved and spurned chief, the deified mortal—did Keoni take the pathway to Tahiti? It appeared so. No trace of a body. No blood. The last ones to have seen him were Logan and Kuahine. And neither was trustworthy.

Freestyle . . . then backstroke . . . tread water . . . freestyle . . . backstroke—take some deep breaths—tread water . . . freestyle . . .

During the first hour, though his eyes already burned badly, he thought at times, *I can go on for days. I just need to hold my course, stroking steady in the water. My body is a vessel, and the island floats, the world spins toward me.* . . . He had swum past the pain of his faulty, apprehensive start. He was in a groove. A good groove.

The water was deep blue and damned beautiful, a sweet break from the dirt and kiawe. A break from the eroded landscape, where he had gotten scratches all over his limbs, where he had stumbled at times as he searched the caves, as he avoided shells that appeared intact— shells that could detonate. Water, at least for now, was a sweet reprieve.

But as colder streams replaced the warm, the first inkling that this challenge may be insurmountable emerged. Hank tried to keep this thought at bay, struggling to keep focused. *Efficient strokes, efficient strokes.* But he couldn't stop his mind . . .

During the second hour—and he only knew it was the second hour because he had taken one last look at his wristwatch, which had become a bother to him, before he cast it aside—a scary numbness set in, a vertiginous *zzzzhhh* synapsing through his limbs. He had used up his glycogen, surely. Startlingly weak, he floated on his back, noticing how cloudless the sky was, thinking *What a fucking beautiful day this is,* waiting for a surge of energy, hoping his starving muscles would be successful in their foraging for fat stores.

Twice he saw airplanes. He waved halfheartedly. Knew there was no chance of him being sighted. He had just been in one, and he knew how tough it was to see any-thing smaller than an ocean liner. Yet he also knew that another search would be launched. For him, this time. That was his ulterior motive. For why wouldn't the

Coast Guard, at the same time, renew their search for Keoni?

Keoni. Destined to be a lifelong friend. Comrade, brother, soulmate . . . leader. But he had crossed too many people. Had become too much of a threat to the powers-that-be. But who would have done him in? The U.S. Navy? The local syndicate?

Too much thought gets you swimming in circles, Hank reasoned. He felt his energy returning, and tried to concentrate . . .

Stroke, steady stroke. Drift, but lightly, featherlightly. Stroke. Breathe deep. Ha. *Breath is strength. Breath is life.*

He had lost sight of Haleakalā. He couldn't figure how. Swim toward the sun, toward the sun. Where is the sun? How can you lose the fucking sun? Be a vessel. A vessel. Virgin. Vestal virgin. What's a vestal virgin? That phrase from a favorite song: *One of sixteen vestal virgins . . . who were leaving for the coast . . .*

Then he jumped, startled. "Wha' was that?" He must have turned a ghastly pale, for *it* had brushed by him again.

The clouds were gone. It was late morning.

These had been beautiful late spring days. A streak, a string, a slew of them. How could so much inner turmoil co-exist with all this external beauty? He had spent the better half of three years in soul-sucking drizzle in Oregon, dark day after dark day, and when he returned to Hawaiʻi he embraced the warmth with gratitude—*excuse me while I kiss the sky.* He was stoked. It was back to year-round sunshine, godly grinds, and a rainbow of faces. He had missed this severely, this blend that had been for most of his life the unquestioned norm. Then, after he got rehabituated to the lovely weather, the ʻono food, the multi-ethnic populace, he began taking it all for granted.

But now, as he stroked steadily in the blaze of sunlight, he recognized how he had internalized Portland, how the darkness had remained within.

As he neared what he thought to be his third hour in the waters between Kahoʻolawe and Maui, Hank felt another burst of energy. He figured that he had already swum farther than those Roughwater Race participants he used to shake his head at when they swam two and a half miles from San Souci to the Hilton Hawaiian shore. He liked watching the race, just for the hell of it. *Fucking idiots,* he'd sometimes mutter, before taking a sip from a can of Coke or a cup of beer. Now he saw them laughing back, knowing who the real idiot was.

He had never in his life seen swimming as serious activity. Had never swam a mile, let alone seven—or eight or nine or twelve, when you consider the current, the jagged path. But his football training helped. He knew about second and third wind. He knew about playing through the pain.

Back at Kaimukī High he was "Good fun Hank," "Take it to the bank Hank," a jokey fun guy. The senior class clown. He received a partial scholarship to play football in Portland. Didn't like it there, but he did get his share of women, mostly pale blondes from the Midwest who had arrived in this cold, dark city for a last-minute dose of the hippiedom they'd been yearning for since adolescence. *You missed Haight-Ashbury by a few hundred miles and a thousand years,* he wanted to tell them. But getting them into bed was a whole lot easier.

There Hank abandoned his comfortable pidgin and fell, chameleon-like, into a variety of West Coast voices. People didn't know what to make of this Latino from Hawaiʻi.

When he returned home after four long years, it didn't take much time for him to pick up where he left off.

But then, politics had changed him. In 1974, when he had returned from "doing time," he found himself protesting the treatment of Hawaiians and other locals the same way he had protested the war. He saw parallels too. He saw people fighting for religious freedom, freedom from outside intervention. He saw people fighting for their homeland.

And the battles escalated. January 1976 saw a series of landings on the island of Kahoʻolawe, the island used by the U.S. Navy for target practice. These acts of civil disobedience gave birth to an explosion of activity and protest. Almost simultaneously, the battle being waged against a developer in the farming communities of Waiāhole and Waikāne had come to a head. It was around this time, in the valley of Waiāhole, that Hank met a woman who insisted on calling him Henry. It struck him then that no one else had called him by his given name for years. It was a name he had long abandoned, a name he no longer used except in the world of documents. And it was the way she said it. A declaration: *You are Henry.*

She was tall, lean, and, for someone who had just turned twenty-two, wore a world-weary face. She was trail- more than street-wise, wary, and resolute.

Now, in the deepest ocean he had ever been in, the deepest shit, one might say, he strove to distract himself by cataloguing his conquests, as if that were the measure of a life. He remembered some of their names—Lisa, Trudy, . . . —remembered their hair color, remembered the favored position even, but he could not see their faces. In his mind, skimming an ocean that was mountains deep, the only woman whose face surfaced with any clarity was the one who called him *Henry.*

In between islands, seemingly in the middle of
nowhere, in the midst of the realization, the bitter
epiphany, that this may be where it all ends for him, he
heard her voice: *Henry.* He felt a bracing tenderness. *I
need to get outa this alive. Need to tell her I love her.*
He mouthed the words as he exhaled, his head turning
to the left, his right hand reaching out, his breathing
regulated. *I need to I need to . . .* He recommitted himself to a long, steady stroke even though stiffness was
setting in. Words came to him with each breath. Then
he found a melody, the dim echo of a soulful refrain:

No more FOO-lin' around, no more RUN-nin' away
No more FOO-lin' around, baby WHY don't you stay
with me tonight . . .

He paused, seeking a rhyme . . .

I won't take flight.

Then it brushed against him again, and Hank shook.
He spun onto his back. "AAAAARRRRRGGGGHHHH!"
he yelled. "WHAT THE FUCK *IS IT?*" He let himself sink
under and fought to look. Thought he saw some puffer
fish. *Okay, okay, relax. Just relax. Gotta keep cool, gotta
swim steadily. No stopping for anything.*
Ninety-eight . . . ninety-nine . . . turn. On his back he took
five deep breaths, then it was *turn. . . .* He started stroking . . .
one . . . two . . . working his way up to a hundred. But too
often his mind drifted, and he kept losing count.

□ □ □

Somewhere in what still might have been the third hour
he floated on his back, his aching eyes closed. The sun

burned red through his eyelids. Hank breathed long and deep. There was so much time to think now, and the clarity was astonishing. He thought about those he felt closest to, for now he understood that he may never see them again. His feelings were as pure as the uncut coke he had walked away from days earlier in disgust. Keoni had always said, *Do your drugs at home. Don't bring the stuff into 'Ohana spaces. We got enough problems with the courts as it is.*

The intense love Henry felt for Kanani—that was her name—surprised him. He was further surprised by the intensity of fondness he felt for his folks . . . his missing friend . . . his close friends—allies in the increasingly messy struggle. This was coupled with extreme hate for the U.S. military, its callous presence, and everything else that seemed foreign to this group of islands, islands he had viewed from the uppermost part of Kahoʻolawe, the Target Island. The epicenter. These islands—the Big Island, Maui, Molokaʻi, Lānaʻi—with Oʻahu, Kauaʻi, and Niʻihau looming over the horizon—formed a dazzling lei. Hank felt a hate even more intense when he thought of those born here who had sold out their own people—who let the struggle disintegrate into petty infighting. Again he was pissed. The same anger that had compelled him to dive into the ocean in the first place now turned him around and fired his strokes.

By the fourth hour he had exhausted all resources, lost track of time and had no concern as to whether it was the fourth or fifth—or tenth hour, for that matter. He had also lost his sense of direction. He backfloated again, eyes again closed, allowing the water to cool his badly burned shoulders. Dehydrated and fantasizing about food, he knew he wouldn't make it to Maui. The colder current had probably carried him too far away from his one ace,

Molokini, the crescent-shaped islet that lay between the two islands.

Hank tried not to think. Thinking led to caring; caring only added to the pain caused by the hundred places in his back that threatened to spasm, the burning sensation in his eyes, the wretched thirst and hunger . . . aching arms, cramping legs . . .

But he stayed calm as he alternated between treading water and floating on his back, as he was doing now, simply allowing the current to carry him, to lull him. Seeing himself in similar repose on the bier, he contemplated his imminent death: what it would mean to whom. Who'd attend his funeral? He thought about the songs he would've liked to have been sent off with: "A Whiter Shade of Pale" . . . "Hi'ilawe" . . . some Beatles . . . maybe "A Day in the Life," that ominous dirge:

I read the news today, oh boy
about a lucky man who made the grade . . .

Then, before it gets too fucking weepy, crank up some Hendrix and some Motown: "All Along the Watchtower," "I Heard It Through the Grapevine," "My Girl,"—*nah, nah. Skip "My Girl." Too fucking sad.* . . . Of course, they'd need to find a body in order to have a funeral.

I can't do this to my folks. I can't disappear like Keoni . . .
Lying on his back, he sang, in a whisper,

I got sunshi-i-ine on a cloudy day
And when it's cold outside, I've got the month of May

He then shouted, slapping a beat on the water, in a mad effort to gain strength,

WE-ELL, I . . . GUESS . . . YOU'D . . . SAY
WHAT CAN MAKE ME FEEL THIS WAY

They found him that way. The 'Ohana, along with other interested parties, had organized a search and the channel was aswarm with boats. They may not have found him if he hadn't been shouting the chorus. Someone claimed he *heard* him first, heard a pitch that pierced the roar of the motor and the lapping waves, and yelled, "Cut the engine."

Hank couldn't reach for the rope so they dropped a net that he could roll into and they dragged him aboard. Like the exhausted ulua and weke he used to catch with his dad, he landed on the hard floor of the fishing boat. Someone lifted his head up and held a Pepsi to his lips. He drank.

Then he whispered something. Very faint. The man holding the can of Pepsi leaned over, putting his ear to Hank's mouth.

The man heard him say, softly, *very* softly, "Coke."

"Coke?" he told the others. "I think he wants a Coke. Not Pepsi."

"All we got is Pepsi."

"Oh, come on now," someone who may have been the captain said. "He's got to be kidding. Or delirious. Fucking guy's dehydrated, almost drowned."

"Hey," someone else shouted, "if you're gonna give him soda, at least de-fizz the damn thing."

Noon

He was back in the water. For the fourth or fifth time, he touched something fleshy and it gave him a start. His immediate thoughts were body, dead body, maybe Keoni's body. Then he saw it was a seaweed-covered, log-sized piece of wood. He grappled with it as if it were a living thing, turning over with it in an embrace that his survival depended upon. Finally, after he had won the match, he was able to rest his arms upon it while he kicked.

Soon after, he saw another log . . . more like a two-by-four. Then a tambourine. More and more wood washed toward him, and with elongated arms he gathered each piece as if it were a precious gem and wrapped the seaweed, which was as lustrous and long as the hair of a reclining Hina, around the wood to hold the unlikely raft together. Then the seaweed began to tear, and he started losing pieces of his precious stock. So he grabbed on to the stiff hemp rope that was attached to his belt. The rope slipped from his hands, yet somehow he maneuvered his body to catch the rope with his bare feet.

As he tied the pieces of wood, it really did become a raft. He reached in front and dragged his body further onto it. A disposable diaper floated by, as well as several plastic bottles, which he snapped up, but mostly it was indecipherable flotsam and debris. He turned and lay supine on the hard wooden raft. Then lit up a joint, and while it tasted wonderful, harsh yet sweet, like coca leaves, it made his mouth unbearably dry. "Water. God, I need water," he whispered as he gazed at an empty plastic bottle.

Almost immediately he felt someone lift his head up and bring a cup to his lips. "For my eyes." He tried to grab the cup but his arm was so stiff he couldn't lift it. So he motioned that he wanted the water poured over his eyes. The man holding his head up emptied the cup on Hank's face. "More. . . . To drink." Another man brought him more water. He felt the hardness of the boat's floor as he drank and drank and drank. He kept saying "More." Finally, he settled back into luxurious stupor.

While he dreamed half-awake in feverish, exhaust-driven delirium—earlier he had vomited the Pepsi, and found he could only hold crackers and water—the fishing boat skipped like a stone moving arrow-straight toward Maui, in striking contrast to what proved to be Hank's inadvertent arc-shaped venture, spiraling toward Lāna'i. Somewhere behind his dream—within which Keoni lay next to him aboard his raft, helping him kick, telling him a joke that had no end—he understood that he would live. He would see the woman who called him Henry. For this he was grateful. He would tell her he loved her, and he'd ask her to marry him. *She has to say yes.* And under the dream, under the joy, knowing now how he may have felt in his last hours, he grieved for Keoni. Did he drown out here? Did somebody have him done away with—for expediency's sake? Either way, what a way to go. Hank sank into deeper, dreamless sleep.

At Mā'alaea, he was awakened by the crew's rough attempts to be delicate as they carried him onto the dock. The ambulance crew was already there, along with a doctor who wore a Target Island t-shirt and surfer trunks. He checked Hank's temperature and blood pressure, and gave him a shot. The paramedics then carried him to the waiting stretcher-and-IV setup, and one of them placed an oxygen mask over his face. After a few deep and long breaths, Hank motioned with his now even stiffer left arm to have the mask removed. The doctor lifted it off.

"Found Keoni?" His voice was a hoarse whisper.

The doctor shook his head. He looked like *he* needed a doctor, like he hadn't slept for a month. The doctor, an 'Ohana supporter, had been one of Keoni's closest friends.

"At least we found *you,* man." He tousled Hank's now dry, curly, salt-caked hair. "You crazy son-of-a-bitch. You should be glad the sharks nevah get you."

"Sharks?" Hank found his voice. "Get sharks out deah?"

"Infested."

"Holy shit . . . *Holy* fucking shit . . . "

Under the oxygen he went, then off to Maui County Hospital.

□ □ □

Midnight

He was alone in his hospital room. He was thirsty and couldn't find a bell to ring, a button to press. "Nurse," he said out loud. "Nurse." He waited; there was no response. He started to get up, and noticed the tube sending yellow liquid into his veins.

He pulled it out.

He found a bathroom, turned on the faucet, cupping his hands to catch the water. He drank and drank and drank.

Then he went to the toilet and peed.

He peered into the hallway, saw a nurse with her back to him looking at a chart. He headed in the other direction. As he walked, he heard a voice yell, "Hey." He did not look back. He pressed an elevator button, but when he saw from the corner of his eye a nurse rapidly walking toward him, he, ignoring a second "Hey," dashed for the stairwell. He ran down to the next floor, skipping steps, and could barely keep ahead of the flying nurse. He kept going down. At each floor landing he would find himself just out of the nurse's reach.

She caught him at the basement level; he had nowhere to go. He was pressed against a door that wouldn't open. She shot a hypodermic into his left cheek and he screamed. He bolted upstairs, limping.

She didn't follow. She just hollered, "You have no pants on."

He exited through the first door he came to, and ran to an elevator and pressed the button. But instead of waiting for the elevator in the empty hallway, he ducked into another room. He looked for clothes but found only a blanket. He wrapped himself in it.

Hank ran back into the hallway and saw that the elevator door was closing. Keoni was in the elevator, waving good-bye. Another elevator, one positioned directly across, arrived. He got in. Every button had been pressed. It opened on every floor, and at every opening he'd see Keoni across the way, waving. The fourth or fifth time this happened, Hank dashed across. "You're alive," he said to Keoni.

"Not really."

"You mean you're dead?"

"Not really." The elevator began moving rapidly downward.

"Where we going?"

"To hell—"

"Christian hell?"

"—with where—"

"Huh?"

"—we're going . . . " Keoni pressed B.

Hank screamed. Eyes shut, he felt as if he were sliding down a chute. He pulled his legs up as he slid sideways, all alone, screaming.

It was a soft landing, like he had been wrapped snug in a blanket and had landed on a bed of feathers. Hank did not want to open his eyes.

Somebody shook him gently. He opened his eyes and saw the nurse. "You're having a bad dream, Mr. Rivera, and— oops, did you wet the bed? Oh, it's your IV. Did you pull it out, you naughty boy? You know we need to keep you hydrated."

The nurse reattached the IV and changed the sheet. She then looked closely at his face. "Your eyes are so red." She left, then returned with eyedrops. She asked Henry to open his eyes wide so she could put some drops in them.

Henry, feeling flustered, sad, but mostly angry, blinked away the excess.

PART I

The House on Tusitala Street

Visitations

She aimed the hose at the hibiscus bush that fronted the large, dilapidated dwelling. She wore a loose Hawaiian print shirt and very faded cut-off jeans. The man, feeling intensely over-dressed in slacks and tucked-in dress shirt, watched her turn off the faucet and begin rolling up the hose. Then she leaned over, as if to pick up something from the thick grass, and he saw that she wore no bra. Her breasts were small, pointed.

The man backed up a few steps and began whistling to announce his presence.

The woman looked up. In one hand she held a minia-ture race car. A red one. She pushed loose strands of hair from her face and smiled.

"Are you . . . Kanani Wong?" the man said.

"Wong is my maiden name."

"So you must be—"

"Yes, Kanani . . . what's this about?"

"Well, I was given your name by a friend of yours. You see, I'm working on a story. About a Hawaiian activist who disappeared mysteriously. About fifteen years ago."

"Keoni . . . " The woman dropped the red race car.

"Huh?"

"That's what *we* called him. Keoni. . . . Why do you want to write about him? Is this an article? You got a movie deal or something?"

19

The man was stung by the hostility beneath her words. "No movie deal. It's not about money or . . . I just think that people need to know his story."

"And you come to *me*? You should be talking to kūpuna."

"I've spoken to Auntie Mary. Auntie Etta. Couple other—and his family, of course."

"You've talked to Cherene and Shirley them?"

"Yeah, and his brothers."

"Keoni's brothers? They don't talk to anybody. And they talked to you?"

The man nodded, then shrugged.

"I'm impressed," she said in a flat voice. She unclipped her dark brown hair, shook her head slightly. The part that fell, a light feathery unfolding, was lighter in color, as if sun-bleached. The woman then grabbed a fistful of what had fallen, twirled it atop of her head, and reapplied the clip. Then, with an undertone of suspicion, she said, "I guess they trust you, eh?"

"Well, they put me through the wringer. Kinda like you're doing now." He scratched his neck.

She looked down and smiled sadly. "Look. I'm sorry. It sounds really good what you're doing. But I don't think I'm the person to talk to. Besides, I—I can't . . . deal with this right now."

"Sure. No problem. Let me leave my card. In case you change your mind."

She took the card, gazed at it for a moment, then dropped the card on the sidewalk. "I don't . . . I don't—" She ran toward the door, then turned to look at the man. She tore open the screen door and entered the house, letting the shaky, loose-hinged, theater-auction prop piece rattle shut.

The man picked up the card and gazed at it. He shook his head, tore it to pieces, and walked away.

Later the woman was sweeping outside on the sidewalk. She saw the business card—pieces of it. "Litterbug," she muttered, then remembered it was she who had dropped it in the first place. She started picking up the pieces, fitting them together. She looked at the name again. It seemed familiar, but she couldn't quite place it.

When the man arrived at home his phone was ringing.

Kanani (naRRafoR)

It was a tale of one huge loss and two grim visitations. I had lost my father, who had been ill for a long time. The stress had taken its toll on me and my sister, but it devastated my mom. When Dad finally succumbed—he had shrunk from his already small frame—there was at least the relief of finality. A closing final chapter, a quiet one for a man who led a quiet life, a peace intruded upon only once, some years back, when he had fought to live where he always had. Painful as it was to see him go, it was worse to see Mom fall apart the way she did. Around the time of the funeral, my sister Leimomi spent all of her time at my parents' house in Waiāhole. Finally, she decided to take Mom in. It was easier that way. Almost immediately Mom started becoming more and more forgetful. She'd get up in the middle of the night and leave the house. She'd be found wandering miles away—like she was trying to get back to the valley she knew. After a couple scary episodes, Momi's husband fixed the doors and windows so she couldn't slip away without us knowing.

While Mom was being locked up in a house, we found we were being kicked out of ours. At first I made more of it than it was worth. It seemed so earth-shattering. After all we'd been through. Yet the logic of it was irrefutable.

The clues had come in quick. The new owners first raised our rent—doubled it, to be true. We paid, reluctantly, because, at least for the time being, it was the least complicated thing to do. We knew we couldn't hold on to the place we had grown so accustomed to. I guess we had known it all along; it wasn't ours to begin with.

Maybe it was time. With Mom going through what doctors say might be the onset of Alzheimer's, I figured it might be time we moved to the countryside. This could relieve Leimomi of some of the burden. Mom could putter around in a garden. She never liked coming into town, especially Waikīkī, and who could blame her?

And during this time of loss and pondering a young man arrived. I initially mistook him for the human face behind the summons, but his mission differed. He was on a quest of his own. He was searching for Keoni, not in the sense that we all searched for the best one among us so many years ago. He was resurrecting Keoni, through the words of others, through the actions in our lives, through . . .

"Why us?" was my answer to both incursions. Both were cruel, initially, but collectively they were the kick in the 'ōkole I needed. And maybe my husband needed that kick too. The lean muscles of our early adult life had atrophied—I guess it comes with age. But we shouldn't have let our brains rot as well. We just weren't sharp anymore. We were no longer cynical scrutinizers of society; we had simply been caught in the wash.

Auwe.

"What we gon' do?" Henry said the day the notice came. He had been uncharacteristically quiet—lying on the sofa, his hands behind his head, probably contemplating

the options. In the dim light the scars on his arms—from
on-the-job cuts and scrapes—were just lines that accom-
panied his highly visible veins.

The boys were at the beach. Always at the beach.

"Well, we gotta move."

"Move where? Shit. Rent is so fricken high nowadays."

"I have a suggestion. The Windward side is cheaper.
Plus, that way we can be closer to Mom. Momi could use
some help. I wouldn't mind being closer to them."

"I dunno, honey. I've never been crazy about that side
of the island. So much rain. Plus, I already gotta spend so
much time sitting in fucking traffic. Shit. I mean, I gon' be
working on the Leeward side for like, the rest of this
decade. Now that I no have to sell fucking shoes."

I said nothing. Henry had apparently thought it
through.

"Eh, no get me wrong," he continued. "I wanna help
take care Mom. . . . Shit, she can stay with us part of the
time, if you like. You know, weekends. An' when you on
break. I jes' think Leeward is the way to go."

"Henry, you know how much the rent is for a two-, let
alone three-bedroom house nowadays? The only place we
could afford would be Wai'anae."

"So, Wai'anae then."

Part of me didn't want to move out there. For one
thing, I grew up on the Windward side. I had never lived
on O'ahu's west side. And—I hated myself for thinking
it—but I was keenly aware that Wai'anae was an econom-
ically depressed area—something I had worked so hard to
get my family away from.

On the other hand, I did have some fond memories of
those days so many years ago when the 'Ohana was in its
infancy. Those innocent days when we were a group of
young idealists who inspired and nurtured a renaissance.

It was more work than fun: exasperating marathon meetings, scraping around for funds. But boy did we party. I can't remember any time in my life that was more teeming with life—until my two babies came along, that is. We worked our asses off, and then we jammed. During those post-meeting pā'inas we went wild. Singing and hula dancing—now that's how you recover a culture.

It saved us. It was what we needed—to heal, to be strong. If evil lurked in some corner, if someone wasn't happy with the goings-on, I wasn't aware of it.

But where would all that be now? A whisper in the wind from the distant past. The 'Ohana probably doesn't even meet there anymore. And it's probably run by a whole new group of people. The Navy's still bombing the island. Is it ever going to end?

All in all, I didn't want to move to Wai'anae. But then we found this lovely three-bedroom cottage in Mākaha, with a big yard and plenty room for Mom and the boys. Then I thought, this is the way it was meant to be.

It was around the time we started packing that this guy came by. He seemed nice, though a little nervous. Henry always says I can put out a mean don't-come-near-me vibe. This guy wanted to compile information on Keoni for his dissertation, which he hoped to turn into a book one day. *Yeah, right,* was my initial reaction. Hell if I'm gonna open up that area of my life. And to some stranger?

But in a weird way, he checked out. He was young, in his mid-twenties perhaps, could have been part Hawaiian—it's hard to tell sometimes, and I was in no mood to ask. He was a little too young to have been part of the Movement, as we called it then, but he was genuinely interested. What changed my head about cooperating was that in the nearly dozen years I'd spent teaching, whenever I'd ask students if they ever heard of Keoni, the man who touched so many lives in such a big way, they'd say *Who?* They had never heard of him. Now, finally, there was someone who wanted to put his story down on the page, perhaps make his legend part of history, mythic undertones and all. We sometimes couldn't help but elevate Keoni to demigod status in our stories about him. Maybe now we could get the story straight.

Maybe.

I gave this journalist, or whatever he was, the cold shoulder at first. Turned him away, shocked as I was by his out-of-the-blue encroachment, and not in the best of moods because of our impending move. If he had been just a shade too persistent, just a shade, I wouldn't have changed my mind and called him. But he played me right. He left his business card. Imagine that, this young guy with a business card. Imagine that, him tearing it to pieces on the sidewalk when I refused to take it.

But when I got over the shock, after I had chased him away, there was one big lingering question in my mind. So I picked up those pieces. And minutes later I was dialing.

"One question. Who gave you my name?"

It didn't register at first when he said *Ginger.* But as soon as he said her last name I was so struck with guilt and pain that I knew immediately that I would cooperate.

"The business card," he said. "It wasn't my idea."

"It's not gonna work with the kind of people you're planning to interview."

"You're right."

"And be wary of using any recording devices. Ask permission first."

"Right."

"And you don't have to agree with everything I say."

"I disagree."

We both paused. Then I laughed softly. He laughed too. He had a soft yet deep and rich laugh.

Mikala's Secret

(Narrator) son of Kanani & Henry

(Waiāhole, Waikīkī, Ala Moana—Fall 1991)

'Analu

Grampa Wong was one real funny guy. Whenevah Mommy an' Daddy took me Gramma and Grampa's house way ovah on da country side, chroo da tunnel even, I use' to sit wit' him in da yard an' watch him talk to da plants. He use' to teach me lotta t'ings. Like how fo' know which side of da bed fo' climb on fo' make shua you sleep good an' dream sweet. O' which side of da bread fo' put da peanut buttah on. How you gotta look good—at da bread, dat is. He always tell me, "If you no can tell one side of da bread from da adda, you not looking hard enough. How you gon' get chroo life wit'out looking good?" He even teach me how fo' pick tangerines. He had one tangerine tree in his yahd. He tell me, "By kala, shape, an' disposition—espeshly disposition."

One time, when I was sitting in da yahd wit' Grampa I wen' notice dat he wen' sit on some fresh birdshit. So I tole him, *Hey Grampa, I t'ink you sitting on birdshit.* Da buggah nevah even move. In fack, he tole me fo' sit on da adda spot of fresh birdshit. He said was good luck fo' sit on da kine bird doodoo. An' he tole me dat whenevah I sit on bird doodoo fo' no tell anybody 'cause dat would spoil da good luck.

26

My grampa use' to tell me t'ings like dat.

An' he use' to say, "Remembah, Mikala"—my name 'Analu, but he always call me Mikala, 'cause dat was his hanai kid braddah's name—"Remembah, I not goin' be heah too long, an' some t'ings I only can tell you once—so lissen good . . . an' remembah."

Inside da house he nevah say da t'ings he tell me outside. He only wink at me o' tickle me—he knew all my tickle-ish places—or sometimes he make me pull out his white hair wit' tweezahs, but dat nevah work 'cause da white part would only spread out mo' and mo' . . . an' da mo' I tweeze 'om, da mo' white. I tole 'om dat planny times, but he still like I do 'em.

One time when we wen' go visit Gramma an' Grampa's house he was sick in bed. Some adda aunties an' uncles was deah. I tot dat was cool 'cause I would get to play wit' my cousins. I get planny cousins.

Anyways, I wen' go peek inside his bedroom an' he was looking kinda tired. But ja'like he knew I was deah an' he wen call my name:

"Mik—Mikala . . . Mikala."

"I stay heah, Grampa," I tole 'om. I was huffing an' puffing 'cause jes' befo' I was playing chasemastah wit' some of my cousins. An' dey real fass.

"Mikala . . . I stay tired of dis ole body. An' dis body tired of me. Pretty soon I not gon' be able fo' move. But no worry. All dat means is I gon' change . . . into one bird, Mikala. No tell nobody now. Dass our final secret."

□ □ □

Was right befo' da funeral dat we wen' go to Ala Moana Shopping Centah. Daddy wen' already try on one suit at da fancy clothes stoah in Kapahulu, and now Mommy needed fo' get one dress fo' her and nice shirts fo' me an' Mākena.

Mommy always take long time shopping and Daddy hate shopping, so he tole her he would take me an' my braddah to Petland—aftah we buy our shirts. So dass what we did. We work fass.

From when I was real small Daddy used to take me to Petland fo' look at da fish. Neon Tetra, Ma'ble' Hatchet, Tigah Bob, da kine catfish dat clean the aquarium glass all day. Me and Mākena use' to always hit the glass fo' make da fish turn direction all at once. Now'days I look at all kine animals, not jes' da fish. Anyways, when I was wand'ring aroun' I came to the birdcages. Had canaries, parrots, parakeets, and one lovebird. All by itself. Had one orange face, wit' green and blue feddahs. Da bird was looking right at me. "Grampa?" I ask 'om. The bird staht making all kine noise. Like was excited. *Tweet-tweet-to-weet! Tweet-tweet-to-weet!* Ja'like was saying *Yeah, it's me, it's me.* Already I stay t'inking, dass Grampa. An' I wanted 'om. I wanted dis bird. Not jes' fo' me. I wanted da lovebird fo' Gramma too. I wanted Grampa fo' be wit' her again. She was gon' live wit' my Auntie Momi folks. But I knew she was lonely.

I wen' stare and stare at da lovebird. Da buggah stare back wit' his head tilted, ja'like Grampa. Had fo' be him. He was on sale fo' one hundred an' fifty dollahs. Dass cheap fo' one granfaddah. In fack, I heard Mommy say to Daddy dat da coffin cos' t'ousans of dollahs. Jes' da coffin. But da coffin only gon' have his body. Da bird get his spirit.

I wen' ask da bird. "Grampa? 'Ass you? You can tell me, Grampa."

Right den Mommy wen' come by wit' planny packages an' stuff. She wen' hand some ovah to Daddy, who was coming from da adda direction. Mommy was saying, "Sorry I took so long. Should we get groceries or should we just pick up—"

Daddy said, "Oh, you bought shoes."

"Yeah." She was smiling. "Leonard gave me half off."

"Buggah bettah give you discount," Daddy was saying. "He owes me bigtime."

I nevah like go. I said, "Can we can we can we buy da bird?" I nevah like tell Mommy dem I tot was Grampa. Dey no would believe.

"Look, Nalu," Mom wen' say, "we can't be buying birds right now."

"But . . . jes' one . . . "

Daddy said, "You heard yo' maddah. We not millionaires."

"Ho mannnnn."

"Yeah, c'mon Nalu." Mākena was jumping in. "We gotta go. I hungry." Dey was all against me.

□ □ □

Was real hard, da nex' few weeks 'cause no had Grampa. An' den we had fo' move.

I got mo' an' mo' worried about da bird. What if someone wen' buy 'om already? What if da buggah wen' die of one broken hot? Gramma was sad too. She needed him.

One day, aftah me and Mākena wen' help Mommy and Daddy pack up t'ings all morning, Mommy tole us we could go to da beach. I guess she figgah 'ass one a da last chances we would get fo' ride waves at Waiks. So I wen' go wit' my braddah fo' bodysurf at Walls. He was one of da best guys already. Da adda guys already talk about him like he one pro. Sometimes when I get out of da watah, and go lie on top da big wide wall—feel good 'cause da cement wall keep da sun's heat, an' I like dat warm feeling—I heah da adda kids talking about Mākena Rivera. Make me feel good, man. I like be ja'like my braddah.

But dis day, I nevah like surf, 'cause da waves was junk. Not much happening. An' I nevah feel like lying on the wall. Mainly, I was t'inking about da bird. I even brought all da money I had—some fi' dollah bills my aunties wen' give me at the funeral dat I was gon' use fo' buy one new boogie board, plus my chree dollahs allowance and some change I wen' grab from da ashtray in Mommy and Daddy's bedroom.

So I stahted walking down Kalakaua Avenue.

I wen' pass da hotel dat Daddy call da Reeched Nixon hotel, 'cause dat's where dis guy Reeched use' to stay when he was on vacation. Den was a few mo' hotels befo' da pink one and den da big one wheah we went fo' one wedding.

I wen' keep on walking. I knew dat the hotel wit' da lighted up elevatah was up da street somewheah, an' dat was near Ala Moana beach and Ala Moana Shopping Centah.

But I couldn't find da hotel wit' da lighted up elevatah. Da road was turning, den splitting in two, an' I nevah know which way fo' go. I wen' pass planny hotels already, but not da one wit' da elevatah. Shit, maybe I wen' pass 'om already. I already wen' walk so fah. Some tourists wen' even ask me if I was lost an' I tot dat was funny 'cause I live heah an' dey no live heah. But was true. I was lost.

"I looking fo' Ala Moana Centah. I gotta meet my Mommy deah." I made da last part up. An' dey pointed. Same direction as I was going.

So I kep' going.

Finally I saw one place I recanize. Was da military place, Fo't De Roosie. I knew dat was by California Pizza and da silvah dome. Den I knew wheah I was. I was happy. An' tired. Man, was far already.

I wen' walk aroun' da bend part, an' den I saw da elevatah. Was moving up. To da Tapa Da Ilikai, whe' we had dinnah one time. You did it, Nalu, I tole myself.

I knew wasn't dat fah now. I wen' keep on going.

Pretty soon I wen' pass da place wheah use' to have twin tyeatahs, den da boat place. Den I was crossing by Ala Moana beach. I could see da shopping centah. Boy oh boy oh boy. Was huge.

Unlike a Deposition

(Waikīkī, Ala Moana—Late Fall 1991)

"This is some huge place." The young, somewhat studious-looking man looks around the cavernous living room. Boxes are everywhere, some bound with twine. Bookshelves are lined all along one long wall, and along a shorter one. If one were to rip the roof off and peer in, the shelves would form a gigantic L. "Man, is this a library?"

"We got rid of a few hundred already. The wife, she book crazy. Gotta read all the damn time. It's a good time to get rid of 'em, since we're moving. Too much dust anyway."

The young man goes to a shelf and picks up a book. "Wow. Eric Ambler. She reads this stuff?"

"Nah, thass me. I like mystery, intrigue, spy stuff. . . . But I finish with these, so if you like 'om, take 'om."

"Really?"

Henry grabs a couple more Eric Ambler books. Hands them over to the man. "Take 'om take 'om. . . . I got Hammett too. You like Dashiell Hammett?"

"I should pay—"

"Pay—you kidding? You helping, brah."

Henry empties out a box half-filled with books. Brings the box alongside the man, who is on his knees browsing. "Anything you like, throw 'om in here. We already wen' put aside those we wanna keep."

The young man gets up and walks along the shelves. Each time he stops to look at a book Henry says, "Take 'om." Sometimes the man says, "You sure?" and Henry says, "Please."

After a few minutes, the man stops, leans against a waist-high shelf, and pulls a pack of Marlboros out of his shirt pocket. Then he looks at what he has done, says, "Geez, I just do this without thinking. On automatic." He pauses, then adds, "Is it okay to smoke?"

"Hey, it's your body. Keep in mind, though, this house is a firetrap." Henry then smiles. "Come to think of it, now may be a good time."

The man puts his cigarettes back in his shirt pocket. "I should quit."

Henry shrugs, then walks to a bookcase on the far end of the living room, gets on his knees as he searches the bottom shelf. "Shit, I forgot about this stuff. There's some good shit here. Here, you gotta check *this* book out." *Doña Flor and Her Two Husbands.*

"I read that."

"Really? Then you must like—"

The man kneels besides Henry. "Sheesh. You got lotta Márquez books."

"Take 'om take 'om take 'om." Henry pulls some books out. The young man goes through them, setting some aside, putting back others. Henry stands up, facing the man, who stands up also. "Actually," Henry says, "I used to smoke, but one day I almost drowned, you see. That put the fire out. Thass when I figured, eh, who needs it?"

"You almost drowned from smoking?"

"It's a long story. Complicated, too."

"I like long stories. That's why I brought tape."

"Come. Come. Befo' we start, lemme show you upstairs."

"Upstairs?"

"Yeah. The bedrooms are upstairs."

The man shakes his head. "They don't make houses like these anymore."

"Fuck no," Henry says as he leads the man up the steps. "Funny, we used to live in one small apartment. One-bedroom. The whole place could fit in the living room—easy. But with two boys, we thought we'd better go for this, eh? Even though kinda run down. Was a good deal back then. Five-fifty a month."

"Shit, that's great."

"Used to be great. . . . Well, here's the bathroom—if you need to go. The boys' bedroom is thataway. Closed off to the human race." Henry walks toward it. Peeks in. "Ey, not too bad. They boxed most a' their junk already.

"Let's go this way." Henry leads the man to the master bedroom. "One more box-filled room."

"I see you haven't packed your stereo yet."

"That's the last thing I'm gonna pack, and the first thing I'm gonna unpack in the new place."

Henry goes to the receiver and turns it on. The FM station is playing "Sweet Home Alabama."

"This song rocks," Henry says.

"Man, you got albums," the man says when he sees an unboxed pile.

"Yeah. My generation's albatross." Henry squats to sift through the LPs. The man squats beside him.

"My dad still has his 8-track player."

"No shit? The buggah work?"

"I dunno. He keeps it in what used to be my room along with his Betamax. And his Victrola. Some silkie shirts from the '30s . . . "

Henry grins. "Fuck. You putting me on."

"No, really. He saves all kinds of things. Thinks they're going to be valuable one day. Say, you got Eric Burdon and the Animals."

"My kinda band."

"Yeah, I'm partial to them too. . . . And the Stones."

"Kinda before your time, uh? Thought you was more the disco and punk generation."

"Yeah, but I spent those years listening to C&K . . . Kalapana."

"I got their stuff too, somewhere in this disorganized pile. I tell you, jes' when I ready to dump all this, I see something like—here we go—*The Best of Judy Collins,* and I'm hearing her singing 'Someday Soon.' How can I throw that in the trash?"

"Then don't."

Henry takes a deep breath. "Well, 'nuff a' this shit. We better get cranking."

"Yep." The young man stands up. He follows Henry down the hallway.

Henry turns back to him. "After we get set up in the new place, we should set up a day where we can jes' play albums all day long."

"You got it," the man says as he follows Henry down the stairwell.

"Olomana . . . Beatles . . . whatever."

"Can't beat the Beatles."

"Nope. No way."

□ □ □

"So why are you folks moving?"

"Well, damn new owners kept raising and raising the rent. Tryin' to drive us out. An' guess what?" Henry turns to face the man. "They succeeded. We gotta be out by the end of the month."

"Gee, maybe I shouldn't be imposing on you right now."

"Nah. Always get time to sit and talk." Henry sizes up the living room area, zeroes in on the coffee table and sofa. "Guess we should do it right here."

The man nods. "The landowners must have plans, huh?"

"Oh, shit yeah. Think about it. This place is zoned for hotel rooms—commercial space. Think they gon' be satisfied with two-story houses? They gon' build something big here. Guarans. My guess is one thirty-story hotel. That way they get a return on their investment, eh? Thass how it works, eh? . . . Shit, when I was a kid all of Waikīkī was like this. Cottages and trees. *The Jungle,* we used to call it. Lotta local people used to live here. Almost all a' that is gone now."

"Too bad."

"Tell me about it."

Henry moves a couple of boxes out of the way, then drags a recliner over by the coffee table and indicates to the man that he sit there. Then he removes some stray clothes and magazines from the sofa and plops himself down. The man begins setting up a tape machine on the coffee table.

"Got an outlet near?"

"Yeah," Henry says while jumping up. He goes to the kitchen, returns with an extension cord. "Here, plug it into this. See if it blows up."

Henry observes as the man tests the machine. The man lays out some handwritten notes on the table, then presses the PLAY and RECORD buttons simultaneously.

"Gee, I hope I can do this right. I not used to—"

"Hey, don't worry. You're gonna do fine." The man presses the PAUSE button. "Seems like it's working. Ready?"

"I guess."

"Well, let's start." The man presses the PAUSE button again.

□ □ □

"This is Tuesday, October 14, 1991. It's 4:15 in the afternoon. I'm talking to Henry Rivera." The man presses the PAUSE button again. "This way I can easily identify the tape later."

"Good move." Again he presses the button.

"So. Can you tell me a little bit about Keoni? Like how you came to know him. How you met him . . . "

"Well . . . boy, this is awkward. . . . Ah, where to begin . . . "

"Take your time."

Long seconds pass. Then Henry says, "Well, I didn't meet him till, shee, I think was late February, or early March . . . hmm, let's see . . 1976. The Waiāhole-Waikāne stuff was heating up. You know, the plans to develop the area. Move all the long-term tenants out." The man nods. "So, let's see, that's right after the court cases, about the time the trespassers were given suspended sentences. Yeah, yeah, that's right. I was outside the courtroom that day. Holding some sign somebody wen' put in my hands. Shit, I didn't even look at what the sign said. I just held it up . . . "

The interviewer is startled by the sound of a kid crying. He looks at Henry. "Should we stop?"

"Nah, nah, nah. Kanani's outside. She can take care of it. Shit, if the world stop ev'rytime one kid cry . . . the tape still going?" The man nods. "Boy, pretty stupid, eh, so far? I bet you nevah know what you was getting into, eh?"

"True. But this is good. You're doing good."

"I dunno. . . . So anyway, I met Keoni there. He came up to me. I was smoking a cigarette. This was way before I quit. He said something like, 'That can kill you. Can I have one?'"

"He smoked?"

"Oh yeah. You nevah know?"

"It's just . . . I dunno. Didn't think he could be—" He hits the Marlboro pack in his shirt pocket. "—as foolish as me."

Henry laughs. "I dunno, man. The buggah wen' light up, like ev'rybody else. Anyway, we had this connection right away. I thought, hey this guy's pretty cool. Didn't know he was running the show. He was so easygoing. An' as I got to know him better, the more I thought, chee, there's something different, you know, special, about this guy. "

"A lot of people share the same feelings."

"You know who you should talk to? You should talk to Glenn Hinaʻole. He live in Kaimukī. In fact, just a few blocks away from here. Buggah knew Keoni from ninth grade. Hung out with him all through high school. They go way back." The man writes the name down.

Kanani steps into the living room. She smiles at the man. "Where's ʻAnalu?" Henry asks.

"He's with Mākena—at the beach."

"Hope big braddah looking out for little braddah."

"I told him to make sure Nalu's in sight."

"Well, Nalu's 'fraid of the deep anyway." Henry looks at the interviewer. "I made him afraid . . . that should take care of the next few years."

"Gee, wha' did you do?"

"Yeah, tell him how you threw the poor kid in," Kanani says.

Henry laughs. "An' I kept pushing his head in. That's how you drown-proof 'om. Teach 'om to respect the ocean."

"That's how you teach them fear . . . " Kanani turns to the man. "As you can see, we don't always agree on strategy."

Henry says, "So who was that crying—outside?"

"What crying?" Kanani says.

Henry and the man look at each other. Henry shrugs. Kanani goes into the kitchen of the large, musty, box- and book-lined house. The two men again look at each other. This time Henry shrugs and they laugh. "Tape still running?"

"Hell, I'm just gonna let it run. I can cut things later."

Kanani returns. She asks the interviewer, "You want a beer or something?" The young man waves *no*. Kanani sits down on the armrest of Henry's big chair.

"When did the troubles begin?"

"Had a lot to do with politicians. Funny the way people connect in this town. Small world squared. Seems like he was being maneuvered. He started having, what you call them, acolytes? Disciples?"

"Parasites," Kanani says. "Hangers-on."

"To me was kinda like, you know that painting, *The Last Supper?*" The writer nods.

"I think everybody knows that painting, Henry."

Henry looks at Kanani. "Wise-ass." He faces the interviewer. "Well, was like the painting, except . . . there's more than one Judas. In fact had Judases all around."

"Maneuvering for power," Kanani says. "It got really weird. I'm sorry. This is Henry's interview. I shouldn't be—"

"No, no," the man says. "This is good. I'm just trying to get information, so the more people . . . " Kanani settles in a bit more.

"On this last trip—" Henry begins to say. Kanani looks at Henry. Then her eyes roll upward.

"Yeah," the interviewer says. "Tell me about that. What was he doing there? Was he connecting with someone?"

"I tell you, that channel between the two islands had more boats than there are tourists walking down Kalākaua Avenue right now. An' this is tourist season. All kinds of shit was goin' on. Fishing boats, zodiacs, naval vessels—you name it. But shit, when you need one. . . . The boat that was supposed to pick up Keoni didn't show. Then there was sightings of smoke on the shore. Far from where Keoni them was supposed to be. Now who was there, if the island's supposed to be uninhabited, eh? How could the other guys have lost him on the trails?"

"These were Logan, Kuahine . . . "

"Yeah, and the so-called 'mystery man.' Three of them in all. That freaks me out to this day: somebody who had just gone along. Those guys say they think he fell—maybe off some cliff—or accidentally detonated a missile. I don't buy that shit at all. Something happened out there."

Kanani shuts her eyes momentarily.

"But," Henry continued, "the lawyers told us, we have no case. No body was found. Get that. No body. Only circumstantial evidence. Hey, circumstantial evidence— thass good enough for me, man."

"The guys with him that night," the interviewer says. "They've been interrogated, right?"

"Couple a times," Henry replies. "Before they went into hiding."

"One of them's still around," Kanani says.

"Oh yeah, thass right. Charlie Kuahine. I think he's working for OHA."

The interviewer jots down something, then looks up at Henry and Kanani. "And the third man?"

Henry and Kanani begin to speak at the same time. They both stop. Kanani tilts her head to defer to her husband.

"No, you go, honey."

Kanani looks at her husband, then the interviewer and says, "Logan and Kuahine swear they don't know who he was."

"Fucking liars," Henry mutters.

"The 'Ohana was never the same without Keoni," Kanani adds. "His disappearance created too much distrust."

"Yeah, and she was in the thick of it," Henry says, indicating his wife. "I wasn't as involved in the day-to-day stuff, yet even then I could see ev'rybody kinda looking at each other . . . watching each other's moves . . . "

Kanani says, "People suspected that organized crime had infiltrated the group, and suspicions became beliefs, and beliefs became facts. Verified or not."

"Shit, Nani, was verified."

She closes her eyes again. "I know."

"Do you think he was murdered?" Henry and Kanani look at each other.

"Stop da tape," Henry says.

"Huh?"

"Stop da tape." The interviewer presses the STOP button.

□ □ □

"This is strictly off the record. Excuse this, but hey, we got two kids." The interviewer nods. "Why was Chung—you know who I talking about? Uncle Cappy?"

The interviewer nods and says, "Cherene folks gave me the lowdown on that . . . the family's theory as to how it went down."

"Thing is, after Keoni disappeared, this guy was showing up at strategy meetings. He never was involved with the 'Ohana before, so how come he was around all of a sudden?"

"Damage control," Kanani mutters.

"Plus, he got his boys, the ones who do the shit work for him. We didn't know it back then. Didn't put it all together till a year or two later, when those same goons started hassling the demonstrators. You know, the Chinatown incident."

"You're talking about organized crime people."

"Organized. Disorganized. With links to the legislature, the courts. That's what we're talking about. Sure you wanna get into this shit?"

The interviewer laughs nervously. "Well, so far none of it is what I thought it would be, but, as I keep telling people, the story's got to be told."

Henry turns to Kanani. "What's the guy's name, the guy on Maui? He was publishing that gay community newspaper. Was one weird name."

"Philpott."

"Yeah, yeah. Philpott. One of Chung's boys threatened him—with a gun—when he published some stuff, speculating on why Keoni disappeared."

"In a gay tabloid?"

"Yeah, Chung's guy, his right-hand man, opened his jacket. Showed Philpott a gun. That's how serious it is, man.

"This happened on Maui?"

"Yeah, Keʻanae. Shit, Philpott had the guts to print what ev'rybody was talking about. The buggah gay, yet he get more guts than all the fucking heteros."

Kanani shakes her head. "Let's not go there, Henry."

"You know what I'm saying. I—"

"Just don't go there."

"Okay, okay. Anyway, Chung's goon supposedly told him, 'You trying to make us look bad?' And this happened right in Keoni's backyard. And these same goons were spreading rumors about how Keoni was one dope dealer—not just one user. Eh, we all know he toked once in a while—fuck, our whole generation did—but pusher? And who's spreading this bullshit?" Henry points his finger to emphasize each word. "The *very* guy who oversees the drug trade in Hawaiʻi."

"So he's your prime suspect . . . in a murder?"

"As far as I know, he gave the order. Guys like these don't get their own hands dirty."

The interviewer says, "This came up when I talked to Cherene and Wayne, Keoni's siblings. Lots of suspicions, but so little that's concrete."

"Well, problem is, we never could *prove* anything. I tell you, had fifty guys ready for shoot 'om if they just had *one* solid piece of evidence. One fucking piece. And then they would go after 'om. It's like when Marley got shot—"

"Bob Marley," Kanani adds.

"Yeah," Henry says, glancing at his wife, "I think he knows which one." Kanani rolls her eyes.

"Shit," Henry continues, "when those fuckahs shot Marley, this was in '78, his boys retaliated. His boys were judge, jury, executioner. They went after the perpetrators and they wen' nail 'om, one by fucking one. Man, the shooters were freaking out. Some of these guys killed themselves. Couldn't handle . . ."

"Henry's been reading about Bob Marley."

"Jes' one solid piece."

Kanani sighs, then gets up. "I better check an' see if the boys are back."

"If they was back they'd be walking in, getting the floor all wet."

"They might be in the back. I just want to check." She leaves.

"Is she okay?"

"Yeah, she all right. Pretty heavy, though, to relive those times . . . chee, fifteen years already . . . " Henry sinks into the sofa. "You can roll tape now."

"Huh?"

"Tape. You can start it again."

"Oh, okay. Good." The interviewer presses the PLAY and RECORD buttons. Then he presses the STOP button. Pops out the cassette. Looks at it. Puts it back in. Presses PLAY and RECORD again. Looks at Henry, smiling, "Got lots of tape left."

Outside, Kanani leans against the clothesline support pole, hugging herself. She gazes at children playing in the next yard.

In the living room the interview continues:

"Finally, Kanani and I just said *fuck it*. It was just getting too weird. Plus, I was tired of tryin' to be there for a struggle

that had gotten so half-assed; we started seeing all our
friends living in houses they bought while we were dedicating
our lives toward 'saving the 'aina.' You know, we came of
age in the sixties. Never bought into those, what-you-call,
middle-class values, but suddenly we were so tired of the
struggle. I mean, not that we wanted to be on the fast track
to material success. For myself, I was just tired of paying
somebody else's fricken mortgage." Henry snickers. "Shit, I
still paying some asshole's fricken mortgage.

"One thing Auntie Ku'ulei told us that drove it all
home: 'Gotta take care family first.' Thass all she said.
We had one kid den, we were both jobless. Thass when I
figured, forget about all these fucking meetings, forget
about all the fucking book work toward some stupid
degree. Time to bring in some cash. That's when I got a
job working construction. Pays the bills, braddah."

"I can relate. I'm paying someone's mortgage, too."

"Well, if you no can get one book deal out of this you can
come work construction with me. You look strong enough."

The interviewer snickers. "I may have to take you up on
that. This is *really* preliminary, you know. The thought of
a book is—I dunno—beyond me right now. At the very
least, though, it's gonna be on the public record. And it's
quite a story."

The phone rings. The two men look at it.

Kanani walks in and picks it up. "Hello."

"This is Ala Moana security," the caller says. "We have
a boy here—"

"Mākena?"

"He says his name is 'Annaloo'? 'Annaloo Rivera'?"

"Can't be. He's at the beach with—" She looks at the
two men.

"He's about seven, eight years old." Kanani hears a
faint "seven" behind the man's voice. "He's wearing a
blue Town & Country t-shirt—"

"And green shorts. Oh, my god." She looks at the two men. "Nalu's at Ala Moana."

"Beach or shopping center?" Henry asks as he starts to get up.

"This is the shopping center, right?" Kanani says into the phone. Then she nods at Henry.

"Well, he's here," the security guard says. "We're right outside of Petland."

"Can I please speak to him?" Kanani says. Henry is standing next to her, squeezing her shoulder.

"Sure," the man says. "Hold on." The interviewer shuts off the tape recorder and stands up too.

"Hello." A child's voice. A sad voice.

"Baby."

"Hi, Mommy."

"What are you doing there?" Kanani is clenching her teeth, closing her eyes tight.

"I not lost. I jes'—"

"How did you get there?"

"I wen' walk."

"Oh, baby. . . . Look, Mommy's coming right now. Okay?"

"Yeah, let's go," Henry says.

"Okay," the voice on the phone says.

"Love you, baby."

"Love you too, Mommy."

The interviewer moves to pack up. Henry says, "Ain't got time for that. Let's jes' go."

"You drive," Kanani says, as the three rush to Kanani's Honda Civic and head toward the shopping center.

□ □ □

"I'm his mother," Kanani says to the uniformed man. "Where is he?" The trio had made their way through the passing crowd in this busy shopping center.

They had come to a screeching halt when they came across the security people standing in front of the pet store.

Two of the security men move to create an opening. 'Analu, standing about belly high to those around him, is sucking on a lollipop.

"How? Why?" Kanani asks as she bends down to her son, pushing strands of hair away from his face. "Why did you come here?"

"I wanted fo' see Grampa," he whispers into her ear.

She cups his face with her hand. "What do you mean, Grampa?"

"Da bird dat was in da stoah," he whispers. "Dat was Grampa. I *know*. 'Cause he tole me. I wasn't suppose' to tell." 'Analu starts to get visibly upset. "Da bird no stay now."

Henry squats down to face his son. "Who told you this?"

"Grampa tole me, befo' he wen' die. He said he was gon' come back as one bird."

Kanani stands up and turns away momentarily. One of the store employees says to her, "He was upset about something. He was running around the store, in tears, saying something about a bird. He started knocking things down. We figured he was lost."

Henry stands up, pats his son's head, reaches for Kanani's shoulder. "We'll pay for the damages," he says. Kanani turns toward him. Her quivering lower lip, her pained eyes signal to Henry that she is struggling to rein in her emotions.

While Henry comforts his wife, the interviewer talks to, then dismisses the guards. He then takes 'Analu to a bench and they both sit down. He is animated as he talks with the boy, attracting Henry's attention. After a few moments Kanani is looking on too. 'Analu is smiling.

Minutes later, the family's back in the car. The interviewer's sitting up front with Henry. Kanani sits with 'Analu in the rear seat. The kid's head is resting on her lap.

"Drop me off at the beach, hon," Kanani says. "I want to get Mākena." Henry nods.

"I can go wit' you, ma?"

"Sure, baby," she says. She tells Henry, "I'll walk back with them."

The two men arrive back at the house. Henry thanks the interviewer for helping out.

"Geez, I didn't do anything. I just went along for the ride."

"Well, you quieted down the kid."

"He's something else. Not too many kids cause such commotion at pet stores."

"Tell me about it," Henry says, looking sheepish for a moment. "What you said to him, by the way? Gee, the way you calmed him down—I could use some pointers."

"Oh, that was nothing." The man shrugs, throws a hand up. "I just—you know . . ." He starts rolling up the microphone wire.

"No, I don't know. I prob'ly woulda yelled at him to shut the fuck up. Please advise. Off the record if you want." The man packs the microphone wire in a case and places the lid on the recorder. Then he looks up.

Henry is squinting at him, a cautionary probing.

The interviewer looks at Henry, exhales as if he were making a large smoke ring, then says, "Okay. . . . This is kinda embarrassing. I told him that death is a freedom bird. I was just making up shit. I told him his grandpa had been trapped in his body so long that the last thing he wanted was to do time in a cage. I chanced it and told him, 'I bet the bird winked at you. To let you know it was him.' And he nodded." The interviewer snickers. "Then I told him that his 'grandpa' had probably been purchased by somebody and had probably escaped already. I thought 'Analu would say, 'what a crock a' shit,' but no, he had this look of wonder in his face. Don't ask me. . . . Then I described how his grandpa had joined other escaped birds in flight. Into the blue sky."

Henry laughs. "Hey, thass pretty good. I tell you, da kid no buy *my* bullshit. Not since he was three. Sheezes."

The interviewer laughs, then says, "Funny thing is, it started sounding real plausible to me."

"Whatchu mean?"

"Well, my thinking is, if you tell a made-up story like you believe it, I mean fucking *believe* it, maybe others will believe it too, huh?

"Maybe I should be interviewing *you*."

Twenty minutes later Kanani walks in with the two boys, the taller one still wet and carrying a body board. The tape recorder and case still lie on the coffee table, along with a large box containing a few books. The two men are nowhere in sight. The two boys head upstairs to shower. As they walk up the stairs, they, along with their mother, who's headed into the kitchen, hear a noise from up above. It sounds like a chair being dragged across the floor. Kanani follows the two boys up the stairs. The sound gets louder: a deep, pulsating *thump thump thump*. When the three of them reach Henry and Kanani's bedroom, they see the two men sitting on the floor amidst a pile of albums. Music is pumping out of the speakers.

"Sorry to make myself at home," the interviewer says.

Henry says, "Ey, whenever you here, it is your home."

The interviewer gazes at the tall fourteen-year-old. "You must be Mākena." He gets on his feet and shakes the kid's hand. "I'm Alika."

□ □ □

In bed, way after midnight

What a day. Brings back memories, huh babe?
About what? Runaway kids or lost friends?
Felt like I was reliving those days.

Yeah. Me too. Kanani rolls over and gazes at Henry's face. He pulls out a hand from under his head and pulls her face toward his until their cheeks touch.

Kanani rolls back.

You think we can trust this guy?
Yeah, yeah. He's cool.
I hope so. We told him so much. She hits his chest. *You, especially.*

You got me into this, Nani.
I know, I know . . . She stares at the ceiling.

I tell you what, though. At this point in my life I ain't gonna worry about who I can trust. Like Alika says, the story gotta get told. Besides, what we got to lose that we haven't lost already?

Oh, . . . everything else.

Beth

(Waikīkī—Early Winter 1991–92)

Kanani

In the summer of '86 a woman moved into the old house next door. Having heard screaming coming from her quarters from day one, I wasn't interested in getting acquainted. Though we traded smiles when we passed along the sidewalk, too often she looked like shit, like she had been up the whole night. So I was wary.

Kids are different. Mākena and 'Analu were out playing with her son and daughter the instant they met. The bigger ones would part the windbreak trees that lined the old wooden fence that separated our lots and climb over. The younger ones were more enterprising. They squeezed between the wood planks, and after a while it had become a gaping, convenient hole. Whenever Beth and I saw each other through the gaps in the trees and the gaping hole, we'd wave. Usually we'd be out in our respective yards, raking the dead leaves, weeding the grass, or watering plants and flowers.

One day, a real hot summer day, we were both out watering and she accidentally sprayed me with her hose. The water came from over the tall trees. It was nice at

50

first, since it was hot out and I was wishing I could find time to take a dip in the ocean. But then I was wearing jeans and a t-shirt, not a swimsuit. When I felt the spray again I got a bit irritated. This neighbor of mine was crossing the line.

When it happened the third time I retaliated. I shot a spray of water over too. *See how you like it.* Of course, I immediately got sprayed again. Annoyed, I dropped the hose and went toward the kid-sized hole. As soon as I parted the thick clusters of leaves for my larger frame, she sprayed me right in the chest. Then she burst out laughing. I had to laugh too. Then I grabbed my hose and fired back. It was war. Before you know it we were both soaking wet.

"I don't know what came over me," she said after we turned off our hoses and took a moment to catch our breaths. "It was so hot . . . " She fanned herself with her free hand, rolling the bottom part of her t-shirt upward, then bunching it up to squeeze the water out. Then she peeled the t-shirt away from her breasts. Her gestures were so natural that I found myself doing the same.

Soon we were spending time at each other's house, trading recipes, jokes, jabs at the local politicians, and, mostly, gossip. Frankly, it was a bit scary at times, the way she knew so much about the goings-on around the neighborhood. The plus side, I remember thinking once, was that if Henry ever decided to fool around, she'd know. Well, maybe that wasn't a plus.

I wasn't much for gossip, mostly because I'd seen all too often how it could get out of hand, how truth would get lost in the impulse to make the story richer—the end result being one huge, juicy lie. But it was different with Beth. I just enjoyed her tales. The way her eyes would light up. The way she'd lower her voice.

We started going for walks around Kapiʻolani Park on Tuesdays and Fridays. There she'd flirt with every good-looking surfer, runner, skater, soccer player—you name it. And she'd give the regulars names: Mr. Pecs . . . Mr. Perfect. . . Mr. Hollywood. If he had a good face and a tight small ass, she let it be known that she was attracted. In this regard I tried to distance myself from her. I was happily married. I never tried to hide my ring.

□ □ □

"Oh, my god," Beth was saying. "Look at him. *Look* at him."

"Can't you be more subtle? Why act like bait when you're swimming among sharks?"

We had stopped by the water fountain behind the bandstand. We were stretching. Beth was using one of the picnic benches to extend her leg. I used to think that men liked it more when women ignored them. That they were turned off by the bolder types. She kept proving me wrong.

Mr. Smiley came by.

"Hmmm," she said. "Hi." Her voice was young-girl gurgly. He smiled, as he always did. Then took off on a run. Not a jog. A run. Like he was on high-octane. Like he was filled up on her.

I hit her shoulder. "You gotta stop doing that. It's embarrassing."

"Oh, come on. I'm just having fun." I had to admit that her attitude was contagious.

"You're getting us into trouble is what you're doing, girl."

"Ho," she said as she stared in the direction of the fading runner, "but he makes me wet."

"You have a husband to do that. . . . Well, at least the follow-through part."

Her eyes lit up. "Speaking of husband . . . " Her tongue wagged back and forth. "Last night . . . "

Uh-oh.

"I got Steve to . . . you know." Big smile on her face. "*Ooh.*" She said that a lot. *Ooh.* Sometimes it was *ah.* In any case, both her *oohs* and *ahs* were very guttural, kind of like a fake cough, like something you'd say while hitting your chest, as she often did.

I knew where she was going. "Did he do what I think he did?"

"Let's just say his tongue musta been—" Her tongue stayed down: "—weally numm aff-ter." That's as subtle as she gets.

Then she quickly added, "Has Henry gone down on you lately?"

I wasn't taken aback, not anymore. My reply was "Not as much as I'd like."

Bad comes with the good, and I was too often reminded of the tragic side to her life. In the more than five years I'd known her I saw her survive two abusive husbands, a string of weird boyfriends, and thyroid cancer. And if that weren't enough, her teenage children were giving her grief.

There was a time after her second marriage crumbled where she was seeing two guys, on alternate nights. Even my usually distracted husband noticed the pattern. It was great for a couple of weeks, she told me later. I guess it was great until that one night when Henry and I heard plates crashing, unidentifiable objects hitting the wall, yelling, what sounded like slaps and punches, and screaming. The screaming was just too much. We had to call the cops.

Later, when her bruises had healed, she thanked me.

One of the two lovers—not the one she fought with—became her third husband. Things seemed to settle down then.

But that was not the end of her troubles.

In the end, at least to this chapter in her life, trouble came, and love had nothing to do with it.

□ □ □

"I'm not leaving. They're gonna have to drag me away."

"They're gonna. You know what you're dealing with."

"I know. Fuckers."

When the deadline had come and gone, Beth had made no attempt to move. She hadn't even packed. Her husband, Steve, a flight attendant, was out of town a lot and couldn't be bothered with the tawdry details of moving or not moving. Beth, meanwhile, began investigating the Itogawa Consortium, the company that had sent out the notices. The more she dug up, the more she dug in.

Moving had been hell for my family. We had accumulated so much during our eight-year stay. Too many books and magazines. But we learned we could do without all the dust and paper. In some ways moving is a good thing, a very good thing.

We had held several garage sales. At first it was mostly books and magazines, the ones we didn't just dump in the trash. Then we had sold off toys, clothes, dishes, pots and pans. Whatever was left we donated to Big Brothers and Sisters, Goodwill, the Salvation Army, the Cerebral Palsy Foundation.

Initially there had been some reluctance, with me, or Henry, or one of the boys wanting to hold on to something for the flimsiest of reasons. Like Henry's LP collection. CD technology had made albums impractical, but again and again I'd find Henry taking an album from the "to dump" pile and shelving it again. Same with the boys. Soon enough, though, this spirit gave way to something stronger. After a few weeks we had made ourselves lean. It had been like fasting. It felt good. Rejuvenating.

What I hated the most was saying good-bye to our neighbors. Our kids had grown up with the neighborhood kids. We had always looked out for each other. Now everyone was leaving.

Except for Beth. Now how was I to know that this woman who had lived next door to me for years, and who in all our conversations had expressed only passing interest in politics, would choose this moment to make her stand, to make an event out of it? How was I to know how strong she'd be when they came? How they'd have to handcuff her and drag her away? How strong she'd be, this forty-year-old woman, to sit in jail, fighting for her right to live where she always had?

Many people made the Itogawa Consortium out to be bandits. Because their economy was doing so well, Japanese corporations had been buying up vast acreage—luxury houses, hotels, golf courses, empty lots—in Hawai'i for several years now. But in her investigations Beth zeroed in on the real culprits—those who brokered these deals. These were people who, in my reckoning, refused to give in to the beauty of the surf at sunrise, unless it was a painting they had bought, or unless they could charge others for a look; these were people who refused to see the effect their decisions and methods had on others, refused to know how the lives of so many were diminished by their insatiable wish for more more more. I knew these people; I had fought them myself once.

I think Beth just wanted to make them see her. Make them know. So while all the other families moved out, Beth stayed. And when she was arrested and then bailed

out of jail, she returned to her house on Tusitala Street.
And insisted on staying.

Despite now living over thirty miles from Waikīkī, my
family often went there to join the weekly gatherings on
her condemned property. We along with others had formed
a motley support group, made up of former neighbors, an
assortment of Beth's friends, and what the press called
"anti-development activists."

The boys loved going back there. Mākena got to
surf at Walls; 'Analu got to hang out with kids he
knew. The gatherings became a rallying point. And
when I helped pass out flyers protesting the eviction of
the one remaining family, it felt like the seventies all
over again.

The news media played it up. Beth became a public
figure. She was misquoted in the newspapers, reduced to
a sound bite on TV. I got anxious at times. *What if she
flashes the camera? Or comes on to a newsman?* But she
stayed in character. It was a critical time, a time to put
away frivolous gestures.

And though I knew where it would end—we were
dealing with powerful forces, after all—I thrived on the
battle. The old juices in me were stirring.

□ □ □

People who live in combustible places shouldn't add fuel to the fire

It was New Year's Eve, a night of ritualistic setting off, a
night where a generation-old tradition made the island of
O'ahu resemble a war zone. It was a night filled with deafening
blasts and what sounded like machine-gun fire. A night of
dazzling displays over harbor skies. There were more fires
started on this night than on any other night of the year.

And this one was huge.

A large house was on fire.

Like us, Beth collected paper. Like us, she had a love for books. And she always used to clip items from the newspapers. Hoarded magazines. When I asked her why, she said to me, "You never know. You might find something valuable."

All someone needed to do was light a match.

The news reports said it was accidental. A sparkler some kid might have thrown in the yard. Some stray aerial. So many people had been lighting up illegal fireworks that night. There were so many fires. But we knew this one was intentional.

She never was a threat, only a nuisance. But they used a bazooka to deal with this mosquito.

The fire raged.

Early New Year's morning, 1992, I parked on the Ala Wai, crossed over to Tusitala, walking through the confetti-like piles of red that covered the sidewalk. Up ahead I saw her, standing alone, arms crossed, facing the charred remains. I could smell the dank odor caused by water poured on burning wood. It coalesced with the freshness of the morning.

She turned and saw me. Christ, she was beaming. "This is so great," she said.

"What? Are you crazy?" Maybe the pressure had been too much.

"Hey, think of what I'm saving on moving expenses."

"But, you've lost everything."

"Only the things that can be replaced."

"You could have been killed."

"That's the beauty of it." With one of her hands she cupped her chin. "Nobody was hurt."

"Luckily."

"We were out at my Mom's," she said, "partying. Heard about it on the news, of all places. It's weird watching a house burn on TV, then realizing it's your own. . . . I came rushing down here and—oh, so many good-looking firemen."

That last comment took some of the load off. I put my arm on her shoulder. "Oh, hon. Can I say 'Happy New Year'?"

"Of course." She smiled, but her eyes were weary. We embraced.

"The thing is," Beth said as she kept one arm around my shoulder and turned toward the blackened frame of the now-roofless house, "they lost. They may not realize it right away. But they lost."

"You think it was arson?"

"What do you think?"

I shrugged. She walked toward the house with no door and entered. I followed her.

"Watch your step, girl," I told her.

The acrid odor stung. In some areas the wood had burned through and we could see pools of muddy water under the house. All color had been consumed into one aggregate blackness. Glass mirrors, steel frames—all melted. Beth picked up the remnants of a book. It dissipated into black flakes.

She put her hand on my shoulder and gently massaged it. "His hand was forced. He revealed his true nature."

I kicked at some rubble. Then I realized that most of the rubble had been books. It had been a great book burning. "Whose hand was forced? You mean the company? Its president?"

"Hardly. Guys like Itogawa have money, but when you *really* look at it, they're cogs in the machine, like the guys who get sent out to do the dirty work. The guy I'm talking about is the irreplaceable part. The orchestrator. The one who expedites the process."

"Who?"

"I have a suspect. He runs a tour company, but that's just a front. His hands are everywhere."

"You don't mean Cappy Chung?" My mind was flashing back some fifteen years. *He's behind all this?*

"Oh, you know him."

Keep cool, Kanani. "Only by reputation."

"Well, he's gonna get his. What goes around, comes around. Even if I can't finish the job myself, someone will pick up where I left off. Hey, it could be a generational battle. It'll all be exposed. We'll win. We'll be vindicated."

It all sounded like one big rationalization to me. "You sound like the people I used to hang with. . . . I don't have that kind of patience. I need to see results sooner than that."

"Hmmm." She kicked the charred remains of a coffee table, which collapsed. "Maybe you better start telling me more about those"—Beth cleared her throat and went into gurgly mode—"people you used to 'hang with.'"

PART II

The Time of the Landings

The Navigator

(Wai'anae—Late Winter 1992; Mākena—Summer 1976)

Kanani

The day I learned of my condition, I felt what I have felt
so many times since—guilt, love, loss, commitment—and
betrayal on top of all that, for since then, for over sixteen
years, I have carried in my deepest, most private sanctuary
a terrible secret.

Keoni was the other one. Of course, no one would
believe this. After he disappeared, just about every other
day some gorgeous woman would come out of the wood-
work and say she had slept with him. Many had, I learned
later. But that was the last bandwagon I'd want to jump
on. The truth is, we did sleep together. Once. Just once. A
lovely, tender, perhaps even inevitable consummation of
what I assumed to be our long-standing attraction to each
other. This was during the time of the landings. I, who
played hard to get while others played it loose, couldn't
say no to him—even though neither I nor he had taken
any precaution. I even knew, and liked, Pi'ilani, the
woman he appeared with in public. I would never do what
I did. But he was different. One slept with him the way
women slept with great warriors in the days of long ago.
Great warriors about to face battle. That wasn't for me.
Peaceful warriors who were about to die? Now that's

more like it. But that wasn't the reason either. I think we were just horny one night; we were in the same locale, the same state of mind.

I knew he wouldn't last. Who knows, maybe he had a death wish. His juggling act—making his way through the labyrinthine assortment of activists, informers, politicians, opportunists, family members, lovers—was more than any-one could handle. For a long time I thought, *wished,* he had simply run off somewhere and made it appear that he'd died.

I remember that late spring day in Mākena . . .

"Pehea ʻoe, Keoni," I said, embracing him. Then I pulled my head back to gaze at his face.

"Maikaʻi. Mahalo, sistah." A cordial beginning. We hadn't seen each other since that day on Oʻahu when we sat talking for hours under the ironwoods at Waimānalo Beach Park. We could have done it then. I had never felt closer. He was so tender, so vulnerable that I just wanted to hold him in my arms.

There, instead of the usual talk regarding the state of affairs in the ʻOhana, or the state of his affairs, he rhapso-dized on his childhood on the Windward side. Before his family moved to Maui. He talked of his parents' struggle to raise five kids on his father's laborer's pay. He told me about how his father got ripped off in a land dispute, some family land, but he talked even more about living on the beach, swimming, bodysurfing, spearfishing, and going to the mountains to feast on the abundant guava, lili-koʻi, mango, and those Java plums that stained your shirt so bad that your mom had to bust out the Clorox. And he talked about learning to dive off the cliff at Makawiliwili just weeks after he'd nearly drowned there, after having slipped into the water.

"I was five or six. Nevah know how to swim then. I sank to the bottom. I found it was solid enough to spring from, so I kicked my way up. But then I went down again. I kept sinking to the bottom and kicking my way back up. Down. Up. Down. Up." He gestured with his hands. "And when I was up I would yell and, shee, nobody heard." He snickered. "My neighbors—they the ones who brought me there, 'cause they wanted to do some fishing—they were too far off. Maybe they figured, ah, let the damn kid drown. He too humbug." He laughed again. "But somewhere during my panic I wen' realize that I could move forward this way. So the next time I wen' touch bottom I kicked not only up, but forward. Kept doing that till I finally could grab onto the rocks. After that experience, boy, I learned to swim right away."

"An' you were five or six?"

"Aroun' there. Prob'ly six."

It was the image of a child struggling to surface, struggling toward a rock, that I fell in love with.

When I walk through the old towns—Keaukaha, Miloli'i—when I go Ka'a'awa side, Wai'anae, Hāna, I see shame, I see hope, I see beautiful people. Not your bulimic-Johnny-Hollywood, plastic-surgeon-to-the-stars, made-for-TV, fifteen-seconds-of-fame type of beauty, but faces that reveal a remarkable inner spirit—the astonishing soul of the 'aina. These people are the survivors, the lineal and literal descendants of a ruined people, a culture that was almost erased. When Kāpena Kuke arrived, there were a million people here, sharing resources, and they had the mind-set, the values, to share them into perpetuity. By the time of the overthrow, after experiencing one hundred and fifteen years of the worst imaginable manifestations of disease, greed, and social Darwinism, after more than a century of horror, less than eighty thousand remained.

Survivors. I'm talking mostly about maka'āinana,
exploited even by their own during this rupture, this
disruption of culture, defeated again and again by the
vilest forms of oppression. These Kanaka survivors still
gave thanks to the ocean gods for the manō, the he'e,
the ulua, the 'opihi, still thanked nature for the
pu'ukenikeni, the lehua, the kī, the hinahina . . . for the
kalo that had been their staple for centuries. They saw
that they lived in the most beautiful place on earth, and
worked to mālama the earth, preserve that beauty. . . .
These were a people of gentle spirit. . . .

But at Mākena it was back-to-business. I was just
another of the women who volunteered in the office, trying
to keep the 'Ohana fiscally above water, which was impos-
sible. Keoni and other so-called leaders, the people in the
inner circle, flew from island to island almost daily and ran
up tremendous bills with the airlines. Then there were the
lawsuits to defend the "trespassers," those who had gone
onto the island without the Navy's permission—to reclaim
their heritage. Our fundraisers, which got old pretty quick
since we were featuring the same three or four music acts all
the time, drew increasingly smaller crowds.

That was how it went during the first few months of
1976, the year America kept imposing its bicentennial cel-
ebrations on us.

It was pain-in-the-ass business, especially since none of
us were accountants or anything like that. When the
money came in, we didn't question the sources. We just
took it, tried to keep our creditors at bay, tried to settle
our accounts. Things would work out magically. I just figured we were blessed.

So privately we were struggling, but our public face
kept winning people over. Consequently—and Keoni had
a lot to do with this—our battle touched the consciousness

of the mainstream. Woke people up. Suddenly our battle was the big one. "Stop the bombing" became a rallying cry of the body politic, even cutting through the usual conservative-versus-liberal, young-versus-old, local-versus-haole dichotomies. It was weird. Suddenly it seemed like *everybody* was on our side. Money started pouring in. Idealistic lawyers came around wanting to represent us—*pro bono*. By that summer, polls showed that the public overwhelmingly supported us in our claims. By then Keoni was clearly seen by the public as being the 'Ohana's chief spokesperson, the one who steered us. He had worked hard behind the scenes for quite a while, but now it was clear that he was the guy people wanted to hear. It was his vision that took us through the rough seas. It was his vision that was the most inspiring—and inspired. He was the one who could articulate the hurt so many of us felt.

> . . . *When I fly over the majestic cliffs of Moloka'i and see Kalaupapa, its ravaged beauty, a place where people, mostly Kanaka, were set off from humanity, exiled, I am overcome with joy and pain: joy that they could find love and comfort during this horrific hour, and find some piece of heaven in what others could only see as a hellish pit; pain that their exile was further proof of man's inhumanity to man, the same ungodly spirit that drives men to forge the weapons of overkill and practice destruction—killer seeds scattered throughout our fragile islands . . .*

Why the Mākena invasion fizzled was a mystery to me then. Of course, now it's so fucking obvious. A few people, people with lots of power, wanted it this way. And from their lofty positions in the state capitol building, from the top floors of the steel and glass towers on Bishop Street, from the ranch estates and Kāhala mansions, and possibly also from the home of the Pacific fleet commander, which brings the Pentagon into the mix, they set it in motion. And motion there was. And it wasn't no *Local Motion*. Coast Guard boats, helicopters, men in fatigues, uniforms, and suits operating with SWAT-team precision sent the little soil there was aswirl as they worked to change the direction of the winds. It wasn't personal. The big guys kept above it all, never getting directly involved. All they had to do really was throw hints about what had to be done, and their lackeys would get the message and go out and do the exacting work of infiltration, intimidation, and basically fucking things up.

> *. . . So we're suing you in accordance with Environmental Protection statutes, including the Safe Water Act, the Natural Sanctuary Act, the Native Rights Act, the Clean Air Act, and the Endangered Species Act. We're looking for more acts to supplement this five-act drama, this Sisyphean tragedy of Shakespearean proportions—to cite your gods. You've always claimed that you're protecting us from outside intervention and don't seem to grasp that the outside interveners were and still are you. Who's protecting us from you? At Mākua, Mōkapu, Pōhakuloa, Lualualei, Kahoʻolawe . . . all we see is evidence of the most heinous crimes against man and nature. Look at your own Declaration of Independence. Your Bill of Rights. You don't seem to see the parallels. Is it because you have too much invested in not seeing them? We're not about to raid the supermarkets and dump tons of Lipton into our precious harbor; we're not polluters. But we are going to wave these leaves and have one hell of a ti party, thank you.*

□ □ □

Tape rolling

"When you enter it's a straight, one-lane road bordered by kiawe and pine. It's dry, somewhat secluded. If you go further along the shoreline, you come to that more secluded area, Little Beach, the place where people just drop their clothes. I tried that. Having come of age during the so-called hippie years, I was anything but ashamed of my body. And I wanted that total tan. Wanted to make those lighter parts of me brown. Seems so crazy now.

"Where was I? Oh, the beach. Well, there isn't much beach, it's such a rocky shoreline. More a'ā than pāhoehoe. But the water. Oh god, the water. Clear, pristine, the most stunning deep blue. It's that color because of the rocks in the shallow areas. In the daytime it was gorgeous; at night, under the stars, it was stunning.

"By June, everything was escalating, and Mākena was the place to be. And what you saw there weren't some naked hippies romping around. Instead there was an assortment of ragged-looking stragglers, people who had set up impromptu camps, people whose backs ached from sleeping on hard ground, people who stopped worrying about make-up and how their hair looked. Some were gathered in small groups; some were just wading in the water, trying to relax for a few moments. Some fell asleep while sitting down or leaning against the trees—everybody was so tired. Those who were more awake were eating leftover sandwiches, chips, whatever snacks they could get their hands on. They drank juice or soft drinks. Or water. Alcohol wasn't allowed.

"This was the ailing heart of a movement at a critical time."

She stops. Her eyes glisten. Alika is not sure whether he should say something. She seems so far into the story that she's forgotten his presence.

"You wanna stop?" he asks softly.

She notices him. She smiles wanly, then says, while shaking her head, "Nah, let's continue . . . let's get through this . . .

"That morning, Keoni spoke with such fire and passion, that I felt even the infiltrators, whoever they were, were moved. And maybe ashamed. I myself had done nothing wrong, yet *I* felt ashamed. For not having done more . . .

"Before giving his speech he was just going around, talking to us individually, shooting the breeze. When he came up to me I hugged him, kissed him on the neck. I whispered, 'You looking tired, Keoni.'

"He grabbed my shoulders, looked at me—big smile on his face—and said in a soft, kind of amusing yet very complicitous way, 'Some people wear you out.' Then he walked on over to Pi'ilani, who had just flown in from O'ahu. She was bringing him the latest news.

"What was to be the biggest and grandest landing, a flotilla of thirty-plus boats, had been scaled down to one—ONE—a one-catamaran adventure. The large boat could carry two hundred protesters easily, but now the skipper was getting nervous about his boat being confiscated. Keoni, unlike his usual self, started giving orders like some mad captain. He dispatched Pi'ilani to Hāna to try to get another boat. He was livid, I tell you.

"The day passed with letdown after letdown. We were basically awaiting word from Pi'ilani. That evening we gathered to eat. First, we gathered in a circle for an evening pule, and this is when Keoni, who began with a prayer, started venting his frustrations. Some press people were around—they knew about the aborted landing by

now. And he knew it—I mean he knew that they knew—
so he spoke with his 'public' voice. It was an angry voice;
it was the voice the media wanted. But frankly, they had
no clue about the private Keoni, and those of us who did
respected it and cherished it and cherished that it was
indeed private. He gave a powerful speech for the press
that evening, but it was nothing compared to the way he
had stirred us that morning."

She pauses again. She seems dazed. Alika is thinking
She is a most beautiful forty-year-old. He can't help but
wonder how beautiful she must have been back then,
some fifteen years ago . . .

□ □ □

". . . They're just fucking with us. Think we're gonna
fold our tents and go home. Well, we've got some news for
them. We've barely started. We had agreed to try it their
way, right?" Keoni was a hula dancer, so his hands always
moved when he talked, articulating what words sometimes could not. "*In* their courts, *at* the state capital. Hir-
ing fucking lawyers. . . . They got us playing *their* game.
Got us *agreeing* to go by the rules of the U.S. courts—with
their enforcers, the military and the police. They don't
want us to cause pilikia by doing this—" he chuckled—
"*illegal* stuff. Hey, what's so illegal about reclaiming one's
homeland, huh? Tell me. What's wrong with wanting to
take care of the land, instead of bombing the shit out of it?
. . . But note, when we agreed to abide by their rules, it did
not mean we'd relinquish all our other strategies, 'cause
we can't lose sight that our aim is to get that island back.
And getting that island back is the first step . . . the first
step in a long, long struggle . . ." He pointed with his
index finger for emphasis. ". . . for dignity, for righteous-
ness, so that our keiki can grow up proud . . ."

People were voicing subdued "right-ons" and "amens"—subdued because our now-sweaty hands were still locked in prayer. I couldn't fight off the chicken skin, though the thrust of the speech was nothing new. Here he was again, trying to fire us up so we'd get through the doldrums—guided by the conviction in his words.

And just when it seemed hopeless, because so many supporters had left, we saw that more were arriving. Word was getting out. The only question was who was faithful, who was committed, or maybe who should be committed.

About two weeks ago, in Honolulu, I had an encounter with Charlie Kuahine. He was a failing law school student, failing perhaps because he was spending all his spare time with the 'Ohana—or more accurately, with Keoni, following him around, always at his side.

Charlie told me, "I don't trust that guy." He was referring to Puhi Cadiz, someone I had inherently relied on, someone who had been around for years—working for welfare rights, prisoner's rights. "Watch out for him," he added. We were standing outside the judiciary building. We had just won a round in Eli's trespassing case. Kuahine was leaning against the Kamehameha statue, his arms folded. Minutes later he was speaking to the press.

I didn't question him at first. I figured he was close to Keoni, so he must know something.

Then Lucy came up to me. Right away she said, "How'd he get to be our spokesman?"

I shrugged. Then I asked her, "Do you trust Puhi?"

She said, "Why? What did he do?"

I was about to tell her about what Kuahine had said when Sherry came rushing down the steps of the judiciary building shouting that the case against Eli had been dropped.

I trusted Lucy with my life, but she was on a plane back to Kaua'i before I could explain to her that the suspicions weren't mine. I wondered what she told others, for after a while it got pretty clear that Puhi, for good or bad, was being left out of the loop.

We won't play by their rules. Of course it wasn't that Keoni would quit going about the legal route—I knew him too well—it was more that he felt an urgency to step up the action, and to make a statement to those political animals who had pushed his tolerance to the limit. An hour later he was talking to those in the nebulous inner circle, those few whom he trusted with his life: "Captain Bullough has bailed. He backed down. Shit! Didn't wanna risk losing his fucking boat."

"Why'd he offer in the first place?" Kuahine asked. "Fucking asshole."

What's Kuahine doing here? I said nothing.

"Well," Keoni said directly to Charlie, "it's an expensive catamaran. Put yourself in his place. Give up your boat for a bunch a rebels with a fucking cause."

"I'd give up my *life*—for the cause," Kuahine said, thrusting his chin up like he was rehearsing for some photo-op.

Melinda and I exchanged looks. *Who is this guy?*

"Look, it's just a minor setback. What we're gonna do is send out a smaller group, which I will hand-pick."

Make good choices, Keoni.

Keoni was playing out a complex strategy: trying to choose those he could rely on the most while not alienating others by placing them in seemingly important but less critical positions. Funny thing is, when I look back on it, he was becoming a politician.

"It's getting pretty dangerous," he continued. "I've even heard rumors about a price on my head." He snickered. "Now's a good time to back out. Believe me, I understand. Especially those of you with keiki. All I can do is ask the kūpuna for strength and take whatever comes." He looked up to the sky, like he was beckoning the gods to give him the strength, the energy to continue.

Later that night, after he'd determined he'd go to Hāna in the morning and get on with that scaled-down landing, some of us retreated to a house in Kīhei that an 'Ohana sympathizer had offered for our use. It was 1 a.m. when Keoni lay near me to rest on the living room carpet. Other people had already claimed the beds. He was out like a light. Breathing hard, yet looking quite at peace. I, on the other hand, couldn't sleep. Thoughts were spinning like helicopter blades in my head. Seemed like I lay awake, or half-awake, for hours. Then, in the middle of the night, I found myself wide awake. It was so uncomfortable on the floor; the bedroll was no bed of roses. Finally, I sat up. Then, as I gazed outside through the sliding glass door, I noticed him standing outside, amidst the anthuriums and the plumeria trees, smoking a cigarette. At first I thought he might be with someone, but he just seemed to be mut-tering to himself. I watched his striking profile for several minutes, thinking of him as a Hawaiian chief who was deeply committed to his people. Then I remembered how he had rejected that construct. "I ain't no *ali'i*. We've had enough problems with that shit," he told any zealous fol-lower who tried to put him on some kind of pedestal.

It seemed that Keoni was coming back inside, but he stopped short and turned sideways, leaning against the frame of the door. I stood up and approached him, saying softly, "Keoni, you okay?" We were both under the door frame, standing both inside and outside this stranger's house.

"Yeah." He motioned for me to step outside with him into the garden. Stars filled the sky; there was no moon.

"That's all? 'Yeah'?" We each had our arms crossed as we gazed at each other. He smirked and I smirked. Then he looked up at the stars, like he was looking for something to guide him, perhaps towards some new path other than the inevitable end he had already foreseen. Then he gazed at me with those dark, penetrating eyes.

"People don't appreciate you enough. All the shit work you do."

"You kidding me, Keoni. You work ten times as hard as anybody."

"Doubt it. I jes' get the press." It sounded like "depress" to me. "Plus, I need to work. Makes me feel alive."

"Well, just stay alive, eh?" I playfully pushed at his shoulder. "We need you."

"Nobody's indispensable."

"You are."

"There's always gonna be somebody to carry on. Hey, we're an 'ohana, a family that extends horizontally—sisters, brothers, cousins, friends—as well as vertically. We're linked to kūpuna, as well as to moʻopuna. What better fucking movement can there be?"

"The royal family's an 'ohana too." I was kidding him. I knew which buttons I could push.

"The royal family hasn't got a clue. To be royal is to be clueless."

"Then how come in one speech you talked about putting a Hawaiian back on the *throne?*"

"Sounds good to me." He smiled. Then he turned serious. "I'm talking about Hawaiians being in control of their destiny. It's a way of thinking. Taking control of your own life. . . . Shit. Here I go . . . " He sighed again. "It's really fucked when you catch yourself talking like there's a microphone in front of your face. Even in private."

"Well, there should be a queen anyway." I smiled sassy at him. "Right?"

He smiled back. "Oh, definitely."

He reached to hug me and I hugged back. Then, still facing me, he held my hands and said, "When I look at 'Ohana members with their keiki I sometimes wish I could settle down, raise children. I *love* kids. I got twelve nephews and nieces . . . last time I counted. My braddah Wayne is quite prolific." He snickered. "I tell you, though, *nothing* in this world is better than seeing their faces lit up."

I held on to his moist hands, not wanting to let go. "You're gonna have yours . . . the wife, the kids, the whole damn thing. Once all this is all over. Then after a while you'll get bored and look for more battles."

We released our mutual holds. He then looked at me, touched his unshaven face, his slight beard, and sadly smiled. "I wish." I gazed at his scratched-up legs, remembering that he often traveled through rugged terrain in his bare feet. He lifted my chin and kissed me. It seemed innocent at first, a light smack on the lips, but then he did it again, and—oh, something about four in the morning and fatigue—every sensation, multiplied. He was nibbling tenderly at my lips, like he wanted to go further, but wasn't sure I'd let him cross that line. We were in uncharted waters.

I began nibbling back and passion just swept over us.

"You are so beautiful, Kanani."

Oh god. This beautiful man is calling me *beautiful.*

"I've been wanting to do that," he added.

"Me too."

Keoni's very touch felt magical. A hand sliding along my arm, my face. I could barely stand the intensity. Now we were kissing wildly. And as we kissed, his hands slid down my sides, caressing my hips, my ass. I was wearing a long baseball t-shirt that was good for sleeping in and not as revealing as a nightgown, but it was, of course, easy access. One of his hands held my waist while the other slipped inside my panties. His fingers traced my butt-crack, down, up, then slid around to the front and stroked my hairs. All the time kissing. His finger—or was it two fingers?— I felt it, them, enter me. *God, I must be so wet.* Uh-oh, I said to myself as his fingers probed, hoping those words wouldn't escape my mouth. We kept kissing, and somehow my panties were down near my knees, and, before long, I was stepping out of them. I wished I had showered.

But then it felt so fresh, with the lingering scent of plumeria and overripe mango; and it seemed so protective, this backyard, with vines spiraling downward. It was dank, and it was dark. The cluster of red, heart-shaped anthuriums seemed to rise from behind him, spikes erect, inviting.

He was pulling off my t-shirt. I yanked his off, then broke the buttons off his shorts as I forced them down. We kissed and fell to our knees; then we lay on our sides, on our bunched clothes, still kissing. We were kissing each other's bodies, arms, neck, fumbling, then he gently straddled me. On his knees, he bent low to kiss my hairs, then he licked my clitoris. *Put it inside!* I wanted to scream. He grabbed his penis and pressed forward, aiming. And missed! "Little low," I whispered, then took matters into my own hands—one hand—and steered him in.

I bit my lips, struggling not to moan. I mean, there were people sleeping in the house, through that open door. As his penis slid in and out, in and out, I kept thinking, *This is crazy. What am I doing?* But it felt so good. Stars were in motion as he gently yet forcefully exploded in me. I came immediately after him, growling, still trying to muffle my moans.

I didn't think about it after it happened. I had convinced myself it was expeditious, a moment of blind passion. And when he disappeared it did not occur to me that he might have left in me, me of all people, the benison of his seed.

Henry complicated matters. Caught in the passion-filled turmoil of love, loss, and fatigue, I was in bed with him less than a week later, after the third night of our search for Keoni, who by then had disappeared somewhere around the island of Kahoʻolawe. Weeks later, when Henry had won me over and I had quietly accepted Keoni's disappearance with the painful yet smug thought that I was, or may have been, his last fuck, I felt the flutter in my belly. Skipping a period had been a clue. Then, more than once inside of Wist Hall, where I was working on getting my teaching certificate, I ran out of class to throw up. I also felt nauseated whenever I smelled seafood. And considering that at the time I worked as a waitress at the Territorial Tavern, there was plenty opportunity for that.

I tried to keep Henry at bay. I was pregnant after all, and I had no idea who the father was. But he was persistent. He was loving, funny, warm, and—what got me—he had risked his life for a friend. The friend who may have fathered the child I couldn't find it in me to abort.

"I'm pregnant," I blurted out one day, ready to face the consequences.

"I love you, Kanani." He rubbed my belly. He wasn't hesitant or taken aback at all. The next day he said, "Marry me." He had never even asked *Who's the father?* I guess he took it for granted that he was.

So I agreed. To marry him, that is.

As the months passed he would sing to the child I carried in my swelling body. He swelled with pride. Then one day, when my belly protruded so much I thought I could never be lean again, he said, "We could name him Keoni."

I wanted to die. "That's putting a lot on the kid," I managed to say.

He looked down for a moment. Then said, "Yeah." He blew out air. "I guess you're right." He was pensive for a moment, then his eyes lit up. "Hey, how about Mākena? It could still be a tribute to Keoni, and also commemorate, well, you know—" He kind of smirked. "—the place where we . . . you know." He smirked again.

All I could think was I was glad we didn't fuck in Poughkeepsie.

I didn't want to remind him that the planned invasion there had failed. And I could never say that he may have been conceived a couple of miles down the road. I simply said, while nodding, "Mākena . . . I think I can live with that."

After that I said yes to everything Henry asked of me. Next to Keoni he was the bravest, most sacrificing man I knew. Plus, I began learning more about all the other girls Keoni had been with, and it made me realize that perhaps I wasn't so special after all.

□ □ □

I screamed. I grasped Henry's hands and squeezed them till he yelled. Fourteen hours of labor. I thought the baby would never come out. No shots, no mind-numbing drugs, I insisted. I want to be aware. I gave in to the episiotomy, though. The topical numbing. Yelled, cut me already! Let's get this damn shit over with!

When the baby was born I figured well, now we'll know. Only thing, the kid ended up looking like me, and till this day, he is slim and tall, like me, rather than husky, like Keoni or his dad—I mean Henry. And his coloring is my darker shade of brown.

But I know who's raised him, and that is irrefutable.

Enríque

(Western Edge of the U.S. Continent—1971–74)

Henry

Off the record?

Oregon and me, we never saw eye to eye. I gave two years for that woeful team. I didn't want attachments. During my two years there I kept my luggage close by. I came close to leaving a lot of times. Sometimes I'd even spin a globe just to see where my fingers would land. I'd always cheated a little, watching that equator line, thinking of its warmth. More often than not, I'd find myself with my finger on the Pacific Ocean, huge as it was, the largest player on the earth's surface.

But then I had made a commitment. To the coach. To my best buddy, Ron Atuaia, who had gone up with me. Us two Kaimukī grads. Alone, I'd a' been sitting in a dorm, hiding from the world. Around Ron, who stood 6' 8" and was built like a brick wall, I could conquer the world. Seemed sometimes like he was the largest player on the earth's surface. When we'd walk around campus, around town, nobody would fuck with us.

When we'd go to some bar or nightclub, people treated us nice. Not only because of Ron's size, but because he was known. He was the team's prize catch. Blue-chipper all the way. In fact I'm sure the only reason the recruiters went after me was they knew how tight we were.

The first year, it was a lot of fun and excitement. So many new things. I had no problem with haoles then. They were my teammates, shit. My classmates. The bullshitters, I tolerated. The chicks, at least the gorgeous ones, I tried to score with. I didn't understand yet how much it was *their* world. I wouldn't understand a lot of this until I returned to Hawai'i.

One thing I didn't want to do, was get too tight with any haole chick. *E pluribus unum,* Ron liked to say, having his own notion of what the phrase meant. *Jes' oof 'om and leave. Don't take any of their shit.*

But then I met this chick from Lewis and Clark. Deb. Deborah. Same spelling as the chick in Blondie. And this Deb was a blonde too. A natural one. Down to the pubes. I had never seen a woman who looked so sexy naked.

But boy did she wear me out.

The thing is, I'm used to being the one making the moves. This one came after me. I never figured out what she was after. Did she just want a football player, any football player? Wasn't money, 'cause she was loaded. She had her own apartment and everything.

Her eyes were something else. One was green, the other blue. I had never seen that before. And this was no contact lens trick. Coming from a place where brown was predominant, I was blown away.

And she liked to write poetry. Most of it was above my head. Either that or I just wasn't interested. I mean the words went well together, but there was no message. Me, I need the message too.

The situation was kinda perfect at first, which was why I kept going back, sleeping over sometimes. She had a roommate. Shit, the first time we got it on, it happened right on the living room floor. She had been massaging my tight shoulder blades, and before you know it, clothes were flying off.

I wasn't about to say, "Hey, let's get some privacy." We just did it on the living room floor. Later on I realized that people show up at her place at any and all times, so we could have been caught *in flagrante delicto*—another favorite phrase of Ron's. He was always spewing out Latin phrases, and going around telling people he was pre-law.

The irony was—I'm talking about Deb—she had this great fucking body, but, geez, I dunno, the sex was like automatic. I mean, she *seemed* thrilled—more than most, I would have to admit—but every encounter we had went the same way: missionary-style fucking, her lifting one leg higher in rhythm to my pumping, softly moaning *uh, uh, uh* with every thrust—thass it.

The strangest part of it all was how she started calling me Enríque. Even though that has *never* been my name, she insisted on calling me that. Now, mind you, I didn't think I had a problem with my Latino identity, especially once I had *found* it, but Enríque never rang right. Maybe sounded too much like *Borinkee*, which always sounded like a putdown to me. Even though now I know where that word came from—the original name of Puerto Rico was Borinquen—in Honolulu in the '60s it sounded pretty nasty:

> *Hey, Borinkee!*
> *What you like, paké who look like one Jap.*
> *Shit, you look like one kanaka-pōpolo.*
> *Eh, fuck you.*
> *Fuck YOOOOOU!*

That's the thing with cultural politics in Hawai'i, hard to sort out what's derogatory and what's not.

And then one spring weekend Deb's parents came down from Seattle to visit. Shit, they started calling me Enríque too. I was wondering, what's up with this family?— all McGovern supporters. Then one night, she and I arrived at her house after going to a Trailblazers game. She switched on the tube. There was this talk show, *Goodnight, America*. The theme song was the Arlo Guthrie version of a Steve Goodman song I really liked. *Cool,* I thought. The star of this late-night show was a feisty lawyer turned muckraking journalist who went by the name of Geraldo. Then I learned we had the same last name. And fuck, Deb was just slobbering over this guy. I twirled my mustache, wondering if there was a connection.

The next day, in the bathroom—she was taking a piss and I was shaving—I said, in reference to the growth under my nose, "Maybe I should shave this off."

She got all worked up. "Oh, for God's sakes no."

Later I told her I was tired of this Enríque business. Told her I'm Hank. Call me that, at least in public. She got to be good about that. But in bed, shit, whenever she got excited, there it was again.

—*Harder, Enríque, harder.* Rolling that *r,* even.

Then when she'd come: —*Oh, En-RRREE-QUEEEEE!*

Shit, and I'm trying to come too, but I'm hearing

—*Bo-RRREEN-KEEEE!*

What the fuck is it with this woman?

Then came spring practice. This was during my sopho-more year, and I was gonna be competing for a starting position the next fall. On this one play, where I slanted off left tackle, this fuckhead 300-pound freshman crushed my foot. At first, I thought I had twisted my ankle; it was so sore and swollen. Then they take x-rays and tell me I got this bone chip injury. Now what the fuck is that, a bone chip? Sounds like nothing. But shit I couldn't walk, and by the time spring practice was over, with me hobbling around on crutches the whole time, I tell you I saw the writing on the wall.

I can't speak for anybody else, but the prospect of spending at least one more season on the bench in this cold, wet, gray place sounded like a fucking season in hell. Ron Atuaia or no Ron Atuaia. Besides, my buddy had gotten involved with some Mormon chick and started going to church instead of bars. *E pluribus* my ass. What was this world coming to? Shit, I figured pretty soon he'd be transferring to fucking BYU.

But this Enríque shit. That was the worst. Felt like I had been defined in some narrow fucking way. Pigeonholed. Predetermined. In this land so large, so populated, this place that had allured me with the promise of choice and opportunity, I felt so fucking alone.

I was a bone chip, cut off, floating on the edge of a continent, immersed in the body politic of America.

I had to get out of there. I had had enough of the damned place, anyway. Too many walking dead in that skid row of theirs. Too many people with that Deb mentality. And too much fucking rain. Shit, even the Indians were pale.

I spun that globe. Got the Pacific again. Tried again, but walked away with the damn thing still spinning. It may be spinning to this day for all I know.

Well, I had no consciousness to speak of yet, 'cause all I did was pack up and catch the fricken Greyhound to Southern California. I desperately needed some sun. I thought, if I like it there, maybe I would transfer to SC or UCLA. Film studies sounded good. Forget about football already.

L.A. Lost angels, urban cowboys, and me. This was the spring of '73. Nixon, Watergate hearings. Mean shit going down.

What saved me was the music. The Doors and Johnny Rivers were the bookends of my early tastes, and I cased the Strip listening for new magic, for even more dynamic fusions of words and music. The Whiskey, the Troubadour, and everywhere in between. Mustache gone by now, I played the part of an urban cowboy. Hung out with mostly white guys, listened to white people music. I scarcely paid attention to Philly soul, or Santana, and I hadn't discovered Springsteen yet. I bought a folk guitar, began taking lessons, trying to emulate these exponents of Cosmic American Music, as some called it. I took music classes at Santa Monica J.C., and practiced chords and scales long into the night, so desperately did I want to be like these California stars. I ended up gigging with some guys I met in lonesome truckstop dives. Even wrote a few songs. They pretty much sucked, though I didn't think so at the time.

After a couple of months of floundering around in the scene, I got to know some guys who were doing session work with Jim Messina and Gram Parsons. I jammed with them a few times in this guy's studio garage. In fact, we were together when we heard that Parsons had OD'd at some inn in the California desert. You prob'ly heard the story. After he died, authorities took his body to LAX. They were gonna send it to Louisiana for burial. Then it disappeared. His diamond-studded corpse fucking disappeared. Then word got around that he had made this pact with his manager: whoever died first had to be taken by the other to Joshua Tree National Monument. So Phil, his manager, and some other dude—Mike something or other; I can't remember last names—they got drunk out of their minds, rented a hearse, and went to LAX to retrieve Gram's body. Fuckers presented false papers, got custody of the body, and took it to the desert. Worse part was, on the way there they got into an accident—hit a wall or something, piss-drunk as they were—then went and got even more drunk, bought a can of gasoline, took the coffin to the desert, poured gas on it, and set it ablaze.

Just one more story from those drug stupor days. Hit close to home, though, that loss. Gram Parsons was a major talent. Major talent.

Booze, drugs, and babes—for good and bad, these came with the music. Crazy days. Rollercoaster highs, freaky fluky lows.

There were times I was so broke I took on any job I could find. For a while I was parking cars. Just like *Enrique* would. But hey, it got me by. Me and all the upcoming screenwriters and rock stars. I lived right in Hollywood, in a bungalow beneath the "D" end of the big sign. Rent was cheap and I soon found out why. The area was overrun with alcoholics, drug addicts, fallen stars. Roaches crawled about the rooms, hallways creaked. I remember this one time, on a cold cold night—cold by my standards anyway—when I pulled out the bedcover from the closet. I covered my stoned, shivering self. And then in the corner of the bedcover I see some dried up blood.

Hollywood. Magical name. Cool sign, up that hill. Down below, nothing but shit.

The thing that got to me the most was that, for me, there was no identifiable community. I mean, sure, there were ethnic enclaves, but you can't pick your ethnicity. Let alone culture. The best someone like me could do was the clubs. But what kinda community is that? Inflated egos and way too much temptation. It's great when you're nineteen or twenty and hot for anything with perky tits and a pleasant face, but at some point even that gets pretty fucking lame.

Community. A place you can identify with, a place you feel a part of. A place where you can raise kids who can grow up knowing their neighbors. That's what I missed

most about Hawai'i. I needed that, and so I came back.
Then I found an 'ohana. It took me a while, but I did. And
then I found love. That took a while too, 'cause, shit,
when the plane landed in Honolulu, after I kissed that
blue sky and let that humidity caress me, I went fucking
wild. Hey, I was twenty-two; what else could I do?

This is off the record, right?

'Cause . . . 'cause shame, eh?

Betrayals after the Fact

(Hāna—Spring 1978)

Kanani

Yes, money had come in in timely fashion. Now some people wanted payback. In dividends. The wrong people wanted a bigger say in matters.

Instinct told me that Kuahine and Cadiz were the key players, working both sides, answering to the power brokers. Instinct told me to be wary of them—even though they seemed to be at odds with each other. You don't get into an inner circle without paying your dues. Besides, an inner circle is made up of people who were there from the start, at the groundbreaking. And neither was. You don't get to hang out with the chiefs and the bosses. But they did.

You don't get to hang out with the main man.

But they did.

And they knew some pretty creepy people. People they'd bring to meetings. A whole different breed. People who would look at you like they wanted to choke you to death. Then they'd break into smiles. It seemed calculated to disorient. In hallways, they'd brush against you—more like bump into you—and say nothing. As if it were the most natural thing. You'd just never know what was meant by the bump, the look, or the snide remark.

88

I called it destabilization. Keoni's presence, his cha-
risma, had been enough to overcome these psyching-out
"gestures." Without Keoni this method of operating
became more pervasive. I could trust Henry, of course.
And Eli, Lucy, Melinda. A few others. But there was a
growing list of people I couldn't for the life of me figure
out.

Worse, Cappy Chung, of all people, wanted in. He
wanted to lead the Movement. He claimed he had gotten
in touch with the Hawaiian identity he had denied for so
long. I guess everybody assumed he was Chinese, a well-
tanned Chinese. What a joke. To finally acknowledge your
race when you see the opportunity to benefit financially.
And to think, even Eli thought Cappy was sincere. Mikahala was a blessing then, 'cause she said *no fucking way*
the loudest. Fresh with her postgraduate degree from
Santa Cruz, fresh from time spent teaching on some reser-
vation in Arizona, she appeared to have the perception
and perspective to see through the political crap.

There was a lot not to like about these infiltrators, but
even within, even among people I like, there were some
very real problems. Maybe we were all too young, but
some of us were just too reckless. Wanting to be Hawaiians so bad after denying that side of ourselves so long.
Some of my best allies began practicing rituals they knew
too little of. They weren't listening to kūpuna. They were
making hoʻokupu to the gods, building koʻa, fishing
shrines. Now they were as westernized as I was, and I
feared for their wholesale turn toward Hawaiian ways
that even our elders scarcely knew. Even my sister Momi,
a Hawaiian educated in Western science, had a deeper
understanding of cultural practices. As an archaeologist,
she had a hands-on approach, had gone on digs throughout the Pacific for over a decade. She had seen similar rituals being practiced firsthand, and knew when something

was not pono. *Just be careful,* I'd tell people, knowing that it was a tough call. What they were doing was revolutionary; why kill that spirit?

Just be careful.

□ □ □

The U.S. Navy was our initial and most obvious enemy. They targeted their missiles on sacred land. But even though we saw it as akin to church bombings, we understood that all they saw was barren land—rocks and dirt.

Then we learned from Keoni that our local politicians were more insidious enemies. They played us. Shifting sides, putting up fingers to test the political winds. No heart there.

The enemy within was toughest to deal with. People you thought you loved, betraying you. It finally came to a head in Hāna, about a year after Keoni's disappearance. . . .

Where people sat in the hall said it all. There was a clear delineation. Sides had been taken, and now, finally, after the differences had brewed for so long, it was time to show where you stood. My memories of the numerous times this group stood in one large circle, to pule, kūkākūkā, or give their manaʻo, were shattered by the sight of people fragmented, sitting in small clusters.

At first it was business as usual. Reports on money woes. Court cases that had brought us together now seemed such a hassle. The void left by Keoni even more apparent. Mikahala tried to run things for awhile, but she was too high makamaka, too tantaran. She fought with and alienated everyone, then finally quit.

Two distinct factions emerged, one that appeared more urban, though that was quite ironic, since this faction insisted on the group keeping true to its grassroots beginnings. The other group, decidedly more *country* in that they were fishermen and hunters, obviously had begun placing more merit on working through the state bureaucracy. All this was complicated by the three *r*'s—romance, religion, and retribution—not to mention infiltration by mainland haole environmentalists, members of organized crime, political lackeys, local yuppie wannabes—you name it . . .

I wished Henry had come. But he said he'd just lose his temper and end up punching somebody. Knowing Henry, that wasn't an unlikely scenario.

Now Eli, facing this audience with microphone in hand, was saying, "We gotta deal with our internal problems. They've been festering too long. And we gotta clean out this sore, this canker that is spreading among us."

People were changing dramatically. One day you're a young Hawaiian military recruit ready to die for Uncle Sam; the next day you're protesting against that same overbearing uncle. One day a Christian, the next day a pagan. Perhaps these pendulum swings were necessary, but the rapidity of these changes was scary. If one's ideology could swing 180 degrees in a day, what would the next day bring?

Eli was saying, "I hear this version and that version. I think the only way we can straighten anything out is to put it all on the floor. Here. Tonight."

"Are you running this meeting?" someone said.

"Nobody's 'running' this meeting. I'm just trying to facilitate—"

"Facilitate? Sounds like you running things."

"Yeah, as always," someone behind me and to my left was muttering.

"Well, I'll sit down and shut my mouth—if that'll get things going. I don't care who's conducting this."

Lucy stood up. Turned toward the audience. "Where's the respect we owe this man? What's wrong with you people?"

That same muttering voice said, "What's wrong with you?" My fists tightened.

"Let one of the kapunas conduct."

"*Ku*punas, not *ka*punas," someone said.

In my mind I'm thinking, adding an *s* is wrong. We don't do plurals that way. If people want to get weird about it.

"We're getting nowhere fast," Eli said.

"Shit. You telling me." That stupid voice again. Who the hell is that? I turned around and glared at this shirtless young man.

"Well," Eli said, trying to be conciliatory, "it seems we're gonna have to let the steering committee confer, so we can . . . decide on how we'll conduct this. Let's take a ten-minute break."

"Smoke break," someone behind me said.

The committee decided that Auntie Rena would conduct the meeting. She was an elder with a shy, toothless smile and a soft, endearing face. Her wise, gentle demeanor commanded respect from everyone. I thought she was a good choice.

But she turned out to be a reluctant leader. After a gentle admonition that everyone treat each other respectfully, she simply went about pointing to people who were raising their hands. She would say, softly, "You. Then you . . . That wahine next."

People were gracious for a while, most speaking to the need for all of us to overcome our differences and work together. I knew this was just warm-up.

After several 'Ohana members gave their mana'o, Steve McKenzie stood up. I knew Steve to be a talented poet, and I had always respected his honesty. Now we were sitting on opposing sides. From where he stood, mike-less, he began:

"I have plenty aloha for everyone here. A few years ago we saw the shape our people were in, and we committed ourselves to various causes—homestead rights, welfare rights, the right to at least some kind of reparation for our ceded lands—and then, finally, we found a focal point and joined forces to stop the bombing of Kohe Mālamalama o Kanaloa, our cherished island Kahoʻolawe . . .

"It's one thing to fight for our rights, sistahs, braddahs, but we've allowed things to get out of whack. Some people have taken things too far."

"How about something specific?" Lucy said.

"I hate to say it, but the way some people are dredging up long-buried gods, for instance. They were buried in the mountains. Now to dig them up through chants, perform hoʻokupu to Lono, Kāne—like we know what we doing. The thing is, we don't have the rituals anymore. They're lost. If you do it wrong . . . you dunno what you fucking with. Sorry Auntie, I no mean to swear . . . but you guys screwing around with things you cannot understand. Shoulda left the gods buried in the mountains."

James Okino stood up. Auntie Rena tried to wave him off. He said, "I'll let you finish, Steve, but, but I just gotta say right now, how we gon' restore our culture if we cannot even restore our pantheon of gods? That is so key."

"I tell you, that kinda stuff jes' . . . jes' goes too far for me."

"Yeah," Wally Amina said, "that kinda shit goes too far for me, too. C'mon. We gotta live in the present."

"Present, my ass." That was Lucy talking.

I saw Eli standing on the side, leaning against the wall, an unlit cigarette between his fingers. He seemed to be sinking down.

"You know that's not the problem," Poʻomaikaʻi Reynolds, whom I barely knew, added. "The problem isn't gods or ideology. Shit man, it's personal. It's just a fucking turf battle. . . . Sorry Auntie. I meant to say it's just a damn turf battle."

He was right. People were snickering, probably because they agreed.

". . . Either that or it's people screwing around with each other's boyfriends, girlfriends, husbands, and wives."

One of the Maui 'Ohana members stood up. "Who you talking about, brah? If you gon' make accusations, back them up."

"I not mentioning names."

"'Cause you one of them." Again it was that smug, back-of-the-schoolroom voice.

"Well," someone near him said, "If you not gon' present proof, then shut the fuck up."

Steve, who was still standing, said, "This is so so sad. Look at us. Look what it's come down to. Call it whatever you want, but I've . . . I've had it." He pointed at the people on my side of the room with both index fingers. *You* take care of Kaho'olawe. You guys so sharp, *you* stop the fucking bombing. Me, I'm outa here. I goin' back Moloka'i and *practice* my culture." His comment reminded me of a bumper sticker I had seen outside when I arrived. *Practicing Hawaiian.*

He got up to leave. So much for plenty aloha. Then about ten others got up and left. Then, in domino fashion, another twenty, thirty more. Altogether, about forty people walked out that night. The 'Ohana split right in half.

The Ballad of Ten Years

(Wai'anae, Ka'a'awa—Early Spring 1992)

Tape rolling

". . . So after the big split the Movement just died?"

"Yeah. For about two years, from early 1978 till about the middle of 1980, it just floundered. I kid you not, the infighting had caused irreparable harm. And, like I said, some of it had nothing to do with politics. Sometimes it was just people who were romantically involved breaking up with each other. Things of that nature. Plus, people were tired of making sacrifices. They needed real jobs."

"I can relate."

"We weren't so young anymore; we were out on our own, raising kids. Maybe it was because so many of us were in our late twenties, early thirties. So Jerrhold becomes a stockbroker. Eddie goes to law school. Some of them were buying houses. Henry and I were quite disillusioned when we found all these people we knew were buying condos and houses, like they had something going for them all along. At the same time Henry and I were struggling just to pay the rent, having to move all the time. Shit, we never settled down until—must have been 1983, when we got that Waikīkī house. One of the few remaining undeveloped blocks in Waikīkī."

Kanani pauses, picks up her glass of water and drinks till the glass is empty.

"You know, people don't talk about class. Nowadays it's always race and ethnicity. Keoni's family was poor, so was Henry's. I think that's why they connected—in the short time they knew each other. My family was a little better off, though my folks had to work their asses off to keep their little farm going. They built a greenhouse and began an orchid business on the side, just so Momi and I could go to private schools. We didn't covet much, unlike—well . . . I dunno why I thought of this, but Henry likes to talk about how the Beatles were working-class. That's why they touched so many."

"A working-class hero is something to be."

"Henry likes to play that song."

"By the time he wrote it John was a multimillionaire."

"He had a lot of heart, though. I think he was lost, even when he got rich. So much pain in his songs."

"Did Keoni have favorite songs?"

"*Kaulana Nā Pua.* No doubt about that one. I think he liked Olomana, Country Comfort, but he was more into the old stuff. Auntie Genoa, Gabby, Atta Isaacs. . . . How did we get here?"

"You were talking about class."

"Oh, yeah. I get sidetracked. Like with my students sometimes. . . . Hey, I bet you grew up somewhat privileged. Middle-class, I mean."

Alika looks sheepish. "What gave me away?"

Kanani shrugs. "I don't know. It's just there in your demeanor."

"Should I wear a scarlet *M*?"

"Nah. Bumbye people think you went to Maryknoll. Speaking of Maryknoll, that's where Eli went to school. Now *his* family's pretty well off, though he's turned his back on all that. Have you seen the shack he lives in?"

"Yeah." Alika chuckles. "I was there two weeks ago. It really is a shack. There's one thing that gives him away, though."

"What?" Kanani chuckles. "The golf clubs under his bed?"

"Close. It's all those bathroom products. The shower's shitty, but he's got Vidal Sassoon shampoo, Jheri Redding conditioner, . . . a styling dryer."

"Well, he's a man on the move. . . . You're pretty observant. What do *we* have in our bathroom?"

Alika looks embarrassed. "I have no idea. Towels that don't match?" He shrugs. "Eli's bathroom stood out, because of the . . . incongruity."

"Close your eyes."

"Huh?"

"Close your eyes."

Alika closes his eyes.

"Describe this room."

"Oh, gosh. Why—"

"It's my turn to ask the questions. Describe this room."

"Okay. Well, it's—this is hard—it's nicely laid out. I'm sitting on a sofa that folds out into a bed."

"What color is it?"

"Brown—sort of."

"Close enough."

"And you're sitting on a rocking chair. Of course there's a coffee table between us. With my tape recorder and notebook, and two clear drinking glasses. There's probably a stain where I spilled coffee earlier. . . . There's a throw rug on the wooden floor. I know 'cause my feet are on it."

"Let's go elsewhere."

"The walls are kind of off-white. The curtains, similar colored . . . the one facing the street is partially open. There's a print on the wall on the kitchen side. Near the clock. It's kinda Gauguin-ish, with two larger-than-life women hovering over a double-hulled canoe. Hmmm. There's way less books than you had in the other place, on two very nice pine shelves that Henry built."

"What kinda books?"

"Some recipe books. A nicely laid out assortment of hardcovers: *The Satanic Verses,* a book by that D.A., Bugliosi? I can't remember the title. It's long. . . . There's some Willie Shakespeare thing. His complete plays, I would guess. . . . Then there's something with the word *Red* in it. The cover is red too. I think the author's Chinese. Mo Yan?"

"Good. But that's only the top shelf. What's below?"

"Family pictures. A great one of your mom and dad. Next to it is a Rivera clan picture . . . uh, and school pictures of the kids . . . some kind of trophy? Below that there's a Random House, no, a Webster's dictionary. Henry and I looked up some word the last time I was here. I remember. We were searching for the word *xenophobia* and couldn't find it because we both thought it started with a *z*."

Kanani gets up and looks at the dictionary. "Amazing. It's a Webster's published by Random House."

"Where'd your hundreds of paperbacks go?"

"In the trash can, in the closet, in the three bedrooms."

"Can I open my eyes now?"

"What am I wearing?"

"The same shirt you wore when I first met you. Faded red, aloha print. And cut-off jeans."

"Open your eyes."

Alika notices Kanani's white capri pants. "Oops."

"You did well. You're very observant. That's good."

"Did I pass the test?"

"A minus. You know that the tape recorder's been running all this time?"

"I'm middle-class. I got lots of tape."

Kanani laughs and says, "Break." Alika stops the tape. Kanani walks into the kitchen and returns with a pitcher of water. She refills the glasses. "Seriously," she says, "you can't judge people by class or race. You know? Like, I can't blame every non-Hawaiian for our woes. And, lemme tell you, there are some Hawaiians that I just—ga—" Kanani shakes her head while speaking—"want nothing to do with. Keoni used to say, 'It's not about race; it's about attitude.'"

"I got that from Pi'ilani. Exact same line."

"Well, I'm sure you've heard it lotsa times."

"Shall I—?" Alika points to the tape machine.

"Yeah. Go ahead." Alika presses RECORD. Kanani sits on the rocking chair.

"He had a way of relating to people. He brought out the best in the worst people. How many people can do that? That's what made him special. Are you getting a picture? I mean, is it coming together, with all these interviews you're doing?"

"The images are getting clearer. I never met him or saw him but I'm starting to feel like I know him. I wish I had known him."

"He was one of a kind. The type that comes once a generation, as Uncle Joe used to say." Suddenly, Kanani's head is down, her jaw is tight. She swallows.

"That's the larger-than-life perspective." Alika turns to gaze at the print on the wall.

"It's hard to resist sometimes. My mom tells these stories, they're all kind of jumbled in her mind now, in her condition, but they're these lesson mo'olelo. There's one where this jealous chief keeps killing the woman he loves, 'cause he thinks she's fooling around. Each time he buries her, these guys—alleged to be her lovers but they're not—they keep unburying her and reviving her. The jealous chief is the one who ends up dead."

"Sounds like quite a lesson. People do self-destruct from jealousy."

"Well, I'm thinking about the story from a different perspective. It's a fable, of course, but wouldn't it be great if Keoni had kept on turning up in some form or other? That's what's so tragic. How come we only get to have one like him?"

"Well, who knows. Maybe there's some kid around who has what it takes."

"And maybe it's a girl."

"Yeah. Or maybe two girls." He again looks at the print of the women posed over the canoe. Kanani turns to look at it too. "You like it?"

"I didn't at first. But it's growing on me."

"Bobby Maeva. That's the artist. Tahitian."

"He's good. In the way that Gauguin is good. Is it cool to like Gauguin?"

"Don't ask me, I'm no art critic."

Alika takes a drink of water, then looks at his watch. "Gee, it's getting late. You think we should stop?"

"Yeah, I don't think I'm—oh my goodness, is the clock right?" She checks her watch. "Oh boy, I gotta get moving." Kanani jumps up. "I gotta go pick up my mom. She's staying over this weekend."

Alika stops the tape and stands up. He picks up his glass and follows Kanani, who has picked up the pitcher of water, into the kitchen.

"How is she, by the way?"

Kanani shakes her head as she opens the fridge. She turns to Alika. "Sometimes she's lucid, other times she doesn't even know where she is. Or what decade it is. Yesterday when Momi was leaving for work, she told her, 'No come home late from school now.'"

"Well, she's a real sweety."

"Yeah. She is."

"Sorry I took so much time."

Kanani gently taps him on the shoulder. "Don't *ever* say that. This is good. It's great what you're doing."

Back in the living room, Kanani and Alika gather his equipment. They do this with great efficiency. Then she walks him to the door.

"I like this place."

"Me too. The layout is just right for us." They embrace, and Alika heads out the door.

Kanani gazes through the curtain, watches Alika put his equipment in the trunk, and whispers, "Thank you."

After Alika leaves, Kanani can't stop her mind. She stands in front of the bathroom mirror, gazing at what she had not noticed before: the crow's feet that now complement the premature bags under her eyes. *Henry says my eyes are more beautiful now.* She puts on lipstick and quickly brushes her hair, all the time her mind running with words for the tape recorder that is no longer there:

I had two kids to raise. Isn't that enough? Had to work. Had to start teaching. Couldn't waste my time dealing with all the petty infighting. Oh, Lucy. What a soul. Eli said she would've been the next Keoni. 'Ohana politics. Too painful and too complicated. My family, my little 'ohana—I had to work on that. Isn't that enough?

The world is filled with problems. And I do care. And I do want to do something. But . . .

Gazing in the mirror, she speaks aloud.

"I retreated."

There you go, Alika, she says to the man no longer there. *That was the eighties for me, in a nutshell. Actually, the timeline was probably more like '78 to '88. Ten years gone by like the snap of a finger, ten years of living in the material world. With the media celebrating the material girl. That was spooky.*

Still gazing in the mirror, Kanani imagines Alika's response:

—*What was spooky, that ten years had passed or that we were living in the Age of Madonna?*
She snickers. —*Both.*

During the long, rear-view-mirrored ride to Ka'a'awa her mind runs and runs. Finally, she turns off Kamehameha Highway and into her sister's driveway.
Didn't think I had slept through so much until I began shaking off the stupor.
Oh, there were clues: Henry's job problems. The always shaky construction industry. Problems with my fellow teachers and their prejudices. No wonder kids are screwed up. I worry about my boys. Pisses me off when I hear all that shit about Hawaiians are like this, Hawaiians are like that. We're people, goddamn it!
To top it all off, Dad falling ill and passing on. Mom, what's going on in that mind of hers? Their entire lives have been a struggle. To what end? No pension, no vacations in Vegas, nothing but struggle. . . . Things are fucked, they're gonna remain fucked, whether I do anything or not.
Is this my legacy? What am I passing on?
If only there were something or someone to light the fire under me. Like the time that construction crew on Maui came across some bones. Boy, did that set off—

□ □ □

(Honolulu 1988)

Kanani

When Henry busted the loose, squeaky screen door I knew something was wrong. I thought oh no, he's been laid off again. Usually he mopes for a day or two, then goes out and hustles some side jobs, cash jobs, to supplement the unemployment checks and he's fine. But I knew Henry well enough to know that it was something else. Something deeper was eating at him. He sulked more than usual. It was a Friday night. I had just assumed we—Henry, me, and the kids—were going to do our usual pick-up-a-quick-meal-and-head-to-the-theater routine. But Henry was dragging his ass. I hated that. If something was bothering him, I wanted him to spill it out.

"What's going on?" I asked him. The kids were upstairs getting ready.

"Fuck. Thass what's going on."

"What is it, Henry?"

He shook his head. I knew him well enough to know that he was simply struggling for a way to articulate a problem. He was always hesitant at first. I had learned through the years that it wasn't just passive-aggressive bullshit.

"There's a bones rally," he finally said.

"A 'bones rally'?" For some reason that didn't sound right. "What do you mean, a 'bones rally'?"

"They stopped construction on Maui."

"Your company? Oh no." He did lose his job.

The boys came downstairs, ready for the movie.

"No, it's not that. I not talking about my fucking job." He shook his head. "Which I still happen to have. . . . It's just—fuck, whose side am I on?"

I knew this dilemma all too well. "Look Henry, you know not many people have the luxury to—"

"C'mon, Nani. We've been over that. It's different this time."

"What? What's different?"

"One stupid jackass on this crew, not ours, was driving his backhoe and *whoop*—he scooped up some bones . . . Hawaiian bones. Probably more than a century old. These guys were clearing the area for that damn hotel they wanna build. You know, the Ritz-Carlton."

"Is that related to the Seibu project? When they wanted to block beach access along Mākena."

"I tell you, I'm in the wrong fucking business."

I was about to say that there are few businesses that are "right" when our older son said, "We gon' movie o' what? Getting late."

"Mākena, Dad and I are talking." He shrugged, picked up the Friday paper, and sat down on the old recliner. 'Analu sat on the arm of the same busted-up chair. Knowing them, they were scoping out different movie options in the Entertainment section.

"These Maui activists," Henry continued, "they pretty well organized. They already forming a burial council. And tonight they're gonna protest at the state capitol."

"Tonight?"

"Yeah, tonight. And guess who's involved?"

"Oh, don't tell me."

"Eli, Lucy, Uncle Joe . . . "

Lucy.

"Shit," Henry said while standing up. "I need a shower." He peeled his filthy shirt off and dropped it on the floor. That wasn't like him.

"We gon' movie o' what?"

"Mākena . . . " I glared at my son. Then I picked up Henry's shirt and followed my husband upstairs.

Lucy, my best friend in the 'Ohana. I hadn't seen her in years. I had lost touch with her when she moved to Maui.

I followed Henry to the bathroom. "So, what? We got two hungry kids downstairs and they're expecting—"

"—to go movie. Yeah, I know, I know. Jes' let me clean up." He peeled his underwear off and jumped in the shower. "Hope get hot water left."

I sat on the closed toilet seat. "You'd rather go to the rally?"

He stuck his head out. "*You* wanna go?"

"Well, I don't know. I just don't know." I didn't know my place anymore. I wasn't into those blood-and-gore movies. *Bloodsport, Terminator* . . . But I was so out of touch with Movement politics.

"I jes' wanna soak in this water for a bit, then I dunno. Actually, getting into one air-conditioned theater sounds good."

"Okay," I said, clapping my hands together and standing up. "Movie it is." I stuck my head in the shower stall. Henry was sudsing himself. "Want me to do your back?" He nodded.

As I scrubbed his back, I kept thinking *Lucy* . . .

Red Heat was showing at the Waikīkī 3 theater, which was within walking distance. We stopped at the nearby Jack-in-the-Box for sandwiches and drinks. Along the way Mākena picked up some mochi crunch at the ABC store, since it cost about double for the same thing in the theater. He and 'Analu liked to add it to their popcorn.

For the first half of the movie I couldn't get my mind off the rally. I kept wondering who had shown up. I knew Melinda was still involved with the Movement. She and Eli were often in the news. Once the movie sunk in, I enjoyed it for its clear lines. I knew who to cheer for. Maybe that's why I don't stay at home.

A huge chunk of me yearned to be at the capitol lawn, yet I remembered too why I was hesitant to interact with some of them. It wasn't the issues; it was personality. Petty as it seems, it had become that kind of world for me.

When we got out of the theater I asked Henry, who had had a refreshing sleep during a good part of the two-hour movie, if we could get the car and go for a ride. Maybe get a late-night snack. He said, "Sounds good. Where?" The kids wanted to go to Zippy's. I said okay, then told Henry that afterwards we should drive by the state capitol building.

People were gathered on the lawn on the Beretania Street side of the building, closer to Richards Street. It was 11:30, and the Māhealani moon lit up downtown Honolulu.

I imagined stepping out and introducing my two sons to some old friends. No one would recognize my eleven-year-old. They hadn't seen him since he was a toddler, and now here was this tall-for-his-age, budding teen. I imagined 'Analu being lost in Lucy Napoleon's cushioning frame.

As our car went past, Henry tooted the horn in support and the boys made shaka signs. I gazed at the signholders. I did see Lucy; she stood alongside the sidewalk. I don't think she saw me.

Then I saw our kupuna, Uncle Joe. When he's there standing next to you, you know you're in the right. His eyes may have been bad, but they seemed to fix on mine—fifty, sixty feet away—and gaze into them without judgment. I turned away.

When Henry turned from Beretania onto Bishop Street, I noticed that the moon was now hidden behind the clouds. Figures, I thought. This was the heart of the financial district, where the shakers and movers reigned in penthouse suites, where lights are on all night. And it's just a short walk from the building where politicians do their bidding. Or else.

Passing by 'Iolani Palace I thought of our imprisoned queen and felt a surge of aloha. I thought, Jesus, these people have stuck it out, while I turned away. Most of them have children too, yet they're not so caught up in day-to-day shit to lose sight of the big picture. *I turned away.* I turned away because there was also some lingering bitterness. Memories of past rifts and the stupid reasons for them. The bottom line is, *I turned away.* Right then I vowed I'd find my way back. Albeit under my own terms.

A few days later I phoned Lucy, who was back on Maui. I wanted to give her my support. It was great talking to her, even though I learned more than I wanted to know about the ongoing factionalism. There was a time when our activist community broke into two distinct camps. Now there were several. Keoni, who conjured up Lono in the minds of many, had brought us together. He was the hub that held the most disparate parts. Now the spokes were flying in every conceivable direction.

That part was disheartening, but I still wanted to help. I told Lucy, I want to help. So we made plans to meet the next time she was on Oʻahu.

After another few days had passed, I called again, thinking I shouldn't put the burden on her. I was itching to get started, ready to see her on Maui. But she wasn't home. Then I found out she was in the hospital. A heart attack, her daughter told me. I was stunned. "Is she reachable at the hospital?" I asked. "I mean, can she talk to anyone?" I was debating whether I could call her there or, if necessary, even fly to Maui to give her comfort. The daughter didn't quite answer. Said she had to take another call, a call from the hospital. She took my number. She didn't call back. Hours later I called. I didn't know if I was talking to fourteen-year-old Scarlett or nineteen-year-old Ginger, so I just asked how her mom was doing. She said her mother had died during surgery.

I was devastated. I crumpled with the pain, doubling over, somehow keeping the phone to my ear. The guilt set in. I couldn't find words. I wanted to rise to the occasion, to at least comfort this young woman, whichever daughter she was, but all that came out of me was "I'm sorry. I am so so sorry."

A few days later my family was flying to Maui for the funeral. Lucy's ashes were to be spread in the ocean off of Mākena. Mākena, my son's namesake place. A place he'd never seen.

Ginger and Scarlett were strong reminders of their mother. I tried to comfort them, but they were better at comforting me. Melinda was happy to see me. *It's been so long*, she said. *So good to see you. Too bad it had to be—* She was busy as hell, since she was running the show. She said Eli was at a conference in Switzerland and couldn't make the funeral.

Uncle Joe, he seemed a broken man.

I met Keoni's mother for the first time there. She sat along with Uncle Joe on chairs set up for kūpuna and close family near the rocky shore. She sat erect, strong. I came over with my sons to pay my respect.

"Come. Kiss Grandma," she said to Mākena when I introduced him to her. I must have turned pale. Then she spoke the same words to 'Analu. All the time Uncle Joe looked on, at me, at the ceremony that followed, quietly, and with eyes that seemed to say, *Hard life . . . rich life.*

Afterwards we drove to our hotel in Kīhei, and passed the house where Keoni and I had made love. Right at that moment, Henry, who had been quiet as he drove the rent-a-car, pointed to his left. "That used to be Lopat's house," he said. "Syndicate guy. One of Uncle Cappy's boys. 'Ohana people used to crash there until they figured out what he was all about." I turned away, toward the mountain. At that moment a passenger in the car ahead must have flicked a cigarette, because ashes burned my face.

□ □ □

(Kaʻaʻawa, Waiʻanae—Early Spring 1992)

"You're gonna just sit in the car?"

Momi, wearing a pareu, is standing next to Kanani's Honda, on the driver's side. Kanani gets out of the car and greets her older sister with a kiss on the cheek.

"All hell's breaking loose, as usual."

"Oh no, what's Mom been doing?"

"No no. That's another story. . . . This is job related. Remember Honokahua?"

"Don't fuck with me. I was just thinking about that."

"Then I guess you do remember."

Kanani and Momi hadn't been the closest of siblings, what with Momi's travels, mostly to archaeological digs, throughout the South Pacific. And even though they lived on the same island for most of the year, they were separated by two mountain ranges. The telephone had been their primary way of interacting, but with their father dying and their mom needing round-the-clock care, they were spending more time together, reestablishing the closeness of their childhood years. Kanani used to follow her two-years-older sister everywhere. Even now, they could communicate complex messages with their eyes and sometimes spoke in code words no one else understood.

Still, Momi's bringing up Honokahua, the location of the Ritz-Carlton, made Kanani shudder.

Hours later, long after her mom, Henry, and the children have gone to bed, Kanani turns off the light and goes to the bed where her husband lies snoring. *He's having a bad dream. This is par for him.* She nudges him so he will turn. *This usually quiets him and makes his dreams less burdensome.*

Still can't sleep. She knows that this state of mind, like an engine that keeps running and running, will be with her for hours, probably till dawn. But she doesn't feel like reading and is sick of dwelling on the past.

So she lies in bed thinking about "the latest," according to Momi.

The H-3 freeway was nearing completion. The latest obstacle was a group of mostly Hawaiians who claimed the road would run right over a sacred site. Some archaeologists claimed otherwise, saying it was not wahi pana. It was common knowledge, though, that some of the archaeologists hired by the state couldn't differentiate the *iwi umauma,* or sternum, of a human female from the *iwi colonelsanderus* lying next to it. Story goes that one archaeologist once claimed to have found some articulated bones of an ancient Hawaiian, except that they turned out to be less old than the tab ring of the Pepsi pop-top lying right next to it.

More than anything, these state archaeologists knew who was paying their salary.

It had already cost taxpayers billions to bore through the mountain to build this freeway—the most expensive ever built, in cost per mile, in the United States—a freeway that would convenience the military more than it would commuters stuck in the gridlock between their Windward homes and Honolulu. The freeway linked military bases, making the transit from Pearl Harbor to the Mōkapu Peninsula a smooth ride. All the while sending an endless stream of cars toward another bottleneck, unless they were headed toward the planned second city, Kapolei.

The plan was obvious. The freeway was a promise of more construction on the Leeward side, a justification for building, from scratch, a new city and a major university. This meant more work for Henry. The downside? What downside? Unless you consider that, in the building of this freeway, the workers had disturbed a heiau, damaged countless indigenous species, and desecrated a mountain.

The hands that moved mountains were showing, or at least the cards they held were.

And people go along. I go along—Kanani's last coherent thought as she finally fades to sleep in the wake of sunrise.

PART III

When the Shark *Bites*

His family had weathered the hurricane just fine, and things were picking up.

The boy eased into the water, not feeling the cold at all. Leashed to the board he lay on, he liked the feel of its polyurethane surface. It was a nice day to catch waves. Seventy-eight degrees, the sign by the bank had flashed.

What he saw later looked dark, smooth, and rubbery, like the tire tube of his bicycle. What he saw later was blood spurting out just below his right knee. The rest of his leg was gone.

His friends carried him to shore; he was still conscious at that point. Seconds later he blacked out.

When the Shark Bites

(Waiʻanae—Spring through Fall 1992)

Mākena

Spring—in the middle of the afternoon

"—So, rather dan being rid of da shark, da people were stuck with many little ones—for deah mistake."

Grandma Wong really hit on those last three words. Then she wen' pause . . . for dramatic effect, I guess, and wen' add, "Dis one of those times. Dis is the time of the manō." She wen' look at my brother ʻAnalu and said, "Da time of da sharks."

Those words ended another of Grandma's chicken skin stories about times past. The stories she told had been passed on to her by her grandmother, who, she often said, heard them from *her* grandmother. Always skipping a generation.

"So, you boys," she said, "be careful in the water. An' watch out for men like Kawelo, who tell you not to go in da water, making you want to go in even more, den turn into sharks and—" She started coughing real bad.

She didn't finish the sentence. She didn't need to. Already ʻAnalu had chicken skin, and even though I was seven years older and not as easily frightened, I felt one chill, too, boy. Me and ʻAnalu, desperate for some sunlight, went out and opted for one land sport—baseball—at

Pililā'au Park. I just got one first-base glove for my fifteenth birthday the week before, and I couldn't wait to break it in.

I dunno if those were the last words Grandma spoke, but from what we found out, she wen' take one nap after we left and she never got up.

That summer

Grandma wen' die in April, and we never go in the water for the entire month of May. But by June, with the heat and all, the ocean we saw every day as we rode along the Wai'anae Coast was, as the song goes, *simply irresistible.* Before you know it we practically lived at Mākaha, spending our days catching wave after wave, and we never let any concerns about sharks, stray surfboards, or wave hogs get in the way.

A couple of times we even wen' camp on the beach with some neighbors. Some families camped all summer. Dad didn't like this at all—I mean the "all summer" part. He said these people were lazy good-for-nothings. "Incorrigibles," he called them. He liked words like that.

Mom saw it differently: "Who can afford the high rents anyway? Why you think *we* had to move out here?"

We used to live in a house in Waikīkī, until some Japanese investors—land sharks, Dad called them—wen' buy the land and then jack the rent up real high.

But it was working out for us, 'cause Dad was making more money now working construction in Waikele than he had made as one shoe store manager at Ala Moana, and Mom was able to teach at a Wai'anae school now. Before, she had to drive to Kāne'ohe every day.

"Well, at least we trying," Dad said. No shit. They were. Mom was teaching summer school and Dad was doing odd jobs on the side, like carpentry, roofing, and electrician-type stuff, so they could save up for that down payment on the house of their dreams in Kapolei, Mililani, Waipiʻo—wherever. They even wen' put their names in a couple of lotteries for affordable housing.

Me and ʻAnalu were bummed when we found out we had to move to Waiʻanae. We knew we would miss body boarding at Walls, chasing pigeons at the zoo, giving tourists wrong directions. And we really were gonna miss those concerts at the Waikīkī Shell. Those were great times. Mom and Dad would hibachi in the park, and they would let me and ʻAnalu surf until dark, until we could only see the malolo leaping up, reflecting the light of the hotels. Then we would shower and change and throw Frisbees, twirl glowies, those fluorescent necklaces, and listen to the music. Mom and Dad liked mellower stuff—local acts like Bruddah Iz, Hapa, Theresa Bright, and singers like James Taylor. So me and ʻAnalu knew what kind of CDs to buy them for Christmas with the money they gave us.

Me and ʻAnalu liked all kinds of music. We both liked when Kapena played reggae, and I thought Willie K was the man, especially when he played like Hendrix. At home we would always play Dad's Bob Marley tapes when he wasn't around. But then ʻAnalu was more into rap than I was, and I was more into grunge and industrial.

When we wen' move to Waiʻanae we thought we would be mobbed by gangs and beaten up. We had heard all the stories. But turned out to be a pretty mellow place. Just dry.

Grandma came to live with us part of the time after Grandpa Wong wen' make. Sometimes her mind was sharp, like when she told me and ʻAnalu stories, but out in the yard she would kinda lose sense of where she was in space and in time. When she wen' die, was only eight months after Grandpa Wong's funeral. Grandpa Wong was mostly Chinese, with little bit Hawaiian. Grandma was mostly

Hawaiian, with little bit Chinese and some haole. Grandpa wanted his ashes scattered near Waiāhole. But Grandma never like. She wanted him buried with her, Christian-style. So they compromised. We scattered *some* of his ashes. The rest she kept in one jar. Now they stay together. Sort of.

Early fall

Summer wen' fly by like one convict breaking out of O-Triple C, and Mom, probably 'cause she kept so busy, was smiling more and mourning less. In the fall, Dad wen' sign up for some classes at West Oʻahu College. Mom was glad 'cause it "kept him out of trouble." By this she meant that he was back to his *incorrigible* habits of hanging out with the boys in somebody's garage, drinking too much beer while watching or talking about football. Actually, this sounded pretty good to me and ʻAnalu. But we knew that this wasn't gonna be the way they would get their dream house. Yeah, *their* dream. For all I could care, sleeping on the beach was fine. It was great, even. Shit, when you see one Waiʻanae sunset after a day of chancing some bone-cracking waves . . . you don't need anything else.

School not only began for Dad; it started for all of us. Mom had her teaching. ʻAnalu started third grade at Mākaha Elementary, me I started my sophomore year at Waiʻanae High, and I guess for Dad it was grade fifteen or sixteen. It was hardest for him. He would work construction from 6:30 to 3:30, come home, shower and change, attend classes in the late afternoon or early evening, come home again, eat, then stay up late studying. Usually he would crash out right at the desk, snoring, drooling, and me or Mom or ʻAnalu would have to wake him up. One time he fell asleep in one awkward position.

His elbows were on the desk, and his head rested in his two palms. When he got up his hands were numb and he couldn't move; he had to call for help. He can be one total spaz, man. We thought that was pretty funny, but Mom, who had to massage out his kinks, felt sorry for him for being tired all the time. Finally, after she bugged him about it for a while, he dropped one class, and was able to hang out a bit with the other fathers on Sundays.

School came pretty easy for me and 'Analu. It's just how it is when your own mom's a teacher, getting on your case from when you start kindergarten. Still, I was content to cruise by, and 'Analu, he just too damn playful. Back at Jefferson Elementary he used to drive all his teachers nuts.

When we wen' switch schools last spring, the first time 'Analu took a math test at Mākaha Elementary he was the first to finish. He aced it. The teacher figured he was cheating. So when me and Dad came to pick him up one day, the teacher, who was leaving school at that time, looked at Dad in his dirty puka t-shirt, work boots, and torn-up jeans, and told him that 'Analu may have cheated on a test. He never say how. Boy, Dad was pissed. He told the teacher, "Who da fuck are you to accuse my boy of cheating? Dis kid can calculate da cost of building a tile wall from start to finish. You know, the problem wit' you fricken Oriental teachahs. You come in from town in yaw fricken BMWs, bringing yaw fricken prejudice—" The teacher went ballistic and stalked away to her old Corolla. Later on I found out that she lived in one low-rise apartment in Waipahu. Then Mom had to go in and try to straighten things out. She wore a matching, two-piece outfit, like some lady lawyer in town would wear, speaking what she called "the language of diplomacy." Whatevers, man. She might have fixed things a little bit, but seems like Dad had already done some psychological damage to the teacher's head.

"Well, bettah her fucking head dan my kid's. Think dey can get away wit' dat kine shit."

"That's not how you fix things. God, Henry." Mom no even scold him for swearing in front of us anymore. Kind of hard. Like we never watch Eddie Murphy in *Raw*, like we no hear it all the time.

"Hey, I know how to fix things. I wen' fix the leak on the roof, right? I wen' fix the garage outlet. Shit, I even made dat damn VCR work again, jes' by staring at 'om." Dad had this smirk on his face. "Next I gon' fix that damn cat outside. I really like fix that cat—howling at night like one fe—" Mom covered his mouth. Me and 'Analu was cracking up. Even she couldn't help but crack up. Fucking Dad.

Wasn't like Dad no had one serious side. He's got more college credits than he knows what to with. I guess he just likes the challenge. And that heavy pidgin stuff, that's just something he turns on and off like one spigot. Seems like standard English is the cold water, and pidgin is when he get hot. Sometimes he mixes it—I guess I do it too—trying to get it right.

Once school was in gear, never take long for the sky to tell us something was up.

First had this suck-ass, super-humid weather; and there were warnings about one hurricane so many miles south of Hawai'i—moving northward. No one wen' take this seriously, except maybe some meteorologists. Then, it was upon us. We got up that morning to Civil Defense sirens. The schools was canceling classes, everybody was jamming the stores, trying fo' buy da kine canned goods, flashlights, batteries, duct tape—and probably insurance. It was total madness.

'Analu was having a good time. It was his first hurricane, since he was born one year after Hurricane 'Iwa happened by. He was more thrilled than scared, and I gotta admit I kind of liked the whole scene too. I mean, hey, compared to school . . .

But the grown-ups, they were dead serious, man—expecting the worst. Dad and Mom were scared that the house was gon' be destroyed. They wondered out loud whether the landlord had insurance. Late in the morning—almost noon, in fact—Grandma and Grandpa Rivera called to tell us to come stay with them in Kaimukī, which would have been much safer than the Waiʻanae shoreline, which always gets hit hard, but Dad said, "No way." He wanted to stay close to home, and be able to gauge the damage as soon as possible.

So, instead, we went to the elementary school gymnasium, where a lotta families had gathered. Here ʻAnalu continued having a great time, running around with kids his age, playing board games. Was great to see him playing with people *his size* for a change, instead of following me around all the time. But then he still wasn't that used to Waiʻanae.

I watched the news on somebody's portable TV, a Sony Watchman. It got boring pretty fast. In my mind I was thinking, *Come on hurricane, hit. Let's get the fucking show on the road.* And it did. At least that's what the news people said. All I could hear was the sound of winds rushing along the coast. In the gym, the lights wen' flicker, but they never go out. The small TV and some radios were our only connection to the destruction outside.

We wen' sleep in the gym that night, and early the next morning went out to check the damage. Turns out we were on one of the luckier streets, probably 'cause we were more inland. Our roof was intact. The X'd windows were fine. Just had this mess in the yard. Sand all over. Somebody's boat had tumbled into our yard, and it was sitting overturned against our garage wall. Our landlord's boat, which was rusty and pretty well had-it, which he just left on the property because he could, was in somebody else's yard. When Dad saw the shiny, blue motorboat, he said, "We should have a hurricane rule: whatevah da hurricane blow in yaw yard is yaws, and whatevah da hurricane blow in somebody else's yard is deahs."

Because our house escaped serious damage, we spent the next few days helping those who didn't come off as well. Dad took a couple of days off so he and his friends could help rebuild roofs, clear roads—that kind of shit. Me and some of the older kids in the area chipped in too. This was good 'cause I was getting pretty restless. I had too much free time in the afternoons. I didn't try out for football—thought I wasn't up to speed—but now I really wanted to play. Now all I could do was wait for basketball season.

The next Saturday, eight days after the hurricane, when things were almost back to normal, me and 'Analu headed out to Mākaha, which was within walking distance. When we was about to go into the water we saw some signs posted:

WARNING: RECENT SHARK ATTACKS.
DO NOT SWIM IN MURKY WATER OR AT NIGHT.

We headed back home. At that time, we didn't notice that there was one new lifeguard. About a week later, when the signs were gone, we wen' walk by the lifeguard station. Then we noticed him. The guys at school had been talking all week about this cool but spooky-looking guy who arrived at the beach every morning in his vintage '59 Impala. It was white, with big tailfins. Already had rumors: that he used to be stationed along the North Shore, that he wen' help save a lotta surfers and tourists from drowning at Waimea and Sunset, and how one day

he failed to save someone and that wen' break his heart.
That's why the sunglasses. To hide the grief. And they
talked about his tattoos. Me and 'Analu saw them now.
He had tattoos on his chest, mostly diamond-shaped and
in rows. On one leg he had a circle of diamonds around
one thigh, and filled-in triangles running from just below
his knee down to his ankle. The other leg had triangles
and what looked like birds in flight. He also had triangle
tattoo bands around both his ankles, and the same design
around his forearms and upper arms. And, of course, he
had those sunglasses on. He looked pretty scary. But
when he spoke to me and 'Analu, his voice was gentle.
He told us, *You boys be careful out deah. No go in too
deep.* And then I remembered Grandma's story about the
Sharkman—Kawelo—who had the mouth of a shark tattooed
on his back. I told 'Analu and he got kind of scared. We
both wen' sit on the beach for a little while thinking about
it. Then we decided to go to the park instead.

We were getting to be pretty good ballplayers.

Late fall

It was around this time that sharks were being sighted
more and more. One surfer lost a big chunk of his board.
The picture in the paper showed him smiling, 'cause the
shark never even touch him. Shit, I would be smiling too.
And for some strange reason it made us feel more confident about taking on the waves. The way we felt was,
even if one shark attacked, the most it would get would be
part of our board—just as long as we stayed on it and
didn't dangle our legs while waiting for the next set.

We really wanted to go out and catch waves, man. The
South Shore peaked in the summer. (I think the Department
of Ed worked that one out with Mother Nature.) But out
on the West and North Shores the waves were just starting

to come up. Plus, things would stay that way all through winter. In school, all the kids were writing surfing essays, drawing surf pictures, and during lunch recess I would hear some guys bragging about the waves they caught. Like one would say, "I caught one eighteen-footah, at Point Panic. I wen' ride down da surface wit my hand out li' dis—" And we knew the buggah was lying 'cause that place never has eighteen-footers. Then another guy wen' talk about how he wen' enter the H.A.S.A. surf meet and came in third place. Nobody wen' believe him until he brought the trophy to school and said, "Wop yaw jaws." His name, Lionel Papa, was etched on it. Just like Dad's third-place karate trophy. "Had on'y t'ree guys," he said to his friends one night when they was drinking in our garage. One of his friends wen' laugh so hard, fucking beer came out of his nose.

Dad kept his trophies in the back of the garage, mostly football trophies from his high school days. He was an all-star tailback. He got a scholarship to one college in Port-land, but he hurt his foot pretty bad and then quit school 'cause he hated the weather in Oregon.

Dad is Puerto Rican, but everybody mistakes him for something else—Portagee, Hawaiian-Chinese, Filipino, Lebanese. . . . Plus, according to Mom, there's some Japanese on his father's side but he doesn't want to acknowledge it. Like he's in denial. The story goes that my great-grandpa was half-Japanese, and his last name was Teraoka. But then along came World War II and he changed it to his mother's family name, Rivera. Mom doesn't usually make up stories, but Dad says thass all bullshit. One day, when me and 'Analu had to fill out the "ethnicity" box on the forms that the school gave us, we never know what fo' put. There was no box for "Puerto Rican." Only had "Other." Dad said, "Mark down 'Part-Hawaiian.' Gotta make dat count." This left three-fourths of what we were unaccounted for, so on the way to school me and 'Analu wen' also check off Chinese and Japanese. Next to the "Japanese" box I wrote "suspect." Then we crossed out "Other," and I watched as 'Analu wrote in "Porto Rican."

The only thing that was keeping 'Analu and me from the choice waves that we saw whenever we cruised down Farrington Highway on our bikes or in Dad or Mom's car was that lifeguard with the tattoos. 'Analu and I began referring to him as "Sharkman." So, because Sharkman was usually stationed at Mākaha, me and 'Analu started surfing at Mā'ili, or sometimes way on the other side, at Yokohama.

I no think we were the only ones affected. 'Cause on Halloween night, when I wen' take 'Analu trick-or-treating around the neighborhood—he went as Eddie Munster; I went as the big brother stuck having to take the kid around—we kept running into kids wearing sunglasses and body tattoos. But I was wondering, did those guys connect him to sharks, the way me and 'Analu did? In the playgrounds everybody was talking about sharks, but I wondered if anybody was connecting the increase in shark sightings to the lifeguard with the tattoos.

Things took one bad turn right after the November election, when this boy got killed by one tiger shark. The shark wen' bite off his leg, right in the shallow water. When me and 'Analu found out it was at Kea'au, which is real close to Mākaha, it really cooled our jets. It was too close, man. Too real. Plus, while I wasn't too keen on this Sharkman business—I still was rational enough to say, *nah, coincidence*—'Analu couldn't handle. He started having nightmares. One time he wen' wake up yelling, "No, Sharkman, no!" Couple times I had to let him bunk with me. This was real hard 'cause the bed is small, and the buggah move around like crazy in his sleep, kicking me, wrapping himself, taking all the blanket.

The kid's death was the talk of the school, if not the whole island. People were talking about killing the sharks, or *not* killing all the sharks 'cause some sharks were like family gods, or 'aumakua. When I wen' try ask Mom about that she just said, "I don't want you and 'Analu going boogie boarding for a while."

Was getting pretty complicated.

And it wasn't till the long Thanksgiving weekend that I began to get one handle on my fear. Was kinda like, you get tired of being afraid. Or you get used to the fear. Or something.

On Thanksgiving Day we went to Grandma and Grandpa Rivera's house in Kaimukī. 'Analu sat with me in the back seat of Mom's Honda Civic, holding the box of homemade pumpkin pie on his lap. As we went around Kahe Point, while Dad up front was saying something about the "fricken pilgrims," 'Analu started singing, softly,

Ovah da rivah and chroo da woods
To grammadda's house we go
Da horse is da way to carry da sleigh . . .

Pretty weird song, I thought, when you riding in one car in near eighty-degree weather. But the stranger thing was, I knew the song too. In fact, it was the only Thanksgiving song I knew. Unless you count "Alice's Restaurant."

Dad took 'Analu's singing as a cue to turn the radio up. It was an oldies-oldies station. We heard the Beatles sing "Love Me Do," which I liked mostly for the spit-sound in the harp, and Buddy Holly wen' sing "Every Day," which Dad knew *all* the words to. I spaced out too much to hear whatever else got played, but it was enough to remind me that I was getting kinda old for these family-type outings. But I also knew that some part of me was gonna miss them too.

At our grandparents house, 'Analu ate so much Spanish
rice and musubi, sweet potatoes and nishime, turkey,
kalua pig, macaroni salad, and pumpkin pie that he had
one major stomachache. Good thing Grandma Rivera is
always prepared. She gave him some Riopan Plus to down
with his 7-Up, and before you know it he was eating rice
again. The best part was I got to hang out with a couple of
my cousins, Joe-boy and Ricky. They were hardcore surfers. They usually rode their boards on the Windward side,
near their house in Ka'a'awa. Lately they had been checking out the North Shore. Joe-boy talked about the eight-
footers he caught the weekend before. He also was talking
about watching Sunny Garcia, Kelly Slater, and some of
the other pros. Shit, I wanted to get my Wave Rebel out
right then.

But the next day when me and 'Analu went out on our
bikes to check out the surf at Mā'ili, we saw that the shark
hunters were out. They had dropped bait on fishing lines
and were trolling the area.

We went to the park.

Nobody was interested in baseball anymore, so we
ended up playing basketball this time, with some guys I
kind of knew from school. It was pretty good for me,
'cause I'm kinda tall for my age, and lean, like Mom. I can
move pretty quick. But 'Analu, he cannot play against the
bigger guys. So he ended up riding swings and making
habut. Man, I was thinking, he gotta start hanging around
with guys his age.

Later in the day we wen' catch one ride to Yokohama.
The waves wasn't that big, but the water looked so cool.
Plus, no had tourists around. Usually you see all these
Sunbird convertibles, but not today. And I never have to
figure out why. Me and 'Analu sat on the beach for almost
half an hour, watching the sets come in. Then I thought,
fuck it, and 'Analu probably thought the same, 'cause we

both went in—for a short swim since we didn't have boards. We didn't last long in the water, though. We kept looking around, feeling jumpy. When we got out we remembered that we had no towels, so we had to dry off on the sand after showering. Once dry, we figured we would go home and act like we were at the park all day.

We really got scoldings from Mom that evening. We forgot that in Wai'anae word gets around pretty fast, so she knew what we had been up to just about as soon as we knew. I mean, she could chronicle our step-by-step movements that day if she wanted to.

She really blasted us: "I told you boys not to go in the water."

"You said not to go boogie boarding," 'Analu said.

"No self-respecting surfah says *boogie* boarding," I said kinda softly.

"Just what I need, two wise-ass kids. Do you *want* to get eaten by sharks?"

"Get real, honey," Dad said. "Dass a one-in-a-million shot."

"Don't go taking their side, Henry. There's a mother out there who's grieving over her dead son. One-in-a-million, hmmph." So the three of us got scoldings. That was good because it was spread out more.

From morning time the next day, Dad was gone. He had gone to Sparkey Lopez's house to watch football, including a game he had missed the day before that Sparkey had taped. Plus, he wanted to check out Sparkey's top-o'-the-line karaoke machine, the one he wen' max out on his credit card to buy. Me and 'Analu, feeling kinda junk for getting Mom all upset, stayed home. We ate turkey sandwiches, played *Cyberblast* on the computer, watched TV—on ESPN they wen' talk about how Jerry "the Shark" Tarkanian was losing too much games. We even did some homework.

In the late afternoon Mom took us to Cornet to shop. While she was checking out the households I went with 'Analu to the games section. He pointed to one new Milton Bradley game next to the *Jeopardy*. It was called *Shark Attack!*

Holy shit, I thought. It's everywhere.

It was dark when we returned, and Dad still wasn't home. Mom began to get worried so she sent me on my bike to Sparkey's house.

When I got to the house it looked deserted, kind of an after-the-hurricane appearance. In the garage had lots of near-empty food plates left, and the rubbish cans was overflowing with paper trash and beer and soda cans. Some of the neighborhood cats were pawing through the thick, black garbage bags, going after chicken bones. Then at the side door I spotted ukumillion slippers and sandals. Then I heard applause and people laughing.

When I wen' step inside I saw that a lot of the neighborhood fathers were there, along with some kids who probably had been sent to call *their* fathers home. Even had some younger, not-married kind guys there . . . including Sharkman. I heard somebody call him Manny.

Sparkey's karaoke machine was a mind blower. Pioneer laser disc setup, Bose speakers—the works. Had lotsa people, mostly men, and they were singing songs from around the '60s—Beatles, Sinatra, Elvis. They were taking turns singing at the mike. Had silly visuals on the Panasonic big-screen TV. Right away I knew was gon' be hard to pull Dad away from this.

Sharkman, or Manny, seemed to be having a great time—drinking, grinding the shellfish pūpū, the batter-fried ulua. He wasn't the only one who was shirtless, but his tattoos made him really stand out. And then I noticed he wasn't wearing his usual sunglasses. Right at that moment he wen' look at me with killer eyes. Shit, was spooky, man. Then somebody wen' hand him the mike. Guess it was his turn for sing. He wen' twirl the mike cord around, then he wen' catch the mike and pull 'om toward his mouth, singing,

> Well, the shark has pretty teeth dear
> and he shows them pearly white
> Just a jackknife has old MacHeath dear
> and he keeps it out of sight

I was watching the words on the video screen:

> When the shark bites with his teeth dear
> scarlet billows start to spread

Shit. This was no Ray Charles commercial for McDonald's. Sounded more like one serial killer song. Manny was really into it. His triangle tattoos moved like waves when he flailed his arms around; his dark eyes were flashing. Great, I thought. Next we gon' get the *Jaws* soundtrack.

Just when he was really belting out the song, around the part about "Lotte Lenya" and "Lucy Brown," 'Analu came by. Mom wen' send him because she was wondering why I was taking so long. We both watched Manny sing his song. I felt 'Analu nudge my arm but I didn't want to make eye contact. The men were cheering Manny on, hollering, singing along too. This song spilled over into another song on the same disc, "Beyond the Sea." This seemed to be Sparkey Lopez's song, the way he took the mike and everybody wen' shut up and listen. It wasn't until this song ended that we were able to approach Dad. We finally got him to go, but only after he sang "Just the Way You Are." Could tell he was drunk 'cause he said, "Dis is fo' ma wife. Honey, you da best," and she wasn't even there.

Dad was up before the rest of us the next morning—to watch the Dolphins play the Bills. During the game he kept telling Mom how great it was yesterday and how she should go over with him to Sparkey's house that afternoon. She was still kinda mad at him for being away all day Saturday and she was giving him a hard time. But Dad really knew how to soften her up, and by noon she was almost willing.

In fact, he was working on her so smooth that they started getting real lovey-dovey, hitting each other on the butt and all that. Me and 'Analu knew what was coming, so we took that chance to dig out. When I wen' slam the door I remembered the time a couple of years ago at our big house in Waikīkī when I sparked 'Analu sitting outside our parents' bedroom, mischief scrawled all over his face. I wen' sit next to him so I could listen too. We heard Daddy go "Ooh, baby . . . yeah, baby . . . " 'Analu started giggling, so I wen' cover his mouth. Then he started to make snorting laugh noises through his nose. I tried to cover his nose too. Then he made one loud fut. We both lost it and we ran out of the house, falling on the grass, tumbling, laughing till I thought I would piss my pants. Then we split. Later, when we came back home, we acted innocent. Nobody said anything.

While Mom and Dad seemed to be getting along just fine, me and 'Analu started having a bad time together almost from the moment we left the house. Actually, now that I look back on it, I was just goading him because I really wanted to hang out with my classmates more, and I wanted him to do the same—hang out with his. So I started hassling him about his Christmas list. He had this list on the computer hard drive for everyone to see. It was titled, *'Analu Rivera's Xmas List*. He was asking for things like Super Nintendo, with the necessary cartridges; WWF action figures; a Town & Country surfboard; more software games for the Macintosh. And that's only the stuff I remembered. So I shouted at him.

"You selfish son-of-a-bitch. What, you like Mommy and Daddy go broke? How dey gon' buy one house if you asking dem fo' buy you so many t'ings, eh? You stupid guacamolehead."

"But, but—" His eyes were getting teary already, but I kept on.

"No 'but-but' me. You jes' gotta learn to ask fo' small, cheap t'ings."

"But I not asking fo' ev'ryt'ing."

"Aah, why donchu get lost. Go. Hang around wit' Jimmy dem. O' dat adda lolo frien' a' yaws. What's-his-name." I pushed him. "Go!"

He wen' look at me with those sad eyes of his. I felt bad, but I never like give in. "Go!" I said again. "Beat it. I goin' down Mākaha. Catch some waves. Swim with da Sharkman."

"I gon' tell Mommy if you go in da watah."

"Fuck it. Tell her. I no give a shit."

"F-f-fuck you." Crack me up, the way he swear. He started running toward the mountain. I ran toward the sea. Before I knew it I was at Mākaha, kind of bummed out.

I sat on the beach. The sets were running from three to five, maybe six, and they were choice. Lotsa swimmers, surfers, and body boarders were out. The more I watched, the more pissed off I got. I was mad at Mom for not letting me and 'Analu go in the water. Especially when I saw a couple of my high school friends out there. And I was mad at myself for being kind of afraid. I was thinking about how Dad always says you gotta fight the fear or the fear gon' eat you. Finally, tired of sitting, I wen' walk toward the bathroom area to get a drink of water.

On the way there I saw the guy Manny. His sunglasses was pushed up above his forehead, and he was looking through binoculars out toward the ocean. Right away I remembered all the sightings from the day before—the Milton Bradley game, the coach's name, Manny and his serial-killer shark song. Was like . . . is there some meaning here? Some warning? When I wen' pass Manny after my drink I noticed he had a walkie-talkie attached to the holster in his waist belt. He was wearing his sunglasses again, the binoculars now hanging from his neck. He saw me looking at him and wen' wave me over. *Oh shit. What the fuck does he want?*

"Hey, you Rivera's kid, eh?" I nodded. I wanted to look into his soul, so to speak, to get some bearings on the guy, but in his sunglasses I only saw one warped image of myself. For no clear reason a thought came to my mind: *He is the Sharkman.* Then he took the sunglasses off, but before I could get one good look at his eyes he wen' block them again with the binoculars.

"Had too much last night," he said to me. "Too much fun, too much drink. . . . Hope I no have to save dose idiots out deah." Then he lowered the binoculars and wen' look straight at me. Boy, was like he wen' burn one puka through me with those eyes. He said, "Jes' got word. The state task force caught some sharks out at Māʻili. I'd t'ink twice about going out deah if I was you."

Man, was just like the guy Kawelo in Grandma's story. He wen' look through his binoculars again. After a minute he turned to me, saying, "Who you t'ink dese manō aftah?" Shit man, I had chicken skin all over. He continued, "Ocean use' to be my refuge . . . my puʻuhonua." Then he wen' pull the walkie-talkie out of the belt holster, and while he was holding it with his fingers he wen' thumb his shorts down a bit, showing the side of his hip.

I saw what he wanted me to see. Just below his left hipbone. A tattoo etched around a tremendous fucking scar.

"Da buggah wen' miss. Jes' got a piece. Maybe he was jes' tryin' fo' warn me, eh?"

And maybe you jes' tryin' fo' warn *me,* I said to myself.

There was some other scarring, on his lower left leg . . . his upper right arm . . . one gash by his ribs—but these were also disguised by the tattoos.

I was just about to ask him *Why the tattoos?* when I heard a car screech to a halt on the highway. "Crazy fucking kid!" the driver yelled. Was 'Analu he was yelling at. Damn kid always careless crossing the highway. And just when I was t'inking of being nicer to him. I told Manny, "I gotta get my braddah."

"Eh, dat kid bettah be careful. Fucking drivers around here, dey no look."

I ran toward the highway.

Me and 'Analu sat on the beach. I was giving him the silent treatment while debating whether to confront my fear in the water or just go home. Thing is, I wanted 'Analu to stay out of the water, period.

Finally I said, "Fuck, I goin' in. I tired of sitting here. And you bettah stay on land, 'cause I was talking to da Sharkman and he like eat you. His last name is . . . Kawelo."

"No lie." He had this sad troubled look. Part of me wanted to hug him and say, "Nah, nah," but I dunno. It's like you gotta finish what you start.

"Lying? You t'ink I lying? Go ask him. He tole me his name is Kawelo . . . Manny Kawelo."

He wen' make one funny face, kind of one pout. I took my t-shirt off, threw 'om on his head, saying, "Watch dis," and took off toward the water.

Oh, man, it's greatest feeling, that first plunge. Like breaking chains. I swam toward the oncoming waves, thinking, *No need board.*

Right away I caught two nice waves and felt like a pro. The water was anything but dangerous to me.

Seems I had caught the tail end of a set. The wait for the next set was long. I was treading water and drifting. I lost track of time. When I looked out at the shore for 'Analu I couldn't see him, though I could see Manny, still peering through those binoculars. I just didn't know what to make of that guy.

Where did Nalu go? Maybe he went to the bathroom. Or home. *Hope he not in the water.*

Then I heard that strange, thrilling roar that wave-catching crowds make when a big one's coming. Like, ev'rybody's in tune.

Was one big set. Real fucking big.

I caught the first wave in. Man, I was flying. I knew that trying to get back out without a board would be nuts, yet I would eat it if I tried to get back in. But I was concerned about 'Analu. I was wondering where the hell he had gone.

As I got closer to shore I still couldn't see him. Then I thought, shit, maybe he did go in the water, and I started to feel this undercurrent.

I instantly felt worse when I saw Manny drop the binoculars and grab his large orange surfboard. I gazed out to where he had been looking, couldn't see anything—the waves just kept coming in. So I started swimming in that direction. I fought and fought the waves. I couldn't get anywhere.

God, I hope it's not my braddah. What have I done? When I wen' look back to see where Manny was headed I saw people just trying to get out of the water. *Oh, man. Dis could be bad.*

Manny was whizzing past me with awesome speed. I didn't know what to think. Was he coming to get me? Was he trying to get 'Analu? Save 'Analu? *What?*

I was gasping for breath, struggling to stay ahead of him, thinking I might be swimming toward my own drowning brother.

Then he was on top of me. He said, "Get yaw damn braddah outa da watah—befo' he drown." I wen' grab his board. "Whatchu doing, stupid? Go get yaw braddah!" I held on. Then he wen' reach back and grab my shoulder, and he held on even when one wave wen' slam us. He was yelling, "What? Yaw whole family stupid? *Dat* way!" He tossed me in the direction of the shoreline.

I was about to turn around to try and fight this tattooed lifeguard when I recognized 'Analu's wild freestyle in the shallow water. I felt comfort for a moment as I stopped to catch my breath. But when I rode the whitewash and swam toward him, it was all guilt and ruminations, man.

Me and 'Analu stood on the sand. Clouds had blocked the sun and our teeth were chattering like crazy. Manny had brought the surfer in and was doing mouth-to-mouth resuscitation. I had to keep reminding myself to breathe. I kept saying *sorry, sorry.*

Turns out 'Analu wen' try to stop Manny from getting out there. He thought Manny was after me. He said he wen' yell *No, Sharkman, no!* and then he wen' tackle Manny from behind in the shallow water. But the enemy wasn't one shark. Was one stray surfboard.

After some scary moments the surfer coughed out water and started breathing on his own. Some people said *'amene.* Or cheered softly and went back to whatever they were doing in the first place. Then the paramedics arrived. They wen' place one oxygen mask over the surfer's face and wen' dress his head wound. Then they wen' carry the surfer, his leash still attached to his foot like one death-tag, into the ambulance.

Manny was on his knees in exhaustion. He was staring at the sand, breathing hard, coughing, spitting. At one point he wen' look at us. His eyes were blood red. His expression said, *Crazy fucking kids*.

Minutes later, two guilt-ridden, sopping wet kids started dawdling home. Neither of us said anything. When we got near our house the sunlight started poking through the clouds. I was looking up, watching how the rays lit up the wiliwili blossoms, when 'Analu said, "Jimmy no was home."

"'Ass okay. . . . Hey, we gotta tell Mom and Dad what wen' happen, you know. No bullshit."

"Dey gon' kill us, yeah?" He was looking at me with those sad, deep-set eyes of his.

"Yeah . . . but dass all right." I put my hand on his shoulder. I noticed that the top of his head reached my chin level. "Hey, you getting tall o' what?" He smiled. I pushed the screen door and we went in to face the music.

When the Wiliwili Blossoms

(Waiʻanae Coast—Early Winter 1992 through
Midsummer 1993)

Mākena

Staging area: Waiʻanae Small Boat Harbor, at sunset

Today was the ignition wires. The 4×4 couldn't start. Yesterday this guy's tires were slashed. All four of them. And the other day another guy got in his Ford pickup and realized that his steering wheel was gone.

This was happening to the shark hunters. While they were trying to eradicate sharks, was like somebody was trying to eradicate *them*. Well, not really, but somebody or some people was trying to scare them away. Even when they tried to post one guard to watch their vehicles, strange stuff kept happening.

Manny was the chief suspect.

I heard rumors that he got pissed off when he found out that some fishermen were taking advantage of the shark scare, catching sharks just to remove their fins and sell them to the restaurants. The fins were worth more than the rest of the shark. And to have room in the boats, that's all these fishermen took, sending the finless shark—hammerhead, tiger, whatever—in the ocean to die.

The tow truck came. Third time in three days.

Because Manny was openly belligerent with the shark hunters, they knew that he had something to do with the vandalism. But they couldn't prove shit.

I got on my bicycle and rode to Mākaha.

□ □ □

Mākaha, at twilight

I had just arrived when I saw this guy who I recognized as one of the shark hunters. He was walking up to Manny, who was standing by his lifeguard station, 47B.

"You behind all da shit dat's happening, eh?" the man said.

"Behind what?" Manny had his arms folded, a crossing of tattoos.

"You know."

"No, I don't know. What you accusing me of? Fuckhead."

"Hey, no call me 'fuckhead.'"

"Sorry. I meant dickhead."

"You t'ink you hot shit, eh, tattoo man? You dunno who you fucking wit'."

"Yeah? Why don't you tell me. Who am I fucking with?"

"If I find any evidence you behind this—"

"What? What you gon' do? Hah?" Manny removed his shades and stared down the man with his killer eyes.

The shark hunter wasn't backing off, the stupid fuck. "Naht'ing. Da cops gon' do it for me. Da law . . . "

"Den bring on the law, you fucking dickhead."

The man nodded. He was shaking with anger. "Hey. I will. No worry, braddah, I fucking will."

"I can't wait."

Another man was approaching. I guess he was the tow truck driver.

"Eh, Joe," he said to the pissed-off guy. "I gotta bring da truck back. We gotta go."

Joe looked back at Manny, pointed his index finger at him, then turned toward the tow truck. He got into the passenger side of the vehicle. As the truck took off, towing the 4×4, I heard Manny say, "I gon' fin and filet *you*."

All that time I was kind of invisible, just one of the kids standing around. I don't think he even saw me.

□ □ □

I like it when the sun goes down, especially after a day in the water, but I was banned from going in. Still I liked to stop at Mākaha Beach, if only to watch the sky change colors before I headed home.

Was getting dark early, being it was December, and just about everybody had gone home. Manny didn't seem to be going anywhere. He just sat in his lifeguard tower, drinking from a bottle that was in a paper bag. I knew he was pau work at five, and it was half past six already.

I went up to him.

"Hey, I sorry, eh, about da adda time."

"What? What you being sorry about? Fuck, why is errrebody so ffffricken sssorry?"

I could have said *sorry I said sorry*, but I was already on one short leash wit' dis guy. Then again, he was drunk. I figured maybe I could take advantage of that. I stood by the steps leading up to the lifeguard's nest where they watch from. I had a lot of questions, like did he have a house? Did he live on the beach? Did he have friends? The question that did come out was:

"How come you got so much tattoos?" I tried to sound innocent and nīele. Not like I was probing.

"Why not?" He pulled the bottle out of the package. He took one last swallow and then he tossed the bottle toward the rubbish can. The bottle hit the edge and broke into pieces. Some pieces fell into the sand. He leaped down, looking pretty agile all of a sudden, and started picking up the pieces.

I started to help.

"Hey, get out—move away. Shit. You gon' get cut. Dass all I fucking need on my conscience." I picked up one of the larger pieces of glass, threw it in the rubbish can, then backed off.

Maybe he had a drinking problem.

"You got the knack for wave riding," he said while digging up a piece of glass.

What?

"You surf good. You get one hearing problem?"

"Oh. T'anks."

"But you can't read waves fo' shit."

"I still kinda new to dis place."

"Dass pretty damn obvious. You—fuck, what is that word? Shit, I gotta quit dis boozin'. Can't even—dat fucking word . . . "

So why do you drink? Where do you live? Do you know what people say about you? You know that all the young chicks and old ladies get the hots for you? Questions, questions, and I didn't know how to ask 'em. When we lived in Waiks I used to talk to anybody—homeless people, tourists who thought I couldn't speak English.

With this guy, every question seemed the wrong one. "Kinda hard, eh, be one lifeguard? People causing all kine trouble."

"You call dat trouble? Shit, I call dat work." I sparked a juicy piece of glass; guarantee deep cut if anybody stepped on it. I stepped a bit closer to it.

"What yaw name?"

"Mākena."

"Nice. Whe' you live?"

"Mākaha."

"You da one-word answer man? 'Mākena . . . Mākaha.'" He thought it was funny. "So whe' you going next, Mākua?"

"I grew up in Waikīkī. My family got evicted."

He shook his head. "Fuck. Da same shit story, again and again. Well, I hope it works out. Given da choice, I rather live out here."

"I kinda miss surfing at Walls."

"Time to graduate, boy." He pointed to the ocean. "Dat's where the real challenge is. Shit, I take any kid who grew up surfing at Walls over some of dese so-called world class surfahs. Dey got heart, man." He looked at me. "*You* got heart."

So I wasn't invisible to him. Eh, it was probably just talk. The buggah was two pints beyond reason.

"I should take you North Shore."

"North Shore?" I gripped the big chunk of glass between my toes.

"Hale'iwa . . . Laniākea, maybe. Shit, we should go right now. Do some night surfing. . . . Oh, I fo'got. Yaw parents. Don't want dem worrying."

"I can't anyway. I'm grounded." I lifted my leg and pretended to scratch.

"Grounded?" He laughed. "Wha' does dat mean?"

"I'm not allowed to go in da watah."

"You mean you stuck on land?"

I nodded, and while he was looking out at the ocean I grabbed the piece of glass with my hand.

"Shit. What a fucking trip . . . what a fucking trip." He stared at the water like I wasn't there anymore.

"I gotta go." He didn't respond. "See ya." He still didn't respond. *Man, this guy's too weird.* I walked away.

A few days after Christmas I ran into him at Tamura Super Market when my mom wen' drag me there with her. I was riding the grocery wagon down the magazine aisle, using one foot to accelerate, and found myself headed straight for him.

"Whoa whoa whoa whoa whoa," he said, stopping the already slowed-down wagon. "Dis one supahmahket, not H-3."

"Sorry." Shit, here we go again.

"Hey, my turn fo' be sorry. About da adda day. I gotta watch my—you know." He made a drinking gesture, his thumb being the liquid going down.

"I nevah notice." I replied, feeling light for a change. He looked like he had cleaned up his act. It was funny seeing him wearing a long-sleeve t-shirt and jeans. You couldn't tell he had all those tattoos.

"Still grounded?"

I nodded.

Manny smiled. He was carrying a small grocery basket. Inside had bread and a pint of Johnny Walker. "Still tied to da 'āina? Well, da waves gon' be deah next week. Next year. Aftah we die. It's all timing anyway, right? An' dass all I can help you with, really. Timing. Da rest, especially all da fancy shit, you get it from somebody else, 'cause dat ain't me."

Mom came up. "Why you always gotta run away with the cart?" She unloaded some frozen meats and vegetables.

I said, "Ma, dis is Manny. He da lifeguard at Mākaha."

Mom shook his hand. She smiled real big. Then she said, "We met once . . . at Sparkey Lopez's house."

"Yeah, that's right. So how's, uh—"

"—Henry."

"Yeah, yeah, yeah. Pretty good singer, da guy."

Mom shrugged. "I dunno. Guess so."

"I was just talking to your son about surfing." My mom smiled again. "The kid's really good." Shit, he sounded different, more like one counselor now. "He's got a gift. He's really articulate in the water."

"Really?" She looked at me, furrowing her brows.

"Oh, absolutely." He winked at me.

Articulate? Where did that come from?

"He's got tons of potential, and I think I could help him realize that potential. Take it to that level." I couldn't believe what I was hearing. And Mom, sheesh, she was smiling again. "On my days off," Manny continued, "I head out to the North Shore. I'd like to take him with me."

Her smile disappeared. "Oh, geez, I—I don't know." She looked at me. "Right now, he's grounded."

"Hey, that's none of my business. I just think he's got the talent."

"Really?" Her eyes lit up. "I—I'll talk to his father."

I dunno what happened that night, but the next day I was out on the North Shore. But I wasn't in the water. In fact we were boardless. This was what Manny called an "exploratory trip." We cruised from Haleʻiwa to Velzyland, passing Waimea, Log Cabins, and Shark's Cove, a place known more for snorkling than for what its name might suggest. At each stop Manny explained the breaks, the reef formation in relation to the tides, and what he called "protocol"—surfers' etiquette, especially when it came to sharing a wave. He explained the ins and outs, the necessary trade-offs. Like the Banzai Pipeline. While it may be famous for its tube rides, it comes with a shallow coral reef. Worse, there's cave formations and you could get caught *under* the coral. Manny said he wasn't gonna take me there until I proved to him that I could read the waves, minimize the danger of a wipeout, hold my breath for minutes without panicking, and he said I should *never* go out there when it's higher than eight feet.

At 'Ehukai we watched some guys get smashed. Each time Manny would tell me what they did wrong. "Da main t'ing is, no get cute," he said. "Cute can kill."

The next day we went to Hale'iwa with boards. Manny wanted me to use one of his. The waves were kinda small, just around one to two. Manny thought that was good, 'cause less surfers to compete with for waves.

He didn't just let me go in; he continued the previous day's lecture. He explained what that bump in the horizon meant. *Articulated* what the shape and color of the clouds said about the conditions. Explained to me how the water color indicated what lay underneath. And the colors weren't just blue or blue-green. There was, like, ukubillion shades. On and on he went. I was kinda paying attention, but I had one eye on the babes passing by with their surfah dude boyfriends. Surfah babes too, not just sunbathers. After the hour-long lecture, we finally got in.

Back at Walls, before I made the switch to one 7' 11" custom board, I used to body board exclusively. The raddest part of body boarding was drop-knee tailslides and projectile aerials. But I had never experienced a full-on tube ride. The bigger board that Manny loaned me was steadier and faster than anything I ever rode before, and when I caught my first barrel, shit, man, I was stoked.

The best part of this new adventure was I had my own personal lifeguard.

The next week we were out at 'Ehukai. The waves were breaking four to six. It was awesome watching Manny and some other guys catching those long tube rides. For me it was hard enough paddling to get out, having to duck dive all the time to avoid getting drilled. For a while I couldn't catch anything. I dunno what it was. Then

Manny came by. He said my timing was off. He told me, "When I say go, you fricken go!"

That's how I caught my first tube ride. It was half-formed; I was sort of in, sort of out at the same time. But shit, the sheer speed of the ride had me laughing. It was so cool. And then I got drilled when it closed in on me. But boy, I was hooked, man. Hooked. I caught a couple more waves. On my last ride, tried to push it a bit; I got cocky. It was UNREAL for a few seconds, then I found myself nose-diving toward coral. I spread-eagled so I would land flat on the water. Shit, this was fun.

After that I went in to shore. Sat and watched Manny catch a few more. Man, he was smooth. Awesome. Rode a tube like it was nobody's business. No fancy stuff; just grace and style.

Fucking all right.

□ □ □

Winter, through early spring

Manny began picking me up early on Saturdays, usually around sunrise. I'd get into his Chevy Impala and off we'd go around the Wai'anae Range. We'd surf for hours, usually at Laniākea, Chun's, sometimes Sunset or Pipe, depending on the size and direction of the swell. I often lost track of Manny, because I would get so into figuring out the waves. Then he would pop up out of the blue and tell me something. He'd point out landmarks on shore to line up on, explain where and how the peak shifted; he would indicate the direction of the rip under the different tide and swell conditions. Manny was teaching me how to read and feel the conditions around me.

Sometimes he'd point to the lines approaching and say exactly what was coming. He'd look at the clouds or gauge the colors on the horizon and predict the weather for the next two weeks. He helped me fine-tune my takeoffs, my barrel riding. One time he saw me trying to go off the top just when the tube was forming. I was just having fun. I took a beating. He just shook his head and smiled. Later, in the car, he reminded me of how humbling the ocean can be. Funny, he and I can both be so quiet, and this one day he got pretty talkative. He went on about attitude, about surfing to make peace with the ocean, "Not to kick its ass, like one goddamn rodeo bull." Then he said, "The last thing you do is go around talking about it. No real champion goes around bragging about it. Think about that."

And speaking of real champs, we saw them all out there from time to time: Shane Dorian, Zane Aikau, Sunny Garcia, Kalani Robb, . . . Fast Eddie and those He'e Nalu guys . . . lotta big names. And they all knew Manny. Wasn't like he was king of the North Shore or anything like that. But you could tell they respected him. Gave him ground, and when they saw me with him they would nod or smile and say *Whassup?*

Not too many of the West Side boyz get to go North Shore the way I got to, and I coulda bragged about it. But I tell you, I always returned home humbled. And boy did I sleep good, dreaming of big blue waves that kept coming and coming, surrounding me.

□ □ □

In the back of the valley

One day, when there wasn't much wave action, we left the beach early and Manny took me to this place where the dirt road ended, way in the back of Wai'anae Valley. The place was just kiawe and scrub, cactus and tall weeds. Then I saw one old abandoned bus with wires all around it. I could hear the hum of generators.

"Home," Manny said.

What? Right then I heard the sound of what must have been five Dobermans. Fuck, I was ready to jump the highest tree—except there were no high trees.

"Relax." Manny clicked the remote he had pulled out of his car. The barking stopped. "No dogs. Jes' one alarm system."

I followed him into the bus. Another alarm went off the minute I stepped inside. Manny pressed a switch by the driver's seat. The alarm stopped.

"Paranoia," he said. "My usual state of mind."

I used to think that he might be Kawelo, that he was capable of turning into one shark and killing innocent swimmers and surfers. Now I was thinking that what he really was might be just as spooky. I just wanted to stay on his good side.

Manny took me to his bus-house a few times after that. He started to trust me, even showed me how to dismantle the various alarms he had set up. One day, a few months later, he showed me a video camera he had set up. It was wired to a battery. He was always recharging batteries during the long drives to the North Shore. He said the camera was to catch intruders. You would never notice it among the cactus and wild grass.

He had all kinds of gadgets; mostly he kept them in one of his two cars. Besides the '59 Impala, which he said he used so people would know he was coming, he had this '89 Civic. This faded blue Civic had a hot but quiet Acura engine. He said he used the Civic when he *didn't* want people to know he was coming.

One day he left me in the bus while he hiked up the mountain range. He had some private place up there. Even I couldn't go.

I just was relaxing, waiting for him so we could go catch some waves, then I noticed this small notebook on the long seat that he used as his bed.

I reached with my feet, using my big and second toes to open it—somewhere in the middle. I moved closer and started reading. The writing was small and hard to decipher, but what I could make out went like this:

Feb 17. Saturday. Just after midnight: What to make of Rep. Bill Anjermann getting into car with Chung at airport?

Feb 24. Saturday. 2200 hours: Sam and Izenhoff having a rendezvous at Kelly's. Been bought off?

Feb 25. Sunday. 1700 hours: S meets with H at harbor. More going down than trolling. Surf's going to be gorgeous.

Feb 27. Tuesday. 1000 hours, give or take a lifetime: Lopez in phone booth near Save-A-Lot. Eyes looking everywhere, sweating profusely. He paces, smokes, sweats for a half hour, then AS comes by. Hands him a paper bag. Money? Drugs? Birdseed?

I turned the page. A tide chart fell out. I slipped it back in and turned a few more pages.

S—married to TL before she moved in with HE. A connection? HE now running the show while HH is doing time. His runners: Ah Sing, Lopez, Kim . . .

EH is a clown, but a dangerous clown. Tight with CC via Kim.

Can't figure: What is S's role???

I turned toward the end of the notebook and
phone numbers. Some were town numbers tha
with 9 or 5. Most started with 696 and 697. V
Coast numbers. One started with 695.

It was mine.

"Int'resting?" My heart jumped. Manny was standing
right over me. This was his Civic entrance.

I nodded. He gently took the notebook out of my
hands. Then he threw it against the back window.

"One rule. Don't fucking get snoopy 'round here,
'kay?" He was stern like how my dad gets when I fuck
up.

I nodded again. *He had my phone number.*

Why wouldn't he? He has to call me now and then.

But . . .

He walked over to retrieve the book. Then he said,
"Know what dis is?"

I shrugged "One diary?"

"Diary? Do I look like one fucking Anne Frank? Do I
look like one fucking diary keeper?"

I shook my head no. I didn't know about this Anne
Frank.

"Da point is, respect my privacy. . . . You go looking
around at yaw parents' stuff?"

I shook my head no, even though that wasn't the total
truth. I knew where Dad kept his *Playboy*s.

He sat down by me. He put his head down, ran his fingers through his hair. Then he stared straight ahead.
"Sometimes people cross a line, go to places dey not quite
ready for—"

I nodded "You mean like Pipeline."

"Exactly."

I sensed a lecture coming, formal tone and all.

"That's how you find yourself in shit you can't get out
of. Seriously. There's some shit you don't ever wanna try

.nrough. Lemme clue you. The world can be a
.k place."

.e went on about dark forces all around. I was listening but things weren't registering. I noticed his eyes were
red. I was thinking, who is S? Is S the same as Sam? Who
is TL? Who is H? And Lopez? The only Lopez I knew of
was Sparkey. Boy, if Manny's watching Sparkey . . . why?
And what the fuck am I doing here?

". . . especially when Pipe'll do it for you." Huh? What
did he just say? He was smiling, the smile of a crazed man.
Did he go up the mountain to get stoned? To harvest?

Made me think he might be talking about some other
kind of pipe.

The next Saturday, at sunrise, Manny picked me up in
his Civic. Lately he'd been using the Civic for the longer
drives—to save on gas, I figured. I thought I should ask
him about some things, 'cause hey, I'm only sixteen. I
don't need this spooky shit. But as we headed around the
range, got on the freeway, then Kunia Road, which
Manny preferred to the H-2, he was really quiet. So I
stayed quiet too.

Then after almost a half hour of silence—no radio,
nothing—I had to say something. It came out, "You one
Fed o' one cop o' something?" *Or?*

He blew out some air. "I'll just say this. I track things
down. I investigate things." That formal tone again.

"Who you work for?"

"Let's not go there. Last thing I need is your parents all
up in arms, thinking I'm leading their son down some dangerous road."

"I understand."

"I work for myself."

"The pay must be shitty."

He laughed. That made me less tens*e*.

"How come you goin' after da shark hunters?"

"Why do you think it's me? Frankly, I don't know who the fuck's doing all the sabotage, but I like it. I wanna shake this mystery man's hand. Those damn hunters, all they can think about is today's profit. They don't give a shit about tomorrow."

"I heard dey cutting off da sharks' fins and selling 'om to rest'raunts."

"Puh. What else is new. Supply and demand, kid. Name o' da game."

I saw an image of a finless shark floundering in the ocean, dying. But it was replaced with images of people being attacked. "Sharks, dey kinda like our natural enemy, right? I mean, dey attack us." I was looking at his scars, the tattoos working along and around them.

"Sometimes we deserve to be attacked. We're the ones invading their habitat. Fucking with the ecosystem, the food chain. We're the ones who don't belong. . . . Look at those longliners—shit, I know people gotta make a living, but—" He shook his head. "An' those gill net fishermen. Greed, I tell you. Jes' plain old greed."

"I heard dey snare endangered species, like turtles—"

"Shit, they snare *everything* in sight. They exhaust the resources. That's *why* sharks have to come closer to the shore, foraging. . . . You factor in global warming, which is the chief reason that fish are swimming at different strata, looking for the temperature range they're used to. So the traditional fishermen can't find fish in their traditional places. No mo' fish, braddah."

"An' what about—"

"Mr. Twenty Questions. You should be a reporter, you so nīele. Is that what they call you in school, Nīele?"

"Somebody else got dat nickname. Dey jes' call me 'Mak,' or 'Maks.'"

By then we were pulling in to Zippy's in Wahiawā. Manny said, "You ate, Maks?" I shook my head. "How many times I gotta tell you, you gotta eat. Can't surf without energy."

When we got back in the car, with our sandwiches and drinks, Manny put his coffee in the holder, started the car, and pulled out, all the while fussing with the radio. Reception is kinda okay in Wahiawā, but once you head down toward Hale'iwa you get nothing but static. Manny popped in a cassette tape. There was no sound. Holding his sandwich with the same left hand that steered the wheel, he fumbled with the dials. Then I heard this guitar that sounded like Jimi Hendrix.

"Better than the Jawaiian crap they've been playing today."

"Jawaiian crap?"

"Mostly crap. Same thing with rap. . . . The good stuff is few and far between."

"What is da good stuff?"

"Fuck, anything that doesn't have that packaged beat, that dumbass, derivative, drum-machine sound. You have to dig to find the good shit. Me, I like backyard jams. Fucking guys with real chops. Passion."

He cranked up the stereo sound. This player, whoever he was, was burning out a guitar solo. It's gotta be Hendrix, I thought. Or maybe it's Stevie Ray Vaughan.

"Hear that? Fire?" The way he said it was FI-YER.

"Sounds pretty good."

"The guitar's smokin', man."

I agreed but I shrugged.

We were quiet for a minute, just listening. We were out of Wahiawā town by now, starting the long downhill drive toward that now visible ocean we both loved. The best view in the world.

"Passion," Manny said. "That's what matters most. Don't lose sight of that." He was sounding formal again. "You have a passion for surfing. To satisfy your soul, right? You know what that feels like, right?" I nodded. "That's your template. It's what you use in all the avenues you pursue. It's got to feel right. Without that to guide you, you're like all those who settle for so way less, who go out and buy everything in sight, thinking that'll fill the emptiness in their souls. They call it a life, but it's fucking paint-by-numbers, man." He spat those last words out. Then took a sip of his coffee.

Back at the ranch

"You may notice I never smoke around here. . . . One match, da whole place blows."

I hadn't noticed because I didn't know he smoked. I looked around. Saw the oil slicks, all the dry kiawe, all the brush. Then, without looking at me he added, "One day, I might ask you to drop dat match."

When it came to surfing, Manny was always direct. From late March onward, we started catching South Shore waves since the North and West were flat and would be so till next fall. But anywhere we went, the site should have been called "Situations." 'Cause that's what he kept putting me in. It was always, *What if?* What if a guy is about to ride right on top of you, what if you can't avoid getting drilled, what if you eat it and get caught underwater for minutes, what if you lose the board . . . what if what if what if . . .

With everything else, Manny was indirect. He liked metaphors, analogies—the kinda stuff English teachers say we need to understand to do good on the SATs.

I slowly caught on. And after a while he knew he could trust me.

The strange part was the more he taught me, the less I could say.

And stranger still, one midsummer day he just didn't show up. He didn't call, didn't leave a message. Nothing. He wasn't even at his lifeguard spot. A new lifeguard was there. Was like he had fallen off the edge of the earth.

I turned toward the end of the notebook and noticed phone numbers. Some were town numbers that began with 9 or 5. Most started with 696 and 697. Wai'anae Coast numbers. One started with 695.

It was mine.

"Int'resting?" My heart jumped. Manny was standing right over me. This was his Civic entrance.

I nodded. He gently took the notebook out of my hands. Then he threw it against the back window.

"One rule. Don't fucking get snoopy 'round here, 'kay?" He was stern like how my dad gets when I fuck up.

I nodded again. *He had my phone number.*

Why wouldn't he? He has to call me now and then.

But . . .

He walked over to retrieve the book. Then he said, "Know what dis is?"

I shrugged "One diary?"

"Diary? Do I look like one fucking Anne Frank? Do I look like one fucking diary keeper?"

I shook my head no. I didn't know about this Anne Frank.

"Da point is, respect my privacy. . . . You go looking around at yaw parents' stuff?"

I shook my head no, even though that wasn't the total truth. I knew where Dad kept his *Playboys*.

He sat down by me. He put his head down, ran his fingers through his hair. Then he stared straight ahead. "Sometimes people cross a line, go to places dey not quite ready for—"

I nodded "You mean like Pipeline."

"Exactly."

I sensed a lecture coming, formal tone and all.

"That's how you find yourself in shit you can't get out of. Seriously. There's some shit you don't ever wanna try

barreling through. Lemme clue you. The world can be a
very dark place."

He went on about dark forces all around. I was listening but things weren't registering. I noticed his eyes were
red. I was thinking, who is S? Is S the same as Sam? Who
is TL? Who is H? And Lopez? The only Lopez I knew of
was Sparkey. Boy, if Manny's watching Sparkey . . . why?
And what the fuck am I doing here?

". . . especially when Pipe'll do it for you." Huh? What
did he just say? He was smiling, the smile of a crazed man.
Did he go up the mountain to get stoned? To harvest?

Made me think he might be talking about some other
kind of pipe.

The next Saturday, at sunrise, Manny picked me up in
his Civic. Lately he'd been using the Civic for the longer
drives—to save on gas, I figured. I thought I should ask
him about some things, 'cause hey, I'm only sixteen. I
don't need this spooky shit. But as we headed around the
range, got on the freeway, then Kunia Road, which
Manny preferred to the H-2, he was really quiet. So I
stayed quiet too.

Then after almost a half hour of silence—no radio,
nothing—I had to say something. It came out, "You one
Fed o' one cop o' something?" *Or?*

He blew out some air. "I'll just say this. I track things
down. I investigate things." That formal tone again.

"Who you work for?"

"Let's not go there. Last thing I need is your parents all
up in arms, thinking I'm leading their son down some dangerous road."

"I understand."

"I work for myself."

"The pay must be shitty."

He laughed. That made me less tense.

The Dance of Twilight

('Iolani Palace grounds, Honolulu—
January 17, 1993)

Kanani

The procession begins at sunset. Figures are shadowy in the loss of light. If a stranger, a tourist, happens upon this tableau, he or she will make little sense of the many small lights shimmering through the haze—the mix of vog and twilight. The stranger will not comprehend the significance of the lights growing larger, will not realize that these were torches lighting the way on a long long road—a road that points to reclamation. Will we ever arrive?

I was once a participant; what am I now? A witness? A beneficiary? It took us a hundred years to get to this point. I keep hoping we can speed up the process. But at least we got here. To this moment.

When those shadowy forces worked to get rid of Keoni, they, like the people of Mānā who tried to destroy Kawelo, failed to see that his ideas would live on in the hearts of thousands. They couldn't kill that. Perhaps that was what Beth spoke of when similar forces torched her house. There's a spirit here.

And it's driven by the chanting. I close my eyes and feel the collective heartbeat. If only for one moment . . .

155

I see the Committee of Safety, one hundred pale-faced armed men moving in with their rifles, ready to take on the darker-skinned palace guards. A few of these pale men had been picnicking with the queen just a few days earlier; now they are seeking her capture. They move quiet in the night as if darkness can hide the foulness of their intent. Where are those loyal to the queen? What has happened to the people, who greatly outnumber these pale-skinned men? What's happened to the warrior spirit?

WHAT'S HAPPENED?

What can you say about a force that so thoroughly disrupts a culture that it cannot find the spirit to retaliate? Wilikoki and Bush are desperately trying to stir people up, imploring them to take up arms. Perhaps their previous failures—not to mention Wilikoki's tendencies toward self-aggrandizement—have put off too many.

Lili'u—isolated in her palace; there is no time, no means for her to retaliate. She has no desire to take up arms. She speaks: *I place my country in the hands of the good people of the United States. They will know what is just and will restore sovereignty. Imua.*

There's a cacophony of voices. There's little I can discern.

I can make out some familiar names: Thurston, Dole, Minister Stevens, President Cleveland . . . then Blount. McKinley.

I hear my husband Henry whispering, "This reenactment is somethin' else, hon. Glad we came."

I'm slow to react. "Yeah," I say out loud. I think I say it out loud. I don't know if I'm saying it out loud or imagining I am saying it out loud. I'm not sure if my husband really spoke.

He did speak. His voice has brought me back from the distance of a hundred years. I see that my two boys are quiet, mesmerized. I want my own space, but I need to be with my family. They are my space.

Colonization is when they distract you from the things that you are passionate about. Who said that? Whose voice is that in the wind? I have stood with my family; I've been passionate about that. But have I turned my back on my culture? Thinking *That's what a life is.* Work, work, and more work. A means. But whose ends am I serving?

Tall grim-visaged monsters turn out to be film cameras. This will be on the news. A sound-bite.

Shadowy figures. It all figures. It's all a shadow play.

I can't concentrate on the proceedings. My mind wanders. And then there's the chanting. I feel the beating of my heart, my sovereign heart. Feel it in my na'au, stemming from my piko, my center. My pulse is the chanting. Whether I like it or not, I am part of this, I am . . . part of this. And we are . . . making history.

We are mocking history.

We're turning history on its sorry ass.

I envision Keoni on the palace steps, speaking to us all. If anyone should be here to witness this, to witness this event, it's him.

Then I remember. He is here.

Devastation Trail

(Wai'anae, Pearl Ridge—Late Winter through
Spring 1993)

Henry Rivera never could get used to those temporary lay-offs. He could still make money doing side jobs on week-ends to complement his unemployment, so that wasn't the problem so much. He thought about taking more night classes at West O'ahu or the UH. He wasn't young any-more and his construction days were numbered. He didn't want to hang on like some over-the-hill ballplayer trying to get that pension; he just wanted out. With Kanani and the boys in school all day, with the boys doing sports in the late afternoons, with Nani putting in extra hours try-ing to fix the broken lives of some students by meeting with their parents—when she wasn't dancing hula, her new passion—Henry simply found himself with too much time on his hands. In the morning, after Nani and the kids went to school, he'd read the newspaper, go through old magazines for articles that commanded his attention—usually there were none—then he'd clean up: wash the dishes, do the laundry, scrub the floors. With hours left before anyone came home, he'd venture out—pick up lunch somewhere, then drive along the coast and around Kahe Point, venture toward Kapolei, Waikele, checking out the new subdivisions going up. Sometimes he'd go to the new Borders store and skim books and magazines or put on headphones in the CD section. *That* he got into, though the highs only brought him lower when he realized how much he missed playing music. He'd head home discouraged. Idleness did not fit him well.

Lily Imura loved her students but was sick of her principal and his not-so-subtle antics. She had applied for a transfer.

One warm afternoon in late February Henry walked into "Miss Imura's" classroom. She was his son's third-grade teacher. This was two weeks into the third quarter and the second-quarter report cards had gone out. 'Analu had gotten his usual A's for music appreciation and PE, but was slipping in all his other subjects. Up to then he had been a steady B student in English, Reading, Science, and Math, and Henry was curious as to the problem.

He had never met the woman before. He went in thinking, *Typical Japanese teacher; I know the type.* Throughout the islands, Hawai'i-bred Japanese, due to their ubiquitous presence in management positions, were thought of as the dominant group, masking the reality of powerful haole cliques. When Henry entered the classroom, with its small desks and chairs, drawings that peppered the walls, he found a disarmingly pretty young woman who professed that 'Analu was her favorite, and that she had to be hard on him because she knew how capable he was.

Lily Imura did not know what to expect from the man with rough hands and searing eyes who suddenly appeared in her room. As soon as he announced he was 'Analu Rivera's father—she had only met the kid's mom at a conference the previous fall—she was relieved. But only slightly.

She had had a terrible day. The principal, who used to praise everything from her teaching methodology to the way she dressed, and who used to treat her with all the charm a balding fifty-two-year-old could muster, was now giving her shit about everything from her methodology to the way she dressed. She had had just about enough of this asshole, and now, the thought of her being lectured by the father of her favorite student just was too much for her to handle.

The minute Henry brought up grades she burst into tears. She brought out her record book, which prominently displayed the basic problem: unfinished assignments. Factor in a little too much playing around in the classroom. As soon as Henry said, "What eight-year-old is not going to play around? That's the problem with you—" she started bawling.

A bewildered Henry began to comfort her. He put a callused hand on her shoulder, and after a moment she looked up at him and said, "It's not your fault, I've just been having—"

"Hey. It's all right. It's all right. I'm on your side."

She gestured, waving her arms back and forth, saying something like *arrrggghhh—damned fucking principal,* and before long she had found a confidant.

Henry discovered that she stayed late in her classroom on a regular basis, so he began to stop by after dropping his younger son off at baseball practice.

Lily had thought about changing her habits and not staying late any more, except that now this man was showing up at her classroom door.

Henry didn't want this complication, yet he needed it badly. There was nothing overtly wrong with his relationship with Kanani, but she was never around. She had become involved not only with the lives of her students, but with the well-being of her community. Henry still thought the world of his wife, and disloyalty had never struck him as an option.

Lily didn't need this complication either. Jake, her off-and-on lawyer boyfriend, was more off lately, and Henry was at least someone she could ask—about men and their idiosyncrasies, how they signal commitment. Plus, he seemed refreshingly honest. He told her early on that while he liked talking to her, he found her a bit too attractive. While she would rant about the sleazy principal, he would say things like, *Hey, what makes me less sleazy? Here I am, a married man, talking to a very attractive single woman. My wife doesn't know. I would question MY motives.*

He wasn't in love with her—he knew that—but there were days when he couldn't stop thinking of her, days when he replayed previous encounters in his mind and then rehearsed what he would say the next time their paths crossed.

Lily thought about him all the time too. It got her mind off Jake, who, though athletic and exceptionally bright in a schooled sort of way, was intensely self-absorbed. She rarely fit into his schedule, which included catching waves or jogging in the morning, followed by an eight-hour workday, then tennis or racquetball, or a workout at the gym, and then back to his office for a couple more hours. On weekends he'd golf or participate in water sports with his friends from high school days, or go to UH games, or attend family functions, or sleep in long and hard. Lily didn't see Henry as a possible replacement, just someone who took the time.

She liked his odd sense of humor, his easy smile.

Henry liked the way she laughed, the way her beautiful face lit up when excited.

After a few encounters, they became more tactile with their good-byes. They'd embrace, kiss each other on the cheek. And one day, their lips met. But even then, they went no further. What would stop Henry was the impracticality of taking it further. Where would they go if they wanted to tear off their clothes and just go at it?

Would they act like high school kids and do it in one of their cars? Get a hotel room?

Henry's house was obviously unthinkable, with kids, his wife, and nosy neighbors. And Lily's apartment was quite far away. Besides, Jake still had a key. What if he popped in on them going at it?

Such speculation on Henry's part seemed wistful. It's not going to happen, he'd say to himself. It's not going to happen. When he realized his concerns were more logistical than moral, he told himself, *put it out of your mind, you degenerate fuck.*

One early March afternoon, as Lily was erasing the lesson on the board, Henry quietly entered the open door. She seemed to sense his presence and twirled around. She held an eraser in each hand and smiled. Then she clapped the erasers together again and again, creating this chalk dust cloud between them, saying, "Did you know I minored in drama?" Henry closed the door and said, in a mock choking voice, "Don't breathe." She lifted her blouse to cover her mouth. Henry lifted his shirt to cover his. He approached her, kissed her as if to resuscitate her, took her by the hand, and led her toward her desk. "Under here," he said as he kicked the chair out of the way. They could barely squeeze under. She gazed at Henry. She was still using her blouse to cover her mouth, exposing her belly and the bottom portion of her bra. Henry began stroking her stomach. They kissed. While his tongue probed her mouth, Henry slid his hands under her skirt and rubbed the front of her panties. Lily reached for his crotch. She fumbled with his jeans, trying to unbutton them. Henry slipped his hand under her panties and stroked her fine pubic hair. Then he reached further. *Oh shit, man, she's so wet.* He yanked her panties down and wondered if he could go down on her without injuring his back.

"This isn't gonna do," Lily said. Henry stopped. Then she said, "We need more space."

They got out from under her desk and looked around, as if wondering *Where?* Lily was already against her desk, so Henry said, "Sit." He kissed her some more, then lifted her skirt and buried his face into her crotch.

"Oh god," she said immediately. "Put it in." Henry was hesitant, thinking from his years with Kanani that women usually need more time to warm up. But there was urgency in her voice. And it wasn't as if she weren't slippery wet. His penis slid right in. Oh, my god, he thought, this feels so good. He came immediately. *Oh shit.*

Meanwhile, she had been energized by his thrusts and started kissing him more and more. He kept pumping but he was already going limp. He felt embarrassed. He wanted to apologize.

It was awkward. She was just getting started and he had nothing left. *Enrique,* he thought disparagingly. Then that thought passed.

Lily must have sensed his awkwardness and said, while stroking his face, "Hey, it happens." She smiled. "It felt good." Then she reached for a Kleenex box. Henry kissed her and pressed his head on her small, still-covered breasts. She stuck some Kleenex between her legs, stood up and slid into her panties while Henry pulled up his boxer shorts and jeans. Then they heard someone whistling outside. Whoever it was then jiggled the doorknob. Henry and Lily froze, looking at each other.

It locks when you close it, she whispered.

Good, he whispered back. There was no place to hide.

The person then knocked. Henry and Lily stayed quiet. He turned his head to look at the door, then looked back at her face. They felt nervous, guilty, complicitous, and aroused. Huge seconds passed. Then the whistling started again and faded.

"Finally," Lily said, still speaking softly. "He's gone."

"The janitor?"

"No. The janitors have keys. It's the fucking principal. He's the whistler. . . . Dammit. I kinda wish he would've caught us. Maybe then he'd get off my back."

"Doubt it. He'd just find a way to use it against you."

"You're right. He would. He's a fucking scumbag."

If he's a scumbag, Henry thought, what am I? He said nothing. After a few minutes he decided it was time to leave. He kissed Lily one more time.

"I, uh . . . "

"Hey, so we did it," she said. "I don't have a problem."

Henry tousled her hair. "Good."

□ □ □

As soon as he was in his car, Henry sank into his seat. *Hoh, man, what the fuck am I doing? How could I—? And why did I have to come so damn quick? Fuck.* He punched the steering wheel. He felt himself sinking, sinking deep. He vowed that he would not see Lily again. Just send a note to her at the school apologizing for his behavior. He decided he would go to 'Analu's baseball practices and offer his help. He didn't care much for the coaches—their style, their tactics—but reminded himself that they were volunteers. Shit, nobody was paying them to come out every afternoon. I could do that too, he thought, at least until the next job starts.

In less than a week he and a crew were supposed to take over a residential project that some previous company was screwing up. Other big jobs loomed as well. In fact, it looked like a shitload of work was coming up. And Henry was determined to go back to school. Maybe study music this time, he thought, though he vaguely remembered hating the music theory class he took at Santa Monica Junior College so long ago. Being a hands-on guy, he missed playing the guitar that gathered dust in the bedroom closet. While he was swimming in thought, a refrain from many years back returned to haunt him:

No more FOO-lin' around, no more RUN-nin' away
No more FOO-lin' around, baby, WHY don't you stay
with me tonight . . . I won't take flight

Oh fuck. How could I . . . ? Why did I . . . ? How . . . ? Why . . . ?

Meanwhile, Lily, alone in her locked classroom, chastised herself. She didn't think to ask if he had a condom. *What if I get pregnant? What then? Oh Jake. Jake, you son of a bitch. It's your fucking fault.*
I need to put a stop to this. I should call him and say—no, I shouldn't even call him.

Late one morning, a few days later, the phone rang at the Rivera household. Henry picked it up and heard a hesitant "hi." Soon it was "I got a free overnight at Ko Olina. A gift from some parents I helped out. That is, if you're interested . . . "
All Henry could say was "When?"
He had been strumming his guitar when Lily called. She must have figured he'd be home alone. He had been practicing a flamenco pattern, trying to get his fingers to work in sync. After the call he began obsessing on his "less-than-exemplary performance" in Lily's classroom. He thought about the tits and ass he'd touched but never seen, the sweet pussy he had only had a quick glimpse of. It had all been too quick. He wanted a sequel, a romantic episode. Just for one night, he convinced himself. For just one night, one night only, he wanted the works.

Ko Olina, the new resort on the other end of the Wai'anae Coast, was a bit of a risk. A little too close to home, so Henry knew he would have to be discreet. Then he thought, *Nobody I know in this area stays at that upscale hotel.* Then it occurred to him, the problem is not who is *staying* there, but who is *working* there.

He arranged to meet Lily three days later, on a Friday. He got off work at three, and had told Kanani he would be home late—probably very late. She probably assumed he was going to spend another night boozing and singing at Sparkey Lopez's house. She seemed too busy with her hula hālau anyway to bother with questions.

□ □ □

"I tole you she wen' minah in drama? She stahted fo' do dis strip show. Damn. Da blouse, da skirt, her bra, her skinny watch."

"Fuck."

"Fuck is right. She on'y had her earrings left. Not to mention her panties. Red, Victoria's Secret panties."

"Well? Did dose come off too? O' was jes' fo' show."

"Whatchu t'ink?"

Josh looked at Henry. "Fuckah." Josh slapped Henry on the shoulder. "How I s'posed ta get work done wit' you telling me all dis stuff? . . . So, what else?"

The two men were resetting a shaky platform that the cement would be poured into. They would do the floors and patio all at once. The crew that had begun the job had set the platform poorly, and part of Henry and Josh's work involved undoing the prior crew's mess. The company was a few days past deadline, and losing money. The supervisor, whose usual style was to leave them alone, kept checking on them to make sure they weren't slacking.

Josh muttered, "An' she one teachah?"
Henry nodded.
"Japanee, too?" Henry nodded again.
"Fuck, sounds way bettah dan goin' Korean bar."
"A lot cheapah too."
"Shit, I know guys who spend five hundred bucks easy at the clubs. Jes' fo' one fricken night. An' dey get shit. Dey hahdly get to touch."
"Fucking nuts. . . . Here, hold dis fo' me." Henry handed Josh the chisel.
"Hey, I t'ink I gon' ask fo' get off work early," Josh said. "I met dis babe."
"Fat chance. I mean about getting off work early. Looks like ovahtime again."
"Fuck." Josh placed the chisel between the wood frame and the packed dirt and Henry began to hammer it. "Jes' no hit my fingahs, eh," Josh said.
"Who woulda thought—?" Henry stopped to survey the structural damage. "Shit, they really screwed up on dis."
"So what, den?" Josh began prying to loosen the wood.
"So we gotta work late."
"No, I mean, what wen' happen? Aftah da chick wen' strip naked."
Henry slapped Josh's forehead with his palm. "Fuck. What else gon' happen when one chick stay naked?"
"Yeah, I know but—chee braddah, some details, please."
"Well, . . . you know."
"How many times?"
Henry made the "OK" sign with his thumb and index, raising three cement-caked fingers. "An' I t'ink she came twice. Unless she was faking."
"Oh, I like when dey fake."
Henry laughed. "You like when dey fake?"
"Shua. All da noise, li' dat. Esta too quiet. Da most she do is hum."

"Hum?" Henry laughed even louder. "What she hum, da 'Close Encounters' theme?" Henry started humming the melody in B-flat. "Hmm-HMM-hmm, mm-hmm-Hmm-HMMMM . . . "

"Fuck you . . . I mean she moan."

The supervisor approached. "Eh, how's it going ovah here? You guys pau fixing da frame?"

"Speaking of moaning," Henry muttered. "Well," Henry said aloud, "dey fucked it up, and, as usual, we gotta unfuck it." He kicked at a piece of wood.

"Well, as long as dey willing fo' cough up da money."

"Yeah, as long."

"If dey like da foundation be solid, dey gotta be willing to pay."

Henry grimaced. "Dass da deal."

"Speaking of money," the supervisor added, "so what, Josh, you gon' clubbing tonight?"

"Dass da plan."

"No spend all yaw fricken paycheck, eh?"

"Well, you can treat me."

"Not on yaw fucking life. I get one mortgage check fo' write."

Josh stood up, holding his lower back. "Ahh, shit. . . . Hey, at least you get one fricken mortgage."

"Hey, you make about da same as me. Jes' figgah." He looked squarely at Josh. "I get alimony . . ." He held up his index finger. ". . . child suppawt." He switched to his middle finger. "T'ing is, I no spend all my money on drinking wit' naked wahines."

"Hey, 'ass only 'cause you cannot. You'd be da firs' in line at Boogie Wondahland if you nevah have yaw fucking mortgage and child suppawt."

*"So, I guess you da lucky one, eh Josh?" The supervisor
began to walk away. "Break's ovah."*
*"I like screw his ex-wife," Josh said to Henry. "See
what da buggah say den."*

Later, when Henry's giving Josh a ride home:
*"Shit, the last time Esta and me did it t'ree times was—
fuck I no t'ink we evah did it t'ree times. Two, yeah, in da
early days. But shit, t'ree . . . fuck, maybe when I was sev-
enteen. . . . Musta been one special night, eh?"*
"Hey, no go blabbing about dis."
*"Blab? Hey, my lips are sealed, braddah. You know my
lips are sealed."*
"Hers weren't." The moment he let that line slip out,
Henry grimaced.
"Dass it. I goin' Blue Cat Lounge tonight."

□ □ □

Shooting the breeze with Josh was one thing; facing
himself was another. At home that evening he and Kanani
made love tenderly. Henry knew that these moments were
most precious, and he wondered why he was putting
everything precious to him at risk. He barely understood
what drove him to her Pearlridge apartment. He never had
to go to the school anymore, since Lily no longer feared
the untimely intrusion of the mysterious (at least to
Henry) Jake. Jake the jock. Jake the lawyer. Into-himself
Jake. Maybe one day, that son-of-a-bitch will hear some
woman's voice, calling him *Jacob,* and he'll stop in his
tracks, skip the Jacuzzi and get out of the health club as
soon as he can, and ask her to marry him. *Who the fuck
are you, Jake, and why are you treating this lovely girl like
shit?*

*And who the fuck are you, Henry? Hank. Hank Hank
Hank Hank Hank.*

It just got to him. One day as he left her apartment, he
got into the elevator, pressed G, for ground, then gazed at
his reflection in the closing doors.

*What the fuck are you doing? She's your son's teacher.
She's not gonna keep her mouth shut. She's got friends.
What you think they do, lunchtime in the cafeteria? They
talk, man. They confide.*

The elevator door opened. Henry saw a woman in a
wheelchair. Pushing from behind was the man who drove
the Handi-van. Henry quickly moved to assist, holding the
elevator open as he got out of the way. The woman smiled
and nodded. Henry nodded too.

Their paths had crossed a couple of times before, as
they were going in or getting out of the building. *Fuck,
people know your routine already. This is out of hand.
Time to put an end to this.*

After each encounter he would check his clothing for
long hair strands, his hands for female odors. He'd dig
into his pants pockets, checking to see that he had his car
keys. He often found loose change, sometimes a useful
mint. Once in a while, a rationalization.

Those Kendrick Girls

(Wai'anae, Pearlridge—Spring through Fall 1993)

A phone call

"I tell you, she's the cutest, most adorable thing in the world. Men still come up to me . . . to look at her."

"Oh, that is great news."

"Yeah, I've adjusted. To being 'grandma.'"

"Oh Jesus, are we that old?"

"Just me. I bet you still look great. I've gained twenty pounds."

"Well, twenty pounds on you would just make you *more* voluptuous.

"That's what I keep telling Steve. . . . He gets a little nervous nowadays when I get on top of him. Thinks I'm gonna crush him."

"Beth, you're incorrigible."

"Thank you."

"You must be the naughtiest grandma on the face of this planet."

"I hope so. It would be so freaking dull otherwise. . . . You know, I've come to the realization that our grandparents were at least as naughty." She clicked her tongue. "Making babies while in their teens. Then, by the time we come along and get to know them, they have this sweet and innocent look. Give me a break."

"So who made you a grandparent? Or is that a dumb question?"

"Heather. She's really straightened out. She's a good mother, surprisingly."

"I'm so glad."

"Oh, me too." Beth went on for a while about little Meredith Malia, her three-month-old granddaughter. And Kanani told Beth about how she had joined a hula hālau on a lark and found it both fun and nurturing. Sometimes hālau members ventured into the hills to gather flowers, ti leaves, hāpu'u ferns.

"I'm so glad you called," Kanani said after they had talked for a while. "God, the way we get caught up in everyday—"

"I know what you mean." Beth then said, "Hmmm . . . " When she spoke again Kanani noted that her voice had shifted to gossip-mode: low, conspiratorial. "Look, there's something I gotta tell you. Remember my sister Helene? She used to come by—"

"Remember? How can I forget? That birthday party at your house? Her in that see-everything dress."

"Hey, I'm her sister; I've had to deal with that all my life. Well, not any more," she added in a teasing voice, "since she's outgained me in the weight department."

"No."

"Oh yeah, she's porked. Uh, anyway, she works at Ko Olina . . . "

Kanani faces her bathroom mirror. Wearing a bathrobe, her hair up, she looks weary, all cried out.

You could deny him sex.

Yeah, so he could go running to her for more.

You could fuck him like no man has ever been fucked. So he knows what he can lose.

I'd rather stab the fucker.

You could wait it out. You could confront him.

What good would confronting him do? Besides, I haven't exactly been up front about everything.

You could get even. Fool around, too.

Yeah, that would do it. I should walk naked on the beach. Better yet, down the street, saying Any takers?

What to do?

□ □ □

Kanani

All I knew about the woman was that she was Asian. Probably Japanese or Chinese. Late twenties, maybe early thirties. Not short by local standards. Maybe 5' 4"—

—According to Beth's sister, the spy.

Well, that narrows it down to a hundred thousand.

One afternoon I was shopping at Pearlridge. When I entered the Honolulu Book Shop, I saw a woman who looked like 'Analu's third-grade teacher. I wasn't sure from her profile, so I went to the other side of where she stood, looking at the display. When I was sure it was her, I tapped her shoulder to say hi. She went pale. Then she smiled, the color slowly returning to her face, though she had this funny look at times, like she was being a little too earnest. We talked about 'Analu for a few minutes. He was doing better in school, and I thanked her for the job she was doing.

As I got in the car, I remembered that Henry had not mentioned Miss Imura lately, though he did say something— when was it, back around March?—about seeing her to discuss the kid's grades. I remember hoping he wouldn't go ballistic on another teacher. And I was glad when he told me it went all right.

While I was driving away from the shopping mall, it occurred to me that she fit Helene's description of the woman she saw with someone who looked like Henry at Ko Olina. Then I thought about how 'Analu's teacher had turned sheet-white.

I sped home. Picture, I was thinking. I need a picture. 'Analu was out playing. Mākena was probably out surfing. Henry wasn't home. Good, 'cause I would have punched his face. I dug up last year's yearbook.

I frantically turned the pages, looking for the faculty photos.

There she was. *Is this the type Henry goes for? Oh, stop it, Kanani.*

I called Ko Olina and found out that Helene was coming on duty soon. I sped there—with the yearbook.

I waited near the front desk until she arrived. I wasn't even sure how I felt about her. Sometimes you do want to kill the messenger. Part of me wanted Helene to say it wasn't Miss Lily Imura. Part of me wanted her to say it was.

So I'd know.

I looked around the lobby, trying to get a good look at every male and female. I was wishing I'd see a Henry lookalike, so I could convince myself it wasn't him that Helene had seen. How many times had she seen Henry anyway, two or three?

Helene saw me and walked up, briskly. She *had* gained weight. Oh, those voluptuous Kendrick girls. There's four of them in all. Korean mother, haole father. All beautiful and bounteous.

She sat down and put her arm around me. I didn't say anything. I just opened the yearbook to the page. Mug photos of teachers.

"That's her," she said, pointing to Lily Imura and nodding. "That's the one. Positive. I have a great memory for faces." She looked at me, saw something in my face, and suddenly she wasn't so pleased with herself. "Sorry." She took my hand. But I didn't need sympathy. I was pissed. I was angry at the whole world.

I thanked her and went home.

"Nalu's teacher called."

"Hmm?" Henry said. Good acting. "What's up? Da kid screwing around?"

No, shithead. You are. "No. She called to remind us to send his—" He looked worried. "'Analu needs to bring in his excursion slip."

"Excursion slip . . ." What a guilty look. "She called about *that*?"

"I guess she wants to be on top of everything." *Ouch.* I had to walk away. I couldn't play this game. I left him to dwell upon it.

He will call her. She will say she hadn't called. Then what'll he do?

□ □ □

Days passed and he never mentioned anything about it. So I don't know if he did call. Maybe it's over. I hope it is.

I got enough on my mind, with my hula, with my two boys and their sports. 'Analu has his Mustang baseball games. Mākena's got his surfing. We all go to the baseball games. It's one nice thing around here. I'm finally getting to know a lot of families from around the area. Some of the kids are future students of mine. It's starting to feel like a community for us.

Not that there isn't a downside, of course. Some parents get a little too excited about the games, grumbling about the umpiring, yelling things that are downright offensive. At least Henry doesn't go that far. He gets upset—that old competitive drive from his football days—but he keeps it to himself. He doesn't yell at the kids, the way the coaches do. He always says, *They gotta keep in mind, it's just a game. They just kids. Let 'em have fun.* Lately, though, he's spending more time helping out these same coaches. Swapping sports stories with them. Chugging down beers after the games and practices.

Of course, I'm also privy to all kinds of Wai'anae gossip. I know which former state legislator is sleeping around with the team mother. I know more than I want to know about certain Bishop Estate trustees. And then there's this couple. Both husband and wife are screwing around. They each know it. Everybody knows it. And I know who's got his eyes on who.

Shit, everybody's doing it. I guess something's wrong with me.

□ □ □

(Pearlridge, Wai'anae—Spring moving through Fall 1993)

Henry drove toward Pearlridge, reliving the disconcerting conversation he had had with his wife.

"Nalu's teacher called," she had said.

And he had said something like, "What's goin' on? Da kid screwing up?"

Then she said something about an excursion slip. *Shit, the boys always bringing home stuff to sign,* he remembered thinking but not saying out loud. *Since when did a teacher call about shit like that?* And after that Kanani said something that chilled his shit: "She wants to be on top of everything."

Henry was going to see Lily. They had already made plans to rendezvous. So he was playing it out, wondering himself where this would go.

As soon as he got to her apartment they made love. They were good at this by now. Knew each other's impulses, preferences. They had established a rhythm. They even shared simultaneous orgasms more than once. But on most occasions, when it was over, Henry wanted to bolt. A crime had been committed; the criminal was eyeing the door . . .

As he buttoned up his jeans Henry asked Lily about the phone call. Lily said "What call?" Henry swallowed spit, then said, "She must've meant Mākena. Must've been one of my other son's teachers." Then he looked at Lily, more at her neck than her eyes, and before he said anything else, she said, "Hey, we didn't expect this to happen."

"I'm sorry."

"Nothing to be sorry about. It's been . . . good for me."

"Hope it doesn't fuck things up with Jake."

She looked Henry in the eyes. "It's already fucked up with Jake. I just hope your wife—" She burst into tears. "I'm okay. It's not what you think." She reached for the Kleenex box.

"I—I love her, you know. I—"

"I just needed someone to talk to. Not one of my women friends—I just needed another perspective. I didn't expect this—"

"Hey, we're still friends, first and above everything else." He wiped her tears. But that gesture was too tender. Her immediate reaction was to kiss the fingers that glided along her cheek. And it made him want to kiss her face, bury himself in her. He pulled his hand away.

"I know," she said, still teary but managing a slight smile. "Us being around each other is . . . " She blew her nose. ". . . kinda dangerous."

"Well, maybe we have to do it by phone then. I mean talk." He looked at her softly beautiful face. Thought about the nicely rounded ass that he had just had his hands on minutes earlier. Sighed. "Right now I got a marriage to straighten out. I can't—"

She nodded. "You got a great kid. A great family. 'Analu needs both of you."

Henry could picture his younger son, and for one brief moment he imagined life without him. That thought, more than anything else, brought him a sense of shame. The conversation was over.

As he left the Pearlridge apartment for the last time and rode down the elevator for the last time, saying hi to the woman in the wheelchair one last time, Henry felt old. *Gonna be forty-one this year. Is it all downhill from now on?*

It hit him that he had been a failure in life. He had failed to finish school. Dismissed it as bullshit. Then he walked away from the causes he thought he believed in. Maybe it was just one person whom he believed in. In any case, he wasn't able to find his way back. He ran away from progressive politics purportedly to build a life. What kind of life has it been? His kids were doing all right, no thanks to him. 'Analu has his coaches, Mākena has that tattooed mentor. And both boys have a mom who's always there for them. *Where does that leave me?*

And of all careers to pick. Construction. Destruction is more like it. He had worked during the boom years. Now the industry was going downhill. Company heads were kissing up to politicians to get those sweet state projects. They were paving over the cane fields, covering the whole damn island with concrete, choking all the greenery. With such finite space, how long would that last? There would be more layoffs eventually.

But something deeper than politics and aesthetics was bothering him. He had betrayed the love of his life. He wanted to own up, confess, suffer in some kind of way. This was no young-man frolic on the beach during spring break. There had been substance to his marriage. Though it had been built on a slightly shaky foundation—he did rush his proposal after learning she was pregnant—they had built something solid.

Solid enough to withstand his indiscretions?

Early that summer Henry signed up for night classes at the University of Hawai'i. He took "History of Philosophy" and "Poetry Workshop." He enjoyed the stimulation.

By fall he was studying music. He picked up and polished his old Martin guitar. Changed the deadened strings and worked the new ones till he had to change those too. He worked on various picking styles—folk, flamenco, bossa nova—and practiced scales, scales, scales. He then took private classical guitar lessons.

He had never cared much for poetry, those squiggly lines on the page, but his creative writing class got him writing, and what he wrote he set to music. He even completed the lyrics to the song that had haunted him for over a decade. Its first phrases had fallen from the sky, for all he knew, while he swam the great ocean. Now, set on the page, it resonated as a reminder of the person he wanted to be:

No more FOO-lin around, no more WAN-d'ring astray
No more FOO-lin' around, baby, WHY don't you stay
  with me tonight . . .

During his "Lily period" he often thought about taking up running. He seemed to be adding an inch to his waistline each year, and he felt more and more self-conscious about it. But he never took to the track, worrying that if Kanani saw him paying more attention than usual to his physical appearance she might get suspicious. But by fall he was huffing it up and down the coast. Sometimes he took a non-coastal route, running the roads that led toward the mountains, seeing a side of Waiʻanae he had never seen before. He passed the Mākaha Resort, those cabanas where the elite took their breaks. Sometimes he heard what he was sure was gunfire. And he frequently ran into signs saying *Warning, Keep out, Military zone, High explosive area, Do not enter . . .*

He did converse with Lily on the phone from time to time, but calls between them became less frequent as his other activities took more and more of his day. The last time they talked—around late September—she told him she was marrying some guy she had met at the church she was now attending.

At least she sounded good.

That same September Josh got caught screwing around with the supervisor's ex-wife. The supe said he didn't give a fuck. In fact, he told Josh he should marry her. Alleviate some of his financial burden. Then told Josh no, he shouldn't marry her. He wouldn't wish that on anyone.

Then, somehow, Esther found out and she left Josh. He's trying to patch things up with her—when he's not screwing the supe's wife or going clubbing.

Meanwhile, Kanani continued with hālau activities. When she wasn't hiking up the hills to gather ti leaves, or helping coordinate fund-raising activities, she danced.

And she went with Henry to the boys' football games. ʻAnalu played in a very tough Waiʻanae Pop Warner league and had made it as a starting right guard. He was stocky, heavy-boned, quite solid. Mākena, lean, tall, with wide surfer shoulders, easily made the Wai'anae High School team but saw little playing time. Henry often got frustrated watching the games, hated that his son rode the bench for most of the game, coming in only when the score was out of reach. But the team was winning, so who could argue? Besides, he knew that Mākena would get a better shot in his senior year.

Kanani's dancing brought out the curves in her lean figure. Henry found himself more attracted to her than he had been since their early days together. But she was always tired at night. She ached more than he did, and let him massage her sore feet and calves. She let him work his way up to her tight hips, her tender butt, her stiff lower back. He'd get aroused, but she rarely showed any interest in taking it further. It drove him crazy.

This is what I get, he thought. This is the price I pay.

A Museum Piece

(Wai'anae, Ala Moana—Late Winter 1994)

"Dad," Mākena shouts. "Phone."

"Who dat? Tell 'om I busy."

"Who dis?" Mākena asks the phone. Then he shouts: "He not saying."

"Shit. Gimme dat." Mākena hands his father the phone. "'Sup?"

After a few seconds he tells Mākena to turn to the news.

"But me an' 'Analu watching wrestling."

"Jes' do it. Channel six."

Mākena aims the remote and presses. The haole anchorman is saying,

> . . . *sennit baskets, known as kā'ai, containing what is believed to be the bones of the high chiefs Līloa, Umi, and Lonoikamakahiki, were stolen from the Bishop Museum over the weekend. The museum had been closed on Monday for fumigation, according to museum spokespersons, so the theft could have occurred anywhere between closing time Friday and early Tuesday morning. Museum officials called the theft of these sacred items "deplorable" and offered a reward for any information leading to their return.*

182

In other news—

"Gimme da remote." Mākena hands the remote to his father, who surfs the news channels. Henry catches the tail end of a related report. The Asian anchorwoman is saying,

> *... said she was appalled that people would do such a thing. She said that the kā'ai belonged to her family. "It shouldn't have been in the museum in the first place," she stated in a phone conversation with our news team reporter. "If retrieved," she said, "these sennit baskets need to be housed in the Royal Mausoleum."*

"Cool, man," Mākena says. "Dey stole da kā'ai."

"I know how fo' kiai," 'Analu states. He throws out a punch and kick.

"'KĀ-'ai,' stupid. Not 'KI-ai.'"

"Quiet, you guys. I tryna listen." Henry channel-surfs but finds that each station has moved on to other news.

Kanani comes from out of the bathroom toweling her hair and sits down. "What's with all the shouting?"

"The kā'ai got stolen," Henry says to her. "From the museum."

"Oh my—you mean the bones Keoni gave ho'okupu to?"

"What's 'ho'okupu'?" Mākena says.

"A tribute, an offering," Kanani mutters. Then she says, to no one in particular, "What is going on?"

Two months later

There's some people you don't see for years, decades even, if you're old enough, and you pick up right where you left off. The connection is still there. For Henry, Peter was one of those people.

Peter was the captain of the small fishing vessel that had rescued Henry eighteen years ago. He had come to see Henry in the hospital that same evening, when the doctors insisted Henry stay overnight for observation. He had even brought Henry a can of Coke.

Peter, a fair-skinned Irish-Hawaiian, lived on Maui, though he was originally from Keaukaha, on the Big Island. Through the years, because of the distance, he and Henry rarely saw each other. But when they did they behaved as if they had been best friends all their lives.

Peter was suffering from a bout of paranoia. He needed to talk to someone, someone he could trust. Some recent events, which for him eerily paralleled the days of illegal landings some eighteen years ago, made him want to turn to an old-days friend. That's how Henry Rivera got the call.

A note had been passed to Henry at a construction site: *Meet me at Ala Moana. Diamond Head side breakwater. Tomorrow. 4 p.m. Board optional. Might wanna bring sunscreen. P.*

Sunscreen? It sounded pretty serious. The clandestine manner in which the message arrived gave Henry chills.

Henry swam the short distance out to the breakwater. The tide was low. This used to be Henry's favorite place to swim, and he often met Peter there when Peter was in town. This is a good place to talk, Henry thought, especially if you're concerned about security. No phone taps, bugs, or hidden cameras.

Two guys were out there, Henry noticed. Peter and . . . who? He swam a few more even strokes till he saw the sand bottom, lifted his goggles, climbed up, and joined the two men. They had a small red cooler with them, filled with canned drinks. Peter offered Henry a Pepsi, then said, "Oh, yeah. I forgot." He put it back in the cooler and brought out a Coke, saying, "On the rocks." Henry grinned and took hold of the ice-cold aluminum can.

"Henry, this is Frankie." They shook hands. It wasn't the grab-each-other's-thumbs-and-hug kind of greeting that he and Peter had exchanged; it was just a handshake. Frankie seemed distrustful, grim. Henry was familiar with this look; it was a look employed by ambitious young men, men trying to find their place in the world, men who saw all strangers as potential rivals. But this guy wasn't very young; he was probably in his mid-thirties. It bothered Henry that the man seemed so familiar yet he couldn't quite place him. One thing he knew for sure, both instinctively and by the way Peter had said it: Frankie wasn't the guy's name.

"So, you've probably heard about what went down regarding the kā'ai."

Holy shit, Henry thought. Is this what this is about? Henry showed a calm face. "I read about it. Sounded cool to me. Was Waipi'o, huh, where they took it, to repatriate—" I better shut up, Henry thought. Let them do the talking.

"Puh," Frankie said, like he was spitting. "Waipi'o." He pulled a zip-lock bag out of his shorts. It contained a pack of Kools. He pulled out a cigarette and offered it to Peter, who declined, and then Henry, who declined also. Frankie then pulled a matchbook from the same bag and lit up.

"That's what I thought," Peter began. "That's what Frankie thought. Thing is, we don't know where it is. There's choke rumors goin' around now." Peter sipped from a can of Budweiser, then continued. "I heard the same stuff you heard. Read the same shit too. So I thought the same. . . . I mean, what the fuck? What the damn thing doing in one drawer in one fricken museum anyway? When I heard that this guy in Kona was having dreams about it—and apparently he either organized the taking of the stuff, or got other people thinking about it until somebody decided to act—I thought, man, imagine the mana those bones still carry . . . to reach out to someone on the Kona side of Moku o Keawe. I mean, we supposed to take care of the bones of our ali'i. So, right on."

Peter finished the beer and crushed the can, placing it back in the cooler. Frankie, ashing his cigarette into the water, stared at the shore.

"So . . . is there a problem?" Henry asked, thinking, we wouldn't be out here if there was no problem. He burped Coca-Cola.

"The problem is I dunno what the problem is, 'cause I dunno what the situation is. Fuck. It just . . . doesn't *feel* right."

"What part doesn't feel right?"

"Imagine this. All goes according to plan. Team One checks out the site, learns exactly where the stuff is kept."

"I heard about that."

"Inside job all the way," Peter said. "Easy to prey on the guilt of Hawaiians who work at the museum."

"And wannabe Hawaiians," Frankie muttered.

"Then," Peter continued, "Team Two goes there one night during the long weekend. And so on and so on. The stuff ends up at the airport—that's what everybody thinks. Goes to either Hilo or Kona. By then that's Team Three or Four."

"Carry-on or luggage?" Henry asked.

"That always gets me. Traditional Hawaiians wouldn't want it x-rayed. On the other hand, sending it through luggage, man . . . "

Peter reached for another Budweiser and pulled the tab. It made a sucking sound and the froth spilled out. Henry felt the burn on this left shoulder and neck. He had forgotten to bring sunscreen. He shifted 180 degrees, trading the beach view for one of the horizon. The blue water looked inviting.

"Had to be carry-on," Frankie said. "Think who's involved. Easy to get the people at the security check to look the other way."

"Nah, the security check's too risky, brah," Peter said. "Cargo all the way. There's lotta Hawaiian baggage handlers . . ."

Who *was* involved? Henry wondered where this drama was headed.

"The short of it is," Peter began again, "artifacts are being sold all the time. Just check out those Internet sites. Recently, one Hawaiian spear went for twenty thousand on the market in England. And it was not a big-deal kind of spear. Was one *ihe laumeki,* a warrior spear, but not something you could connect to ali'i, not something with this kind of mana. . . . The point is—"

Frankie jumped in: "—the monetary value for what was taken from the museum is said to be in the millions."

"I figured that, but—" Henry was thinking no Hawaiian would risk the wrath of the gods—for any amount of money. But then he thought, why would I think that, having seen—. "You're saying that the whole thing might have been engineered to make a sale?"

"We hope not," Peter said. "But that's the latest rumor."

"Okay, let me sort this out. The kā'ai can be sold for a million plus—easy. Somebody, maybe even a Hawaiian, has made a killing on the sale. So, what are we doing here? Other than talking. I mean, I like talking story, but—"

Peter exhaled a long breath. "Well, your sister-in-law could help with some details."

"Details?"

"She has all these connections with museum employees. Plus, she's Hawaiian. Thing is, I don't know her that well, and she's tight with information. We could use some . . . verification."

"I can talk to her. No problem. But something tells me there's more to this. More than you telling me."

Peter sighed. Took a long look at Frankie, who was taking one last drag from his cigarette. Frankie then flicked the butt into the water.

"Eh, no pollute."

"I'm giving ho'okupu to Kanaloa."

"Bullshit." Peter shook his head, then turned to Henry. "If what we said is true, we think we know who engineered it all. Think. Who has the power to make the museum people look the other way?"

"Someone who has operatives working in the museum," Frankie answered. "And can make judges overturn cases."

Peter looked Henry in the eye. "Maybe even someone who could make Keoni disappear."

"Uncle Cappy?" Henry said, and as he said this he saw a moray eel slither past. He shivered in the heat.

"No. Not Uncle Cappy."

Henry was puzzled. Peter had always agreed with Henry that Cappy Chung was the chief suspect in Keoni's disappearance.

"Think. Who controls the funding?"

"I dunno. Who? Oh, you mean somebody in politics." Henry thought for a minute, then found an obvious answer. "Miyahira."

"Congratulations," Peter said. "You get the prize."

"Fucker is old, though," Henry said. "Shouldn't he be retired already?"

"Tell me," Peter said, "what's the average age of our U.S. senators?"

"I have no idea. What, eighty?"

"Seems like it, eh? That's one profession where people seem to have zero interest in retiring. My theory is they live long, defy death, 'cause they can't let go of the power they've accumulated. Look at that guy, Strom Thurmond, from South Carolina, or wherevers. What, he ninety-something years old, right? Fucker prob'ly gets up at five every morning, ready to go. An' he ain't getting up for no pussy."

"Money," Frankie muttered, "the ultimate aphrodisiac."

"Tell me about it."

"Tell him about the Princess," Peter said.

"You tell 'om."

"She called Uncle Cappy. Said she wanted her kā'ai back. Like it was hers in the first place. She was pissed off at the museum for being so careless. With Chung and Miyahira so tight, essentially she's asking the thief to help find the goods he stole. What a crock."

"If your theory is true."

"Yeah, if. . . . You see, that's what gets me, Henry. Years ago we swore that if we ever found proof that Uncle Cappy had Keoni killed, we would get him ourselves. Gut him like the fucking pig he is. But we never found real evidence. We let it slide, went back to our lives. And now look, he's still doing shit."

"Plus, he's grooming another generation," Frankie said.

Henry, facing the beach again, saw a school of baby akule in the water. "By the way, whose bones are in the kā'ai? Anybody know for sure?"

"Shit, it's most likely Līloa and 'Umi. But it could also be Hakāu, or Kauhola. And lotta people wanna believe that Lonoikamakahiki's there."

Lono, Henry thought. They were talking about chiefs who walked these shores over four hundred years ago. Chiefs brought to life in the mo'olelo of Samuel Kamakau . . .

"I'm pretty sure that Lono's bones are there too," Frankie said.

"That's the chief that Keoni folks made hoʻokupu to," Henry muttered, remembering his wife's words.

"Maybe even Keaou's bones are in it," Frankie continued. "The point is, whether it's his bones or Lono's or whoever, those caskets hold the bones of Big Island aliʻi . . . and no way Oʻahu gon' control that. Why is it that the most urbanized, colonized bunch has such a stranglehold on our heritage?"

Then he added, "There's lots of unresolved issues between islands. Sovereignty is a way for each island to establish autonomy. And be like the old days, before those damned Kamehamehas empowered the haole."

The venom in his words stiffened Henry. "So the Kamehamehas are the bad guys."

"Where I come from," Frankie said.

"And where is that?" Henry was more and more curious about this Frankie.

"A very Hawaiian place."

Later, when Frankie had swum back, muttering something about being late for a meeting, Henry, who was about to leave also, said to Peter, "What's his beef?"

"Eh, he's all right. His family is involved in a fight for some other museum artifacts. The ones taken from Forbes Cave. Ever heard of NAGPRA?"

"Oh yeah, stands for Native—"

"The Native American Graves Protection and Repatriation Act."

"Yeah, I've heard Leimomi talk about that."

"Well, Frankie's family is claiming lineal descent. They have a valid claim. And the reason he's so pissed all the time is his family lost a huge chunk of land—you know, one of those adverse possession situations—and he's trying to find legal help to get the land back. That's what I respect about him. He wants the land. He ain't interested in money. Except that unless he finds legal help he's gonna need some huge bucks, just to fight the case."

"Oh, that sucks, man."

"Yeah, truly. Funny part is, you'd think he could do it himself. Fucker spent two years in law school, before dropping out.

"Really?"

"Yep."

Now Henry was pretty sure he knew who "Frankie" was.

Look Out Old
Macky's Back

(Wai'anae—Late Spring 1994)

Mākena

I hadn't seen Manny since last summer, since the day he insisted that the board he'd been letting me use was mine to keep, and then told me, *Time to get your license, kid, so you can drive to the North Shore.* He must have gone out of state. Maybe out of the country.

He had missed the whole football season, and for a while I used to imagine telling him what was up. In my mind I would be sitting in his big Impala telling him about the catch I made in a key game. Or about the time our quarterback got picked off, and I nailed that safety and he fumbled the ball. Actually, those were the only two memorable plays I made all season. Mostly I sat on the bench, trying to keep the game in focus and not drift off. Coach said I was a talented wide receiver, but Randy, the guy ahead of me, was a second-year All-State player. My Wai'anae team came in first in the OIA, then made it all the way to the state championship against St. Louis. Of course, they wen' cream our asses.

Coach tells me that with Randy graduating, next year's my year. He has me on a weight-training program, tells me it'll pay off big. Of course, he wants me to quit surfing.

Doesn't want me cracking my head or something. But the buggah no understand: surfing is life.

One afternoon, I was on foot, turning down my street from Farrington Highway and one car wen' pull alongside. I figured could be my mom or dad, so I dropped the cigarette and stepped on the lit part. Now I ain't hooked, but it's good to have a toke once in a while. I save the really good stuff for weekends. Maui Wowee. Ganja.

It was Manny, driving his old Impala. I ducked to peer into the passenger window.

"Been looking for you," he said. "Get in."

"Whe' we going?"

"To the next level. If you ready for it."

I didn't know what he meant, but I nodded. I got in the car. I had forgotten how roomy it was.

"Where's your schoolbooks?"

"No mo'."

"What about homework?"

"No mo'. Only had math. I did 'om in school."

"Fucking D.O.E." Manny shook his head. "How's the surfing? You been getting out there, I hope."

"'Tsall right. Mostly I been going to Mākaha. Sometimes Yokohama. Not like da Nort' Shore, but at leas' I can bike to dose places.

"Still no mo' license."

"I got 'om, but no mo' car. My folks only let me use da car fo' pick up 'Analu from baseball practice. O' fo' go store when dey need somet'ing."

"Well, right now, I gotta take you to the mountain. Then we surf."

Next thing I knew we were at his place.

He did his usual routine with alarms and shit, and I followed him into the bus. The tattoo on his back—I never really looked at that one up close before—had uneven brown and black streaks kind of moving outward from the center. I had chicken skin from looking at it. I don't know why. Maybe I had seen it before. Or dreamed it before.

"Things are happening," Manny said as soon as he sat down. "Processes are in motion."

What was he talking about? "Whe' you been?"

"Around. Now I need to take you to the mountain," he said again. "You ready for that?"

"Shoots." Mostly, I was curious. I always imagined that he had this great stash up somewhere. Pakalōlō growing large like trees. Right in the military's backyard. But from the way he was speaking, it sounded like it was something else.

Manny handed me a canteen that was in a belt holder, and some trail mix. "Gonna need strength." I put the trail mix in my shorts pocket. "How's your shoes?" he said as we stepped out of the bus.

"Fine," I said. It was a weight-training day, so I was still wearing my Adidas cross-trainers instead of my usual slippers. I liked my shoes 'cause they were comfortable. Manny was barefoot, though he carried a pair of shoes, the laces tied together, around his neck.

We didn't go back into the car. Manny just started walking toward the mountain, which looked far away, and I followed. Early on, Manny broke off a kiawe branch and used it as kind of a walking stick. He would step on pieces of broken glass or walk through thorny bushes like it was nothing.

For a while it was just a dusty, dirty area. Very dry, and real hot. Then we came across a long fence topped by barbed wire. It blocked off a road, or that's what I thought at first. Manny went straight to a spot along the fence where we could easily crawl under. We crossed the road, then crawled under a similar spot on the other side. It was then I realized that we were on private property.

"Whose property is this?"

"Nobody owns the land. But the U.S. military claims it's theirs. As natives, you and I jes' claiming our access rights. Right?"

I nodded. *Fuck, I hope I no get into trouble.*

Then we came across these mounds. They turned out to be a weapons storage facility. *Oh, shit. Is this why we're here?* Manny walked right by them, heading more north than east now, not far off the road.

The mountain looked like it was covered only with dry, wild grass. But as we moved northeast it got more lush. 'Ōhi'a, eucalyptus and pine trees, and lots of cactus. Plus, it was rocky like hell. By now my canteen was empty and it seemed to be getting late. I was hoping I would get home before dark. I didn't want Mom and Dad wondering where the fuck their son was. But I had to trust Manny.

Suddenly we were going downhill, carefully, into a gulch filled with vines that had huge sucking leaves. There were also different kinds of ferns mixed with the cactus. Then we came to this place where a waterfall might have been—if it ever rained. The streambed was dry and pebbly.

"Not much rain here anymore," Manny said.

Tell me about it.

"Hundred of years ago, this place must have had lots of rain, lots of water. The names of places in this area reflect that. Of course, during the plantation era, those sons-of-missionaries used to siphon off the little that did come. And look now. Somebody must have pissed off the gods, eh?"

"Big time."

"So the gods took the water elsewhere." Manny hesitated, then said, "It's my dream to bring water back."

"How's that gonna happen?" I used to always hear Mom and Dad talking about water problems on the Windward side, where Grandma folks used to live. Plantation owners had created a ditch—Waiāhole Ditch—that brought water to the Leeward side. I guess this was for the sugar plantations, like Manny said, and the pineapple plantations down Kunia side. Nowadays, according to my dad, it's for golf courses and all the residential developments going up.

"Beats the shit out of me. It's a dream. I jes' do what I can do. Leave your stuff here and follow me." I put the empty canteen down, along with the snack pack.

It was almost vertical, the climb. I did what Manny did. I hung on tightly to rocks, hanging on to roots that stuck out like the roots of the orchid plants Grandma and Grandpa Wong used to grow. I would check first if they might be loose, all the time thinking *What the fuck am I doing? What the fuck am I doing here?*

After several minutes of scary climbing, I saw Manny standing on this ledge above me. He reached down and pulled me up like I weighed nothing. There was just enough room to sit, catch our breath. Manny then moved this boulder that appeared unmovable, unless you had a backhoe. Manny pushed it aside like it was papier-mâché. Turns out the boulder was hollowed out on one side, and not as heavy as it looked. But shit, it wasn't light either.

I was looking at a dark crevice, one that seemed to end right away. But that was part of the deception. I watched Manny as he moved another rock, revealing a low and very dark tunnel.

For the next few minutes we crawled. Ate dirt, I tell you. Wasn't scary, what I saw, was more of a revelation. I guess I shouldn't say more. There's been enough of this stuff on the news. And I tell you, man, by the time we crawled out, put the hollowed-out boulder back, and climbed our way down, when I looked up at the cliff and saw the precarious rock formation, I knew the earth was telling me something. And I knew I had to start paying attention.

We sat down on some boulders and drank water from a container that Manny had stashed up there. Then Manny started talking like he had never talked before.

"When I was a kid," he began, "I lived in Wai'anae for a while. Like you, I was into the ocean, I had no idea that all this stuff existed. And I don't jes' mean the caves and shit, but all the military facilities. Then my family moved to Wahiawā. Schofield Barracks, even though it was a few blocks away, it didn't exist for me. I was too preoccupied with getting out to Hale'iwa every day, hitchhiking with my board. Jes' had to get to where the surf was breaking.

"Then I got this job. I was in high school then, needed pocket cash 'cause my folks weren't giving it to me. The only jobs available were, da kine, busboy, dishwasher, or groundskeeper. Minimum-wage jobs. I figured if I'm gonna work for shit, it may as well be outdoors, so I applied for and got this groundskeeping job. It was at Schofield Barracks. So I became part of the grounds crew there. I used to mow the officers' lawns, water the endless trees. After a while I figured out that jes' about everybody in the crew had places where they could hide out and jes' cruise. I used to hang with this guy, Tommy LaBenz. He was a year younger than me. We used to hide out near the firing ranges. Nobody would ever think to look for us there. Sometimes we'd wander around. I liked the head of my crew, this guy Manuel Salcedo. Old Filipino man. Funny guy. He had a rascal smile, and always wore an L.A. Dodgers cap. He'd always make sure we did some work at least. But after a while he would go to *his* hideout and leave us to our wits.

"Sad thing is, two weeks before he was gonna retire and start collecting that pension he had worked all his life for, he sat at a bus stop on California Avenue. It was his day off; he was catching the bus to town, as he always did. Then all of a sudden this car came flying down the avenue— the brakes had failed—and it jes' crashed into the bus stop. I heard Manuel died instantly.

"If that wasn't bad enough, a few months after that Tommy and some of his cousins were goofing around at Nuʻuanu Pali. They had found an abandoned grocery cart up there and were taking turns pushing each other around in it. I guess they lost control of it when it was Tommy's turn to ride, 'cause over he went. Over the fucking Pali. Shit. One more warrior gone.

"This was hard to take, I tell you. I was sixteen, going on seventeen—about the same age as you. I remember being bummed for the longest time, wondering what it all meant. Wondering if there was any justice in the world. I was still working at Schofield. I started going off-road, after doing my usual two-three hours of work, traveling among the trees. All that time I didn't even know that the main road in Schofield, Trimble Road, became Kolekole Road as it went through the Waiʻanae Range, then became Lualualei Naval Road, which took you all the way to Farrington Highway, Nānākuli side. That blew me away. Made me start readjusting the maps in my head. The lay of the land was so intriguing I began to wander all over the damn place. Got to know the area like nobody else. Found so many hiding places. Knew where I could pick fruit, berries, if I got hungry." Manny looked around. "Learned how to survive out here."

"Thass how you found this cave?"

"Well, not exactly. I would say the cave found me. One day I saw this old man. Another old man. And funny, he had the same kinda walk as Manuel, a slow, easy-going lope. I was curious, wondering what he could be doing on military land that was so out of the way. So I followed him. At first I was real careful. I watched him struggle to climb the same cliff we just climbed. One time he slipped, almost fell down. I thought, shit, what if he fall? He gon' die out here, all alone.

"So I walked to the bottom of the cliff and said, 'Papa, you need help?'

"He wen' look down, saw me, and said, 'It's about time.'

"It's about time," Manny repeated. "So he showed me the place I jes' showed you. And that was that. After that, I would always look for him, especially around the area of the cave, but—" Manny shrugged, holding his palms out. "So I jes' figured I would never see him again. I tell you, I wasn't about to enter that cave alone.

"Then one day, when I was near this very spot, I heard a scream. A woman's scream. I ran toward the road and saw this girl being pulled out of this car, being attacked by three guys. Crew-topped grunts. Without thinking I just charged. I was seventeen. I thought I could kick ass. Especially haole ass. I hit this one guy so hard he fell back into the bush. Then I charged this other guy, to tackle him, and we both went down. That was my mistake. While I was down wrestling him the third guy stabbed me on the side. I rolled over in pain. I was on my back when he came toward me. I kicked him in the nuts as hard as I could and he dropped the knife. I reached for the knife but the shithead I had knocked into the bushes stepped on my arm and *he* grabbed the knife. He went nuts, man. He started swinging the knife real wild, cutting my arms, my legs, my chest. . . . The girl—the third guy was holding her—she was screaming the whole time. Then the guy with the knife stabbed my arm and hit an artery. Shit, my blood started shooting up, like a fricken geyser. Then he kicked me in the throat and I started choking, gasping for air. At that point they panicked. They grabbed the girl—her clothes were all torn up—dragged her in the car and took off."

Holy fucking shit.

"I was losing blood fast. I tore off my t-shirt and tied my upper arm. I figured that was my only hope. At first it didn't seem to work. Blood kept shooting out, in spurts. So I made the tourniquet tighter. I was dizzy already. And then finally the blood stopped. Then I felt the agony of the other stab wound, the big slice along my hip."

"So it wasn't a shark," I said.

Manny looked me in the eye. "I showed you my shark wound. Now I'm telling you how I got the rest." He took a deep breath.

"Then I lost consciousness. Next thing I knew, the old man, that same old man, was treating my wounds. He was using what I thought was juice from the cactus, but was probably aloe. He nursed me, stayed with me for two days in the hills, using his shirt to keep me warm at night. The nights were fucking *cold*, I tell you. He gave me some stuff to drink. Some kind of tea he made. I tell you, it knocked me out. Then—I guess this was the third day—I woke up and he was gone. I thought he had left me there and thought I would never see him again. Thought I would die and join Manuel and Tommy. I was already thinking, gee, that wouldn't be too bad."

Manny cleared his throat, then drank some water. "Turns out he had gone back to wherever he lived and put some wheels on this paddleboard that he dragged all the way up here. It took a lot out of him. I mean, we're talking about a guy who's at least eighty years old. Man, he looked so wiped out.

"He lifted me up, asked me if I could walk. Every step was pain, but we got to the road. I almost shit when I saw the road again, thinking what if those guys came back, checking to make sure I was dead? Anyway, he strapped me to this paddleboard on wheels, tied himself to the board, and used his own body for drag. Imagine that, this old guy pulling against the downhill grade, easing me down the hill. For over four miles."

Manny stopped. Closed his eyes, pinching the bridge of his nose with his thumb and index finger.

"By the time we got to the bottom he was in worse shape then I was, and we still had a ways to go. We crashed for the night in the bushes. The next morning, we hiked the rest of the way, me limping, him dragging his legs. Finally we got to his house. It's that dilapidated shack near my bus. Thass where I recuperated.

"His house. Now that was something. Could tell right away he was a fisherman. He had throw nets all over the place. He told me that he had lived in that same spot for about thirty years, which was when the U.S. Army chased his family out of Mākua. You know, so they could practice their bombing. I tell you, this guy had ancestral ties to the whole Wai'anae Coast. I learned later that after his wife died, his children all split. They all went to live in Honolulu, or to one of the other islands. One of them moved to Vegas. None of them wanted to live the life of a fisherman-farmer.

"He kept giving me this tea he made, from I don't know what. He was an herb gatherer too, the way I figure. Anyway, whatever it was he was giving me knocked me out. Seems I slept for days. An' from time to time I would wake up—I couldn't shake off the drowsiness—an' I would hear this humming sound. Really weird. I would feel this tingly feeling on my skin. The lightest breeze would sting. Of course, it turns out he had been tattooing me. He was using India ink and this gun that was powered by a generator. Mind you, I learned later on that he was expert at carving designs into wood. Not bodies. I was his living, breathing guinea pig. When I recovered he told me that he wanted to create a network of tattoos to disguise my scars. He said I was too young to go around so disfigured. Now, of course, I'm a different kind of marked man.

"The old man also told me he wanted the tattoos to tell a story—one he wouldn't divulge, of course. He jes' said I'll figure it out in time. He said because of this scar—" Manny pointed to a diagonal scar on his chest opposite his heart—"he chose to invert and elongate the usual kōnane design that warriors wore on the left side of their chests. So instead of a checkerboard look it would be more diamond-shaped. The arm stuff is warrior bands, with a shark teeth motif. Supposed to protect me in the water." He smirked and snorted. "On my legs, birds in flight. Note there's one solo bird."

"What about the stuff on your back?" Those jagged lines, moving out from the center. They didn't seem to fit.

"What stuff?" Manny twisted his head, like he was trying to see what was on his back.

"You kidding me, right?"

He just stared at me for a moment. Then he had this look, like he was remembering something, speaking more softly. "While the old man did all this tattooing he got weaker and weaker, and funny, I was getting stronger and stronger. I began to wonder if this was his intention. And I wondered if he had willed himself to live only long enough to finish the task. But that kinda thinking, I don't know. Like I'm supposed to be special. I was a nobody.

"Anyway, by the time he was finished tattooing me he was too sick to eat. Then he started puking blood. He had an old car, a '59 Impala—yeah, the same one. I had the hardest time getting the engine to turn. When I finally got it going, I drove him to the hospital. The diagnosis was cancer. Terminal. The doctor said it had spread through his body."

Manny stood up. "Oh fuck, 'nuff a this shit."

I nodded. Manny offered me one more swallow from the plastic container. I drank. Then he drank.

We walked a bit and came to a road. It was bordered by the same kind of barbed-wire-topped, chain-link fences we had seen almost two hours earlier. I didn't make the connection at first, but slowly realized that this was the same road.

It was *the* road.

Manny slipped on his shoes. "We're gonna run this. You think you can handle? Four miles, downhill all the way." It sounded far, but I nodded. "I'll race you down," he said after he tied his laces, and took off.

Oh man, who woulda thought it would be so much fun. The road was so fucking steep. I couldn't stop my legs, man. Shit, we were flying. The wind blasted our faces. It wasn't even work. I bet we were doing four-minute miles, easy. Just flying downhill. We got to the bottom in no time. At that point Manny looked at me and cracked up. I must've had a shit-eating grin on my face.

Back in the bus, Manny pulled a 7-Up out of his icebox. Boy, after all that climbing and running and walking, it hit the spot. I finished the can so fast that Manny threw me another one.

Manny didn't seem tired at all, as he drank slowly from a bottle of Michelob.

"That's my training," he said, "the run back. My favorite run, though, is through Ka'ena Point."

"Man, that area's pretty treacherous. Not my idea of fun."

"You want fun? Try it with a flashlight at night. Plus, think of how much quicker you can get to the North Shore than if you drive around the Wai'anae Range."

"But that only takes you to Mokulēʻia. You still got a ways to go to get to Haleʻiwa, let alone ʻEhukai."

"It's still a lot quicker to run to Mokulēʻia than it is to drive around the whole damn mountain range."

"I guess."

"So the old man died?"

Manny closed his eyes and nodded.

"His bones up there, too?" I got chicken skin, thinking about what I had seen earlier.

Manny shook his head. He was pretty quiet now, but it wasn't weird. Then he said, "His family had him cremated. I was a stranger. I had no say in the matter. . . . You know, funny, I jes' remembered. He had all these phonograph albums—78 rpm. You know what I'm talking about?"

"Yeah, the speed. Our player only get 45 and 33."

"What, in the age of CDs you guys play albums?"

"My dad's stuff. He no like get rid of 'om."

"He had all these old records. Old Hawaiian stuff, jazz, blues. He used to play these tunes while working on me with his tattoo gun. The needle on his player used to skip a lot, it was so old."

"Maybe he used it as a tattoo needle."

"Yeah, right. You really one clown. . . . Anyway, later on, after he died, I tried to find a needle to replace it, but no electronics place carried something that ancient. Then, in the army, I learned how to make one myself."

I was stunned. "You were in the army?"

"Surprised?"

"Yeah."

"Well, when you're eighteen, and you got no future, and somebody's telling you to be all that you can be. . . . The real reason is, I wanted to get those guys."

"Who? Oh, you mean the guys who—"

Manny nodded. "Nothing like a stint in army intelligence to get the information you need."

"Holy shit. You was one soldier."

"That wasn't the initial plan. I was really fricken naïve in those days. After I recovered—thanks to the old man—I went to press charges. I talked to this lawyer, supposedly a family friend. All I learned was that I wasn't supposed to be on military property. *I* was the trespasser. So I got no help.

"But I remembered certain things about the car. I remembered the model, the California license plate. And, of course, I remembered the girl. . . . Through some family contacts with the police station, I learned that she had pressed charges. But what the military often does, I found out, is relocate soldiers who commit criminal acts on civilians. You fuck with your fellow soldiers, you're brought up for court-martial. You fuck with civilians, you get a vacation in some other part of the world. You fuck with dark-skinned civilians—" He paused. "I need more beer." He pulled another Michelob out of the icebox. It was his third bottle.

"So did you find them?"

Manny finished a long sip, then said, "Took me awhile, but I caught up with them, one by one. Second Lieutenant Nelson was the easiest to find. He was still on this island. Had married a local girl. He used to beat up on her. So she left him. I beat the shit out of him. Broke his jaw and a couple of his fingers. Fucking weak bastard when it comes to picking on someone his own size.

"Corporal Montero, same thing, though I had to go to fucking Oklahoma to track him down. I broke his fingers too . . .

"Now the guy I really wanted was Olvey. PFC Martin J. Olvey. The guy who cut me up. Fucking U.S. Army couldn't control that guy. They had kicked him out. Fuck, even those baby killers didn't wanna be associated with a scumbag like him.

"Him I woulda killed, I know I would've. You see, I had set out to kill all three, but found that I didn't have it in me—the killer instinct. But this guy Olvey, I could've. He had a record of felonies a page and a half long. Rapes, thefts, burglaries, assault and battery, you name it.

"Know where I found him?"

I shrugged.

Manny snickered. "In jail. Fucking guy was already in jail. Plus, he was in a fucking wheelchair. The story goes, he broke into the *wrong* house. The guy who lived in it was a card-carrying member of the NRA. He shot Olvey twice, once when he was turning to flee. Hit him right in the spine. Olvey's crippled for life. And serving life, for his catalogue of crimes.

"I went to see him, you know. Convinced the authorities that I was a relative passing through. I watched as they wheeled him in. He had no idea who I was. I told him I was the fucking ghost of Christmas past. I told him he was a lucky son-of-a-bitch. . . . And you know what he said?"

"What he said?"

"He said, 'I don't know who the fuck you are, but I wish you *would* do me in. Be a lot better than living like this in this shithole.'

"I opened my shirt, to show him the scars, but the fucker only paid attention to the tattoos. I told him, 'I hope you live a fucking *long* life, motherfucker,' and then I left."

"He didn't know who you was?"

"Fucker had no clue."

"Hard fo' imagine you being one soldier."

Manny was in his own world, staring ahead, muttering. "I was seventeen when it happened. The girl, I dunno, sixteen? You don't do shit like that to people and get away with it." Then he suddenly snapped out of it. "Hey, getting late, eh?"

I looked at my watch. "Holy shit! I gotta get home!"

Manny snickered. "Shit is right. Ay-ya, kid gon' be grounded again." He pulled out a cell phone from his backpack.

The Line Forms
on the Right

(Leeward Side—Late Spring 1994)

Henry

Shit, man, this sucks. After one bust-ass day in the ditch-digging universe—I swear I'm switching careers, man—the last fucking thing I need is a fucking traffic jam. *Shit!*

And Friday's always the worst. Way worse when it's fucking humid and the fucking air conditioner's gone kaput, and way way worse when it's the start of a fucking three-day weekend, and way way way worse when these motherfucking assholes don't know how to drive! Move it, shithead!

Talk about fucking snag, talk about deep shit, I am in it. Kanani looked so sweet in bed this morning. Before I headed out I kissed her and rubbed her butt, but instead of pulling away like she usually does, she pushed her ass hard against my hand and said, "Tonight."

And I can't get fucking home.

I turn on the radio, channel-surf for some good sounds since the cassette player's been eating tapes lately, and hear the traffic-watch guy saying it's backed up from the Keʻeaumoku Street overpass to Pearl City. Shit. Fricken H-1, I hate you, you fucking concrete beast.

208

I'm a fast-lane guy all the way. I don't need this shit. At least I know how to fucking drive. Not like these damn clowns I stay stuck with. Shit, why the hell people so damn slow to make their move? I tell you, like, what is the fucking problem? The guy in front of you wen' move, so you move! No fucking count to five first, dammit. Some people have no regard . . .

So I just gotta sit here in the damn heat and breathe these obnoxious fumes.

Fucking *days* go by on this suck-ass freeway. And me I'm just waiting to get off—in more ways than one, when I remember what's waiting for me back home. If I ever get home. Oh look now, this jackass in his all-terrain suburban terrorist vehicle, blocking everybody 'cause all of a sudden he remembers he's near his exit and in the left lane when he should have been ON THE RIGHT!

"DICKHEAD!"

Of course, he can't hear 'cause his windows rolled up, 'cause the fucker's got AIR CONDITIONING. Asshole.

I should sell cars. I got some sales experience. At least that way I can pounce on the first affordable air-con job that I see. "PLAN AHEAD, FUCKER, OR STAY HOME. WHAT DA FUCK YOU DOING ON DA ROAD ANY-WAY?" Fuck, I wish he could hear me.

Then worse, I see now that they've coned this whole damn stretch again. Why? Why on a Friday? Why at the start of a three-day weekend? Why, when it's humid as hell and the air conditioner's a piece of shit and there's no fucking song to soothe my sorry soul on any frickass station in town! Whywhywhywhywhy?

The only thing that's good about living in Wai'anae is once you get past that fricken Pearlridge to Waikele bottle-neck, the cars finally start getting scarce. All those fricken suburbanites are gone, back to their fricken homes in Mililani, Waipio Gentry. . . . Suddenly you're doing eighty and feelin' the wind.

But then sometimes when you get around Kahe Point, you gotta be careful 'cause all of a sudden you can find yourself coming to a full-on stop, a fucking foot-easy-on-the-brake-so-you-no-skid-but-still-abrupt-fucking *halt*. That's when you learn how easy it is to trap this whole coastal community, a community that's relegated to one fucking access route. And that's how it's gonna stay, unless the damn Army is gonna open up Kolekole Pass. Unless there's a fleet of fucking ferries to take you around the point. It's either that or swim.

And, fuck, I've done that already.

Bad traffic all along Farrington Highway. A hostage situation, and the hostage is me. Somebody tell me why.

Good. Starting to clear. Car's beginning to move. Looks like a three-car accident. Not much damage. They finally got the cars moved to the side. Poor fuckers. Insurance going skyrocket. Everybody's rubbernecking, including me. Well, at least nobody look hurt. Traffic still moving a bit slow, but hey, it's moving.

Shit, better stop for groceries. Get it over with. Getting dark already, and fuck me if I have to venture out again. Plus, an air-conditioning break would be nice.

I pull into Tamura's. I dunno if Kanani went shopping today, but I hate it when we run out of the basics: bread, milk, toilet paper, oranges, and shit. Maybe poi, if fresh. But never more than ten items. That's my policy. That way I don't need a cart; just a fricken basket.

I cannot fucking believe it. The damn express line not moving. Some idiot is probably asking for a price check.

Shit shit *shit*. There's always some fuckhead. Just pay the damn money. They rippin' you off already, fuck. Just cut your losses and dig out. But no, no. You gotta save that fucking dime or quarter.

Fuck me. *I* need a price check, 'cause the price that damn cashier rang up on the 12-roll pack of MD doesn't begin to match the price that made me grab that damn pack of toilet paper in the first place. Now everybody in line is pissed off with *me*.

I don't even wanna look at them. I hate that raising-the-eyebrow thing they do. Or the way they make like it's okay when I know they fucking pissed off. Shit, I would be.

Finally, finally, finally, I'm on that last stretch toward Mākaha. The sun is down; the sky lit up, orange sherbet on my left, above the long stretch of horizon, blueberry yogurt on my right, above the mountains. People already camping out on the beach for the weekend. For the rest of the year, in some cases. Or at least until the authorities come and do what they have always done: kick Hawaiians off of the land. These happy campers know what it's all about. They know that this fast-lane, rat-race life is bullshit.

Just before I can make that last turn into my street, I get stuck behind some shithead making a left turn. I bet the damn traffic department plans it that way. Fuck! They send guys out and tell them, *Eh, turn left so you can block the drivers behind you. This is one field test, brah, to track traffic patterns. Worst-case scenario and blah blah blah. Now back to my coffee break.*

Sometimes when I get home I'm wound so tight. I'm ready to snap. Snap. Snap. Yet I hate bringing all that shit

home. I hate it when Nani sees it in my face. Like, *Uh-oh,
hard day.*

Fuck, hard day. Hard life.

□ □ □

Henry pushes open the door with his ass. He kicks the
door shut behind him. Then he carries two packages of
groceries into the kitchen and plops them on the counter.
Pulls out the 12-roll pack of toilet paper, drop-kicks it
into the living room, picks it up, then goes to the bathroom to piss.

*Home and nobody to complain to. Fucking Friday traf-
fic. Too many idiots on the road. Fuck. Coning off lanes
on a Friday . . .*

Henry heads back to the kitchen and begins putting
away groceries. He leaves the Lion coffee and bread on the
counter. Puts the brown sugar and can of corned beef hash
on the pine shelves that he built when they had first
moved in. Little improvements. Then he puts the eggs and
milk in the fridge.

*Not just the air conditioning. Fucking left blinker no
work, oil leaking from the engine, cassette player all
hemajang. Mo' worse, the rust. . . . Time to dump this
piece of shit.*

He falls back into the sofa. Picks up the remote. Presses
the MUTE button, then, as the picture starts to come on,
walks toward the bedroom, comes out in boxer shorts,
and heads to the bathroom.

*Stuck in the express line. Now what's wrong with that
fucking picture?*

Henry jumps in the shower. Steams the dirt and stress
out. *Kanani should be done soon. She's picking up Nalu
from practice. Boy, I miss those days when we'd leave the*

boys with my folks for awhile. Waikīkī days. Shower sex, bedroom sex. Nowadays it's—

He lathers, basks in the heat, shampoos his hair. *Don't know why Mākena's not home. Or maybe he came home and went out again. Fuck, I just hope the kid ain't doing drugs. Hope he knows better. Fucking world's dangerous. Needles. HIV. Sure hope he ain't screwing around. Don't need some knocked-up girl knocking on our door. But shit, he's seventeen. What else he going be up to?. . .*

Hope our "date" is still on. Shit, I would jerk off right now—got so much saved up—but fuck if I'm gonna stroke my dick with these callused hands.

Henry comes out of the shower fresh, rejuvenated. *No work this weekend. Good. Really need the break.* He puts on his boxer shorts, wipes off the steamed mirror, reaches for the comb.

Henry walks into the living room. *Home alone. I should bust out my guitar. Nah. Jes' ease up fo' couple a minutes. Relax.*

He notices that the answering machine light is blinking. He sighs, gets up, and goes over and presses the PLAY button.

3:54—Henry, I'm gonna be getting home late. If you get home early enough, you might want to check on Nalu at baseball practice. Okay? See you soon, I hope.

4:35—Henry, this is Mom. Call me when you get in. Bye.

4:55—Hi everybody. Alika here. It's been a while. I got some stuff I want to show you guys. Uh . . . uh, I'll call later. Or you can call me. . . . Well, actually I'm on the road. I'll call again later. See ya.

5:57—Me again. Traffic is horrors. Must be an accident. I'm really running late. Can you get Nalu? Did Alika

*call? I'm not sure, but I think he might be bringing some
documents over. I'll try his house. Bye.*

Henry remembers that he had turned on the TV earlier.
He picks up the remote, channel-surfs with the MUTE still
on as the phone messages continue.

Kanani is on the answering machine for the third time,
telling Henry that if he's tired and Mākena is home, have
him go pick up his brother. Then,

*6:43—Manny here. Got your son with me. He was
helping me with some things. Uh . . . sorry we took so
long. We're on our way.*

Right then two cars arrive in the garage.

One of them is Kanani's Honda Civic. The other car is
familiar too. In fact, everyone in Wai'anae recognizes
Manny's white '59 Impala.

Earlier, the setting sun had streamed the Wai'anae sky
with a light orange hue. Now it was blue and starless.

Kanani comes out of her car carrying two large bags of
groceries. Manny jumps out of his car. *No that's Mākena.
He was driving.* Manny's sitting in the passenger seat. He
makes no attempt to get out of the car until he sees Kanani
struggling with her packages. Then he jumps out and
takes one of the packages out of her hands. They exchange
smiles.

Henry notices for the first time how his son's shaped
like Manny. Well-muscled upper body. Lean waist. *Surfing's really beefing him up. Plus, he's been lifting at school
for football.*

"You're in your underwear," Kanani says as she kisses
her husband. Henry is leaning against the door, holding it
open. "Alika's coming."

"What?" *How did my house become Grand Central
Station?* "Tonight?" Henry whispers.

"He was planning to come here tomorrow night," she
says softly. "But then he called and asked if we could do it

tonight, 'cause of some concert or something. Said he has some stuff he wants to show us."

"I thought—you know."

Kanani looks sheepish. "Sorry. . . . Tomorrow?"

Disheartened, Henry nods.

Manny says, "Nice shorts" to Henry as carries the bag in. He follows Kanani to the kitchen. Mākena stands by himself outside, staring oceanward.

Henry goes to the kitchen.

"Can you stay for dinner?" Kanani is asking Manny.

"Uh, I can't. I have to—"

"Stay," she demands.

Then she looks at Henry and says, "Where's Nalu?" Henry can't think straight. He feels exhaustion setting in.

"Oh shit," Kanani says, closing her eyes.

"I'll get him," Henry mutters, thinking, when will this day end?

"Where is he?" Manny says.

"Wai'anae High School. The baseball field. Practice just ended."

"I tell you what. I'll go get him. You folks relax. Take your time. I'll take Mākena with me." Kanani and Henry look at him. "I'll be back," he says. Manny and Mākena leave.

Kanani and Henry look at each other. "He reminds me of somebody," Henry says. "I jes' can't figure out who."

Kanani nods. "I should get dinner started."

Kanani goes into the kitchen to start the rice, then joins Henry in the bedroom, where he's gone to change into a t-shirt and shorts. She slips off her work clothes. Henry, whose back is to her, sees his wife in the mirror. She is down to bra and panties, digging in her clothes drawer. He buttons his shorts, then walks up to her. From behind he unfastens her bra. She turns around, her ass closing the drawer. She watches as he slips off her panties. As she steps out of them he bends to kiss her pubic hair, parting it where the line forms, then rises to kiss each nipple. Then they are eye to eye.

"Sorry 'bout the change in plans."

"Can't help, I guess. When's Alika coming?"

"He said around seven."

"What time is it?"

"Seven." She leans back while he holds her. "You look tired. Hard day?"

"Extremely hard." Henry feels like he could melt into the floor, he's so relaxed and fatigued.

Kanani grabs his shorts. "It sure is. My goodness. . . . Hmm, you smell clean."

Henry kisses her lips, then, as she closes her eyes, each lid, each cheek. "Mmm . . . I not that tired." More kisses. "Alika's always late, right?"

Kanani leans back, sizes up her husband. "I know *that* look," she says. "Okay, five minutes. We've got five minutes. Lock the door."

Baseball Batman

(Wai'anae—Late Spring 1994)

'Analu

I like sitting in da dugout aftah one game, especially one game whe' we wen' smash da adda team. But today was only one scrimmage game. No count in da standings.

I guess dass why Mommy dem nevah come.

Shit, getting dahk a'ready. Coach Allen stay waiting wit' me. I wen' help him hose down da field and rake da dirt. Errebody else went home already.

Usually dey no fo'get me. Unless somet'ing weird happen. I no care so much. Dis jes' practice. But I hate when dey miss my games. Like last week, when I wen' hit one triple in da second inning and by da time Mommy and Daddy wen' come was already da fawt' inning. When dey foun' out dey wen' congrajulate me. But dass diff'rent from seeing da actual t'ing. I know my dad went aroun' asking if somebody wen' videotape 'om. But even if he get da tape, when he gon' get time fo' watch?

I guess I shouldn't complain. Some of my teammates, dey parents no even come. Not even once.

Da barrel of da bat feel good in my hands. I pound da handle paht on the ground.

Mākena, he hahdly come too. Dass 'cause he stay always surfing, o' goin' to da weight room. Hanging out wit' his school buddies.

Coach Allen said he like me staht pitching. I dunno. He said I get da strongest arm on da team. But, shit, what if I no mo' control? What if I walk o' bean ev'ry battah? How dat gon' help da team?

"I should call your folks," Coach says. "What yaw numbah?"

"695-2227."

"Thass easy to remembah." I watch him walk to da pay phone. He walk funny. Dad says he look like Booboo. Especially when he stay wit' Coach Dave, who's big and tall and has one big pon-pon. Dad say togeddah dey look like Yogi and Booboo.

Jes' when he entah da phone booth, I see Mākena running up. "Whe' Mommy dem?" I tell 'om.

"Dey stay home. C'mon, we catching one ride." He pick up my baseball bag.

"Gotta tell coach."

"I told 'om already."

I grab my bat. *BATMAN*, I sing to myself. *Dudu-ludu-dudu-ludu, dudu-ludu-dudu-ludu, BATMAN*. Den I remembah my jacket. I pull my jacket off da chain-link fence and tie da sleeves aroun' my neck. I chase aftah my braddah. I bet I can run as fass as him now. I wave bye to Coach Allen. Coach Booboo. "We gon' movie tonight?" I yell to Mākena. My jacket is flying like one cape. *Yeah yeah yeah*, I heah him saying. But I no see Mommy o' Daddy's car. I see—

"'Ass da Sh—"

Mākena, he stop right in his tracksan' I run right into him. "Come on." He push me forward. "Cut dat shit out. He's cool."

The Search for the Mole

(Wai'anae—Late Spring 1994)

"Sorry to ruin your Friday," Alika says to Henry as he arrives with cake box in hand. Henry is sitting at the front edge of the garage, firing up the hibachi. "I mentioned to Kanani I had scored these tickets to the Makaha Sons concert tomorrow night, so she insisted I come tonight. I could have—"

"It's cool, braddah. No problem. In fact, the kids going out."

"Yeah, that's what she told me."

Henry puts crumpled up pieces of newspaper on top of the coals. He pours some Quick-Lite fluid on the paper. "Nani'll be right out. She's taking a shower." Henry lights a match. Flames shoot up high. "Oh, and this guy, Manny. Nani invited him for dinner. He's the lifeguard that's supposedly turning Mākena into a world-class surfer. I think he's cool."

"And if we start talking about, you know, sensitive stuff?"

"We jes' gotta be discreet, I guess. I no think he'll stay long. Once he leaves we can really talk."

Henry looks at the tan cake box. "What dat, haupia?" Alika lifts his eyebrows twice, then smiles. "Better put 'om in da fridge, eh?" Alika nods.

The two men leave the dying flames and walk in the house and into the kitchen. They come out with chips, guacamole dip, beer, and sodas. They set up a folding table and some chairs. Henry adds more crumpled newspaper, then squirts more Quick-Lite on the coals. Instantly, flames shoot up again.

□ □ □

"Hey, looks good, the shrimp," Manny says when he arrives in his Civic with the two boys.

"This the only way to do it," Henry says.

Manny drops poké and beer on the table.

"Howzit Uncle Lika," 'Analu says. "Man, you should see his house. His house is one bus."

"Take off your shoes before you go in the house," Henry says to 'Analu. "You two clowns," he says to 'Analu and Mākena, "soon as yaw mom pau, hit the shower."

"I like go first!" 'Analu says. "He gon' use up all da hot watah."

"Go first, den," Mākena says.

While 'Analu removes his cleats and socks, and heads into the house, Henry removes the shrimp from the grill, placing them on a plate.

"Hey, you pretty filthy too," Henry says to Mākena, who's lingering in the garage, picking at the chips and dip. "Whe' you been?"

"Hiking." Mākena removes his shoes and socks. His socks are covered with brown dirt. He tiptoes into the house.

"Hiking? Sheesh. I thought you was a water man all the way." Henry turns to the men. "Alika, this is Manny. Manny, Alika." The two shake hands. Henry, using a pair of chopsticks, stokes the fire.

"Where's yaw Impala?" Henry asks.

"Takes up too much space. Sorry we took so long."

"Not a problem." Henry puts two steaks on the grill.

"Alika?" Manny says, as he turns to face him. "Hmmm. You part Hawaiian?"

"About as much as Keanu Reeves."

Manny smiles, then opens the packs of tako and ahi poké. He pulls two Buds from the plastic holder and offers them to Henry and Alika. Alika declines. Henry grabs a can. Manny pops open a can for himself.

"Keanu Reeves," Henry says. "Heard he started a rock band. Plays bass."

"Dogstar," Alika says.

"Mākena's friend Keith—he's a cousin or something."

"To Keanu?" Alika says.

"Yeah. But hardly knows him."

Manny snickers. The two men look at him. "What?" Henry says.

"Nothing."

"You got some cool tattoos," Alika says. He is looking at the triangle shapes and bird symbols on Manny's legs.

"Show 'om da rest," Henry says. Manny hesitates, then rolls up his sleeves and lifts up his t-shirt.

"Holy shit," Alika says. "Aw, man. That's—wow."

"Story of my life."

Alika looks bewildered. Manny continues: "When Kāpena Kuke, you know, Captain Cook, when he came he and his boys thought Hawaiians had no written language. That supposedly made us 'primitive.' Yet you look at the paintings of Hawaiians from that time. The elaborate stylings on their bodies. You look at other evidence . . . mummified remains. . . . We did write . . . on our bodies. And on pōhaku . . . "

"You watch, Manny," Henry says, "Alika gon' start taking notes."

"Not on his body, I hope."

'Analu comes running out of the bathroom, wearing only BVDs, a big blue towel on his shoulders. He runs back and forth between the kitchen and the bedroom, shout-singing, *BATMA-A-AN. Dudu-ludu-dudu-ludu, dudu-ludu-dudu-ludu BATMA-A-AN.* Mākena quietly enters the bathroom. The humming sound emanating from his parents' bedroom is Kanani's styling dryer.

'Analu runs out into the garage, extending his Batman routine. "Second base. Third base."

"Whoa whoa whoa. Ease up," Henry says as 'Analu runs into Manny.

"Home," Manny says.

'Analu turns toward the front door, says, "To da Batcave, Robin," and runs back in.

Everyone's out in the garage. Kanani is dressed casually, in t-shirt and shorts, but her hair is silky smooth, shiny. The boys are picking at the various pūpū.

"Why don't you kids just eat here?" Kanani says. "There's lots of food."

"Da movie gon' staht soon," Mākena says. "We can eat in da t'yetah."

Henry hands a twenty to Mākena, who leaves his hand out. Henry pulls a five out of his wallet and places it on top of the twenty. Mākena pockets the bills, muttering "thanks." Henry then holds up the keys to Kanani's Honda, but when Mākena reaches for them, he pulls them back. "So you can drive standard now?"

"Jes' little bit. He—" indicating Manny with a turn of his head—"was showing me."

"Yeah, I saw that. So you wanna take my car?"

"That piece of shit?"

Henry shakes his head as he hands the keys to his son. "Drive slow, eh? No reason to hurry. Any problems, call." Mākena nods. Then Henry says to Manny and Alika, "Spoiled, these kids."

Manny says, "Nothing like settling down and raising kids."

Kanani chokes on a taco chip. She coughs, then waves her hand like it's nothing. But then coughs again. And again. Her eyes tear up. Henry rubs and pats her back. Alika runs into the house and comes out with a cup of water for her.

□ □ □

They had been shooting the breeze for hours. They were stuffed from the poké, the chips, the guacamole dip, the carrot and celery sticks, the rice, the shrimp, the steak, and the beer. On top of all this they devoured the haupia cake that Alika had brought, and smoked some pakalōlō, which Manny had offered. Kanani passed on the latter, concerned as she was about setting an example for the kids, who would be home at any moment.

"I trust him," Kanani says to Alika as they carry the dishes in, leaving Henry and Manny in the garage. "I don't think we need to hide anything."

"Your call."

Out in the garage, Henry and Manny bask in the glow of the hibachi fire. Every minute or so, Henry, using wooden chopsticks, sloughs off ashes from the coals. Fatigue is hitting him hard. He feels a little drunk, a bit spacey, but mostly he feels content. "You still go Sparkey's house?" he says to Manny.

Manny is slow to react. After a good half-minute he says, "Not really. Not since it's become a hangout for thugs."

"Yeah. . . . I mean hah? What you mean?"

"All those syndicate guys. . . . You know."

Henry shakes off some stupor, leans forward. "No, I don't know. Fuck. Like who?"

"Oh, gosh. Sal 'Da Looza' Souza, Johnny Chinen, Jorge Kamana, Perry Smith."

"You mean all those yokozunas?"

"Well, they not all sumo-size. Look at Sparkey. Scrawny as shit."

"You not telling me Sparkey is syndicate."

Manny shakes his head. "Not really. He's more a wannabe. I think they just humor him 'cause he's useful at times."

"How you know all this?"

"You find out all kindsa things being a lifeguard. . . . I was also a fireman in my prior life. You think only detectives get good information, try hanging around a fire station. By the way, this guy Alika. What's his story?"

"Oh, he's a university guy. He's been working on a Ph.D. in history. I guess he's kind of a journalist too. He's published in *The Weekly,* that airline magazine *Hana Hou*—places like that."

"Yeah? What does he write about?"

"Oh, mostly cultural stuff. His dissertation is on Hawaiian activism in the late '70s. He's focusing on one of the guys who disappeared back then. Supposedly drowned off of Kaho'olawe."

Manny utters a name.

"Oh, so you heard about him."

Manny nods.

"Anyhow, thass how we got to know Alika. He's been interviewing us and other people for long time now."

Manny looks meditative. "No shit? Wow. . . . That's something. That's really something. . . . You trust this guy?"

"Alika? Sure. Why, is there a reason not to?"

"Oh, no, no. I jes'. . . . Ah, fuck, too much pakalōlō." Manny laughs. "Hard to be coherent. I jes' didn't know what your connection was. He seems cool."

Henry smiles when he thinks that all this questioning is coming from someone who keeps his cards so close, they've become the diamonds tattooed on his chest. "That's a

Hawaiian thing, eh, connectedness?" Henry says. "When a Hawaiian asks, 'Who you?' he's asking who, what are you related to, right?"

"It's a damn good way of relating to the universe, doncha think?"

"Couldn't agree more." Henry had a vision of an unconnected soul wandering through barren terrain. After a pause he says, "Who you connected to?"

"Oh, nobody. Everybody."

Kanani and Alika come back out. Alika heads toward his car, opens his trunk. Pulls out a briefcase.

"He not taping tonight, I hope," Henry says.

"Let's go inside," Kanani says.

Henry taps the charcoal with the chopsticks. "Aw. So nice out here." He takes a deep breath, then hops up and holds the door for the others.

Alika says to him. "I want you guys to hear some stuff."

"I guess I should head home," Manny says.

"No no no," Henry says. "Stay. I think you wanna hear this."

"Listen."

Henry, Kanani, and Manny all lean forward as Alika presses PLAY. He adjusts the VOLUME and BASS/TREBLE slides.

"You have her permission?" Kanani says.

"Oh, she wants people to hear it."

Alika presses PAUSE. "By the way, I don't play anybody's tapes without asking permission first. I wouldn't play your tapes—"

"We trust you, Lika," Henry says. "Get on with it." Alika nods and presses PLAY again.

"So I'd been working there for like three weeks, armed with his mementos . . . "

Alika presses PAUSE. "This is Pi'ilani. Keoni's girlfriend. She's talking about her search for some mysterious
woman that had been involved with Keoni. It's not
because she was jealous or anything like that. Pi'ilani
thought that this woman might have some valuable information about his disappearance. To give you an idea of
the lengths she went to, she applied for a job that she was
way overqualified for, just so she could get into that office
in the DLNR building. 'Cause that's where the woman
was supposed to be working."

"Did she find her?" Henry asks.

"You'll hear what happened on the tape."

"All this time," Kanani says, "all these years, I thought
she just wanted to forget about it. Forget about him."
Alika presses PLAY.

*"I knew he'd been getting the inside scoops from some-
body in this office. And I'm thinking, who can it be? It
wasn't a guy—the letters were obviously written in a
woman's voice—"*

PAUSE.

"Those are the letters Keoni's mom passed on to her."

PLAY.

"You could tell that?"

"That's your voice," Manny says. Alika nods.

*"Oh, it was obvious. The tone. So affectionate. I
mean—"*

The voice on the machine pauses.

*"—you oughta know. Men, they try to hide their feel-
ings, even when they're close. They always opt for humor,
like they need to set some kind of protective screen. I
guess a prophylactic over their vulnerability . . ."*

"Condom-nation," Henry mutters. The others groan.

*". . . Women, generally, don't do that. You give me
a book of essays—essays now, not poems—poetry is
different—then you white-out all the names, and I can*

*point out to you every one that was written by a female.
I guarantee it."*

"She's right," Kanani says.

*"I'd like to take you up on that, but . . . on with the
story?"*

"Yeah. I'm sorry."

"My fault. I shouldn't interrupt."

*"So, anyway, I eliminated all the men. Then, as the days
went by, I was able to eliminate most of the women. Most of
them had zero political consciousness. Mostly secretaries—
though I didn't just count them out because they were
secretaries."*

"Mm-hmm. Go on."

*"Anyway, then I eliminated a few because of their age. I
felt it had to be someone of his generation. The way things
were phrased . . . the attraction factor . . . and, of course,
it had to be someone who knew at least some Hawaiian. I
felt silly, goin' aroun' saying, Pehea 'oe, or talking about
the limu kohu like it was the most natural thing. Before
you know it I was down to three suspects."*

"She's good," Henry says, right over her next words.

"Sounds like a detective," Manny adds.

"Quiet, guys, we missing stuff," Kanani says.

"I'll play it back." Alika presses buttons.

"—s down to three." After the word "three," Alika
presses STOP. Then PLAY.

*"Melanie—even though she was a few years younger, I
think I kept her in 'cause she was a . . . a woman of considerable attributes."*

"Attributes?"

*"She was a 'babe,' as you men say . . . so it was down to
Melanie, Malia, and Sophie. Then it got hard. Malia was
not very friendly, so it was hard to get any bearings on her.
She always seemed bitter about something. Sophie was
warm. Like the letter writer. I guess I wanted it to be her."*

"So how'd you figure it out?"

"Well, I tried to get more intimate with them. I had lunch with Melanie. Oh, I tell you, she's funny. And a real hot-cha type. You know, the kind that throws out these pheromones. Men come on to her all the time. But I don't think she's promiscuous. Anyway, I never had lunch with Sophie, but I'd stop by Sophie's desk at least once a day. She was the office manager, so I often had to see her about other matters. Anyway, we'd get into these long conversations. You know how it is in state offices. Work one hour, talk story for two. Well, this office was like that, squared. Work for half an hour, talk for four. It was awful. Seems nobody worked, 'cept maybe Malia and a few others. My instincts told me it had to be either Sophie or Malia. And because Malia was hard to approach, I figured if I got to know Sophie well, I'd be able to verify that it was or wasn't her without having to deal with Malia. Keep in mind, Melanie was not really off my list of suspects yet.

"And then, one day as I was passing by Malia's desk when she was out to lunch or something, I noticed some doodlings, and it dawned on me—"

"The handwriting?"

"Yeah. See how bad a detective I am. I bet you would have figured it out the first day."

"Oh, I don't think so."

"It was obviously Malia. Same curlicue l's, the way she crossed her t's . . . and i's."

"Crossed her eyes?"

"Ouch."

"That's me. She just hit me," Alika whispers.

"We figured that out," Henry says.

"Dotted them. . . . Well, it was a very left-handed, you know, kinda backwards style—though she was right-handed—"

"So you went up to her."

"And I just said, 'so you're Keoni's friend.' She looked scared, so right away I added, 'I'm not jealous. I need your help.'"

"Did she warm up to you?"

"Oh, yeah, she was the real warm one, the genuine one. Sophie, it turns out, seemed nice, but she was a backstabber. No wonder Malia was unhappy there. You see, Malia had lived on the Big Island for a while. She and Keoni had become, as she put it, occasional lovers. He didn't come by that often, but when he did, they had their hideaway. More than anything for him it was a retreat, in the mountains, for when he needed to get his head straight. It sounded idyllic; I got jealous hearing it. She was renting this place in Hōlualoa, really out of the way. You know the road huh? Winding. Well, you couldn't drive up to her place. You had to park on the road, and hike the rest of the way.

"According to Malia, it was paradise. Avocado, papaya, mango, banana, you name it, growing in front and back of the house. Potted plants all over the veranda. She really hated having to move back to O'ahu, but the owner needed the place back. He had separated from his wife, I think.

"Then back in Honolulu, because of her archaeology background, she got hired at the museum, which she said was a great place at first, with Puku'i and Williamson and Emory all there, but then she lost her job—something about budget cuts. This was several years before the big housecleaning, when that new guy came in. Then, after being unemployed for a few months, she got hired at this fledgling Historical Sites Commission office. And its offices were in the same building, on the same floor, as the also newly established Governor's Commission on Crime."

"The GCC."

"Can you make it louder?" Manny says. Alika complies.

"*Yeah. So, to make it short, she got cozy with one of the commission's researchers, and before you know it she was passing Keoni whatever inside information she could get ahold of, which wasn't much—at least at first. . . . Things like how some developer got some sweetheart deal in some land swap. The commission was looking at campaign donation discrepancies too, but it was mostly land stuff.*"

"*Weren't most of these land deals legitimate? What I'm saying is, it's not considered a crime to buy a piece of property and then turn around and sell it for a profit.*"

"*True. In the private sector, it's not really a crime. Unethical, maybe, but not illegal. I guess it depends where you draw the line. But when you have political power, that's something else entirely. I'm talking about the power to alter land use designations, the power to broker deals that benefit select friends, that's abuse. And that* is *criminal.*"

"*Is this what the GCC was looking at?*"

"*You see, where they came from was another, um, another part of the equation. These commissioners, they grew up privileged. Most went to private schools. These were young, idealistic lawyers, and their notion of a criminal is, you know, some sleazy guy walking down Hotel Street with chains around his neck, wearing shades even at night, going to strip clubs. . . . But the more these commissioners investigated, the more they came to see the criminals were people who looked like them, people who dressed like them, people who worked in the same building as they did. In fact, in some cases they found themselves investigating the very people that brought them on board.*"

"*How did that happen? I mean, why would any powerful politician appoint people who would make him—or her—the subject of their investigation?*"

"*Hubris? I dunno. I think they really believed the investigation would stay at a low level.*"

"*And Malia was feeding all this to Keoni, right?*"

"*Yeah. You see, he was doing his own investigating. Going after the Navy with environmental protection laws is one thing. Going after state senators, judges, the leaders of both political parties, that gets pretty heavy. . . . You know, he disappeared just when he had gotten enough evidence of criminal activity together to go public with it.*"

"*Did anybody see this evidence?*"

"*I don't think so. If someone did, they're not talking now. We went through his files, looking at every piece of paper. You see, he kept extensive notes. That was his habit always. But there was nothing. We came to the conclusion that his files had been ransacked. While we were busy searching for Keoni, someone was going through his house, destroying or stealing all the evidence.*"

"*You have any idea who?*"

"*Coulda been anybody. There's a real, uh, what's the word . . . there's a 'small world' quality to all of this too.*"

"*You mean the way people are connected?*"

"*Yeah. Like when I found out that Malia is related to Senator Miyahira by marriage. I guess he's married to her auntie. Oh, don't worry. She can't stand him; she'd love to see him get his due. And Miyahira's daughter, Lori, you know she used to date Charlie Kuahine.*"

"That's one motherfucker I'd like to nail," Henry says.

Alika stops the tape. Henry and Kanani are looking at each other knowingly. Alika says to Manny, "Kuahine was one of the last guys to see Keoni alive." Then he says to the others, "I was gonna ask Pi'ilani more about him, and see if she knew anything about that third guy." Alika looks again at Manny. "There's one guy we've never been able to identify. He gave the people on the boat a false name. The thinking is, Kuahine brought him along, convinced Keoni that he'd be useful. . . . Anyway, I was about to bring this up and Pi'ilani's phone rang. I tell you, we jumped out of our chairs . . .

"The caller was her Mom. I waited while she talked to her, but you know how it is sometimes. . . . I was running late for another interview, so I had to leave. So that was it. That was the interview . . .

"But she did give me all this stuff." Alika pulls out a reddish-brown accordion-type folder from his backpack. As soon as he puts it on the coffee table, Manny gets up and walks out of the house.

"What jes' happened?" Henry says. "Did he leave?"

"That's weird," Kanani says. "It's not like him."

"Gee whiz," Alika adds. "You think it was 'cause of what we were talking about? What was I thinking? These islands are so small, he could be related to Charlie Kuahine. Or—"

Outside a door slams.

"He lives in a bus, you know," Henry says. "Fuck, I wonder if he drives it around."

"Those tattoos of his," Alika mutters. "I've never seen—"

The screen door pops open. Manny walks back in and drops a coffee-stained manila folder on the table. "Cross-reference," he says.

□ □ □

Kanani sits cross-legged on the floor, her back against the wall with the Maeva print. She is silent, reading from the reddish-brown folder Pi'ilani had given to Alika. The three men sit on the floor around the coffee table, talking. Papers from Manny's and Alika's files are scattered about.

"Note what happened at the college level," Alika is saying.

"Man," Henry says, "they're all here."

"Yeah," Alika says. "That's how it goes. The pattern. These guys knew each other from way back, small-kid time in some cases. One guy ends up being a state senator, the other a syndicate goon. With their common background it's easy to reestablish contact, help each other get farther along. It gets far more serious with the law school, though. Look at *this* graduating class. Our ex-governor's graduating class. Maybe no outright criminal types, but the way these guys have been taking care of each other has been devastating to the state."

As Henry looks through pictures of the graduating class, he is reminded of "Frankie," the guy Peter had brought with him. What law school class was he with? What connections did *he* have? Henry had never felt right about that encounter. *Fake name, what kind of shit is that?* His family was supposedly screwed on some land deal, but—the vibe. Because of this *vibe,* Henry never connected them up with his sister-in-law Leimomi, and he regretfully distanced himself from his buddy Peter.

Manny's coffee-stained wreck of a manila folder presents intimate details of coffee-shop meetings, dock-side encounters, and such. "Guys like Chung are always discreet," Manny explains to the other two. "But his boys, they're reckless. So if I want to learn something, I follow the underlings. I see who they're talking to, who they're meeting with."

"I can't decipher a lot of this," Henry says as he pores through Manny's notes.

"You try writing in the dark," Manny says while yawning. "Here, lemme connect the dots for you." None of the men notice that Kanani has retreated to the bedroom.

□ □ □

"You mean, this guy Evans has his own operation?" Henry tries to stifle a yawn. He's way beyond exhaustion, but feels a second wind coming.

"That angle is hard to piece together. He does seem to operate outside of the Chung/Miyahira sphere. But with their consent. Now why would the big guys allow this loose cannon to operate?"

"He must be doing something that serves their purposes," Alika says. He then adds, "To state the obvious."

"Yeah, but what?"

"I used to think it was his involvement with commercial fishing," Manny says.

"That could be a connection."

"Yeah, but then I learned that he was only interested 'cause a couple of his brothers are fishermen themselves. His family's huge. He's like the oldest of seven brothers."

"I heard that Miyahira is on record against the longliners," Alika says.

Manny smirks. "That's his M.O. He's the master at playing both sides."

"Motherfucker," Henry says. "Too bad Sparkey's in with those guys."

"Yeah," Manny says, "he's such a fuck-up."

'Analu and Mākena walk in.

"So how was the movie?" Henry says.

"Pretty good," 'Analu says. "*Mayjah League II* was sold out, so we went fo' see *Da Crow.*"

"Pearlridge was supah-crowded," Mākena adds. "Fricken long, da lines."

"Brandon Lee," Henry says. "Shit, they had to finish the movie without him."

"Suspicious accident, eh?" Alika says.

"Was the movie R-rated?" Henry asks.

"I dunno." 'Analu shrugs his shoulders.

"Must have been R-rated, then." Henry shakes his head. "You kids want haupia cake?"

"Shoots."

Henry and the boys head toward the kitchen. "Gee, where's Mom?" Henry says. He leaves the boys with the cake and goes into the bedroom. He finds Kanani sitting on the bed. "The boys are—hey, whass wrong?" Her eyes are puffy, her cheeks wet. The accordion folder is on the carpet at her feet, sheets of paper scattered all across the bed where they had made love just hours earlier.

"I'm all right," she says.

"You don't look all right."

Oh, Henry . . .

Kamehameha Day

(Honolulu—June 11, 1994)

Malia

There's a story I could tell, one of murder, betrayal, and intrigue, one of passion, madness, and delight, one that enraptures, challenges, involves . . . once you hear it, it becomes a part of you—you can't let it go. You can try to. You can hide behind your job, get busy, rationalize the hell out of your existence, but way down, deep, it's always there, nagging at you . . .

At lunch, talking about a lunch some 18 years previous

"Keoni and I had gone to a restaurant—more like a hole-in-the-wall place. It was the kind of place he liked. Removed, nothing fancy, like a jump back in time, perhaps to more innocent days—if there's such a thing. Amidst the pungent odors of watercress and onions and smoked fish, he started telling me why he invited me here. He said he had heard about a contract on his life. He said his brother had flown in from the Big Island to tell him word was out that the local syndicate was after him. That he'd soon be a grease spot on some sidewalk, like that senator who dared betray Chung a few years ago."

236

"Quit, then. It's not worth it. I mean, what are all these sacrifices for? Cadiz's a jerk. You can't fucking trust Kuahine. And Logan . . . I mean, like, what is he all about?"

"The thing is, it's not about them guys. I can't just quit."

The waitress, a fifty-ish woman wearing heavy blue eye shadow and long false eyelashes, took our order. Poi and corned beef and rice and chicken luʻau . . . haupia. "And water, please," I added before she left.

"You wanna get coffee too?" I asked him. "The coffee's shit here."

"I've been mainlining way too much caffeine." Keoni said, but his thoughts seemed elsewhere.

"Yeah, and you wanna be healthy when the hitmen come." I was immediately sorry. I reached for his hand. "I should just shut the fuck up. I'm sorry."

He held my hand and patted it with his other hand. "Hey, don't say sorry. I need you saying what you think. I need you to keep me straight."

"I thought it was the other way around."

"Then we just talked about other things. He said he wanted to spend time on the Big Island. Take a break, if that was possible. But, you know how these things go. Soon it was back to politics.

"He laid out this elaborate network, explaining how it operated, and to what ends. It sounded like the Watergate affair, actually I'm thinking of the movie *All the President's Men*, you know when Woodward and Bernstein are finding that the cover-up goes higher and higher. Same thing, Hawaiian style."

"I can't believe the governor's involved."

"Let's not be naive, Malia. You have too much faith in politicians. And when you say top, you gotta think, what

is the top? Is the governorship really a position of power?
Or is it the illusion of power? What you see is not what
you get. The governor does his bidding. As does our won-
derful U.S. senator, and a bunch of chickenshit legislators.
Now, mind you, there are other networks. And sometimes
these networks crisscross. The mayor's got quite a net-
work himself. But this guy's got it down. His network
reaches a lot farther."

"This is just way over my head, Keoni."

"Malia, I'm not asking you to believe—"

"It's not that I don't—"

"I'm just asking you to keep a copy of the file. And
when the time comes—"

"I don't like where this is going. You're not gonna die."

"Hey." He grabbed my hand. "This is just a precaution.
In fact, look at it this way. It might save me. . . . I mean, if
they know that several people have copies of this stuff,
they'd know that killing me won't stop the story, right?"

"Right. . . . What should I do with—"

"And right then, he walked in. Uncle Cappy. Like he
knew. This is too weird, I was thinking. What the fuck
is going on? I had chicken skin on my chicken skin.
The timing of it. I tell you, he has this Darth Vader
kind of presence—not that I thought so then. I don't
think *Star Wars* had even come out yet. . . . So he nods
at Keoni. And Keoni nods back. It's not like they
hadn't encountered one another before. Then Keoni
turned to me with this expression I'd never seen . . . a
combination of concern mixed with . . . "

Malia shook her head.

". . . fatalism? Anyway, Keoni closed his eyes, took a
deep breath, and in seconds he was calm. I mean really
really calm. And then he said, real soft, 'Fuck.' Then he
laughed. The laugh was real. He wasn't faking it.

"Then the food came, right on cue. I couldn't eat much, but Keoni scarfed his down like it was his last meal . . .

"It *was* his last meal."

Then Malia began crying, heavy heaving sobs. It was as if this was the first time she could grieve after all these years. She was choking on her sobs, only managing to sputter out. "And that fucking lowlife, fucking scum—there he was, sitting, with that smug fucking grin of his!"

"Are you all right? We could do this later."

Malia did not bother to look up. "What's the point? Here. Just—just take the damn stuff. Please. I don't want it anymore."

Malia handed Alika an old, edge-worn manila envelope. "Pi'ilani has the rest. Just take it."

Malia and Alika left the restaurant perhaps the same way Keoni and Malia had left their restaurant some eighteen years earlier. Alika was aware that death loomed over every step, yet in visualizing, tracing, the death walk, Keoni's inexorable, premature steps toward his ultimate destiny, he strangely found himself revitalized. There was energy in his step. He had been averaging five hours of sleep a night for nearly three years now. *That's supposed to ruin you.* Yet he felt strong; his thoughts were clear. He was privy to riveting information. People who were hesitant at first would start telling him things they didn't even tell their spouses. They trusted him, and he wasn't about to abuse that trust. For anything.

Some he considered to be dear friends: Eli, Melinda, the Rivera family and their tattooed friend . . . Pi'ilani . . .

Mostly, he felt close to a guy he had never met. He had been gathering information, hearing story after story of incident after incident; he had spent countless hours sorting these bits, resolving contradictions, piecing it all together. A picture was emerging, getting sharper each day. So much reason to burn the candle from both ends and sideways.

Keoni, long-distance, had touched him too.

□ □ □

A conversation, phone booth to phone booth

"Couple questions. In the mid-eighties, the Feds had busted all these syndicate guys, right? A whole bunch of them are in jail."

"Yeah, but they were expendable."

"Well, it's made things pretty quiet these last few years. You know, we don't read about people being shot on the street in Chinatown or wherever. Makes me wonder a few things. One, is power so consolidated that there is no threat, no underling trying to undermine his bosses?"

"That's an interesting observation. I never thought of that. What I do know is many of the battles are being played out on more legitimate fronts. You know, people think just because guys like Chung and Miyahira are old, that that's that. But look at the recent scandal involving Miyahira's daughter. Not Lori, uh . . . Louise. Her law firm had a non-bid contract with the state's retirement fund. And her husband had a company that administered the state's deferred-compensation plans."

"You know that Chung has shares in that?"

"Why am I not surprised? And then Louise gets nominated for a judgeship. Geez, why shake down merchants when you can raid the state's treasures legitimately?"

"Manny keeps saying, follow the money."

"Like in *All the President's Men*."

"I guess."

"Reminds me what Rich Cooper told me. You know, he's the former investigative reporter for the *Advertiser*.

His wife teaches at my school. It sounded weird, but he said to pay attention to the power struggle between our two big banks. He said watch how the politicians line up."

"That's where you have *lots* of money."

"Loads of money . . ."

"You know I heard an interesting thing about Kuahine. Something that may make Henry reconsider wanting to get his ass."

"What?"

"According to Pi'ilani, in the mid-eighties, when all the busts were going down, he walked into the local FBI office and told people there that he'd do anything to help them nail Chung. And if you remember, around that time Chung got real nervous. His lawyer called a press conference; they were expecting indictments. Of course, nothing came of that, I guess 'cause he's got judges, politicians, media people all in his back pocket. But it was interesting to learn that about Kuahine."

"I just don't know who to trust. You know? That's what's so scary. Like, for example, the idea of going to the FBI. I don't think I can trust the FBI in these circumstances. I know Henry doesn't. . . . I always remember, nobody trusted Puhi—all because of what Charlie Kuahine told *me* one day. Because of *me*, he was isolated. Of course, he had such an overbearing style, and he always carried his stash with him. But what do I find out? As time went on, his commitment got stronger. And undeniable. He made more sacrifices than anybody, excepting Keoni, of course. He really grew. Shit, aren't we allowed to grow? To change?"

"What's Puhi doing now? I'd really like to talk to him."

"Oh, you don't know? He died. Last year. Poor guy had a massive heart attack. . . . I tell you, he had a massive heart and we found out too late."

"Oh, boy. . . . Shit."

"Well, get cracking on that dissertation. Don't you have a deadline?"

"I can't worry about a deadline. The information Manny's given me is taking it in another direction."

"So it's worked out good. I'm glad you're connecting with him."

"Yeah. He's given me a better framework. Things are falling in place. Funny, you know, I talked to him a few times. I'd call him or he'd call me. It's always by phone. Then, I dunno, suddenly no calls. He never answers his cell phone."

"I've heard that he does that. Disappears for a while."

"He has this friend Sam. I've never met him, but Manny said he could fill me in on syndicate stuff."

"Hey, you better be careful."

"I'm always careful. By the way, did you read about President Chun?"

"You mean the trustees stripping him of his powers?"

"Yeah. It reminded me of something Henry said to me once."

"What did my husband tell you?"

"He said, 'You can spend seventeen thousand dollars on a Hawaiian kid every year and you still not going turn him into one haole.'"

"That's a great imitation. . . . The sad truth is we do turn haole. All of us, to some extent, and years later we wonder how it happened. At that point some of us start reexamining our lives. I've seen that time and time again these last twenty years. Time and time again."

So you're back. About time.

How's the surfing?

Every day. Waves or no waves.

Ready to take it to the next level?

Shit. How many levels get?

As many as it takes.

What is it this time?

I want you to enter the contest.

Contest? All dis time you been saying dat contests are bullshit. You always tell me "Surfing's about satisfying your soul. Not awards."

Look, I see the way you pay attention to contest results all the time, keeping track of who got the best waves that day. Which is all it is, right? Who caught the best waves on that day.

Nah. It's not my thing.

If it isn't, it isn't. But I think you wanna find out how you can do against some of the best. An' if you don't find out, I tell you it's gonna haunt you.

The young man shrugs and starts walking away.

Hey.

What?

It doesn't mean you're gonna lose your soul, you know, the tattooed man says. Jes' to find out.

The Runner-up

(Haleʻiwa—Late Fall 1994)

Mākena

I was at this party. Hoh, had lotta surfah dudes, surfah chicks, posers, and ragers. Was at this beach house in Haleʻiwa. The house was basic: natural wood exterior, drywall interior. Hurricane come, thass it. Was the perfect kine house fo' party, though. Big, with plenty rooms. No mo' furniture. Just cheap carpet all around, so not too bad if you puke or spill beer.

This was my senior year, and my life was cruisin' an' surfin' and babes. So when me and Keith arrived earlier, we were stunned by the starry-eyed babes wandering in and out of the house. Seems like we had stumbled upon a coven of bitchen witches, man. Surfer girls. Swimsuit model look-alikes. Rumor was that a couple of them had speaking roles on *The Byrds of Paradise* series. Keith started making his moves and I lost track of him right away. Me, I wanted things to settle down more. I was kinda like, scouting the scene—before I made my own moves.

Joints were being passed around—on one fucking tray, man! I made one stray comment to this dude about being busted, and he pointed to a guy who was toking and drinking and said he was one off-duty cop.

I never like people think I no do stuff, so I toked. I didn't inhale too much, though, and I didn't hold the smoke in too long. Still, I got pretty damned stony. And thirsty.

First I drank some Pepsi, but then I found myself drinking beer on tap. There were kegs and cases of beer, more than enough to go around. And with Jawaiian-reggae music thumping mega-loud through direct-reflecting speakers, the feeling was irie.

And then the band showed up. They did Jane's Addiction and Dance Hall Crashers type stuff. Mosh-pit music. Wasn't my thing. Was too fuckin' loud. Besides, it started getting crowded with drunk guys banging into each other, so I had to go outside. Some guys were ripped, man. I mean really, really ripped. I had slowed down on my beer intake, so I only qualified for one "really."

Outside was more mellow. I stood on the mix of Astroturf and grass and looked up. The night sky was awesome. Out here in this cool North Shore town, far away from the city, you can really see the stars. There weren't that many clouds, but enough to chase the moon into hiding.

There were platters loaded with food laid out on two long tables that were under this big sheet of blue tarp, which was tied by rope to some support beams on the house side, and onto some aluminum poles that had been spiked into the ground on the Astroturf side.

When I went to check out the food, all the 'ono grinds—chicken wings, poké, sushi, li hing mui pineapple chunks, and other shit—I found myself standing on another big sheet of blue tarp. This one covered the part of the ground that was under the overhanging tarp. If you stood right in the middle, it was blue up, blue down, blue all around. Like being inside and outside at the same time.

The grass-mixed-with-Astroturf lawn area, the area not covered with tarp, was huge. Cars were parked all over this area, all kinds of ways. I noticed there were mostly classic cars, old Mustangs and T-birds, Porsches and Saabs, Beamers, plus some brands I didn't know. When Keith and I arrived in his beat-up old Datsun surf-mobile, we made sure we parked down the road a bit.

Every time I tried to get to the food, I found myself stumbling across or being introduced to familiar-looking people. TV newspeople. Bit actors. Guys I recognized from surf magazines (couple of them even knew my name). Celebrities, I guess. Then there was this one guy who someone said was a Hollywood screenwriter. This was *his* beach house. He was talking to this guy who had written a novel, according to Keith, who showed up by my side with his t-shirt wrapped around his head.

"No lie," I told him. "One novel? Fuck. Hard enough fo' write one t'ree-page paypah fo' English."

"Eh, dass what I heard, brah. And he was published in . . . what dat magazine? . . . *Details*."

"*Details*?" I shrugged.

"Yeah, you know. The magazine. Like *GQ*."

"Whoa."

Then Keith caught the scent of this super-hot babe in bikini top and cut-off shorts. He howled like a werewolf, then staggered off on her trail.

The screenwriter was heavy into conversation with the host. Probably writer talk. As I walked by, with one foot on the edge of the blue tarp and the other on the Astroturf, the host grabbed me by the arm, and said in a loud voice, "You're Mākena."

I nodded as I gazed out at the two smiling haole dudes. The host was this short guy who wore a black tank top and shorts. His chest and even his upper back were really fucking hairy. And he was losing hair at the top of his head. I knew where it was going. The other guy had this "*Ed Wood—Go!*" t-shirt on, which confused me at first, then I thought it was pretty cool. He had long, long brown-turning-blonde hair. He looked like an older version of one of those male models in those slick magazine ads. He was about an inch shorter than me. I'm exactly six feet tall.

Was getting surreal already. I was thinking, maybe it's the weed starting to hit. Seems like the two guys were staring at me—smiling at me—for minutes. All I could think of to say was "T'anks eh, fo' letting us use your house."

"Hey, man. That's what it's about. Say," he continued, pointing his index at me, "you sure caught an awesome ride today." He turned to the novelist guy. "This is the guy." Pointing at me again. "He's the one I was telling you about, the one who got spat out of that awesome tube during that awesome set."

It had been a long, rough day. This morning, during the contest, so many surfers got worked bad. Especially during my heat. I tell you, I almost ate it a few times. Conditions were heavy. I was just trying to survive.

The novelist guy had his Heineken bottle in his right hand, so he stuck out his left, fingers out, pinkie up, thumb down. I figured he wanted me to shake it so I did. "Awesome." He stared at me, smiling. Smiling a little too long.

"Uh—I . . . got lucky." He looked at the host and continued the conversation they were having.

I hadn't brought my eyeglasses with me—by the way, I'm kinda nearsighted; my dad says that's the price for reading too much. I left my glasses in Keith's Datsun 'cause, well, no look too cool, huh? Unless it's Oakley's or something. So while the two writer guys were pretty much in focus, the background was hazy. I could tell the makes of the cars parked in the yard only by their shapes, and unless I squinted, I couldn't even make out the license plates.

"Man, if I lived here I would never get any writing done," the blondish guy was saying.

"I know what you mean," the host said. "I'd have twice, three times the projects, I'd have projects up the wazoo if I were still in Santa Barbara . . . let alone Malibu." He held his drink up. "Aah, but what the hell."

"To hell," the blondish writer said, holding his drink up too. I started to lift my drink up too, but stopped halfway. I dunno if they noticed. They both drank.

I was looking for a smooth way to exit, but, boy, was like my legs were heavy, and was like, I was not in control. So I just watched them in conversation, sort of the way people watch tennis or ping-pong matches.

"So like I was saying, there's always a lack of story."

"I know what you mean . . . "

"But visually it's right up there."

"Exactly."

I had no clue as to what they were talking about.

"What you guys talking about?" I heard myself say that, but my ears seemed plugged, my head seemed stuffed. It came out so soft I don't know if anybody heard me.

"I mean, even *Endless Summer II*. Shit, my kid could write a better script—"

Endless Summer II. Yeah, it wasn't that great. Okay, I getting my bearings now.

"I read ya."

"—in about two days."

"Don't need to convince me."

"You know, if I can just get Scripps-Howard to approve the collaboration—"

Scrips? Movie scripts?

"—thing is, they're funny about approving people who're not in the guild."

"Well, if you get the go-ahead," the blondish writer said. "You got my number."

The host held up his bottle. "To year-round sunshine, dazzling young women, and fat paychecks. To the good life."

"Here's to it." The blondish dude clinked glasses with the hairy-bald one. I looked at my half-filled bottle, half expecting one of them to say to the other, *He's still here?*

"Plus, we could cast some Rell Sunn type . . . "

"You mean like this one?"

I swear, at that moment the most gorgeous woman I had ever seen in my life walked up to us.

"Desiree," the host said.

She reminded me of Tia Carrere. She had the same kinda glow. She was wearing a pareu and holding a glass of what looked to be red wine.

"You're right," the novelist told the screenwriter host, who had his arm around her already. "She does look like a cross between Carrere and Carrera. Or did you say Nia and Tia?" She rolled her eyes.

"Yeah, the Nia, the Tia . . . the *Santa Maria*." The host beamed.

"Makes you feel like Columbus, don't it? I tell ya, Hawai'i's got the patent on great-looking chicks."

"And this one's a talented actress. She just did a show at that theater at—" He looked at her.

"—Chaminade," she finished.

He turned to her. She was all smiles and light. "What was the name of that . . . performance?"

I only could make out the word "angels." I leaned a little closer and heard her say it wasn't acting so much as it was dancing.

I couldn't believe I was still standing there. Woulda been nice if they'd've introduced me, maybe even told her about the barrel ride that got me the First Runner-up award. I had to check to see if my body was still there.

Then I started hoping that she *wouldn't* notice me. Here I was, standing there so fucking silent and stony and stupid, fidgeting from the grass, watching what looked like some outtake from *Wayne's World*. Man, the pakalōlō was doing shit to my head.

Apparently, she didn't notice.

"So which of you guys is gonna write a script with *me* in mind?" she asked. Her smile was more a smirk now.

"I'm working on it already," the novelist said.

"My agent's sending the script around," the hairy guy said. Then he added, "I mean it."

He's got an agent.

I took small swallows from my nearly empty bottle, gazed out toward the car-covered lawn to make like I was caught up in something.

"Why aren't you in Hollywood?" the novelist said.

"Oh God. L.A.'s so creepy."

"Hey, what's wrong with creepy?"

"Well, I mean . . . sleazy."

Creepy. Sleazy. Weren't there five more dwarfs?

"I don't know," she continued. "I'll go back up if my agent says something's up. Otherwise I'm happy here."

She's got an agent too.

I swallowed. I could feel a burning sensation going down my stomach, practically to my groin.

"Weren't you in Aspen for a while?" the screenwriter host said. "Skiing, or whatever it is they do up there?"

She got even more sparkly when he said that, if that was possible. What's that song on my dad's Springsteen tape?

Blinded by the light.
Cut loose like a deuce, another runner in the night.

Great teeth, I thought. I took a swallow of what was left. "I was in Aspen, then Denver. I stayed with my cousin. She took me to the slopes."

"Break a leg?" the novelist guy said.

"You're supposed to say that when I'm going *on* stage." She hit him on the shoulder. "Not when I go *skiing*."

My stomach felt queasy. Maybe food would help. I caught the whiff of fried chicken. *How do I cut loose?*

The bottle was empty. *Shit.* I looked at my watch. 12:24. I'm gonna walk away in exactly two minutes, no matter how awkward it might seem.

I started thinking about how I should do it. Just walk away? Come up with a good exit line? Like, *I'm gonna get another beer. Anybody want some?* But if I said that and they said *Yeah*, I'd have to come back. Then I'd be right back where I started.

12:26. Okay, okay, just two more minutes. For real this time. The queasiness felt more like nausea now.

"Oh, by the way, this is Mākena." The host's words were so direct and loud they blasted through my stupor. "Mākena," he said, gesturing toward the beautiful woman, "Desiree." She held her hand out. I took it. "What was your last name?" the host said. "Riviéra?"

The nausea increased. Things were starting to spin. It must have been that last swallow. Put me over the edge.

"Riv— Riv—awaugghghghg." I was heaving up a mess of yellow-whitish stuff on the blue tarp where it met the green Astroturf.

I heard somebody—must have been the novelist—say, "an auspicious debut," or maybe he said, "a river of puke." I must have blacked out for a moment.

When I came to, I found that Desiree was holding me by my arm and shoulder and was walking me to the bathroom inside the house to wash up. I figured that the two writers were supervising a quick cleanup.

I guess I did get her attention. Man, I shouldn't have drank that beer so fast—especially since I hadn't eaten for hours. And where the fuck is Keith?

In the bathroom I rinsed my mouth in the sink. Desiree then pulled some toilet paper from the roll and started to wipe the cuff ends of my long-sleeve t-shirt. I just pulled them away from her and placed them under the warm-running tap. I rubbed soap on the cuff sleeves, then rinsed them out.

She sat on the closed toilet seat.

"How old are you?"

I noticed that she didn't say *How old you?* Full-on local style. She probably wouldn't say *Whassup?* either. So I followed her lead. "Seventeen," I said as I looked at my bloodless face in the mirror. "I'm gonna be eighteen in a few months. Why?"

"Kinda young to be puking your guts out on beer, huh?"

"And grass. Don't forget. Grass too." I gargled. Then I grabbed the bottle of Listerine that probably was provided for such occasions and gargled some more. Too young to smoke, too stoned to party, I thought to myself. More than anything else I wanted my head either foggier or clearer. None of this in-between shit.

"I didn't like the way they were ignoring you."

"Ignoring me? Who?"

"You know who."

"I didn't notice."

She got up from the toilet seat, mumbling something that sounded like, "Maybe they should have ignored you, with that chip on your shoulder," and lifted the lid. At first I thought, is this lady gonna take a piss in front of me? Instead I watched as she poured her red wine into the toilet and flushed.

Shit. Should've gone with my football buddies to see *Pulp Fiction*.

Then she said, "Wanna go outside and get some air?"

"I dunno. Is it past curfew?"

"Okay, have it your way." She got up and left the bathroom. Desiree, covering her ears, bumped her way through the dancing, pot-smoking, beer-spilling crowd, and I did the same. She walked out through sliding doors that faced the ocean, then on through the yard and onto the sand. The moon had finally broken away from the clouds. It was almost full.

I dunno if she knew I was following her, but pretty soon I was walking beside her. "And how old are *you?*"

She stopped. She looked me straight in the face and smirked. "Nineteen."

"Nineteen? When did you graduate?" It was weird not saying *When you wen' grad?*

"A year ago. From Punahou. I was probably last in my class." She walked on. I followed.

"Well, I got six months to go . . . at Wai'anae." Punahou, the school for rich kids. Mostly haole kids, though Desiree was no white girl. She looked Hawaiian, Asian, maybe some haole mixed in there too.

Wai'anae, where all us Hawaiians live. Mostly poor Hawaiians. By whose design?

"I know."

"What you mean, you know?" I felt slightly headachy, but at least I was starting to think straight.

She grinned at me. "I just know."

That threw me off. It was like she had something on me. Or worse, maybe with her high-makamaka private school background, she knew what a lowlife I was, and was just playing with me.

Why else was she giving me all this attention? Maybe she had a thing for losers who throw up at parties. I felt like I was in that tube ride again. I had no idea if I was going to pull through or really get pounded. But I had to keep going.

"You know, I have some cousins who go to Wai'anae. I think one of them is graduating this year. Do you know Maile Thompson?"

Didn't ring a bell, though I knew a couple of Mailes. "Not really. It's a big school."

"Well, maybe I'll see you graduation night."

That sounded more local. I pictured her standing with my family, taking pictures with us. Yeah, right. Fat fucking chance.

As we walked on, the sand felt cool between my toes. The ocean waves were washing in broken pieces of the moon. I tried scooping some up.

"I've done it too," she said as her hand brushed against mine.

"Done what?"

"Puked at a party. In fact, I puked in that very same house. Right on that stupid Astroturf. That's probably why they have the tarp now." She turned to look at me again. "So I can relate."

"So what? You go parties there a lot?"

"This is my first one in a while. I know Arlen, the guy who lives there."

"The short, hairy guy?"

She smirked. "If you wanna put it that way."

All of a sudden I wondered if she had heard anything about my performance that day. I mean, if she hangs around with those dudes, she might know I had placed second in my age group—Lincoln Chase won—and lotta people, including the judges, thought I had the day's best ride. *Luckiest* ride is what it was. Eh, she probably has no idea. . . . So why then? I couldn't figure—

So where's your boyfriend? I wanted to say out loud. Just to get it out. He probably some Hui O He'e Nalu tough-ass surfah dude. Better yet, some young, hot-shit Hollywood producer or lawyer who's in L.A. getting laid while she's here in Hawai'i—probably doing the same thing. Well, as my buddy Keith always says, don't invest anything. Just get your rocks off.

Seems we walked a mile in the Wai'anae direction. I was thinking, if we kept going in this direction, we'd get through Ka'ena Point in a couple of hours and I could just call Dad to come pick me up at Yokohama.

The night was still. Quiet. Just us and the waves and the stars and the moon. Desiree's cheeks sparkling in the moonlight.

"You need to work on your selection." I almost shook. That's what Manny always says. It's always, *No get too excited. Be patient. That's the only way.*

"What?" I said to her.

"Wave selection. That's why my jerk-of-a-cousin beat you, you know."

I stopped in my tracks, looked straight at her. "Wait a minute. Who are you?"

"Never mind, who am I. I do know a *little* about surfing."

Something clicked when she said that. "What's your full name?"

"Desiree Kanoe Ku'uipolani Tiepel. It's just a name."

"Yeah, sure. And your dad is just 'Ace.'" Ace Tiepel, the surfing legend. The guy who went out when the waves were biggest. Twenty, thirty footers. Sunset. Waimea. Maverick's.

"No no no. You've got the wrong girl. I'm not his daughter. Jenny's his daughter." Then she added, "She's my cousin. She used to be my surfing partner.

Now she's at Colorado State, majoring in haole boy-friends."

"Haole boyfriends?"

"Actually, she wants to be a physical therapist. There's a lot of work there. With all the skiers."

Right then I had these images of some woman massaging some guy in one ski lodge. It was me being massaged by Desiree. Then the director yelled "Cut!" and turned to the Hollywood screenwriter and the novelist. Then he said, "We need a rewrite." Was this a movie I had seen? I felt a little less stony, but there was a *movie* feel to everything around me. The scenery, the colors, the girl.

"Wave selection?"

"I think you would have won . . . " She stopped in her tracks. Looked me straight in the eyes. "I'm sorry. I got no business acting like a coach. I can't come close to surfing the way you do."

"Sounds good, though. It's good advice. Wave choices."

We sat on the sand for a while, quiet.

"Didn't somebody mention you being a dancer?" I said to disturb the silence.

"Well, I do a form of dancing called Butoh."

"I've heard a' that."

"Really? What do you know about it?"

"Um. Well, it's Japanese. I know that for sure. I think it emerged in the fifties. I know it was sometime after World War II. After Hiroshima. You empty yourself of thought and just move intuitively." I was bullshitting a bit, mixing Manny's surf philosophy with stuff my dad used to tell me about karate. Same culture, I figured.

"Boy, you got some interesting sides to your, uh, personality."

"I dunno. I jes' read stuff.

Desiree stood up. "Well, like anything, it keeps evolving. The way we do it now is a far cry from what it used to be back then."

"Do what?" I had lost the train.

She rolled her eyes. "Butoh."

"Oh yeah."

"And Butoh isn't exactly lively dancing, you know." Desiree burped. She put her hand on her chest. "Excuse me. The wine . . . " After a moment she continued. "Most often it's improvisational. Usually slow movements. The dancer's body, searching for a form. And we usually perform naked."

"Naked? Whoa." I fell back on the sand.

"Just kidding. Thought that would get your attention. Our costumes vary, but in our most recent performance we wore white sports panties and painted our bodies white. Believe me, it's not as sexy as it sounds. Here—I'll show you something."

She got up and stood at the ocean's edge, facing me. She started moving in real slow motion. Her face was a blank. I felt thickheaded, watching as she took at least a minute just to artfully lift one leg, while at the same time reaching out with her arms.

The setting was perfect. Dark, sparkly ocean. Moonlight beam. Then she turned around, her back toward me, facing the water, and started to untie her pareu, unfastening the knot behind her neck. This was like when you press the slo-mo on the VCR, but without the shakiness. She was so smooth. This was such a tease, man. Wish I had brought my glasses.

Seems like it took ages before she turned around and I could see the top part of her tits. I could see where the tan line ended and the whiter part showed, almost to her nipples. But it wasn't as sexy as you might think, 'cause of the dead look in her face. In fact, because of the lighting I wasn't even sure she was flashing part of her tits, wasn't even sure she was not showing her nipples. Was so weird.

Then she stopped, smiled, and the speed was right again. She said, while pressing the untied ends of her pareu against her chest, "Wild, huh? It takes a lot of discipline." Man, she was just so beautiful, in real time. "Say, why don't we go for a swim? Before I could react she was stripping off her pareu, and running in the water. I know this movie, I thought. When I realized I was thinking *Jaws,* I thought, *Oh no, not that shit again.*

When she dove into the face of a wave, holding her pareu in one hand, I thought, *Boy, what a loss that would be,* then tore off my shirt and chased her in.

I dove under some whitewash, then came up standing in the shallow water. I didn't see her. Then I felt a tug at my leg. She was pulling me under. Then I came back up and there she was, arms crossed, wearing nothing but panties, laughing. Where'd her pareu go? Then she pulled her pareu from between her knees and wrapped it around her waist, looking at me the whole time.

Inviting me.

Shaking like crazy, I crossed over to her. I put my hands on her hips. She put her arms around my neck and drew me in. *Oh shit oh shit oh shit.* I kissed her and she kissed back. We were shaking from the cold, but our tongues kept going at it. The waves kept knocking at us, and finally we tumbled over. When I came up I grabbed her hand and pulled her close. I still couldn't stop the shaking. Then I slid one of my hands through the opening in her pareu and felt her panties. Then I slid my hand under and felt her butt crack. I was thinking *Ohboyohboyohboy. Hollywood. Hollywood.* Oh man, this was the best tube ride yet . . . was like everything in my life had led to this moment. The fucking screenwriter should be taking *this* scene around. I was livin' it, man. I was fucking livin' it.

We fell again with the next wave. I got up and chased her toward the shore. Then she fell to her knees right near the shoreline, leaned forward and started throwing up. I held her by the waist and patted her back as she puked all this liquid. She must've swallowed water.

Afterwards she rinsed her mouth with the salt water and I led her to the dry sand. Then I picked up my shirt and covered her. She kept shaking and shaking. Was like she had taken my shaking and had made it her own. I wanted so badly to make love to her, but she didn't look too interested right then. She rested her head on my lap for a while, while my mind insisted on making it all seem like a movie. I was so outside of myself. *What kinda shit did I smoke?* I still was expecting some director to yell "Cut."

I had no idea what I was supposed to do next. Was like nobody gave me the script for the rest of the scene. I couldn't help but think *I am not worthy* as I waited for her to make the moves, figuring she was too sick to continue making out. So all I did was pat and rub her back.

"I hate that fucker," she said all of a sudden.

"Who?"

She didn't respond right away. She had her hands over her head. Her elbows rested on her knees. "Arlen."

"What, the hairy guy? Eh, no worry 'bout him." I rubbed her shoulders and neck, feeling something in my groin. Maybe still get chance, I thought.

"He dumped me . . . " She started sobbing now. "After making me pregnant. . . . I had to, I had to—" Now she was bawling, holding her stomach. I didn't know if the pain was more from throwing up or from reliving what she had to do.

"Hey. It's all right. It's all right." I still rubbed her, but my desire was gone. Fucking guy. Now I knew who was writing the script, man. Shit. Shit. Fucking guy.

After a long soothing silence, we got up and walked the long walk back to the beach house. I let her wear my t-shirt over her retied but still damp pareu. It was good timing because by the time we got back, it had started to drizzle. And shit, I was fucking cold. Desiree and I followed the path around the side of the house and walked to the front. Seems she just wanted to get outa town. Or into town. She looked around at the cars—there weren't many left—like she was wondering which one was hers. I was wondering too. Was it the red T-bird with the top down? It looked like it always stayed down, even when it rained. Was it the black Porsche? I followed her as she walked toward this baby blue Miata. She turned, pulled off the t-shirt and handed it to me, saying, "Thanks."

"For what?"

"For staying with me . . . while I made a fool— "

"You did the same . . . for me." She nodded, her eyes glassy. *What is she on?* She fired up the engine.

"Look. I . . . gotta go."

"Sure you can drive all right?"

As she nodded she backed up into the tall chain-link fence, though she had no reason for being in reverse. She paused a bit, looking kinda uncertain, then waved bye and drove off.

"Drive carefully," I whispered, feeling the light rain on my face, waving as the baby blue Miata faded into the night.

I put on my shirt. The one she had worn. Then I went back to the house, feeling hungry and ornery, like if I ran into a certain writer I would blast his fucking face.

The hungry part was stronger. I didn't find any writer or host, just some wasted dudes hanging out in the kitchen. There I sparked a plate full of chicken wings and ate all of them. Was so fucking 'ono. Then I drank a Coke and burped so hard I felt it shooting up my nose. That felt good too. I was getting my strength back.

In the living room the mega-loud band was breaking down. Some DJ type was taking over, taking the music down a few levels. There weren't that many people around by now. Just the mess they had left behind. Plates, cups, bottles, which people used as ashtrays, were all over the place. The few who were left sat on the couches and chairs, either making out or passed out. All the surfah types were gone, or crashed out in one of the bedrooms, needing a bit of sleep before checking out the waves at sunrise. I skidded through the sliding door, went looking for Keith. One of the wasted dudes in the kitchen had said he had gone out on the sand. I would have passed him earlier if he had gone south, so I headed north.

I couldn't find him, so I returned to the house. I stood against a wall, absorbing the music. Reenergizing.

Then I moved from room to room, looking for Keith, finding people in various states of stoniness, various states of undress, finding everyone but him.

I burst out the front door and found myself standing under the blue tarp. Blue up, blue down, blue all around. It was eerie more than irie, this feeling of being outside yet inside.

I was kinda like scouting the scene, contemplating my next move, an ending to this unfinished script, when the novelist guy with the "*Ed Wood—Go!*" t-shirt bumped me as he backed up out of the front door. He was saying bye to someone. He was also preoccupied with this surfa chick, who had a hand in his back pocket while his hand rubbed her ass. "Living the dream," I muttered as I got out of their way. He and the girl walked, I mean staggered, across the Astroturf lawn toward the Porsche and climbed in. After a moment he got out, shouting, "Where's my keys? Where the fuck are my keys?" He checked his pockets, then headed back toward the house.

"They're here, Jim, in the ashtray!" the girl in the car yelled, but he was just out of hearing range, so she got out of the Porsche and stumbled toward the house to get him. I knew that would take a while.

There were only three people, all local guys, outside at the time. They were sitting on folding chairs under the tarp, leaning back with their legs on the food table, totally engrossed in conversation. They didn't notice me unfastening the rope that was tied to the aluminum pole—I had lots of rope now—and stringing it through a loop on the edge of the tarp that lay on the ground. As quick as I could, I unraveled the remaining rope toward the Porsche. I could barely get it to reach the black car, but when I did I yanked hard, muttering, "C'mon, gimme some slack."

After checking again to make sure no one was looking, I looped the rope around the rear fender and tied the tightest double knot I could make. I stepped away from the car, and quietly, nonchalantly in the drizzle that was hardly even a drizzle by now, walked toward the front door. Just when I reached to open it, Keith burst out. I jumped.

"Scared da shit outa you, eh?" he said. "Whassup?"

"Where's your babe?"

"Which one?"

"Which *one*?"

"Da one you was chasing."

"Oh, dat one. I lost track of her."

Just then, the blondish-haired novelist came out with the girl, making out as they walked past us.

"Oh shit," Keith whispered and I now recognized her as the one he had been chasing after earlier that evening. "Fuck."

"Watch dis," I told him as they went to the car.

"Fucking asshole," Keith was saying.

"Like we're any different."

"We *are* different."

We were standing on the tarp, watching this Hollywood movie, watching this dude and his dudette fall into the Porsche. I didn't know if the rope would give or hold, but I had to warn Keith.

I was just about to say *Check out the rope* when the novelist floored the accelerator, and all that came out of my mouth was *JUMP!* and we jumped. Then we rolled. It happened lightning quick, but I saw it all in slo-mo. I saw blue all around me as I rolled. I saw chairs crashing, paper plates, bottles and other shit just flying from the falling tables. I got a blurred sense of three caught-off-guard characters who were falling and stumbling too, laughing and moaning—stunned sober. For them it was a wave from out of nowhere, a big fucking blue wave. They ate it, while Keith and I barreled through. Keith roared.

The Porsche not only took two huge pieces of tarp, it took a bit of the house too. I guess the part of the rope that had been tied to that beam was fastened awfully tight. The beam had broken off and part of an eave sank a foot or two.

Arlen came storming out, saying "What the—?" before being stunned into silence by the mess.

What I saw was a beautiful night sky, an ocean of stars.

□ □ □

"You guys all right?" Arlen said.

"We coulda been hurt, you know," Keith said in a scolding voice as he got up. "Shit, I dunno whass wrong wit' your friend. Fuckah almost wen' kill us."

I remained on the ground, using all the strength I had to not laugh. I mimicked Keith's grim look.

"Hey, I'm really sorry, guys. I dunno what got into him."

"It's cool," I had to say. "We'll be okay."

*I bit my knuckles to hold in the laughter, and while
Keith maintained his game face, we watched Arlen as he
started to check out all the flotsam and jetsam shit. Then
he checked on the trio who really coulda gotten hurt. His
hands were in prayer mode when he apologized.*

They were okay. I was glad for that.

*Keith and I helped three annoyed guys pick up the chairs
and tables and helped them gather some of the stray mess.
Arlen kept apologizing, kept wondering how it happened.*

*Funny thing is those three dudes just sat down and con-
tinued their conversation. Like nothing happened. Like
they just had one more story to tell. Arlen went back
inside, probably to deal with more mess.*

"Sucking Keith," I whispered to him.

*"You should talk. Shit man, I t'ought you was gon' be
boring."*

"An' I t'ought you was gon' be scoring."

"I was."

*I looked at my watch. Shit. Quarter to four. "Well,
brah, 'nuff excitement for me. I'm ready to split this
grungy scene."*

"Yeah, but let's go out da back way."

"Why?" Keith didn't answer.

*We followed a stone path that went around the house
and led to the beach. A girl, in silhouette, stood against
the backdrop of the shore. She had been waiting for Keith.
"Sucking guy." And I thought I was orchestrating this. I
punched his arm.*

I remembered her from a Byrds of Paradise *episode. She
was this pidgin-speaking classmate of Jennifer Love-
Hewitt. She spoke this stupid-sounding pidgin, boy. Some
kind of Hollywood version. Keith began telling her what
just went down. Of course, he made up shit and the farther
we got from the house, the more crazy the story got. Pretty
soon it was Keith's story, and I was enjoying it like I was*

hearing it for the first time. After a while I was laughing so hard I could hardly breathe. My stomach was hurting.

We snuck through someone's yard, found the street where the rusty surf-mobile awaited, and got in that old Datsun. They sat in the front while I commandeered the back seat.

"You know dat dis guy almost won today's—I mean yestahday's event?" Keith told the girl. "You know, da one at Pipeline?"

"Cool," she said. "I'm impressed." She turned to smile at me.

"Yeah, he was da runner-up," Keith added.

I nodded, thinking, Tell me about it.

I was too tired to think. The girl's fading smile reminded me of Desiree's smile, before she said bye to me. I wondered if she had made it to her destination okay. Wondered about the novelist. Could he still be dragging all that tarp? What kind of spin was he putting to his night?

I closed my eyes and saw nothing but blue—spinning, swirling blue. I had to smile.

"Your friend's looking tired," I heard the girl up front say to Keith. "Think he's gonna crash."

"Fuck crash," I said abruptly. I crawled through the back door window, ignoring Keith's Hey what the fuck? *comment. I managed to climb on the roof of the slow-moving car. I kept my knees bent, pretending to ride, feeling the wind.*

How was I to know Keith would hit the brakes just when I was hanging ten on his car roof? I flew forward, first hitting the hood, then found myself doing 360s on asphalt.

I have to be cruel. I have to tell you something. I had an affair. He kept saying that in his head. He feared the gods were punishing his family for his indiscretions.

I have crushing news for you. He may not be your son. If he needs blood, . . . She feared telling him, especially after all these years. Now she feared not telling him even more. She feared that the gods were punishing her family for her not being forthright from the start.

In their minds they worked equations like, in his case: *What if the boy comes to and I lose my family for fessing up?*

Equations like, in her case: *How can I do this to Henry? After all these years. What if Mākena dies? Do I tell him then? He may not have been yours to begin with.*

God help me, she said, her deeply buried Catholic upbringing rising to the surface.

God help me, he said, more as a catch-all for *whatever* was out there.

Only akua sabe. Uncle Joe's words.

Both wondered through it all if their family—if they—could survive this.

Magic Man/Under Partly Cloudy Skies

(Kahuku—Late Fall 1994/
Waiāhole Valley—New Year's Day, 1978)

Kanani

He has good friends, that's one thing I can say about him. They came with flowers and cards and kind words. His buddy Keith agonized as much as we did. "Was my fault, Auntie. My fault," he kept saying to me.

Henry was uncharacteristically quiet. And all I could do was pace the corridors of the hospital while they worked to revive him. I cursed, I pleaded, I begged. I was ashamed that I could not handle the situation better.

In the span of eight months I had lost both parents. Isn't that enough? No. I need to be punished more. If so, akua, punish ME! Not my son. Not my son.

We were survivors. We had survived evictions, betrayals, cutting losses. But our wounds had healed. Scars, I can deal with scars. I just can't deal with losing my son. No god is—

"His condition is stable," the doctor, a neurosurgeon, said yesterday.

What does that mean?

"Looks like he'll be all right. All tests point to that. His body has suffered severe trauma. A coma is its way of getting the deep rest it needs."

I didn't like his use of the word "it." I told the doctor, "But some people don't come out of comas."

"That's true . . . but we're optimistic. Cautiously optimistic."

I looked at Henry. I had never seen him so distraught. He was insane with guilt. Outwardly he was blaming his casual attitude toward booze and drugs, especially when we learned that Mākena reeked of alcohol when he was brought in, and later tested positive for marijuana.

I suspected that a major part of Henry's guilt had to do with one Lily Imura. I couldn't hate him for that anymore. It used to bother me now and then. Long after I knew in my heart it was over, I would sometimes dwell on it and let it eat me up. Now, if anything, it seemed irrelevant, silly.

"Stop beating yourself up, honey." I rubbed his shoulder.

"I shoulda . . . if I knew . . . "

"How could we know?"

"The kid means everything to me."

"He means everything to all of us." I turned to look at 'Analu, who was asleep on two chairs that were pushed together. I used to sleep like that as a kid at my cousins' house. 'Analu didn't want to go with Grandpa and Grandma Rivera, when they left. He too had a stake in this horrifying vigil that found me, the lapsed Catholic, down on my knees begging for divine assistance.

Henry pressed his back against a pillar, slid down till he was in a low squat, looking utterly exhausted. I had finally gotten some sleep in the afternoon, just crashing out in the waiting room.

"Why don't you nap?" He shook his head.

Henry never could stand the suffering of others. Even animals. He couldn't shoot for sport like his friends did.

Even fishing was hard for him to handle. I could tell he wanted to swallow all the pain, take all the blame. Mākena was deep in some ocean of his own creation. Henry wanted to be in the water rescuing him, pulling him out from wherever he was.

And so did I. For two days I've been pacing the corridors, tabulating my losses: Mom and Dad. Lucy and Uncle Joe . . . Keoni . . . Two days. It's been nearly forty-eight hours since Keith called. It was a quarter after four in the morning when the phone rang. It had to be bad news. My fear was that it was one of Henry's parents. Considering how old they were. . . . And I thought Mākena was asleep in bed. I could hear the panic in Keith's voice. He fumbled for words, saying, *Mākena fell off da car roof, Auntie. He—I was driving—the brakes—I nevah know—was my fault—* and we rushed over. Then we waited. We heard little from the doctors. In desperation we called Eli long-distance. He said he'd be flying in the next morning. Told us not to worry about the doctors; they were as good as they come.

In the room next door, there lay another young man, also in a coma. Today his heart stopped beating and the place went crazy. Doctors and nurses were rushing in, sending people out, some of them hysterical.

And they revived him. But for how long?

The nurse in blue came by. Asked us if we could wait outside while she checked Mākena's vital signs. Like earlier, she allowed 'Analu to continue to nap near his brother. Poor kid.

Henry and I stepped into the hospital corridor.

"What time is it?" he asked. I was staring at the clock on the wall.

"4 a.m."

"I'll go get some coffee," he said. I nodded. He started to walk down the hall. He turned. "Want anything else?" I shook my head. "You okay?" I nodded but thought, *How can I be?*

He came up, reached out to the back of my head, and gently pressed his forehead to mine. "He'll be all right. Da kid's strong."

"Hope so."

The nurse in blue came out. "He's doing quite well. It's just a matter of time. You can go in." Those words were utterly devoid of meaning to me. I took a deep breath as I walked into the room.

I was struck by the smell of ginger, 'ilima, and pīkake, emanating from the leis and flowers Mākena's friends had brought these last two days. There was another scent too. Could it have been those purple-streaked white flowers that Manny dropped off yesterday? Two half flowers. Naupaka, he had said. From the mountain and from the sea. I hadn't had any chance to pick up anything. And although I was looking at my son, lying there hooked up to wires and tubes, IV units, and a respirator, in my fatigue it was a lush valley I succumbed to . . .

□ □ □

Beneath partly cloudy skies I carefully walked up the valley trail to the house I had grown up in. It had been so long since I'd lived here. For years I had lived in dorms, first at Kamehameha, then at Palo Alto, where I went for my first two years of college, then at the UH, when I found I had to return to Hawai'i. Too much was happening.

Mākena was wrapped in a blanket in my arms. I tired easily.

First I looked to see if anyone was in the orchid-filled greenhouse, the place where Momi and I used to play when we were kids. No one was there. Then I saw my mother stooped over in the vegetable garden, which was surrounded by ti leaves and plumeria.

"Hi, Ma."

"Nani—" She lit up. "Bring dat boy heah."

I carefully handed the fragile new life to her. "You sure you strong enough, Ma?"

"Fo' carry one baby? No get silly." She held him in one arm and grasped my neck with her free arm. We embraced, with the sleeping infant between us. "So good to see you folks."

"Good to see you, Ma."

Dad came from a wilder part of the garden, a part that edged into the forest. Here there were mangoes, guava, and liliko'i. Dad must have been feeding the stray birds, as he always does. Sparrows, doves, and mynah birds fluttered behind him. There was more of a bend to Dad's walk, and it struck me that he had aged so. Is that what the struggle against the developer had done? He beamed when he saw Mākena and quickly reached to hold him.

"Wait yaw turn," Mom said. "I jes' got him."

He looked at me and smiled. Oh boy, did he lose another tooth?

"Let's go inside," Mom said.

I expected the house to be immaculate. No matter how sick she was, Mom always kept things in order. And now that Dad was retired I guessed he helped also.

But it wasn't quite so. Mom apologized for the "mess." It was slight, but it bothered me. It was a sign of wearing away.

I sat on the couch with Dad. Mom sat on her rocking chair, humming a lullaby as she held the sleeping baby.

"Henry's coming. He went to Haʻiku to see Uncle Sam Lono first." It always seemed odd to me that we all called him Uncle Sam. He was a kahuna lapaʻau, and nothing like his American counterpart. He was an elder blessed with wisdom, yet he was famous for his dirty jokes; he had gone blind, but that hardly slowed him.

"If Henry went foʻ see Sam Lono," Dad said, "we not gonʻ see him till Fawt aʻ July," Dad said. He got up and headed toward the kitchen. To make tea, I presumed.

"He'll be here. . . . He bettah."

The Waikāne-Waiāhole struggle had narrowed the gap between my parents and me. Having grown up on the music of the times, and having bought into the counterculture and all its attitude and fashion, I had little patience for farm life and less for Mom and Dad. A couple years previous, Jasper Simeona, a developer who had donated considerable sums toward the governor's reelection campaign in '74, made moves to drive all the farmers out—in the name of urbanization and housing, which in reality would knock more than a few into the homeless category, since the houses Simeona's people would build would not be affordable. Thus far, neither the public hearings nor the court injunctions could stop this powerful hui, this business-government coalition that abused the very constitutional rights they hid behind when convenient, the very rights they steamrolled over when others claimed them too.

This time we were gonna make sure that what happened to the pig farmers in Kalama Valley, the plantation workers at Ota Camp, and so many others wouldn't happen to us. Aligned with the old-time farmers, we organized. When that didn't work, we mobilized. We weren't the type to run into the hills and fight as guerrillas, though those who saw action in Vietnam were ready for that course of action too. But we were determined and poised to fight.

Hawai'i's community-at-large, most of them a mere one or two generations removed from the feudalism of the plantations, still bought into egalitarian dreams. Even the governor had a plantation past, a memory of being a second-class citizen. So when it all came to a head, when farmers and their backers brought out their hunting rifles and showed their resolve, the governor stepped in and said, "Enough. The farmers will retain their leases." For now.

Not that the governor was a magnanimous or charitable man. He was simply a practical man who listened to his advisors and was convinced that an outright war would undermine years of the hui's work—and with so much more work to be done, so many more friends to make rich.

Of course, the governor's move pissed off the guy who really ran the show, the guy whom the governor, not to mention the banking consortium, answered to. The guy whom Keoni found around the corner of every bad deal that had gone down, the man at the heart of this coalition.

For precious minutes my parents were alive and vital. Then they dissipated. A grim reminder that they were dead.

I couldn't accept it happening to my own son. "No. No. No!" I caught myself saying out loud.

The kid's eyelids started fluttering. I went up to him and stroked his hair. "Ma's here, baby." *Oh c'mon, kid, wake up!* I brought a pīkake lei to his nose. "Wake up, Mākena." As a baby he loved to smell flowers. Even fake ones, like the time he was about one or two and he put his nose to Henry's mom's silk flower arrangement and said, "'Mell good."

And Grandma Rivera said, "Oh, you little faker."

My parents were suddenly vibrant when Henry walked in . . .

Henry did have his priorities straight and arrived within the hour, just after Mākena had started screaming. Mom couldn't stop his screaming. Dad couldn't stop his scream-ing. But when the baby heard his father's voice he shut up. And when he saw his father's silly expression he began cooing.

"Wow," Dad said. "You da magic man, eh?"

Henry picked up Mākena and began singing, quite ten-derly, "Do you believe in magic, in a young girl's heart . . . ," waltzing around the house with the baby in his arms. He could liven up every room he walked into. I don't know what it was. He exuded life, energy. . . . He could get my mother up dancing. She'd say, "No, Henry, my leg soah." Next thing you know she's twirling around like a sixteen-year-old. It's like how he'd sing slack key numbers with the boys. All those hapa-haole and Hawaiian songs. How did he know all those songs? He didn't speak Hawaiian, but sang as if he did.

□ □ □

Downstairs, after leaving the cafeteria, Henry, hold-ing two paper cups filled with black coffee, paced back and forth, practicing his confession. "She didn't mean anything . . . " *Man, that sounds so bullshit.* "It hap-pened. I'm sorry. I'm so so truly sorry. I love you. I always have and always will." He shook his head. *Like she needs to hear that shit now, you fuck.* "Fuck-head." He closed his eyes for a moment, embracing the fatigue, the guilt, the self-hatred. *Oh, man. Why this?*

A few minutes later he was back in the elevator, riding up. He let his knees collapse, slid down in the corner. As the elevator inched up toward the fifth floor, Henry sank even more, not caring that he spilled coffee on his pants.

He was remembering Mākena in diapers, laughing as he took his first steps in their small apartment. He remembered Mākena dressed as Robin that one strange Halloween night. Remembered how they foiled a car thief and ended up cruising the strip looking for, of all things, gum. He remembered the pride he felt when Mākena perfected his jump shot. Then he saw his son's sheepish look after he had hit the brakes too hard—on the day Henry took him out for his first driving lesson.

When the elevator door opened, Henry slid back up and sighed.

□ □ □

Kanani

I might have dozed off for a bit. I had been leaning against the sliding glass door, fumbling with the beaded curtain cord as if it were a rosary, and, engulfed again by flower smells, I succumbed to my exhaustion . . .

With my eyes closed I felt that a light had been turned on.

I was reluctant to open my eyes, for I felt Keoni's presence. When I opened my eyes I saw a whisper of a presence, a ghostly presence. All my life I had heard about yet never seen the Marchers of the Night; I had heard the lurid tales of sorcery conducted by kahuna 'ana'ana, yet never witnessed any magic, black or white; I had also heard of Menehune sightings, especially on Kaua'i, where those stories thrive. I had put them all in the corner of my bookshelf brain that allowed for the unbelievable, the unverifiable. But Keoni was here. I closed my eyes again and this time I saw him distinctly. He wore a white shirt and white pants, like how others had nervously described his apparition in the days after his disappearance. He smiled at me—more a smirk, really, a sheepish, engaging smirk that undercut his haunting, haunted eyes—and he raised his hand as in a wave. His eyes were reassuring. I felt my mouth caught in a sad half-smile, and my lips began to tremble. Then my whole body. Like I was saying no to him. But I wasn't saying no. I was just shaking. My hand—I had no control over it—it reached out.

But he wasn't there. I opened my eyes to the dimly lit room. *Damn you! The wound still hasn't healed!*

In my shaken state I looked at Mākena. *Oh, oh, my god, his eyes are open.*

"Ma?"

I raced up to him, "Yes, yes, it's me, baby. It's me." His right hand reached for my neck and pulled me down. He was so strong. Again I stroked his hair. "Oh, Mākena . . . sweetheart . . . "

While he held on to my neck I used my free hand to ring for the nurse.

By the time she arrived I had pulled my head free from my son's vise-like grip and let him squeeze my hand. The nurse looked Filipina, or Guamanian—I hadn't noticed that before. Mākena saw her and said, "Hey Auntie, whass up?"

She said, "Well, look who's awake and talking."

"He thinks you're somebody else."

She checked his pulse. "Good. . . . The pulse, I mean. Considering his injury, it's common that they get their—" She looked at me and gestured with her finger, a back-and-forth movement. "—their wires crossed." She was local, I was sure, but had this Holly Hunter, marbles-in-her-mouth way of speaking, part

Columbia School of Broadcasting, part southern belle. She checked Mākena's eyes.

"Good. Good. Good! No dilation." I wanted to take her to lunch. Be her best friend. "I'll go get the doctor." She started to leave, then turned to face me. "This is very good news."

"Thank you. Thank you." I went over to Mākena, and again he grabbed me in a vise grip.

"I love you, Ma."

"I love you, too, baby."

Henry walked in with the coffee. I pulled myself from my son's grip.

"Hey, magic man. . . . He's up. I think he'll be all right."

"Magic man?"

He had no clue. I grabbed the two cups from him and set them on the flower-filled table. Henry came up to the bed.

"'Sup, Uncle Jimmy?"

"'Uncle Jimmy?' Whatchu talkin' about? I not Uncle Jimmy." Henry's cousin Jimmy, an HPD patrolman, had been dead for five years, shot while chasing down a robber. Henry looked at me, shaking his head in befuddlement, then back at Mākena. "Dad. I'm Dad."

"I know dat. . . . Hey . . . Dad."

"What? I'm right here."

"I love you, Dad."

"I love you too, boy. We all love you." Henry gave me that look again.

"Hey, Dad." Mākena's voice now sounded conspiratorial: soft, a bit higher in pitch.

"What?" Henry matched the pitch.

"What I doin' heah?"

I looked over at 'Analu on the two chairs. His eyes were wide open. Since when? He was smiling. "Good dream?" I asked him.

He nodded. "Mākena wen' chrow me one touchdown pass and we won da game."

The staff doctor came by, and with no hesitation took Mākena off the respirator. He sensed my apprehension and said to me, "He's been breathing on his own all this time. This was just a precaution." After thoroughly checking our son, he explained, unfortunately not in layman's terms, the recovery process. He told Henry and me that while there should be no lasting damage, it would take about a year for everything to be all right with Mākena's head. Between now and then he'd have to get therapy to speed up the healing process, and we'd have to expect that he'll get confused about things, get events and people mixed up.

"So nothing new, then," Henry said, trying desperately, I assumed, to bring levity to this day.

I was too thankful to ask for more, too exhausted to be amused.

Before we left the hospital I learned that the young man in the room next door wasn't going to make it. He had had a seizure and was brain-dead. I couldn't help but wonder whether some mean-spirited demon was going eeny, meeny, miny, moe—that awful rhyme—back and forth, from Mākena to the young man, a man who had a girlfriend and a child. Why couldn't both of them survive? I thanked Kane, Lono, Jesus, all the akua out there, for letting me have my son . . . but the uneasiness lingered. I said mahalo, mahalo, but as heartfelt as my thank-yous were I couldn't help but feel guilty that my son was spared while another mother was stung with grief.

□ □ □

Mākena had to give up football. (So that's the bargain, I couldn't help but calculate. That's the sacrifice.) No chance he'll ever play it at UH or some mainland college as he dreamed. And no watersports—except therapeutic swimming. And that has to be done in a pool. No ocean for this boy. Not for a while.

Two days later, Eli, who was again passing through O'ahu, came over to the hospital. We got him to translate, at least in part, what the staff doctor had said.

"You see, it was a contra-coup injury. The human brain is a soft, pulpy mass floating in liquid. . . . " I cringed as he spoke. "When Mākena's head hit the asphalt, the brain itself hit the side *opposite* the impact area. That caused the concussion . . . and that's why he lost consciousness. He's looking good, but we have to monitor him for a while. It'll be a year or so before it can be determined that he's clear of any lasting damage. The physical therapy that Dr. Ikeda prescribed is gonna help."

"Does he really need physical therapy?" I ventured. "He's strong . . . his coordination seems fine."

"But he could so easily slip back. You'll see. He'll have difficulty figuring out his left hand from his right. Things we take for granted will stump him. He'll continue to get people mixed up, call them by the wrong name. That's par for the course. Hey, the overall prognosis is great. I just wanna be extra careful."

Henry, who had been quiet, said, "Yeah. No sense taking risks. He's got a long life ahead. Rush into things, you jes' make matters worse."

"Right," Eli said. He looked at us. Then pulled out his prescription tablet and a pen. "I tell you, right now I'm more concerned about you two," he said as he wrote. "God, you look like war vets. PTSD. I'm gonna have the nurse give you some samples. It's gonna take more than Aleve, and this should do it. He handed me the prescription. "I'm gonna have the nurse give you some samples. You need sleep. You know, hiamoe."

I nodded and hugged him. "Thanks, Eli. Thanks for everything."

He and Henry shook hands, then they embraced. "Eh, no shame bill us now." Henry said. "Plane trips and all. I don't want you footing the bill for—"

"Bill you guys?" Eli snickered. "Bill you guys?" He started to walk away, saying, "I gotta go check this kid—he's here from Moloka'i. Real nice kid. Got stomach cancer." He turned around to face us. He was twirling his stethoscope. "Bill you guys?" He spun around, saying, "Get some sleep."

Mākena sat quiet in the back seat of the car—dreaming, it seemed. During the long ride from the hospital in Kahuku to our house in Wai'anae we left the radio off. Henry drove slower than usual, right at or just below the speed limit. Cars roared by us going over seventy-five, disturbed at the way our family sedan was dragging its ass on the wide open freeway. Henry and I only spoke on occasion and 'Analu fell asleep. Near Kapolei, 'Analu woke up and asked me to pop in some reggae. I was hesitant. I felt like we needed the holiness of quietude right now, on this long ride home, like when Henry and I brought our boys home as newborns. But when I turned my head to the left to check how Mākena was doing, he said, "Yeah. Some music, Ma." For a moment I had had this vision of a two-day-old Mākena—too small for the child seat we had bought, too fragile to be carried, he had to be propped up with towels. But this two-day-old child was now the seventeen-year-old who reminded me, "Yeah. Some music, Ma."

The only reggae in the cassette-filled glove compartment was a tape that was labeled "Marley." I popped it in. There was silence, so I fast-forwarded the tape. The car's player has a silence sensor. It stops between songs. When it did stop, the song that came on was "Buffalo Soldier." It wasn't the reggae version. I pressed the fast-forward button again. This time when the tape stopped there was only silence. I had thought that "Stir It Up" was next.

The boys were getting impatient. "C'mon, Ma. Jes' play 'om. Any song."

"I'm trying."

Henry snorted. "That's the end a' da tape." With his eyes on the road he popped out the cassette, flipped it over and popped it in again, saying, "Yaw mom fired as DJ."

Magic man had struck again. Henry placed his right hand on the hand brake. I reached for his hand and squeezed it tightly. He looked at me and I gazed back. "Love you," I mouthed. He squeezed my hand.

The Wai'anae Coast never looked more beautiful. More comforting. We were headed home. The mountains, the beautiful ocean, were a welcome sign as we passed Nanakuli, Ma'ili, and headed toward Wai'anae town. Dazed as I was, I wanted to latch onto every detail, every landmark.

McDonald's, the Mall, Tamura's, the schools on both sides of the main drag. 'Analu got excited when he saw a couple of boys he knew, Joey and Ryan, riding skateboards: *Hey, look at 'om doing loops on the sidewalk.* He kept his gaze to the right, toward the stores, the houses, the Wai'anae Range, while his quiet, contemplative brother gazed oceanward. As we ventured toward Mākaha, Robert Nesta Marley, blessedly reassuring, sang

Rise up this mornin', smile with the rising sun
Three little birds . . . pitched by my doorstep.
Singin' sweet songs, of melodies pure and true,
  sayin'
"This is my message to you, whoo, hoo."

Singin', don't worry . . . 'bout a thing
'Cause every little thing's gonna be all right
Saying don't worry . . .

PART IV

A Spark Is Struck

Sparkey's Tail

(Wai'anae—Early Spring 1995)

Henry

The desperate call came at a desperate time. It was almost midnight. Kanani and 'Analu had gone to bed. Mākena was watching *Saturday Night Live,* channel-surfing during commercials.

"Hate to call you li' dis. But. I sorry, man. T'ings happen an' you know . . . "

"Sparkey?"

Silence. Then a quiet "Yeah."

"Whass wrong, brah?"

"I need money fucking bad. Really bad."

Shit shit shit. "Ah, how much?"

"Chee. . . . T'ree, fo' t'ousand."

Ouch. "Ho-o-o, Sparkey, dass a shitload a money."

"You telling me. Fuck, I'm dead."

"Is dis . . . is dis from gambling?"

Silence. Then, "Yeah. . . . Shit, nobody like help me. Bully would help, but he stay tight. An' Sam, he only get a couple hundred. . . . I gon' die. I gon' down, man. Dey gon' eliminate da middle man."

"What?"

"Me. Da middle man."

Henry didn't know whether to laugh or cry. "Look, Spark. Maybe I can scrape up a couple a bills. Two, maybe t'ree hundred. Dass all I good for, man. Really. If you can get some adda guys—"

"Hey, man, I appreciate it. I really really appreciate it, man. Braddah, you one true friend. If I could I would *give* you my karaoke machine, but, shit, I gotta sell dat too."

That hit Henry hard. No more of those wild beer-fests at the Lopez house. He hadn't been there in a while. Ever since Manny had told him about the kinds of people going in and out of that house. But he had relished his moments there. Loved the space it put him in. And the couple of times he got his wife there and her surprising everyone, Henry included, with a knack for country blues.

Later that night Henry sat up in bed thinking about his first encounter with Sparkey, a lean stranger who wore a ragged t-shirt and holey jeans. He held a cigarette between two shaky fingers and was hanging around outside the Save-A-Lot supermarket. This was shortly after Henry and his family had moved to Wai'anae. Henry was about to get groceries. He figured that the guy approaching him wanted a handout. But Sparkey's first words to him were

Hey, like score some land?

What?

I got some good land on the Big Island I stay unloading fo' two t'ousand an acre.

Was he a drug dealer or pimp talking in code? *Nah. I not interested in buying land right now. Especially on one adda island. Cannot be here and build there.*

Eh, I might be moving some quality O'ahu land any day now.

Everything sounded illegal with Sparkey.

Call me when you got it. At least I can go see it.

Eh, I could show you da Big Island land right now. We go catch one plane. My treat.

Well, I gotta pick up my wife. 'Sides, like I said, I live on DIS island, so—

Dat gon' be yaw getaway home one day. Not yaw MAIN place.

Another guy comes up. *Hey Joe,* Sparkey says, *I stay unloading some quality acres.*

The guy waves him off, looking at him like, *You fo' real o' what?*

That was Sparkey, all right. And despite the weird shit, Henry thought of him as a friend. Henry never figured out this land business, but it seemed that for this guy, money ebbed and flowed like the tides. Sometimes he'd be dressed in clothes that were practically rags. Then he'd be dressed to the nines in some sleek outfit. For a while he was driving an old pickup that looked like it would break down any minute. Next time you saw him it was a new Cutlass Supreme.

Henry even remembered Sparkey carrying around a boom box with crappy speakers. Then he heard that Sparkey had spent a few grand on this elaborate karaoke system.

Henry scraped up three hundred by postponing some bill paying and by counting on a side job he had lined up the morning after the call. His work buddy Josh threw in another hundred.

But Sparkey never came for the money.

The Ultimate Salesman

(Oʻahu—Spring 1995)

Sparkey

I goin' down. How I gon' get away wit' dis? Dis one total fucking setup, man. I already wen' dump planny t'ings in my life: girlfriends, rubbish, da kine 'opala. . . . Deah was even da time I had fo' dump all dis unbought sweetbread. I was about twelve years old. I couldn't sell 'om fo' da school's fun'raisah. Wasn't my style, back den, fo' knock on doors, asking people fo' pay inflated prices fo' somet'ing dey can get fo' half da price at da store. But because of dat incident I wen' swear I would learn fo' sell anyt'ing, dat I would become da ultimate salesman. An' to some extent I did. When I was pau wit' school I stahted selling cars, stereos, fun'raising tickets. Den I wen' move up to land and drugs, da big score kine stuff. Sometimes my pockets would be so fucking loaded wit cash, I would have to unload most of it. I used to hide 'om in my house, but, shit, what if I get burglarized? So I stahted burying da cash—in double o' triple layahs of zip-lock bags. I nevah did trust banks—dey only get robbed. By guys I know, even. An' da manini int'rest? Fuck, it ain't worth it.

I remembah driving to Kailua from my folks' house in Pauoa. Jes' dumping all dat 'ono Buck's sweetbread at

Bellow's—on military land. Right in da scrub grass near da ocean, where da ground is all dirt mixed wit' sand.

I felt bad, wasting so much bread, li' dat. But who would eat two-week-old stale bread? I said, *Heah, birds. Grinds.* An' I left it for dem.

One adda time we was making one float fo' da senior year homecoming at Roosevelt. Was at somebody's house. I fo'get who. I was helping make all these paypah flowahs fo' da float. Man, we filled box aftah box wit' paypah flowahs. Was cool 'cause dass how you meet some pretty nice chicks. An' den we wen' pile all da stuff in cahs and go to da place—Aileen's house I t'ink was—where we wen' put togeddah da float. Boy, was jes' right. Jes' enuff flowahs fo' covah da wire mesh. In fact, some places was jes' barely covered. An' I had tot we had made more dan enuff. Den one day, like weeks, maybe months later, I wen' open my trunk. Deah was two full boxes of paypah flowahs. I wen' forget fo' unload my car, distracted as I was by all da chicks an' da flirting and shit. I had no reason fo' open my trunk befo' dat, an' I had no idea.

Wasn't like was one big deal. Da float still wen' look all right. Da job still got done. Dough I'm sure people was t'inking, *Didn't we make mo flowahs?* Was like having one stringy lei, rather than one full one where no can see da string at all.

So deah I was at Bellow's again—I guess dat was becoming my personal dumping ground—getting rid of hundreds of paypah flowahs. Now I truly was one littah-bug, dumping all dis paypah. I felt littlebit guilty, but I figured da world gon' recova from dis. Dis not one oil spill, dis not aerosol in da ozone, dis just paypah. Prob'ly organic.

An' nevah hurt at all, not like da time I had to dump my pet cat in da Kapālama incinerator. Felt like shit, man, dumping one fucking kitten in the rubbish dat they was burning up. I nevah do naht'ing wrong, for once. Who tell dat fucking Calvin fo' lay one distempered baby cat on me? From all his cat's littah, I get da one dat gon' run aroun' in circles, make noises all night and den fucking drop dead.

But deah's like a karma to all dis dumping, 'cause man, who woulda tot dat I would fuck up so bad on one drug deal and owe my life to dat prick Harley Evans? Who woulda tot dat my life would be on da line 'cause a one stupid fucking debt?

An' who but Harley Evans would t'ink of such a nasty way fo' forgive me da loan? He tole me, *We not gon' kill you if you do dis fo' me.*

I was wondering what I was getting into. I tole 'om, *I may be stuck right now, an' I may have run outa choices, but I radda die dan kill somebody.*

An' Harley say, *It's naht'ing like dat, brah. You no have to kill nobody.*

An' I was confused. 'Cause gotta be somet'ing huge. Harley Evans, he no forgive loans, wheddah you do his laundry, launder his money, or even suck his cock, like I heard he made Brian's wife do. Harley is not a kind, forgiving man.

What den?

He's already dead. You jes' gotta get rid of da body.

So dis guy, I don't fucking know who, is in my trunk. It's not sweetbread or flowahs, brah. It's somebody who yestahday was one living breathing human fucking being. He get one bullet wound in his face. He get t'ree more in his chest area. He's cold, man. We had to pound da rigah mortis out jes' fo' get him in da trunk. I use' to work in one mortuary. Dead bodies no scare me. In fack da only time I ever got scared shitless in the morgue was when me and dis guy Bobby was lifting dis dead old lady face up onto da gurney, and she wen' wake up. Fucking lady woke up! She was suppose' to be dead. Dead and delivered to da morgue. Her eyes was wide open, man. Now *I* wouldn't have panicked. I wouldn't. But fucking Bobby, da buggah wen' haul ass outa da morgue. An' man, deah *I* was hauling ass aftah him. Shit, we left dat poor lady lying deah—all alone—prob'ly trying to figgah out why she was deah in da first place. Lucky t'ing she nevah get one heart attack and die right deah on da spot. But den if you gotta die, what mo' convenient place . . .

I heard when dey took her home she was shaking like anyt'ing. Least she was alive. An' den dey fired our asses. Shit, we was ready fo' quit anyway.

I drive aroun' an' aroun' fo' I dunno how many hours, man, in this fricken Nova dat gon' be up fo' sale in a day or two, 'cause shit if I gon' keep dis fucking ass-dragging Chevy aftah tonight. I no even like stop fo' food o' go store o' even get gas, dough I running low, 'cause, shit, what if somebody reckanize me? Link me to whe' dey foun' da body? Eh, I watch movies. I know how cops operate.

I wen' ask Harley, where should I bury da body?

He jes' say, *If I knew where, I would bury da fuckah myself. An' put you right on top a' him. So unless you want a contract out on yaw fucked up head, you bettah do one good job. If they EVAH find the body, man . . .*

I cruise da Windward Coast. Bellows get soft dirt, I stay t'inking. Easy fo' dig. But shit, when I get deah I see cahs all ovah da place. An' couples making out in dem. *Shit.* What dis world coming to?

I head up toward da Pali Tunnel.

Along one dark side of Nu'uanu Pali Drive I drag da body outa da trunk. It's totally fricken dark. Totally spooky. Shit, I no even dare carry pork aroun' here. One t'ing Sparkey Lopez nevah gon' do is fuck wit' da gods.

I pull dis small flashlight outa da glove compahtment. I have to hold 'om wit' my mout'. Da light seem so bright, dough, in all dis darkness. I stay t'inking, shit, I gon' get caught. Well, if I get caught, I get caught. Nah, nah, no can t'ink li' dat. No can t'ink li' dat.

I cannot fucking do time.

So I drag dat damn body. I walking backwards, so shit, I gotta turn my head ev'ry few seconds. I can heah da running watah. It's getting loudah. I jes' keep wondering, how much more? How long can I drag dis fucking dead body? My mouth soah too, from da way I gotta hold da flashlight. I gotta stop ev'ry couple of minutes, jes' fo' catch my breat', give my mout' a break.

Oh man. I should jes' give it up, but shit, dis is a mattah of survival. My survival.

Finally finally finally I see da stream. I drop da body on da ground. I shine da flashlight on da watah. Good, one fucking pond. I sit on one bouldah. Good time fo' light up. Shit! My cigarettes stay in da fricken cah!

I try turning off da flashlight. Whoa, fucking spooky. I turn it back on fast.

Shit, now I gotta go get da cement bag an' rope.

On my way back, I stay t'inking, dis place good. Da rain gon' cavah da tracks. Aroun' heah always raining. As long as da body no get buoyant an' start floating around, like it's saying, "Hey. Look. Dat damn Sparkey Lopez, da ultimate dumpah, wen' put me heah. If you dig deeper you gon' find sweetbread, flowahs, an' one dead pussycat too."

When I get back to da Nova, I drag da cement bag outa da back seat. Dat was all I had in my yahd dat was heavy.

Fuck, what was I t'inking? Dis is too damn heavy. Niney-fo' pounds, says on da bag. Fuck, I stay sweating enuff already. Shit, no wondah da fucking cah was dragging its ass up da damn highway.

I put da bag on da ground, den pull da rope an' some garbage bags out of my trunk. Dis fricken rope was in my closet. I no even remembah how it got deah. Maybe I was gon' hang myself. Maybe I *should* hang myself.

I put da rope an' garbage bags on da cement bag, pick da whole t'ing up, an' staht my slow walk toward da body. At least dis time I can go forwards. Jes' when I staht going, I remembah, cigarette. So I drop da whole t'ing, go back to da cah, an' pull out my pack of Marlboros.

Excep' I no mo matches. *Fuck!* An' I cannot be dealing wit' da cah cigarette lightah right now. Fuck fuck fuck. *Shit!*

I put da flashlight back in my mout' an' lif' dat damn cement bag an' da rope. Fuck, dis worse dan dragging da body. Cannot drag dis.

I t'ink I fucking die ev'ry t'ree minutes—carrying dis damn fricken bag. Gotta keep stopping, gotta catch my breat'.

Fuck. Dis taking so long I not even sure da body gon' still be deah. Maybe da fuckah tired a' being dead, tired of waiting, so he jes' walk away.

In fack I t'ink saw dat in one movie.

Da body still deah. Now what? I drop da cement bag right on top 'om, watch da dust kicking up. Cannot hurt da fuckah anyways. Den I tie da rope aroun' an' aroun'. Each time I go 'roun' I gotta lif' da body up little bit, jes' enuff so I can drag da rope undah.

I check my Indiglo watch. Fo' in da morning already. I pull out dis note dat I wen' compose wit' my left hand fo' disguise da handwriting. It's wrapped in t'ree layahs of zip-lock bags—dope bags. Da note says, HARLEY EVANS DID THIS TO ME.

Jes' in case.

If I go down, Harley go down too. I stuff da note in da dead guy's pocket.

Den I pull one of da garbage bags ovah da body, from da head down. Dese bags are t'ree mils t'ick, man. Dis da good kine. Was on sale at Sack 'n Save.

Shit. Da bag only reach down to his fucking knees. So I take one adda garbage bag an' staht from da feet and work up. Shit, man, I shoulda opted fo' cremation.

I can hahdly push da body ovah. So fricken heavy. But I still sked dat he not heavy enuff. I start t'inking maybe I shoulda cut him to pieces. I start picturing anadda scenario. One slice-and-dice scenario. Den fucking mosquitoes start biting an' dat jes' about kills it. All dis an' mosquito bites too? Fuck me.

I finally shove da body ovah da cliff. I figgah I can come back da next day—dis aftahnoon, actually—aftah I take one long fricken nap. I gon' bring one scuba mask an' dive as deep as I can an' see how it's doing. An' I gon' bring some net o' chain an' some mo' weights. As long as nobody watching. Dis body nevah gon' come up.

I stay itchy an' nervous all da way back to da fucking cah. I hoping no cop wen' stop by fo' wondah what my cah doing heah in da middle of da fricken night. I stay in deep enuff shit already.

Good. Da coast look clear.

I get in da cah. Release da brakes. Let 'om roll back-ward down da hill little bit. Hahdly can see, since I no have my lights on. When I spark one driveway, I turn da steering wheel one hahd left fo' spin da cah into it, den let da momentum carry da cah—going forward now—down da hill.

I do all dis wit'out firing da engine.

Den I turn da key. Hoh, da buggah purrs. Da buggah ride smooth now. Empty of its burden, I guess. I punch in da cigarette lightah an' light up. Gee, maybe I should keep da cah.

I put in gas on Vineyard, pay cash so no mo' paypah trail, den get on da H-1 fo' da long drive back to Wai'anae. Fuck, I space out fo' da whole drive. I no even turn on da radio.

When I get home I scrub da Chevy ovah and ovah. Den I take one long, hot showah, sitting down in da stall, letting da watah wash ovah me. I am so fricken tired, I jes' fall on da fucking bed, wearing only my bebedees.

By da time I get up, shit, stay dark again. What da fuck? I stay, da kine, disoriental fo' a while. Den I look at my watch. Shit, I wen' sleep fifteen hours! Worse, I nevah make it back to the dumping ground.

I go in da living room, look at my choice karaoke machine, an' t'ink, *You, you fuckah, you got me into dis mess.*

If I only wen' save some of da fricken cash dat went into dis—

I turn it on. I staht playing my favorite CD: *The Best of Bobby Darin.* I turn up da volume and staht singing: "Dream Lover, until then . . . ," clearing my t'roat until I sound okay. Den it's "Splish Splash, I was takin' a bath . . . " —my favorite song, small-kid time, da one I use' to sing in da showah night aftah night.

I dance aroun' in my bebedees, ja' like Tom Cruise. Da song go by so fast. Den it's "Oh, the shark has pretty teeth, dear/An' he shows them pearly white. . . . " I add more bass, push da treble all da way up. Man, dis is sonic heaven.

No, no, heaven is what follows. Da heart-stoppah, da classic, my all-time favorite song:

Somewhere . . . beyond the sea
Somewhere waiting for me
If I could fly like birds up high
Then straight to your arms I'd go sailing

Gee, whatevah happen to Bobby Darin? Heard da buggah wen' die. O' maybe I confusing him wit' Sam Cooke. Maybe dey bote dead, dead as da guy I jes' wen' dump in da pond. In any case, wherevah you are, braddah Bobby, you da man. You are da man.

I so tired my voice come out real raspy-smooth. Kinda like John Lennon. Kinda soulful. I fricken tired, but I no like stop. Da mo' I sing, da bettah I feel. I staht feeling really good. I feel like nobody can take dis away from me now. I'm a changed man. It's time to walk da straight line. No mo' crazy shit. Fuck, I no even feel like goin' to chicken fights. Gambling is too damn dangerous. Maybe jes' da fi' dollah kine, on NFL games. Addawise, shit, I'm cured. I don't need all da bullshit. I jes' wanna sing. I jes' wanna keep on singing, man.

Except dat I stay starving. So I make some pancakes from da ready-made battah I always buy at Liliha Bakery, an' fry some strips of bacon an' t'ree eggs. Den I make some Lion coffee. Oh, man, ev'ryt'ing smell so good.

An' ev'ryt'ing *taste* so fucking good. So 'ono, man. I nevah know I was dis hungry. I scarf it down fast.

Aftahwards I sit on da sofa, contemplating my new life. I no care what kine job I gon' have. I willing to work my ass off ev'ry day. Construction, maintenance, whatevah. As long as I can sing my songs and eat 'ono grinds.

Den I hit the sack again.

I open my eyes and Harley stay right in my face. *Shit. Fuck. What time is it?*

"Where you wen' bury da body?" He's standing right ovah me. I dunno how he got in.

"I nevah bury 'om." He stay glaring at me. I sit up. "What time is it?" I scratch my nuts.

"Little past midnight, fuckhead. Where's da body? Whatchu mean you nevah bury 'om?"

"I did bettah." I smile. Harley, he smile too, real big. I tell him about da pond way up Nu'uanu. "Not Jackass Ginger," I tell 'om. "Little bit above dat. I dunno if get one name." I tell him how da buggah stay weighed down. He look pleased. He tell me, "Good, da buggah gon' decompose fastah." Den he say, "Hey, we go celebrate. Let's go fo' a ride, man." An' I say, "Okay. What da hell." Den he says, "Gee, get dressed. You not gon' out like dat."

I grab one pair of jeans, put 'om on, an' pick up da shirt dat stay on my rocking chair. Harley stay checking out my karaoke machine.

"Man, I gotta spend mo' time ovah here." He turns to me. "Not now, dough. Let's go."

While I stay buttoning my shirt I close da door behind us. I wondah again how he got in. I always make sure da doors and windows stay locked. I get deadbolts an' ev'ryt'ing.

We no get into Harley's Cadillac. He like I take my Chevy. He tell me I should drive. His parasite buddy,

Alfred, his gopher and mayjah intimidatah, jumps in on da passenger side.

Harley, he no get in. He jes' say, "I gon' pick up some beer and poké first. Meet you guys. . . . Tell 'om whe' fo' go, Al."

Al nods, looking straight ahead. "To da beach," he tell me. "Yokohama."

Harley follow us out on the road, an' when I turn right on Farrington Highway, da buggah turn left. I stay t'inking, he coulda stayed behind us and buy da booze at da Mākaha 7-Eleven. Plus, he not da type fo' pick up stuff fo' anybody else. *Shit*. Somet'ing's wrong here.

"So, like, what's da deal?" I say to Al. I ease up on da gas pedal.

"Da deal? What deal?"

"What is dis about?"

"Pahty time, man. Jes' keep driving. Like mo' dan five miles an hour."

It hits me now. "Why me?"

"What you talkin' about?"

"You know what I mean. Be straight wit' me, Al."

"I dunno what you talkin' about. Like I said, man, it's pahty time."

"Den how come Harley no like be pahty to it, hah? Whe' you planning fo' bury *me*?"

"You talk too fricken much." Da buggah slide down in his seat, like he stay planning fo' nod off.

"Is dat da reason? Is dat what Harley t'ink? Hey, I nevah did rat on anybody. Evah. I have *nevah* been one snitch in my whole life an' you know it, man."

"Talk-talk-talk. Talk-talk-talk. Shit, if Harley wanted you dead he would do it himself. . . . You too paranoid, brah. Keep asking questions an' I *have* to shoot you."

"Hey, hey, sorry. You know, I jes' tired, man. I no can t'ink straight." I pick up speed. Twenty-five, then thirty miles per hour. Dat's as fast as I wanna go.

By da time we arrived at da beach, da paranoia is back. T'ing is, Harley nevah forgives a loan. Who was I tryna fool? Harley will make you do stuff, dirty shit, but once you in his debt, you always always owe him. Dass how he got to be Harley Evans.

We walk along da sand. Gee, da stars, so pretty. Da ocean, so peaceful. I feel like singing.

> *Somewhere, beyond the sea,*
>   *somewhere, waiting for me . . .*

I look back, an' sure enough, Alfred has his gun out. Look like one nine millameetah. My heart sinks.

I need time. "Before you shoot me . . . "

"I said, I not gon' shoot you." He points wit' his gun toward de ocean. "I jes' want you to go for a swim."

"Bullshit."

"No bullshit."

"You want me to drown?"

"Well, dass up to you. I dunno how good you swim. You might survive."

"You gon' make sure of dat, eh? . . . Lemme jes' tell you something first." *You fucking has-been stooge.* "Harley's fingerprints are all ovah da dead guy. I made sure a' dat."

"Bullshit. You wouldn't know how to make sure a' dat." He points da gun at my face.

"An' da only way you can undo da damage is to pull up dat body, man, if you can find it, and remove da evidence. An' furdamo', da only way you can find da body is wit' my help."

"Bullshit."

"T'ink about it." I *have* to sell him on dis.

"You bettah be wrong, you slimy shit."

"Why? What you gon' do if I wrong? Kill me?" *Damn loozah son-of-a-bitch.*

"Start swimming."

It ain't working. *C'mon, Spark, you can talk one guy on welfare into buying one Mercedes.* "Look, braddah, let's figgah somet'ing out." I need some bargaining space, man. "Why should we all go down?"

"Jes' you. Nobody gon' catch Harley. He's *too* smooth. Staht swimming."

"C'mon. You know dis can work fo' ev'rybody. Let's figgah somet'ing out. . . . I got one nice piece o' land. An' I not talking about Pondarosa Pines."

"Fuck you an' yaw damn land."

Fuck you and yaw land. Fuck you and yaw land. I've heard dat too many times. "Hey, wait, wait. You know I got da best music setup on da Wai'anae Coast. Fucking Bose speakahs, man. Surround-sound. *Bose.* Da whole t'ing, all yaws. Fo' naht'ing."

"I got my own."

"I bet it's not Bose."

"Fuck. You don't even know. You t'ink you da on'y jackass dat got direct-reflecting speakahs? Hah?" He waves da gun, motioning fo' me to entah da watah.

"Why? What kine you get?"

"I got one Yamaha CD playah, one Technics receivah, two Bose direct-reflecting speakahs, a couple of Altec/Lansings. . . ." He raises his hand way ovah his head. "Huge fucking speakahs."

"Well, imagine if you add mo' Bose speakahs to dat. Multiple speakahs in ev'ry room, braddah. 'Magine the sound you can get wit' my Pioneer surround-sound receivah with video inputs. Not jes' audio, brah. An' da bes' paht is . . . *karaoke* . . . "

"You know what? You convinced me, brah. 'Cause right aftah we done heah I gon' back yaw house and pick 'om up. Fo' free."

"'Ass what I mean, fo' free. You lemme go and it's yaws, man. If you jes' take 'om, shit, dass grand larceny."

"You dumb shit. Harley saw yaw setup. You t'ink he don't have plans fo' 'om already? Fo' all I know, he stay at yaw house right now, taking 'om apart and loading his cah."

I gotta play my trump card. "Hey, I got friends. Friends who gon' figgah out what happened."

"Friends, shit."

Dat was my ace. An' he jes' wen' piss on dat ace an' da buggah stay dissolving. Disinagrading. I get chicken skin. *Friends, shit.* Dass so fuckin' true. I got no real friends. I mean, I tot Harley an' Big Al was my friends.

Alfred finally figgah out I stay tryin' fo' stall him. All of a sudden, he real pissed off. He stay waving da gun again. "Get in da fucking watah!"

I keep my clothes on and step into da ocean. Hoh shit, so fricken cold! *Fuck!* Den I staht hearing da song in my head again. It warms me up little bit.

> *Somewhere . . . beyond the sea*
> *somewhere waitin' for me*

I staht singing out loud:

> *My lover stands on golden sands*
> *and watches da ships dat go sailing . . .*

"Eh, fuck," Al says. "Shut up 'fo' you wake up all da fish."

I sing loudah, working da inflection, swaying and snapping my fingahs. Dis one audition I gotta fucking pass.

> *It's far . . . beyon' da stars*
> *it's near beyon' da moon*
> *I know—*

Da buggah raise his gun and aim 'om at me so I shut up. I hold my hands up, an' da wave almos' knock me down. I keep singing da words, inside my head. It's da only comfort I have right now. Finally, I turn around an' jump in toward da incoming waves, manini-kine waves. I not one good swimmah. Shit, I haven't been in da watah in ages. I look back and dat fucking Alfred he stay waving me on. I staht t'inking, fuck, I ain't gon' drown, man. I can wade long time, all night if I have to, till da early morning surfahs come out. He cannot do shit den.

If I have to go down, I taking somebody wit' me.

I turn on my back an' look towards da shore. Shit, he stay stripping down. He get some kinda object in his hand. An' no look like da gun. Look mo' like one billy club.

Shit. Dis is it. I goin' out fighting, man. I'm fucking tired but I mo' tired of playing dese fucking shit-ass games. Where da fuck did it get me? I jes' gon' wait fo' da buggah. I gon' wear 'om out, da fucking fat shit. I gon' float on my back, resting—until he come an' try finish me off.

But I sked. What if no work? Dis is fo' real, man. Shit, I no like die. An' what now? Look like *two* guys coming aftah me. Shit, must be Harley. Unless I hallucinating. Man, da eye play tricks on you when yaw life is passing you by.

I stay waiting, but kinda moving little bit, drifting back an' left, den mo' back an' left, den back an' right. Zigging an' a zagging, splishing an' a splashing. I figgah, let 'om get tired tryna catch me. Fucking guy outa shape anyway. I hope he die from one fricken heart attack.

But, shit, he stay swimming strong. An' jes' when I figure *Dis is it, stupid, you blew it, you fucking dead, you da dumpee,* jes' as Al is almos' on me, somet'ing come from undah da watah and pulls him down. *Holy shit!* Jes' wen'

I figure *I* goin' down, *he* goes down. . . . All I see is bubbles an' signs of some undahwatah struggle.

I no feel any relief, man, 'cause I stay swimming sideways and t'inking *SHARK!* and I tell you, I stay ready to shit my fricken pants. I'm freaking out, man. I gon' be da next to go when dis turn into one fucking feeding frenzy. *Hoh man.* I ain't out of da woods yet. Not by a long shot. An' I too fucking sked fo' be happy about Alfred's fate.

Funny t'ing, I no see blood. Instead I see somebody swimming towards me. Can't be Al. Shit, I hope it's not Harley.

Manny? Look like Manny. *What da fuck would he be doing out here? Is he in on dis?*

"You can swim?" da fuckah says. Not even "Hi."

I shaking so fucking much I hahdly can nod.

"Good," he tell me, "'cause I fucking exhausted. Let's go."

"Wheah?"

"Out."

"So I can get shot o' something? Harley gon' get me." I stay treading watah ferociously. He hahdly moving.

"Jes' follow me. Harley ain't gon' do shit to nobody."

Man, I knew dis Manny was one strange cookie. Fuck, I no even know who's side he on. Like dose WWF wreslahs. He musta killed Al, so he cannot be on deah side. So I figgah I got naht'ing to lose.

When we out of da watah, he tell me, "Get in the car." He no mean mine. He referring to one adda cah, which turns out to be Alfred's. One dat was prob'ly left here all along. Part a' da plan. Manny lays out one double-folded beach towel on da seat fo' my wet ass, an' drives to one place deep in da valley, kind of like one hideout, like we goin' to da Batcave o' somet'ing.

The place isn't dat impressive, dough. Turns out to be one old bus dat he stay using fo' living quartahs. Like some adda jobless guys I know. But it's wired like naht'ing I've evah seen, with alarms dat he gotta shut off befo' he let me even come close. We rinse off wit' one hose, den he tell me fo' go sleep, dat tomorrow gon' be one big day. *Yeah, like today was easy.* He already on his cellular.

"Who you talking to?" He jes' shake his head.

At about six in da morning—still dark—he wake me up an' say, "Wear dis." I look at da clothes, an whadaya know, look like fit. "Lucky thing I get one friend your size . . . taller than you, dough, so I think you gotta roll up da pants. . . . Evah been to da Caribbean?"

"Where dat?" I get one image of cruise ships.

He smiles. "Heard of Puerto Rico?"

"Potta Rico? Hey, my stepfaddah Potta Rican. I grew up on pa'tele, gandule rice, bacalao." Shit, I miss dat stuff. Almost as much as I miss one good night's sleep.

"Think of being able to eat food like that and having no Harley Evans to bother you."

"Hey, what a minute. You talkin' about me . . . " I choke. ". . . leaving Hawai'i?"

"Jes' for little while. Until we nail that fricken Harley. Here." He hand me one cup coffee.

I take a sip. Hoh, da hot. "You one cop?"

He shake his head.

"I bet you working for da Feds. You working fo' da Feds, eh?"

"Fuck no."

"Who, den?"

"The cops and me have an understanding. If they don't fuck with me, I don't fuck with them."

"How come you—"

"Look, we ain't got time for Q an' A. Let's jes' say that some relationships come in handy."

I get dressed an' den we step out of da bus. Da yahd, if you can call it one yahd, look like had one huge oil spill. One fucking enviramento nightmare. Except fo' da bushes an' cactus. "I bet you know all kine shit, hah?"

He look straight at me. "Another day, brah."

"You really t'ink you can get me off dis rock? What if people come aftah me? Harley's boys, dey watch da airport too."

"They're not gonna look for you if they think you dead. Right? Think about it. Alfred is shark shit by now, but they're not gonna find any trace of *him* at Yokohama. Jes' traces of *you*." He smiles. "And before we get rid of his car, we have to have you donate a few drops of blood."

"How come?"

"We need to plant a trail. A false trail. Jes' a few drops."

"Fuck. I hate bleed."

"Hey, I'd do it for you, but it's gotta be your blood . . . your DNA. To save your fricken life."

Den it hits me, da magnitude of his help. Fo' one degenerate fuck like me. Why?

I let him prick my fingah. I no like look. We leave a few drops on da drivah's seat. An' in da trunk. Den we get into one Honda Civic.

"Who's cah dis?" I say while I strap on da seatbelt.

"Mine."

"What about Al's cah?"

"What about it? No worry, I got a friend coming. He'll take care of it."

"You know what? Why you no take my karaoke machine . . . an' ev'ryt'ing dat comes wit' it."

"Is it all paid for?"

"I paid fo' it cash."

"Mmmm. Maybe my friend could, um . . . repossess it."
He looks at me. "To pay your funeral bill, of course . . .
Or, maybe he can jes' hold onto it. Hmmm. Then again I
could ship it to Puerto Rico."

Potta Rico. Sounded scary and beautiful at da same
time. "Nah, nah, jes' sell 'om, man. . . . I really appreciate
dis, man. Braddah . . ." I grab his shoulder. "I love you fo'
saving my sorry ass."

Manny puts his hand on my hand. "You need to duck
out of sight until we get out of Wai'anae."

I unfasten da seatbelt an' slip down in da seat.

"I got some stuff for you in the trunk. Carry-on stuff. It's
like American Express. You can't leave home without it."

"Aftah you drop me off, you gon' go aftah Harley?"

"Not yet," he says. "I got a plane to catch too."

"Whe' you goin'?"

"Nevada."

Nevada? "You mean, Vegas?"

Da buggah snickah. Den he say, "I'm a gambler, but not that
kind of gambler. . . . I jes' need to leave till things cool off."

*Yeah, you dumb shit. He wen' kill somebody. To save
yaw dumb ass.*

"I'll be back soon enough. Lots of unfinished business.
Right now we gotta stop at a friend's house and give you a
makeover."

Two hours laytah me an' Manny stay flyin' on Conti-
nental Flight 451 to L.A. Manny stay sitting way in da
back. I'm almos' in da middle, but I get one window seat.
We can't let on dat we know each adda.

Fucking seating is tight. I t'ink next time I gon' fly one
adda airline. *Next time.* An' can hahdly see da damn
screen. Shit, I hope dey show one junk movie, so I no need
watch.

When we reach L.A. I gotta change planes an' fly to
New Orleans. Da Mardi Gras place. Den across to dat
island dat Manny wen' show me on a map. Fuck, I
nevah know Cuba was dat close to Potta Rico. An' so
big . . .

I get one new look, one new ID, and fifteen hundred in
cash. I also have one job waiting fo' me in one place called
Ponce. I dunno how he did it, but Manny really wen' sell
me on dis crazy adventure. I feel reborn. I feel like one
changed man.

But I feeling kinda sad, too. I hoping I no miss Hawai'i
too much. I hope I can return befo' long. 'Cause, man, I
get fam'ly here. Shit, I get memories here. An' at least one
friend.

I look out da window fo' try an' see da ocean, but I
only see clouds. White and pink. Maybe dass what dey
mean when dey say scarlet billows. Fuck, I wish I had one
vocabalary, but I use' to jes' fuck aroun' in school.

I guess we stay somewhere *beyond* the sea. All dose
songs stahting to make sense. I guess traveling's good. I
glance back at Manny. I fight da urge to give 'om one
shaka sign—my way of saying *t'anks, brah*. He stay
wearing shades. Can't tell if he looking back at me o'
sleeping. Den da plane shake. Fucking turbalence. Jes'
when da flight attendants was gon' staht da meal service.
Shee, da plane shaking like anyt'ing now. Seatbelt sign
stay on. Da flight attendant walking down da aisle, seeing if we stay belted. I wink at her. She smile, but dass
paht of her job.

I ain't worried, 'cause if deah's a God, he wouldn't take dis
plane down, not wit' one babe like da flight attendant o' one
cool guy like Manny aboard. An' even we did crash, if we
ended up in da watah, I can't t'ink of anybody I'd raddah be
out in da ocean wit' dan Manny. So I jes' sit back an' close
my eyes. 'Cause I can finally relax now.

A Spark Is Struck

(Wai'anae—Spring 1995)

Henry

Twelve of us walked up to Evans' house. Sam, Sparkey's brother Dave, Jerome, Skip, Bully, and I dunno who else. Half of us still in black pants, black shoes, and white dress shirts. We would have been the pallbearers, had there been a body to bury.

"We like talk to Harley," Sam told Tweety, Harley's girlfriend.

Sam, a former cop who was now a private investigator, was gonna do most of the talking. I stood right next to him. When we left the beach ceremony on foot and walked to the 7-Eleven—funny, one guy runs out of smokes and eleven guys cross the road with him—all the while we were talking about Sparkey. Everybody had stories. Sparkey was a fuck-up, but we loved the guy. The thing that pissed me off most was there wasn't even a body, just traces of him: a shirt and blood stains police found in a car near Yokohama. Shit, the family had no body to identify . . . or claim . . . or say farewell to—just like Keoni's family so long ago. That's the sickest part, man. I was a little afraid, coming here, but now the fear was gone.

One thing about Harley, he may be a dirty operator, a fucking slimewad, but the fuck-ass has no fear. He came out by himself. He didn't even have his trademark silkie shirt on yet. He was buttoning it as he stepped outside.

Already I could see curtains moving in the nearby houses.

"Sheezus," he said, smiling, "what brings you all heah?" He turned to the house. "Tweety, bring some beeah."

"We don't wanna drink, Harley," Sam said. "We jes' came fo' tell you to get out of Wai'anae." I didn't really know Sam, but I liked his style. "We know you had somet'ing to do wit' Sparkey's death—"

Harley held his hands up. "Whoa, whoa, whoa. Hold on. I had *naht*'ing to do wit' Sparkey. Sparkey had choke enemies, man. You guys should at least do some checking first."

"Name one," I said, right when somebody else said, "We did."

Harley looked at me. Probably wondered who the fuck I was. He shrugged his shoulders, held his palms open. I could see scars and bruises on his veiny arms, marks that I bet if one were to follow them, led inevitably to Sparkey's fatal end.

"Look, you fucking piece of criminal shit—" Dave started to say.

"Hey, yaw braddah was da criminal—"

Sam held Dave from stepping forward. I had never met any of Sparkey's kin before. He lived alone, though I heard he entertained women, ones he picked up at various clubs, from time to time. At the funeral there were lots and lots of his relatives.

Just then, from the makai direction, a large, navy-blue Oldsmobile rolled slowly up the street.

"Look like your goons have arrived," Sam said.

It hit me then that I was staring death in the face. As much as I am drawn toward confrontations, I suddenly wanted this one to stay as cool as possible. I remembered stories of how Harley and his boys took care of some judge, which was how Harley had beaten a previous murder rap. Fear was back, abating my anger.

Then a little girl, about five years old, wearing a dirty t-shirt and shorts, came walking up the road's edge, pulling behind her a string attached to a wooden duck that made a *quack-quack* noise when the wheels turned. I probably was the only one who entertained the thought that the duck might be a bomb. *Quack-quack.* I dunno what the other guys were thinking, but something about this moment, this seemingly innocent act, made everybody freeze. *Quack-quack, quack-quack, quack-quack.* Nobody seemed to know what to do as she took forever to cross between Harley and the rest of us. The duck would fall, and she would stop, set it right, then start pulling it again. *Quack-quack, quack-quack.* Each time the duck fell over I cringed, half-expecting it to explode, taking all of us with it.

Then she stopped right between Harley and our group. We all had been silent for what seemed like minutes, watching her. The car had come to a full stop too. But the driver had left the engine idling. Something's gonna blow, I thought. The *quack-quack*ing duck, the men in the Olds, Harley—something. The mood was too rife with tension for it not to. My eyes were on the duck. I fought the urge to run and grab it and fling it as far as I could.

Then the little girl spoke: "You having one meeting, Uncle Hahley?"

"Yeah, Honey-girl . . . one meeting."

"What about?"

Harley smiled, and said, "About bad little girls who ask questions." The buggah sneered at her playfully, his hands outstretched, his fingers made to look like claws, and he took some quick steps toward her. She started running, pulling the fallen duck, laughing in play-acting fear.

"Mommy," she shrieked. "Uncle Hahley said he gon' catch me-e-e-e-e!"

And into her mother's arms. The mom had come out of the house next door. Ohh, what a tortured and pretty face. A few years ago she may have been her high school's homecoming queen, or at least one of the princesses. But there was a defeated quality to her appearance.

She looked at us, then Harley. She knew better than to say anything. She stood there, braless, mute, her breasts already loose and sagging beneath her ragged tank top. Her shorts also too loose, her shoulders sloping forward. Her hair looked unwashed, like it had been pinned up in a hurry. She pulled back some loose strands of her brown hair, showing in her cool yet concerned expression a quiet reconciliation with the cards she got dealt, and took the kid into the house.

No one said anything, but it looked like Harley now had the upper hand. He appeared more confident, relaxed. No doubt, his boys had weapons, perhaps an arsenal. And us guys, so foolish, we just had numbers. Maybe Sam had a gun, but I couldn't see one on him.

"So, ah," Harley said, "where were we?"

Just then a black '59 Impala with large tailfins came cruising down the road from the mauka direction. It rolled slowly toward the Olds, until the bumpers were against each other. *Shit.* It's my tattooed friend. Mr. Here-One-Day, Gone-the-Next. The paint job on his car had thrown me. It made his arrival more ominous, even though it was daylight. He cut his engine and the driver of the Olds cut his engine too. Manny, shirtless, as usual, got out of his car. *Oh, shit! He has a fucking shotgun!* Oh man, it's really gonna blow now.

Ignoring the guys in the Olds, Manny aimed the gun at Harley's face. Harley's goons had their revolvers out. Shit, this world is too damn violent. I should just walk away. Throw my hands up and say, *fuck this shit.*

Get real, Henry. I started thinking about plan B. As soon as the shooting starts, I run low and dive through the bushes, roll over and over away from the scene, and get clean out of there. Highly implausible, but the only weapon I got is my mind and IT AIN'T WORKING TOO WELL!

Manny spoke. He was still aiming the gun at Harley. "I can only guarantee one t'ing, Harley. Any o' dem—" Manny nodded toward the car—"any of your fucking lowlife stooges make the slightest fricken move . . . and *you* gon' follow Sparkey." Manny turned his chin a bit toward us. "Da pallbearers already here."

Those words struck a chord with Harley. He snickered and looked down, sliding his left rubber slipper back and forth on the dirt.

"So, what's your call?" Manny added.

Harley gestured with a hand wave, like he was erasing a smudge on a chalkboard with his palm. The guys in the Olds put their guns down. The driver fired up the engine. They seemed quite relaxed, scarily professional about it all. I recognized the one in the front passenger seat. He used to go to Sparkey's house. He was at the funeral, too. Knowing how things operate in Wai'anae, he had probably grown up and hung out with some of the guys I now stood with. The driver slowly backed up, swung the car around, and cruised down the road. Manny went back to his car. Before getting in, he looked at Sam. "Got it undah control?" Sam nodded. Manny got into his car, lay the gun at his side, and sat there with his eyes closed, like he was going to nap.

"Well," Sam said, "back to our discussion."

"Why you guys wanna make it hard?" Harley said. "Sparkey's dead . . . right? From what you tell me. An' I telling you I had *naht*'ing fo' do wit' it. Zero."

"Eh, we not *stupid*, Harley. Da cops may be stupid, but, fuck, we know. So we giving you one fucking chance. You looking at da neighborhood watch of Wai'anae, man. An' us guys," Sam stabbed the air with his index finger, punctuating each syllable, "we voted you out."

I glanced at Manny in his car. His eyes were closed. Did he nod out?

Tweety came by the door, smoking a cigarette, her foot keeping the screen door from closing. Like the neighbor woman, there was that cheapness about her that took away from what might have been stunning beauty. More fucking waste.

Harley spat on the ground. "How much time you giving me?"

"How much time you gave my braddah, hah?" Dave said, as he stepped forward. "Hah?" Sam yanked him back.

Harley held his hands up, showing palm. "Okay. Okay. Let's say in two weeks I'm outa heah. Fuck, I'm totally innocent. You gotta at least gimme time fo' straighten t'ings out, right? I mean, fuck, I'm outa here. Who wants to live in one fucking vigilante community—"

"Vigilante, your ass," someone said.

"You got two days. Fawty-eight hours. An' no even T'INK"—Sam raised his index finger "—no even T'INK of any kind of retaliation, man." Those words seemed to stir Manny. He opened his eyes and gazed at Harley. "If anyt'ing, ANYT'ING, happen to ANY one of dese boys heah, or our friends and families, I PERSONALLY guarantee . . . you one dead man."

"Hey. Keep it cool, man. I'm outa here. I'm gone."

Harley was on his way to his beach house in Haleʻiwa
that evening. Lucky for him he was in between the two
places. Because that night both his houses exploded in
flames. In Waiʻanae neighbors saw what looked like a
freshly painted, black '59 Impala roll by. The stereo in the
car was so loud it woke up the entire neighborhood.
Somebody said it was all Rolling Stones songs—playing at
earth-shaking volume. Later some neighbors were argu-
ing, one of them claiming the songs were "Paint It Black"
and "Gimme Shelter"; another insisted it was "Playing
with Fire" and "Tumbling Dice." Still another insisted it
was live versions of those songs. One neighbor said the
driver, wearing all black, including gloves, and a wool-type
cap that covered most of his face, poured gasoline around
the yard, threw a lighted match, and stood there to watch
it burn, burn, burn. He only took off when the sirens came
close.

The same thing happened soon after in Haleʻiwa. The
key difference in this case was the silence. No one heard or
saw a damn thing.

And then a boat in the small boat harbor burst into flames.

□ □ □

Police found four bodies in the area surrounding
Manny's bus, which had been torched. The bus was now a
burnt-out, bullet-riddled shell. The forensics people had
a field day. Later, when the scorched bodies were identi-
fied, authorities learned that these men were associates of
one Harley Evans.

Detectives are looking for Harley, who's been in hiding. A body was fished out of the Nuʻuanu Stream—
deep shoeprints and dragmarks in the area had aroused
suspicion. This unidentified victim was also linked to
Harley.

Another Harley associate, Alfred Kim, is missing. It was his car that was found with Sparkey's blood in it. Police have lots of questions.

And the Property Damage Unit is investigating the fires, which everyone knows were caused by arson. But nobody's talking. I mean we talk amongst each other, neighbor to neighbor, but nobody's giving the police anything. Nobody's giving them shit.

ʻAwa Interlude

Three men sat on three sides of a rectangular lau hala mat made of the most excellent weave. Each man faced the center, where they had placed a poi pounder, an ipu pueo, a large, exquisitely shaped koa bowl, four coconut shell bowls, and a dipper—also made of coconut.

The koa bowl was half full with ʻawa. One of the men took the kīʻoʻe, the dipper, and stirred the numbing, intoxicating froth.

This same man scooped out liquid portions with the kīʻoʻe and poured them into the four smaller bowls. The three men lifted the bowls to their lips and drank.

A fourth man arrived. His head was covered by a hood. He walked around the mat, embracing each man. The older man, the one who had stirred the ʻawa, handed a bowl to this fourth man, who had just sat down, like the others, cross-legged on the mat.

"Drink," the older man said. The hooded man stirred the pale yellow mixture with a finger and he too drank.

The man slipped off his hood, unzipped his parka, and took the garment off. There were tattoos on his arms, legs, chest, and back.

The four men continued to drink from their bowls, the older man refilling them every now and then.

After a while this older man spoke:
"Remember, we never asked you to cause pilikia. We only asked that you help set things right."
The tattooed man nodded.

"We never wanted you in jail. Enough of our people . . . "

"That's not your problem."

"It is our problem," one of the other men said. He was young, lean, his body toughened by outdoor labor.

"We hear you have an accomplice," the older man continued.

"He wanted to help. He's been very helpful."

"We didn't want anyone else involved."

"But he's special. He's my—"

"Leave him out of it. You work alone. Understand?"

The man with the tattoos nodded. "Right."

The third man, the eldest of the three, who had been quiet the entire time, said, "We never told you to flatten tires or remove steering wheels from cars . . . "

"Or ignition wires," the younger man added, smirking.

"Never."

"We never told you," the oldest continued, "to take drastic steps. Even in retaliation for the destruction of our 'aumakua, even for the careless disregard for life."

"Never."

"We never told you to take up weapons of destruction."

"No, never."

"We will never ever ask you to take a life. No matter how corrupt that life is."

The tattooed man is quiet.

"Of course, we are concerned with the level of corruption rampant along this coast. We simply want our 'ohana free of corrupters."

"Exactly."

"Construction workers are digging up the bones of our ancestors again. We don't want you to get involved with that."

"I won't be."

"Military personnel have found bones on Kohe Mālamalama o Kanaloa."

"I've heard."

"People are playing jurisdictional games."

"As always."

"Ignore the matter."

"As always."

The tattooed man stood up. "Is that it?"

"It's also come to my attention that you've been taking notes."

The tattooed man points to his head. "It's mostly here."

"Have you been taking notes?"

"Only to keep track of—"

"More pilikia," the younger man said.

"Burn them. And stop writing things down."

"Never write about us," the second oldest said.

"Never."

The tattooed man put his parka back on, lifted the hood over his head. He got up and again embraced each of the three men, then left.

The man with the coconut dipper spooned out 'awa, refilling all four bowls. The three who sat there drank, while the bowl that the tattooed man had drunk from sat there brimming.

Na Wai E Hoʻōla I Nā Iwi?

(Oʻahu and Kahoʻolawe—Late Spring 1995)

The family of the deceased gathered around the large stone at midnight. They had paid a thousand dollars for this ceremony. They had come to a sacred place, the launching point for the souls of the dead. The west and north shores met here—kissed, caressed, pounded. Rocks lined the ocean's floor in curious formation. Surfers rarely challenged the treacherous waves, the cutting reefs, the danger zone that was Kaʻena Point.

But the family was on land. These were English-speaking, pidgin-speaking Hawaiians who knew only fragments of the language of their ancestors, and they listened with warm hearts to this man they thought of as an attendant priest—a kahu, or even kahuna. And they listened to him chant. In this sacred hour.

This "kahuna" had grown up in a high-class residential area in East Honolulu. After graduating from Kamehameha, quite close to the top of his class, he took one of the many scholarships offered by the richest school in the United States and went to Mills College. There he didn't fare well. He had fallen in love with a beautiful haole woman in his religion class. They dated for a while. When she lost interest in him, it broke his heart. The cold, rainy weather only added to his misery. Finally he transferred to the University of Hawai'i, where he graduated in political science in 1986. *In this sacred hour.*

During the same year that musicians throughout the Western hemisphere declared they weren't gonna play Sun City, he frolicked on the beach of Waikīkī, looking for a woman who would fill the void created by the blonde woman back at Mills. After a year of partying—drinking too much beer, snorting too much coke—he applied to several law schools. Georgetown took him. *In this sacred hour.*

When bones of ancient Hawaiians were being dug up at Honokahua, Kalama Housseman was living in the District of Columbia, getting quite chummy with one of Hawai'i's representatives to Congress. This representative later set Housseman up with an internship with a circuit court judge back in Hawai'i. So he interned. And partied. For the next two summers. *In this sacred hour.*

Whereas in the profane hours of the fall and spring semesters he sweated out his classes and exams.

In D.C., he fell in love with a woman in a Virginia senator's office. He loved the lilt of her Southern drawl, the way it seemed to convey a stand-by-your-man ethic. He appealed to her ambition, promised her the world, and convinced her to return to Hawai'i with him.

In 1991, when Congress passed the Native American Graves Protection and Repatriation Act, or NAGPRA, Housseman claimed to have been instrumental in its passage and immediately formed a hui that would see to the repatriation of Hawaiian bones. He became, in a few short years, a spiritual leader, a self-designated kahuna to whom Hawaiians with less education turned, to see that things were done right. To his followers he appeared to be one of the enlightened ones.

In this sacred hour.

The family of the deceased felt they were getting their money's worth. Housseman's chant was carried in the wind. The air was humid, the sky threatening thunder. Every distant light seen by family members, whether the reflection of a watch face or a flashlight being carried by a soldier pissing on the shore of Keawaʻula Bay, was seen as a soul making its passage.

A man with deep-set eyes looked on, content. He had asked permission of his subordinate—these were ironic times—to come witness this ceremony. The man with deep-set eyes, the head of the department, a man whose restrained activism had made him an unlikely political appointee (a masterstroke on the part of the governor, who knew to keep his enemies close), had no inkling as to the degree of verisimilitude contained in this event; it looked authentic enough. And although complaints had come from other sectors— even his leading archaeologist, Leimomi Luʻuwai-Wong, had complained to him—he was too busy putting out fires in other divisions to worry about the subtleties of ritual.

Leimomi stood a hundred yards away, her arms folded. She could hear pieces of the chant—a phrase here, another there. She knew that her familiarity with the Hawaiian language, while limited, went deeper than Housseman's, and as she watched this young man, a rising star in the political world, play loose with sacred ritual, she wished there were a TV camera present. But then she had stopped praying that people be held accountable. Because she knew better. *In this sacred hour.*

Two weeks later

"Maaaaa! Telephonnnne! Auntie Momi!"

Kanani comes out of the bathroom, closing her robe. "I'll get it in the bedroom . . ." Kanani picks up the phone on her dresser. "What's up, sis?"

"I have some news that might just blow you away."

Kanani closes the bedroom door. "Is this gonna take long?"

"No, but you might wanna sit down."

Kanani sits on her bed, letting her robe fall open.

"We were going over one of the most artifact-filled sites on the island, when we came across some bones. And these weren't goat bones. At first we thought, this is the guy who disappeared a few months back. Remember that story? His wife had said he never came back from fishing. He was thought to have drowned. Then authorities started getting curious about the wife. Found out she was running around with some other guy."

"Yeah, I remember."

"I wasn't the first one on the scene. Maui police and a couple Navy officers were there. And John, the Navy archaeologist. When I got there they seemed to have already agreed that it was a recent murder victim, so Maui County would take over. They have jurisdiction."

"At least until Housseman comes along, right?" Kanani, feeling a little impatient, stands up and grabs the hair brush on her vanity. She starts brushing her wet hair in front of the mirror while her sister continues.

"Well, that's just one of the glitches. This time it's way more complicated than that."

"How so?"

"For one thing, the Feds might wanna claim jurisdiction also, since the Navy is still involved with the target island—supervising the clean-up. And there's something else."

"What?"

"Well, I could tell right off that these bones had been there for ten at least, probably closer to twenty years."

Kanani drops the hair brush. "No." She sees her face in the mirror, turns from the sight. "You're not thinking—"

"Well, sis. You never know. Anything's possible."

"You're suggesting that after all the searches, after all the years of people tramping around—"

"Hey, we're still finding new artifacts. There's so many caves, gulches. . . . I mean, it's only a thought. A big *What if?* I'd really like to do some testing."

"Would they let you?" Kanani sits on the bed again, closing her robe, fingering the phone line.

"Not unless I steal it. Right now, the bones are on Maui. Housseman is flying there to look."

"Mr. Jurisdiction himself. Is he gonna claim that they're ancient?"

"Well, he can't do that. Not this time. But he will claim that the bones are Hawaiian."

"And are they?"

"Oh yeah. Sure are. Just ask da kanaka archaeologist. And . . . whoever it was, was murdered . . . "

"Murdered?"

"There was a bullet hole in the skull. I'm ninety-nine-point-nine percent sure it's a bullet hole."

"Can anything be done? I mean, to stop Housseman."

"Well, we could support Maui County's jurisdictional claims. We're talking about a homicide, Nani. *Whoever* the bones belong to."

"Oh boy, here we go. Another turf battle."

"It doesn't end. It may *seem* like a legitimate turf battle, but we know what's going on. Same as with the Forbes Cave stuff."

"That shit is scary. I mean, people are dying. You don't screw around with—"

"Well, unless we're willing to steal what could be Keoni's bones . . ."

There it is. Uttered. The thought given life.

Kanani inhales deeply. Exhales. "You're kidding, right? I mean about stealing it."

"I wish I weren't."

Kanani's robe falls open. At that moment she remembers too vividly Keoni's hands touching the same breasts the mirror now exposes.

"I hate to say it again, but . . . if you had told Henry from day one . . ."

"I know, I know. Instead of day ten thousand."

"Or never."

"Well, 'never' could work . . . if I were sure that Henry was Mākena's real father."

"Then it would be no problem."

"But I'm not sure. That's the thing. And to tell him at this point—"

"Oh, he'd be crushed."

"It would kill him."

Mākena, who's been listening on the other line, quietly hangs up when his kid brother enters the house.

Two days later

"So when Kalama Housseman came, he wasn't about to wait out the process. Remember, he's a lawyer, though a non-practicing lawyer. . . . He wrapped the bones in white kapa. He was headed for the helicopter to take him and the iwi to O'ahu, when Eli arrived. Eli confronted him. Told him, would Keoni have approved of this process? And suddenly there was this silence. Everybody seemed to arrive at the same notion. I mean *everybody* was on the same page. We were all acting like we *knew* it was Keoni's bones.

"Anyway, Housseman just said *Yes, he would've*, and headed for the helicopter. Eli cut him off. Housseman starting yelling at him: 'We can't let them x-ray the skeletal remains of Hawaiians. That's sacrilege!' Then Eli said, 'We don't know they're Hawaiian. The only way we only know for sure is through DNA—' And Housseman goes, 'My heart tells me these are the bones of a Hawaiian. That's all I need to know. And these haoles'—I guess he was referring to the pilot, the two Navy representatives, and of course, my co-worker, Myrna. Those were the only haoles there—he said, 'these haoles, they don't understand.'

"That's when Eli said, 'What if they're Keoni's bones? I think we *need* to find out. We need to know.' And Housseman goes, 'Keoni was Hawaiian. We can't subject his bones to DNA testing because it's sacrilege. It would destroy his mana.'"

"His mana *was* destroyed," Kanani says to her sister. "His mana would increase, if we could verify—. We need to know. His family needs to know."

"I agree. With the family we're talking lineal descent. And that can override all other claims. What we got is a Catch-22 situation."

"Wha' do you mean?"

"They can't claim lineal descent unless they know it's Keoni's bones. Plus, I don't see anybody rushing out to tell the family what they think they've found. They may never know. . . . You know what Housseman said to Eli—as he was about to board the plane?"

"What?"

"He said—you're not gonna believe this—he said, 'We cannot give up our hard-earned rights in an attempt to solve some modern-day crime.'

"At that point I couldn't keep my mouth shut. I yelled at him. I said, 'Not even when the victim is Hawaiian?' And he said, 'It's not pono.' I tell you, I wanted to pono his ass. Then he took off. Eli looked at me and said, 'If vindicating Keoni is not pono, if solving his murder is not right, then I don't know what the fuck is.'"

"So even Eli turned around on this."

"I tell you, it's a tough call . . . every which way you look at it."

The next day

". . . from what I heard, something got to Housseman during the flight. I heard he got real nervous. He was shaking like crazy, like he was suddenly afraid to fly."

"Maybe was Keoni's mana."

"Hey, you never know. I'm not one to disbelieve. Anyway, by the time he got to Oʻahu he was a fucking nervous wreck. . . . Now comes the really bizarre part. Hope you ready for this."

"Am I?" Kanani put a hand to her chest.

"Here goes. . . . You know I was kidding about stealing the bones, right?"

"Don't tell me you changed your mind."

"I didn't. But somebody did. They're gone."

"WHAT?"

"Disappeared."

"Fucking Housseman."

"No, it's not him."

"How can it not be? He's so devious. He's just gonna make it look like somebody else did it. While he's stashing them somewhere."

"Well, if you've seen him lately, you would know he ain't making this up. He hasn't slept. He's a total wreck. I almost pity him."

"The bones are . . . gone?"

"Stolen. Just like the kāʻai. Maybe by the same people."

"But . . . why?"

"Who knows? If we know who, then we know why. Could be some group who, like Housseman, doesn't want the bones x-rayed, or DNA'd. I mean, we could be talking

about AHOLA, OHA, Hawaiian Homes, Hui ʻŌiwi. . . .
There's even some woman claiming her ancestors came
from Kahoʻolawe. She's saying the bones are hers—lineal
descent again. Hey, I just had a thought. What if Keoni's
Hāna friends took the bones? You know *they're* capable."

A day later

"And guess what?"
   "I don't wanna know."
   "This you might. Housseman quit."
   "He quit?"
   "Yeah," Leimomi says while snickering. "He gave Mike
his resignation . . . and took a job with Bishop Estate."
   "Hmmph. That's where he belongs."

Graduation Day

(Wai'anae—Spring Yielding to Summer 1995)

Wai'anae High School's graduation was held on campus.

It was a joyous day for most. Seventy percent had graduated. Mākena, who graduated thirty-second in his class, had won an essay contest and was even cited for his surfing achievement several months earlier. He was planning to attend the University of Hawai'i. Everyone in school had treated him exceptionally kindly since the accident; he was excused from physical education, even though he didn't want to be, and he took a Polynesian instruments class instead. He picked up well on the 'ukulele. The class traveled to elementary schools in the Leeward District, playing the likes of "Surf Pā'ina," "Puamana," "You, Ku'uipo," "Coconut Girl," "La Bamba," and Nirvana's "Come as You Are," which this mostly male class sang in unison. They also played instrumental versions of "Europa," "Kawaipunahele," and "I'll Remember You" (the latter to placate the teacher, a big Kui Lee fan). One day Mākena found "Mack the Knife" in one of his dad's songbooks and asked the teacher if he, Mākena, could arrange it for the class. He got help from his father, who had also graduated, a month earlier—not because he wanted to, necessarily, but because in his stints at various colleges in the last twenty-four years he had accumulated far more than the requisite number of credit hours. The arrangement of the song was

328

sparse and clean, and the teacher, Mr. Yanagihara, was sufficiently impressed.

So the class learned this song too.

For Mākena, it was a way of paying homage to a dead friend.

□ □ □

Shortly after the confrontation between Harley and the pallbearers, Manny had apparently returned home. After he had disabled the alarms, four men, the same four who were in the Olds, came toward him with guns. Manny leaped into his bus as they fired, and came out with a gun himself, shooting with deadly accuracy. He managed to hit all four while he went unscathed, but as he approached one of the dying men—speaking on a cell phone at the same time—and got on one knee to lift the man's head to perhaps help him breathe, a shot rang out. A hazy figure, sneaking up from behind, had hit Manny in the back—the tattoo, black and brown lines radiating from a center, perhaps too tantalizing a target to resist.

That's how Mākena, Sam, and Alika had pieced it together, with the help of the videotape they pulled out of Manny's surveillance camera. Early that evening Alika had gone to see Manny. Since the night they met at the Rivera house, they had kept in touch, trading information. But this marked the first time that Alika was going to Manny's bus-home. And he needed help finding the place, so he brought Mākena along.

They came upon a gruesome sight. Bodies all over the place. Mākena ran up to Manny, who lay on his back next to the man he had knelt over to assist. Manny was barely alive, his eyes glazed and teary. His gun and cell phone lay next to him. When he heard Mākena call his name he smiled, then whispered, "It's about time." Then, in a voice scarcely audible, he said what sounded like "Someone's coming—" He coughed. "Water . . . home."

Manny coughed again, then seemed to gasp for breath. It was his last breath. Mākena pounded his chest, blew air into his lungs, but a crying jag took over. Alika also tried CPR. They failed to bring him back. Mākena, his head pressed against the black diamonds on Manny's still warm chest, had to be pulled away by his companion.

A motorbike approached. Alika picked up Manny's gun. He and Mākena tried to duck in the bushes, but it was too late.

"Stand behind me," Alika said to Mākena as he held the gun at his side.

The man, who wore a dark parka in the dim light, climbed off the bike and, as if he didn't see the other two, ran toward Manny. He knelt down, felt for a pulse, and shook his head. He closed Manny's eyes as Mākena and Alika approached, cautiously. He then pressed his forehead against Manny's. After a moment he picked Manny's cell phone up from the ground and stood to face the other two.

"I need your help," he began. "Manny had called me. Said he had killed these guys who tried to ambush him. We were talking when I heard the shot. . . . He knew he wouldn't make it, and wanted me here to cover up his tracks. Destroy all evidence of his death. 'Cheat them out of their victory,' he said. I shot here from the harbor as fast as I could. I was still talking to him while on my way here. He kept going on about needing to be buried at sea." He shook his head again. "Fuck!"

"You wanted our help," Alika managed to say.

"Yeah," he said as he looked around, scanning what looked like a war zone, "please." Then he added, "I know who did this." He looked at Mākena, who was sniffling every now and then. "You must be Henry's kid." Mākena nodded. "And you—" He looked at Alika.

"Alika." Alika handed him Manny's gun.

The man put the gun in the pocket of his shorts, and held out his hand. "I'm Sam. Manny's like a brother to me." They shook hands. "We got a clean-up job to do."

The three men dragged Manny's body and placed it in the trunk of the Impala, setting it against Manny's shotgun. They then ransacked the bus, taking anything they considered to be of value. Or useful. Or evidence. The items included U.S. Army dog tags, keys, sunglasses, some records—78 rpm. Manny's two surfboards posed a dilemma, since the car with the racks, the Civic, was nowhere to be seen. While Mākena looked for a place in the nearby bushes to hide the boards, the other two gathered some clothing, Manny's notebooks, a half-filled gasoline container, and an empty one. They used a thick blue blanket to wrap most of the loose items.

As the three men walked toward the cars, Alika's dull-red Subaru and Manny's black Impala, Alika carried the bundle while Sam poured gasoline throughout the area. Sam told Alika to drive the Impala and asked Mākena if he could handle the Subaru. Mākena nodded. Sam then pulled a book of matches out of his jeans. Mākena said, "Let me do it."

Sam handed him the matches.

Alika got into Manny's car; Mākena jumped into the Subaru. Sam hopped on his motorbike. All three fired up their engines.

Mākena lit the entire book of matches and threw it out the window.

They took off as the place ignited. The bus was an instant inferno. The oil-spattered area surrounding it, which contained the bodies of the four men, burst aflame.

Suddenly, Mākena hit the brakes and jumped out. Sam and Alika stopped. Sam hopped off his bike and came running after him. "We gotta get outa here. Now!"

"Camera," Mākena said as he ran just ahead of the flames that were spreading toward the shrubbery. "He has a camera." Mākena dug his hands between cacti and into an already burning bush and yanked the surveillance camera out. Then he and Sam made a mad dash toward their vehicles.

Mākena, the camera on the seat next to him, sobbed as he followed the other two out toward the coastal road. Just before Mākaha Valley Road met Farrington Highway, Sam slowed to a stop and the others stopped behind him. Alika and Mākena got out of the cars.

"I'm leaving the bike here. I need you to get on home, kid. I can drop you off near your house."

"No way. Whe'evah you guys going, I going."

"It's too dangerous."

"I no give a shit. If I die, I die."

"Please. Don't do this."

"Yeah, Mākena," Alika chimed. "You should go home."

"Fuck no!"

"Look," Sam said. "We can't waste time."

Mākena looked straight at him. "Let's go then."

Sam sighed, muttering, "Your folks are gonna kill me." He put his fingertips to his temples. "Okay, here's the plan . . . "

As he spoke he removed some clothing from the blue bundle. Then he took off his parka. He wore no shirt underneath.

"Holy shit." Alika and Mākena saw the tattoos on Sam's upper arms, back, and chest. They were almost as intricate as Manny's.

After Sam put on a black shirt and black pants, he slipped on Manny's shades. Then he put on a navy-blue wool cap. The transformation was complete.

The black Impala moved inexorably down the strip of coastal highway that evening, the Subaru and the motor-bike left behind for the time being.

"The most important thing we need to remember," Sam explained to Mākena, who sat up front with him, and Alika, who sat in the spacious back seat, "is to convince people that Manny's still alive. . . . Those we can't convince, we'll just have to fricken *haunt*."

They pulled in behind a gas station. Alika ran over to fill the two containers.

"You okay?" Sam said to Mākena. Mākena's legs were pumping nervously, his hands under his armpits.

"I'm fine. Jes' raring to go."

Sam lit a cigarette. Mākena opened the glove compartment and pored over Manny's cassette tapes. When Alika jumped in with the two filled containers, they proceeded toward Harley Evans' house.

Later that evening they returned to the other vehicles. They removed the items from the blue blanket, then used the blanket to wrap Manny's stiffening body and proceeded, with Alika now driving, toward the harbor.

When they passed a fishing boat whose bow was emblazoned with the title *Bottom Feeder*, Sam told the other two that the boat belonged to Harley's fisherman brother, J. D. Evans. When Alika commented on the appropriateness of the name, Sam said, "Balls. They all got balls."

They moved on until they reached the slip of Sam's boat. Sam jumped out of the car and hopped on the boat. When he gave the signal, Alika and Mākena hauled the blanketed body aboard. Sam, who had left his boat keys with the motorbike, hot-wired the ignition, and off they went.

The diesel smell gave Mākena a headache, so Sam suggested he go down into the cabin for a while. There Mākena saw a shelf filled with odd souvenirs: nets and hooks of all sorts, plastic tubes, empty bottles of all sizes. He also saw a stack of pamphlets and magazines. The letters WWF on the top pamphlet drew his attention. Mākena picked the pamphlet up and saw the phrase *Journal of the World Wildlife Federation.* "Endangered species," he muttered when he saw the accompanying photos. He browsed through magazines on fisheries and longlining. After that he took another look around the cabin. On its floor, by a small door—everything seemed miniaturized— Mākena saw a steering wheel and ignition wires. He then noticed that his headache was gone and went back up.

"We're heading out toward Ka'ena Point!" Sam was shouting to Alika over the roaring engine.

"That's the launching place for the souls of the dead!" Alika shouted back.

"Yeah, I know!"

After wrapping the blanketed body with the anchor line and cutting that line, the three men held hands and prayed; then together they threw Manny's corpse overboard.

And proceeded to Hale'iwa.

□ □ □

During the tedium of inspirational speeches that were the fare for graduation ceremonies, Mākena relived those heart-rending moments. Now the speeches were over, and the procession would begin. The graduates marched forth—girls first, then the boys—in alphabetical order. As each young woman and young man reached the podium, her or his name was announced. Every name was applauded. For some there were yells and cheers.

Then the seniors were told to flip their tassels, from left to right.

The graduates were told to proceed in orderly fashion to the football field and to look for the alphabet letter that corresponded to their last names. Family and friends would be there to greet them.

There was no order to this, as exuberant graduates waded through the thick masses, trying to find a letter, a face, distracted by those they didn't expect to find and yet knew. Mostly, the graduates found each other, greeting each other with hugs, kisses, high-fives, and handshakes. Some even shed tears as they embraced people, some they only dimly recognized. Envelopes filled their hands and leis covered their faces. The flower smells were intoxicating.

And that was about as intoxicated as Mākena would be allowed to get that night. While his old buddy Keith had dropped a tab of Ecstacy before the ceremony, and was planning to party all night, Mākena was under parental and doctor's orders to play it straight. It would be a long time before he'd be allowed to taste alcohol again. He didn't mind; the thought of drinking beer made him nauseous.

As he stood dazed under the *R* sign, caught in the mix of leis, tears, and thanks, there appeared before him a beautiful young woman. Those around him gave way, opening up space.

Her appearance seemed to freeze all motion. *Who is this mascaraed woman?*

A dim phrase from months back entered Mākena's consciousness. *Maybe I'll attend your graduation.* Still, Mākena couldn't quite place her.

She walked up to him, presented him with a maile lei and embraced him, whispering, "I didn't know you got hurt . . . that night. . . . I am *so* sorry. I would've been there."

She then grabbed his hand and smiled. Mākena struggled to make the connection. It wasn't easy, conscious as he was of curious onlookers. He knew it had to do with that night in Haleʻiwa. Keith had talked about that night quite often, but he never knew what to make of Keith's wild stories, a different version with each retelling, the only constants being a beautiful woman and an ocean of blue tarp.

Then something clicked, some synapse leap, and Mākena said, "How's your cousin?"

"My cousin?"

"Yeah. She still massaging guys in Aspen, or whe'evahs?"

"You remember *that*?" She laughed. "Jenny's fine. In fact she's back. Attending UH. Missed the ocean too much."

"I know how that feels." *What is this lady's name?* "Ah, I'm goin' to UH. I might see her there." *Did I score with her or something? Doubt it.* A memory flash: ocean, stars. A kiss. But something didn't sit right.

Then he noticed something else about her. She seemed heavier, rosier, than she was in the dim corridors of his memory.

Desiree put her hands on her belly. "Yes, I'm pregnant." Then she said, "And engaged. Somebody I met. Not a producer or writer or ANY Hollywood type. In fact, he's a lot like you."

"Oh yeah?" Mākena smiled. "What's that? My type." Slow, bewitching motions in shallow waters danced in his memory.

"Well, he's a surfer, of course. He's mostly like you in that he's not pretentious. He's kind, bright, endearing . . . my goodness, you're turning red."

□ □ □

Mākena

The morning after the night Manny died I just couldn't get out of bed. I told my folks I was sick. Dad came home early from work that day and noticed the scratches and burn marks on my arm. He knew I had been with Alika; he knew I had gone to Manny's house. He didn't say anything at first, just got some aloe, and dabbed it carefully on my arms. He didn't know where the real pain was.

He told me to wear a long-sleeved shirt. "No let your mom see your arms. . . . I dunno what you got yourself into, kid. I jes' hope it's done."

"It's done. Promise." I couldn't tell him about Manny. Or about what I did with Sam and Alika. He patted me on the back.

About a week later, when I could wear short sleeves again, he asked me, as I rode with him to the store,

"Did you start the fire . . . or put it out?"

I hesitated. "Both, I guess." Metaphorically speaking.

"I know we no talk that much any more, and thass fine, thass jes' part of growing up. But what's been going down lately is pretty serious shit. Thass why I curious as to what part you played in this. And why."

I tried, I wanted to, but . . . I couldn't. *I have to keep Manny alive.*

"You don't have to be specific. Jes' tell me this. Are you in any kind of trouble? 'Cause you know I'd do anything to help."

"I not in trouble, Dad. It's finished."

"Alika, he cool head, but Manny, even though I like and respect him, he's got this vigilante streak. Don't let him be dragging you into places . . . you know . . . "

I just nodded, thinking, as I had been thinking for nearly a month now, *This may not be my real dad.* Then as we turned into the shopping center, Dad said, "Jes' tell me one more thing."

"What?"

"What you did, was it teenage craziness or was there a good reason for it? You know I love you, . . . no matter what your answer is."

I looked at him straight in the eyes. "There was reason."

I loved my Dad. That's why it was so painful. Hiding things from him. I had to look away.

He stopped the car, pulled up the brakes. "Thass all I need to know."

Nickelodeon has a show called *My Three Sons*. My own show would be called *My Three Fathers* . . .

First, there's the one I never met. But it's like he's always been around. He's the guy everybody talks about, the guy who raised the bar, I guess, for being a true modern-day Hawaiian. He risked his life for a cause. . . . He's the guy my mom and auntie were talking about on the phone one day. He might be my blood father. I have a lot of aloha for this . . . this stranger. I don't blame him for not being around, 'cause by dying he became a spirit guide for generations to come.

I'm just blown away when I think of that.

Then there was the guy who was more like a friend. He taught me what the stakes were. And he showed me what could happen when you up the ante. He took risks. He even put me at risk. But thass cool. I love him for what he showed me 'cause he showed me possibilities. Then he died. And when he died I had to grow up. Fast.

Then there's Henry Rivera. He's always been around, so I kind of take him for granted. But my love for him cuts deepest. He's no star, though sometimes when he's strumming his guitar and singing, I think he imagines being one. There's not gonna be stories told about him, at least not the kind you hear about guys like Manny, or Uncle Keoni. He just puts his guitar down after a while, and gets back to the grind—to provide for Mom, 'Analu, and me. He busts his ass day and night. To raise a family.

That's not glamorous, like the life of Uncle Keoni—man, it's hard to call him "uncle" now. There's even songs about him. And the stories about Manny make him seem like a real life Batman, or maybe his Hawaiian equivalent, Pe'a Pe'a, with hideaway caves and a car that looked like the Batmobile after he and I painted it black one day . . .

But there are stories about Henry Rivera. They may not get told, but I know them. I've even been in some.

Batman and Robin

(Waikīkī—1984)

Mākena

We was on da roof of da building, in our capes and masks. Daddy was da main crime fightah. I was his side-kick. We was helping da police catch da criminal mastah-minds who been breaking into cahs all aroun' da area. One of da policemans was Daddy's cousin. I called him Uncle Jim.

"Eh, boy. No go near da edge now."

I was sked go near da edge. I wen' adjust my Robin mask fo' see bettah. When I was small, real real small, Daddy stay telling me, he use' to take me go trick-o-treat and ev'rytime I use' to walk into walls 'cause my mask was crooked. Daddy is da Caped Crusader. I wanted fo' be dat. But he said I too small. So I had to be Robin.

"Way before Batman there was this guy called the Green Hornet. And his sidekick—you know what I mean by sidekick?"

"He could kick from his side." I showed my daddy how.

"Yeah. But sidekick also means pahtnah."

"Like Robin?"

"Yeah, yeah, you got it. But kine of a lessah, or smallah pahtnah. . . . So anyway, the Green Hornet's sidekick, or paht-nah, was Kato."

340

"Kay-toe," I say.

"Yeah. 'Kay-toe,' 'cause haoles, dey no can pronounce Japanee names. An' dey cannot tell one paké from one Japanee."

"Sometimes I cannot tell."

"You gon' learn. Anyway, where was I? So dis Kato guy was played by . . . none other dan . . . Bruce Lee."

"Bruce Lee? Da real Bruce Lee?"

"Da one an' only. An' Bruce Lee, when he played Kato on dis TV show, *The Green Hornet,* da buggah move so quick, he had to slow down his moves, jes' so da camera could catch his moves. Dass da t'ing wit' Bruce Lee. His hands moved fastah dan da eye can see."

"Wow. Fo' real?"

"Would I lie to you, my son, my son? . . . An' he could kick Burt Ward's ass. You know Burt Ward, da original Robin?"

"He da one on Nickelodeon."

"I guess. Anyway, to improve ratings back in the old days da TV guys wen' set up one fight between Kato and Robin, meaning Bruce Lee versus Burt Ward. Dass kinda like Arnold Schwarzenegger fighting da kid in *Wondah Years.* What's his name?"

I nevah know his name so my shoulders went up and down.

"Well, *Batman* was da more popular series—in fact, dass why it's still showing—"

"*BANG. POP.*"

"—so da producers, dey wanted Robin for win. An' it was like, give me a break. Nobody would believe that, Bruce Lee, the best martial artist of his time, maybe all time, would let Robin kick his ass. Would you?"

My head wen' shake no.

"An' Bruce Lee let it be known dat he wasn't gonna take shit from Burt Ward. So he made da buggah real nervous. You know, like practicing his supahfast blows on da set, giving Burt Ward da eye, acting like he might lose control. So you figgah . . . how Hollywood gon' deal wit' dis dilemma, dis, ah . . . , problem? Hah? T'ink about it. Burt Ward is da biggah stah, but nobody in deah right mind gon' believe he could beat Bruce Lee. So you know what happens? Da studio guys finally decided to let da match end in one draw."

"One draw? One draw? Dat sucks."

"I shit you not. And you know what wen' happen to Bruce Lee aftah that?"

"He wen' die?"

"No, I mean, befo' he died."

"He made movies, da kine wheah the words and the mouth no match."

"Yeah, the mouth go, 'Goong chow-wah' and what you hear is, 'I must revenge my family.' But damn good movies anyway. Best martial arts movies evah."

"You gon' teach me martial arts, Daddy?"

"When da time comes, grasshopper . . . "

"Why you call me grasshopper?"

"Nemmind. . . . When the time comes, I will explain dat too. . . . I want you to learn from one paké master, like Bruce Lee."

"Bruce Lee was paké?"

"Every day of his Chinese life. Ja' like Grampa Wong. Like you, in part. Hard to find da Chinese in you, though."

"I no *feel* Chinese."

"No look at me. *I* dunno what Chinese supposed to feel like. Dat's Mom's side a' da show. She get da kine, ah, Chinese eyes. Pretty eyes. You get—I dunno what you get. Chop suey eyes."

"How come Green Hornet not on TV?"

"Canceled." Daddy stay looking at something below. I try fo' look too, but he hold me back so I no fall ovah. Den he whispah to me: "Look, look. Look what happening, down below. Shit, I cannot believe dey would have da guts to come back."

Now Daddy stay carrying me, holding me aroun' my stomach. Spooky, look down.

"Bad guys," I said, real soft so dey no can hear.

"Looks like it." Daddy was talking soft too. Den da car alarm went off. Den wen' stop real quick. "Boy. Dat guy moves fast."

"Ja' like Bruce Lee."

"Stay here. An' no get close to the edge." Daddy ran to da adda side of da building and he wen' whistle real loud. Da guy was taking off in da stolen cah an' already Uncle Jimmy was behind 'om.

Daddy came back by me. "Wow, dat paid off big time. Who woulda t'ought dey'd go for da bait?

"Bait?"

"Well, I guess it's time to head back, eh?"

"But but, I tot, I tot WE was gon' catch da bad guys who wen' steal our cah stereo."

"You saw Uncle Jimmy take off, eh?" I nodded my head. "He gon' catch 'om. We did our paht."

"Hoh man. Dis sucks . . . " I wen' put my head down. "Sucks mo' dan one draw."

Daddy wen' rub my head. He made my mask all crooked. "We cannot be reckless. What if he had one weapon? We gotta live to fight anadda day, right?"

I still was habut. "Right," I wen' say. I was kicking da loose gravel on da rooftop.

"We did our job. An' dat's da role we crime stoppers have to play."

"But."

"No. No no no no. No more 'buts' from you. Dis is not glamorous work. You want glamorous work, you be one Hollywood actor."

I wen' punch da air. *"BAM. POW."*

When we wen' reach home, I wen' ring da doorbell. Den I wen' yell, "Trick o' treat!"

Mommy wen' open da door. She was carrying 'Analu. Daddy call him "Da little tit-sucker."

Mommy said, "Gee, about time you two got back."

"We was out stopping crime. We wen' help Uncle Jimmy dem catch one criminal who was as fass as Bruce Lee."

"Oh, that's good." Den she wen' look at Daddy, an' her eyebrows went way up.

We went inside da house. All da candy in da bowl was gone. An' my bag dat was full of candy was empty.

"Whe' my candy?"

"So many kids were coming. We ran out. I had to give some of it away, baby." She wen' look at Daddy.

"Hoh-oh man." I t'rew down my Robin mask.

"No worry. I saved some for you. It's in the icebox . . . You couldn't possibly eat all of it, Mākena."

"Yeah, kid. You know we not gon' let you eat dat many sweets."

I wen' open da icebox. Still had some left. But no had bubble gum. Bubble gum is my favorite. "You—" I was crying, I was so mad. "You wen' give away all my GUM!" I wen' run upstairs and I wen' dive on top my bed, hiding my head undah da blanket an' pillow.

Mommy wen' come and she wen' sit on top my bed. "I'm sorry. I didn't know that the bubble gum was your favorite. If you like I can send Daddy to the ABC store."

"I no like ABC stoah gum." I was keeping my head undah da pillow.

"It's probably the same. The candy people give away is store-bought. Where do you think it comes from?"

"I no like bawt candy."

I could hear Daddy coming upstairs. I wen' peek little bit. He was carrying 'Analu now. "Let 'om sleep it off," he was telling Mommy. I no was even tired. Wasn't dat late.

"You know what?" Daddy was telling Mommy. "ABC was giving away candy—I think some gum too. Maybe Robin like put on his mask an' go trick o' treat with me."

"It's late. Tomorrow's a school day."

"Well, if a certain kid gets a move on we can still get there."

I wen' get up, wipe my face wit' da blanket. Den I wen' run downstairs an' put on my Robin mask.

Daddy an' me went to da ABC stoah. Had lotta people out, still trick-o-treating. In fact was mostly old people in costumes.

In da stoah we wen' look at da bowl of candy. No had gum. I wanted fo' cry. Daddy said, "Let's go, quick."

"No."

"I said 'let's go.'" He was mad, so I wen' follow him. We went to da next ABC stoah. Still no had. An' da next an' da next. All along Kalakaua Avenue. Finally, I was so tired already. Feel like we wen' walk ten miles.

"I t'ink dis is the last ABC store in Waikīkī" Daddy was saying when we wen' come to one stoah dat looked like all da adda ones.

I almost nevah like walk in. None of da adda stoahs had. Why would dis one?

No had. An' da bowl was almost empty.

Daddy was talking to da stoahman an' pointing to da bowl. I dunno what he said to da man, 'cause I was too tired and I stahted wandering aroun'. I couldn't even be habut already.

Den da man wen' go in da back and came out wit' one box full of gum, an' wen pour DA WHOLE BOX into da bowl.

I wen' stand in front of da bowl, watching it fill up. I was smiling so much, I couldn't hide my teet'.

I only wen' grab aroun' five. Dat was 'nuff.

Testing the Waters

(Wai'anae—Summer 1995)

An' Daddy wen' horseyback me home, Mākena whispers as he adjusts his goggles, which he wears over his extended-wear contact lenses—a graduation present from his parents. *They just grateful I survived my senior year.* The doctor had given him the go-ahead to swim, but reminded him that he was not ready yet to catch any wave higher than a one-foot bump.

It's been a calm, hazy day at Kea'au. No surf, and not many left on the beach. Mākena relishes days like these, alone in the water. He's seen hammerhead sharks, small ones. They never bother. He's also seen mempachi and moano, and every now and then a silvery school of baby akule.

On this summer day, when the sun has fallen and the hazy but full moon brings assurances of no rain, he sees a shadow below. He gasps, then casually starts swimming toward the shore. The shadow seems to follow him, and he knows it can't be his shadow. There's no one else in the water, at this late time, just a couple of stragglers on the shore. *Can't panic. The way it's moving, it could get to me in a second.* He calmly shifts his angle, swims slowly, easily, careful not to disturb the water. *Don't panic. Relax.* The shadow disappears.

He's all chicken bumps. He tries to maintain an even breath, a calming cadence in the face of terror. *Can't panic. Not now. Where the fuck did it go?* He can't resist the urge to look under.

At first he sees nothing. Just some limu, sand, and rocks below. *Scary. Where is it?*

Then he sees the shark. It seems to be retreating. *Wait, it's turning back. Is this shark an ancestral guardian, or am I dinner?*

Another shadowy sight engages his periphery. He sees wings, or what seem to be wings, like those of a large bird, but deep in the blue water. He forgets about the shark.

It has legs and a tail. A huge body.

This turtle, a hawksbill, is articulate, majestic in the water, more than he could ever be. Mākena is fascinated. It swims upward in beautiful bird-like strokes.

And the manō follows.

The scenario unfolds in slo-mo: the honu turning on its side, its belly facing the manō, cutting into the path of this tiger shark. Mākena's cry, a searing Nooooooo!, is swallowed up. Mākena then sees, on the shell, or carapace, of this honu'ea, a very familiar design: irregular brown and black streaks radiating from the center.

Something tells him there is a larger design. He can't think straight but he intuits understanding. He is frightened, yet secure. Lines of memory crisscross in his brain, symbols registering but not quite, a message sent but not received, and yet . . . a message.

The shark turns away.

Mākena rises. *Can't panic.* He surfaces, gasping for air. He sucks in deep, but swallows water. He's not prepared for the slapping wave and takes in more water. He coughs and coughs and coughs. His heart pounds. Refusing to look under again, he swims toward the shore.

Can't panic. He takes a deep breath with every other stroke.

Can't panic. He finds a rhythm. A steady stroke. *It's been so long.*

I refuse to panic.

When he reaches shore, he places his towel over his shoulders and allows the shivers to overtake him. He can't stop his teeth from chattering. He crosses his arms, rubbing himself. Then he falls back and rolls back and forth on the sand to deal with the hurt that has come surging back. After a while the hurting and shaking stops.

Darkness is coming. And he'll need its cover.

To hide a set of bones wrapped in white tapa, in a cave deep in the overlap of mountains, above a ravine where green maile once grew, during a time eons ago when this dry region was blessed with rain.

To bury a videotape. Soul-wrenching footage of a man facing terrible odds. *The way he moved. He almost pulled it off. If it weren't for that coward who snuck up from behind.* Better to bury it, Sam had said, than to let people know he's gone.

To bury some notebooks, notebooks whose words have been burned into his memory. *Sam's got the information he needs.* He is confident that neurons will no longer misfire, that the synapses are the meaningful empty spaces in his now-healed skull where he will be able to retrieve what's necessary.

And he has to do these things alone. He had been afraid, hesitant, but no longer.

He gets on his bike.

Passing the bullet-riddled, burnt-out shell of a city bus, he abandons the bike and starts to run with the bundled items. He follows the path carved by Manny's frequent journeys to the mountain. He moves warily—can't risk an ankle twist, or worse, a fall.

Someone is chasing him, shouting to him. He runs as fast as he can, but the bundle . . .

An arm grabs him. It's his father, gasping, out of breath. He's in his jogging clothes—old gray t-shirt, black shorts, dirt-streaked New Balance shoes. "Whe' da hell you going? I been tryna—catch—I saw you back—" He takes a deep breath.

"I jes' goin' on a hike."

"You wouldn't be—" He stops to catch his breath. "—running—" He stops again. "—that fast—" One more breath. "—if you was jes' hiking." He rests his hands on his knees, takes another breath. "What's that in the bag?"

"Naht'ing."

"No 'naht'ing' me. Is this some kinda drug shit going on? Is that what Manny has you doing? Harvesting pakalōlō? I tell you, if you dealing, or working for one dealer, I will kick your fucking ass."

"Why you always gotta misread what I do? First t'ing you t'ink is—"

"Mākena, how can I not think that? You've been busted, kid. An' look at you, you think this no look suspicious?"

"You no understand. I have to—I have to—"

"Have to what? What da hell's going on?" Henry, his arms on his hips, his gray t-shirt dark with sweat, glares at his son. Mākena looks down.

"Bones, Dad. Dese are da bones."

"What bones?"

"Uncle Keoni's bones."

"What da hell you talkin' about?"

"His bones."

"Don't joke around with shit like that."

Mākena lays the bundle on the ground. Opens it. Pulls out the tapa-wrapped bones.

"You want me to open it?" Mākena says angrily.

Henry is about to nod, but as he runs a hand over the crisp cloth small bumps appear all over his arms. He shudders. "Holy shit!" He rubs his arms. "What just happened?"

Mākena shrugs.

"You talking about the iwi they found on Kahoʻolawe? The one that disappeared?"

Mākena nods.

"How? Why?"

Mākena shrugs.

"Who put you up to this? Manny? Look, you gotta tell me."

Mākena shuts his eyes. "He's dead, Dad. Manny's dead. Harley's boys—dey wen' kill 'om. Harley wen' kill 'om." Mākena pulls out the set of notebooks, the videotape. "Dis is his stuff. I gotta hide 'om."

Henry grimaces. He closes his eyes, puts a hand to his chest. "Oh, man. This is . . . Manny, dead. . . . " He closes his eyes. "You mean, that night?"

"Yeah. Dat night. Had one gunfight at Manny's place. Five against one. Manny got four of 'om."

"And the fires?"

"Was me, Manny's friend Sam, and Alika. Sam said we gotta hide da fact dat Manny was dead. We wen' dump his body in da ocean. Off Kaʻena Point."

"Sam? . . . I think I know Sam. . . . Geez."

Mākena starts to rewrap the bundle.

Henry watches his son. "An' now *you* have what might be Keoni's bones? Did Sam put you up to this?"

"Was da adda way around. I wen' ask him fo' help. We wen' break into Kalama Housseman's trailer. Alika wen' help us."

"Alika?" Henry throws his hands up. "Good god. What is going on? . . . And you, why? Why you?"

"Why? Ev'rybody fighting fo' his bones. Ev'rybody saying, jurisdiction, jurisdiction. But dey no really give a shit. Nobody, not one person showing any respect." Mākena swallows spit. "It's like with Gram."

"Gram? Gram of what?"

"Gram Parsons. You tole me da story, planny times, about how his friends when bury him in da desert. 'Cause dey had one pact."

"Gram Parsons? . . . But that was a pact between *friends*. You didn't even know Keoni. An' I don't think you're a lineal descendant, kid."

"Not according to Mom and Auntie Momi. I heard dem talkin' about Uncle Keoni. Dey was saying he might be my . . . my real dad."

Henry snickers. "Mākena. You're recovering from a concussion. Think about it. You probably heard wrong."

"I know what dey said."

Henry squints, probing his son's face. "Look, you're my son. I, of all people, should know. . . . Uncle Keoni disappeared way before—" He stops, ponders, his eyes looking out toward the horizon, gazing back nearly twenty years. *When did she announce to me that she was pregnant? Was soon after he disappeared, in June.* "She was despondent over his disappearance," he mutters, without realizing he's muttering. "But who wasn't?" Then he remembers the look in her face when he suggested they name the child Keoni. *Didn't know that look then, but I know that look all too well now.*

Shit, it's possible.

Henry feels sick. He feels a sensory overload. Too much data. Way too much to assimilate. He shuts his eyes tight. *Why didn't she tell me?*

"Dad."

I guess we all lead secret lives. Christ, how'd it get so complicated?

"Dad."

Maybe I should have been Enrique boy, a jíbaro in the mountains of Puerto Rico. Why'd my grandparents have to come here?

"Dad."

Henry finally hears his son. He looks at his son, tall and grown up. *When did that happen?* "You *know*," he says, trying to stay composed, "you know this is news to me, this stuff about Keoni. And Manny, good god—"

"Sorry, Dad."

"Me, too."

Henry covers his face with his hands, then interlaces his fingers.

Mākena places a hand on his father's shoulder. "You my dad. You gon' always be my dad. I'm a Rivera. . . . Dad. You okay?"

Seeds planted, so long ago. Desperate swims toward fertile shores. The 'Alalakeiki Channel. Funny, 'alala keiki means "child's wail." Peter had told him that. It's named for the plaintive cry seamen had heard there.

Whose seed made that landing? To be in competition with—

Henry looks at his son. "Some kids ask for cars for graduation. You, you jes' wanna set things right." He looks to the sky, then at the bundle. "That," Henry says, "that could be Keoni's bones?"

"Yeah."

Henry smirks, wanly. "An' you actually have a place for it?"

Mākena nods again. "A cave. Up in the hills."

"He would like the view." Henry fights to stave off tears. He rubs the area between his nose and upper lip, a place where a mustache once grew.

It's not a contest, Henry tells himself. This child belongs to all of us, to none of us. Whatever's been passed on to him, by whatever means, is gonna have to be played out in this complicated, modern world.

"Dad?"

It can't be easy for him either.

"Dad."

What is my role?

"Getting dark, Dad," Mākena says, swallowing as he speaks.

Henry, his mind still spinning with thoughts, tensions, matters unresolved, nods. "Go. Do what you gotta do." They embrace, hard.

Mākena picks up the bundle.

"Gon' take long, you know. I gon' be home late. I hope Ma not gon' be mad."

"I'll take care of it." *You just take care of yourself.*

Mākena hugs his father one more time, then begins his long, slow uphill run. Henry watches him hitch the bundle over his shoulder, watches him until he disappears up the solitary road.

HAʻINA
Itʻs a Wrap

(Waikīkī—Fall 2000)

Late afternoon

A man and a very pregnant woman walk along Kuhio Avenue, passing the shops and tourists. They have come from the movie theater on Seaside Avenue and are headed in the Diamond Head direction.

Hoh, glad we only had to pay four bucks.

Escapism. Just what I needed, actually.

Speaking of escapism, did you know that Arlen got funding from Sundance?

No shit? How the—? How the fuck did he pull that off?

How else? Connections.

Thought you were gonna say talent.

They cross Kānekapōlei Street.

Isn't it great not to have to study for a change?

What a luxury. But I'm gonna have to find some real work soon. Especially with baby coming.

We can manage, you know—hey, where are we going?

The man pulls the woman by the arm across the street.

Where else? To the car.

The car's not this far down.

Well, we'll get to it just the same. You need the exercise.

355

I've had enough exercise.

Indulge me, then.

He leads her down a dimly lit side street. The sign says Tusitala Street.

The man and woman pause when they come to several acres of vacant land. There's a fence around the property. On the street side, where the sidewalk is overgrown with weeds, there's two signs posted. One says NO TRESPASSING. The other announces that a hotel will be built there. The accompanying graphic on this sign shows a twenty-story building featuring a large swimming pool. Several sentences in very small print list the amenities. Both signs are old, rusted, threatening to fall.

Weeds and trees grow high on this vacant land.

Among the weeds there are aluminum soda cans; bottles, most of them broken; dirty paper plates; empty oil cans; countless cigarette butts; a deflated volleyball; matchbook covers; pieces of cloth. . . . There is a hole in the fence where one could squeeze through, to retrieve a ball or a Frisbee, or to urinate. You can tell by the scorched areas that there have been fires here.

The man squeezes through the hole. His pregnant wife says, *Alika, why are you going in there? It's filthy. I bet there's rats, mongooses.*

Just wanna see something. He steps gingerly through the tall weeds, says, *Geez, Lauren, a used condom.*

You pick it up and I'm leaving you here. Leaving you, period.

Alika continues his slow, deliberate trek through the weeds, bending down at times to look closer at the ground. He shouts to Lauren: *They used to live here, you know.*

Who? Her arms are crossed, resting on her large round belly.

The Riveras. This is where their house was. When they got evicted.

Lauren's arms drop. *No shit.*

□ □ □

Birds flock to the large trees on this property. The accumulation of years of birdshit, along with the added fuel of debris, has made the area combustible. On two occasions a carelessly thrown match has started a fire, and on those occasions firemen easily extinguished the blaze. Still, the Waikīkī unit fire department captain has complained to his superiors about this piece of ruinate land. His complaints have been echoed by the neighborhood board. Mostly they think of the property as an eyesore, especially considering how they, with the help of the Hawai'i Visitors & Convention Bureau, are in the process of revitalizing Waikīkī in hopes of increasing the tourist trade.

Who owns this? passersby have repeatedly asked. The rest of the conversation usually goes this way:

Some Japanese corporation. They had big plans, but then the bottom dropped on their economy. You know the story.

But isn't it costing them money to leave it sitting here like this?

Well, it's cheaper than building.

□ □ □

Sunset

Alika and Lauren are sitting in the car, a rusty, barely functional, faded-red Subaru. They are parked alongside the Ala Wai canal.

Next time let's pay for parking.

You hate these long walks.

Not as much as you hate paying the three bucks.

If not more. It's such a rip-off. Alika taps out a beat on the steering wheel. *So Arlen got the money, eh?*

Good things come to those who hustle.

I just hope he can make a decent movie. What script is he doing, Endless Summer III?

No, I think he eighty-sixed that one a while ago. It's still a surf movie, from what I heard, but there's an actual storyline.

Written by Skip?

Nah. Skip skipped outa town. Along with his Baywatch *buddies.*

Baywatch, Alika whispers as he shakes his head. *One thing I gotta say about Arlen, at least he considers local actors. And they're not just relegated to the backdrop.*

Well, when you live with Pi'ilani for a while, it's gotta change you.

Alika sighs. *Yeah . . .*

Sorry, I don't mean to take you back there.

No, it's good. I think a part of me is always "back there."

You think we'll ever see Manny again? Not that I've ever seen him, but—you know what I mean.

Lauren, . . . Alika blows out air. *There's one part of the story I never told you.*

It's all right. I know. It's touchy stuff.

But I don't wanna keep anything fom you.

I understand.

We were sworn to secrecy, you know.

Alika. I understand.

It's about Manny . . .

□ □ □

Twilight

Lauren and Alika sit in the car, silent except when Lauren holds a Kleenex to her nose and blows.

You must be hungry, Alika says after a while.

No. I'm fine. She's kicking, though.

She. Alika snickers.

Well, I'm hoping she's a girl, Lauren says somberly. *God, do we need women . . . to set a better tone. . . . Look where revenge takes you.*

You're right. Even Sam ended up . . . reassessing his moves.

I mean, what is that? Faking one guy's death, faking one guy's life.

I'm sorry.

And why are you apologizing?

I dunno.

So what's the ledger now? Is there a score? Fifty to two in favor of the bad guys?

Alika, his hands locked behind his neck, appears disheartened as he stares straight ahead. Lauren reaches for Alika's right shoulder with her right hand, and squeezes.

I'm sorry. Me and my big fucking mouth.

They got levels, we got levels too, Alika says after a while. *Contingency plans.*

Levels? What? Who?

That's what Sam told me once. . . . That's why he's been so slow to proceed, just to make sure it's done right. To get the best results. Alika fires the engine. *You know, I gotta believe in the guy. Gotta believe in something. . . . He's created a network. "Net" is the key word. If all goes well, we'll—he'll—catch some of the big players.*

You mean, like the movie we just saw.

Sometimes life does imitate art.

So it really wasn't escapist for you.
Alika shakes his head slowly. *Nope. No escape.*
We better get going. Before the engine overheats.
Alika pulls the car out into the boulevard.
The car has come to a halt. A scattering of red lights up ahead. Neon. Indigo. Colors of a city at night. Lauren gazes to her right. The moonlight shimmers on the gently moving water. Beautiful to look at, but she knows the canal water is foul.
I hate to ask, but if Evans talks, you think they'll let him off the hook?
No way. No fucking way. He's too big a catch. Frankly, if they only get him *I'll be happy.*
But he's gotten off twice already. I don't think any judge has the guts to put him away. Judges fear for their lives too.
Well, from what I've heard, he's pissed off too many people. He's really gonna get nailed this time.
Too bad you guys buried some key evidence.
To keep Manny alive. Tap, tap, tap, on the steering wheel.
To keep Manny alive.
That was the trade-off. But we're still gonna get the motherfucker. You know why?
No, why?
Sparkey Lopez.
You mean Lazarus?
Yep. You see, after Sam tracked him down in Puerto Rico, he begged Sam to let him come back. It isn't that he missed Hawaiʻi so much. He just has this hard-on for nailing Harley.
He's taking a huge risk being here. The light's green.
He's been meeting with the Feds. Talking up a storm.
The light's green, Alika. Someone's horn blasts.
Telling them quite a story. Alika accelerates, then turns on the radio. *I tell you, Sparkey's singing.*

Acknowledgments

I would like to thank Walden Robert Cassotto (Bobby Darin), Lizabeth Ball, Davianna McGregor, Terrilee Kekoʻolani-Raymond, Adolph Helm, Georganne Nordstrom, and members of the Protect Kahoʻolawe ʻOhana for inspiring some of the passages in this novel. I would like to thank the "spot editors," Joel Kam, Kahikina de Silva, and EMRJ, for checking to make sure I got the words right. Thanks also to Eric Komori, for technical support, and to Paul Lyons, Cynthia Franklin, and Cristina Bacchilega for their valuable help with minutiae.

Many thanks to Dennis Kawaharada, for his perceptive reading and sharp though restrained critiquing of the entire draft. And thanks to the staff at UH Press, especially Masako Ikeda, and the crew at Publication Services, for their care and concern with my ever-evolving manuscript.

And thank you, Holly, for nursing the manuscript through each vital phase.

Hey J.O.